Dell Books by Libby Sydes

ONLY WITH YOU
ANNALISE
STOLEN DREAMS

"I WANT EVERYTHING,"

she said, without regard for how foolish she might sound. "A knight on a white horse who will sweep me away and love me forever."

"Fairy tales. Fantasy," he replied softly. "I'm no knight, Jenny, just a man."

She felt his hand at the small of her back, pulling her closer, deeper into him. However improper, she wanted to be there, safe and protected by him, stirred by the virility of his body in such a compromising position.

"Kiss me, Ian," she said softly. "Kiss me like you love me, then I'll go to sleep."

He didn't want sleep, he wanted her. "You have no idea how dangerous that would be right now."

"I don't care," she said. "You're a strong man, Ian. I'm certain you can control yourself enough to grant me that one wish without my having to suffer the consequences."

His grin was pained. "You have entirely too much trust."

"Only with you," she whispered. "I trust only you."

ONLY WITH YOU

RAVE REVIEWS FOR LIBBY SYDES AND HER PREVIOUS NOVELS

ANNALISE

"In Laura Kinsale style, Libby Sydes has penned a dark, intensely emotional and very powerful romance that grips the reader and holds you in her web until the very end."—*Romantic Times*

"BRAVO! Libby Sydes deserves many honors for this book. I could not put it down!"—*Romance Reviews*

"AN INTENSELY EMOTIONAL BOOK . . . beautifully written with strong characterizations and a gripping plot."—*Old Book Barn Gazette*

STOLEN DREAMS

"You'll be captivated by the mounting sexual tension . . . Libby Sydes whisks readers away into a novel that instantly grabs your attention."
—*Romantic Times*

"A WONDERFUL TALE, seething with deep, dark emotions. Hunter is a dangerous and thoroughly sexy hero."—*Rendezvous*

LIBBY SYDES

Only With You

A Dell Book

Published by
Dell Publishing
a division of
Bantam Doubleday Dell Publishing Group, Inc.
1540 Broadway
New York, New York 10036

If you purchased this book without a cover you should be aware that this book is stolen property. It was reported as "unsold and destroyed" to the publisher and neither the author nor the publisher has received any payment for this "stripped book."

Copyright © 1997 by Libby Sydes

All rights reserved. No part of this book may be reproduced or transmitted in any form or by any means, electronic or mechanical, including photocopying, recording, or by any information storage and retrieval system, without the written permission of the Publisher, except where permitted by law.

The trademark Dell® is registered in the U.S. Patent and Trademark Office.

ISBN: 0-440-22233-8

Printed in the United States of America

Published simultaneously in Canada

April 1998

10 9 8 7 6 5 4 3 2 1

WCD

To my agent, Sue Yuen
For everything

Women are creatures without which there is no comfortable living . . . it is true what is wont to be said of governments, that bad ones are better than none.
—JOHN COTTON

Women are superior creations, without which there would be nothing valuable in this world. Including men.
—GRANNY DELANEY

Prologue

Mississippi, 1861

THE SCENT OF HONEYSUCKLE FLOATED ON THE BREEZE, thick and lazy as summer. Jennifer Delaney dangled her feet over the edge of the dock, her toes barely touching the water. The sun beat down on her bare shoulders, making her skin hot and sticky. Things were all stirred up in the nation, Papa had said so, but the South would set everything to rights. There was a war brewing, she had heard, but it seemed far away—Manassas and Shiloh, places more talked about than real. Papa was getting more worried though and their neighbor, Patrick Thorne, had sent some of his prized horses to help the Army of the Confederacy.

Jenny tipped her head back to catch the brightest of the sun's rays. Mama would scold for a week over the new crop of freckles across her nose, but every querulous word was worth the feel of freedom on her face.

She kicked up a spray of water and watched the glistening shower of droplets rain down. Spanish moss dripped from surrounding cypress trees, dusty gray against rough brown bark. She plucked a strand and wound it around her finger like a wedding ring.

She was going to get worse than a scolding if she got caught out here in nothing but her wet unmentionables, but she didn't care. A good swim was worth a hard lecture every now and then, or so Granny said.

Jenny picked up the journal beside her and leafed through a few more pages. She loved Granny's witty, oftentimes irreverent, writings. The book was forbidden for reasons she didn't exactly understand, but she read it anyway. It was her only link to the kindred soul who had passed away the very day Jenny was born and for whom she was named.

Granny had survived the birth of ten children, a revolutionary war for independence, yellow fever, smallpox, and even the bite from a dog. But she had not survived the birth of one tiny great-great-grandchild.

"A century is too old, and this is too many generations!" she had stated emphatically from the bed where she had been an invalid for a year. "It is a waste of time and energy to have to worry if every breath is my last."

In her grandest show of rebellion and complete authority yet, Granny waited until she heard the thin high wail of the new baby, waited until she heard that it was a girl named for her, then folded her arms over her chest and went. Just like that. Jenny had heard the story retold a hundred times and still had trouble believing it. Yet never once had the facts altered in the retelling.

Only With You

The hot Southern sun baked the thin cotton chemise on Jenny's slender frame. Twenty more minutes and her underclothes would be dry. She could don her dress without anyone being the wiser.

A snapping turtle swam up near the dock and poked its head out, then dove beneath the surface again. A snake slithered behind, hardly stirring the water. Jenny brought her knees up fast.

A water moccasin was nothing to get brave over, even if she had turned thirteen yesterday and was on the verge of becoming a woman. She wouldn't have her coming-out ball for a few more years, but she would get to attend her cousin Camellia's debut this fall. She would even be allowed to dance with Papa. She peeked back down at the moccasin. It wasn't as bad as a coral snake or a cottonmouth but was dangerous nonetheless.

She curled her toes over the warm wood of the pier and propped her arms on her knees, then her chin on her arms, and sighed. Summer was her favorite time, her very favorite, and the Yankees were going to ruin it.

Gathering up Granny's journal, she rose. Her chemise was as dry as it was going to get on a sweaty June day. She plucked it away from her budding chest, then gathered up her clothes from the dock. The boards blistered the bottom of her feet, and she decided to leave off her shoes to toughen them up a bit for the fun days ahead.

Mama wouldn't like that either. Jenny could hear her now, grinding away at the last of her childhood freedom. *Jennifer Delaney, you are a disgrace. A Delaney from South Carolina, even one transplanted into Mississippi, does not go traipsing across the countryside in bare feet behaving like common trash.*

Maybe not, but Jenny wouldn't be called a sissy by her older brother, Sam, or his friends. She slipped on her petticoats, then pulled her dress over her head. Mama was like that, every inch a lady. Fierce as a general running her household but helpless as a kitten around men. Jenny had never seen anyone change hats as easily and predictably as her mother. The woman could stare down a recalcitrant slave at twenty paces but grew faint and wilting around a spider when there was a man around.

Jenny shook her head. She was her mother's only daughter and a grave disappointment. Not that it mattered much. Her mama was a fair disappointment to Jenny too. She had finished doing up her buttons and was making a knot of her sash when the yelling started.

"Jenny . . . Jennnnnny! Come quick!" Samuel Delaney burst through the underbrush like a raging bull.

"Sam!" she scolded, sounding so much like Mama she cringed. "What in tarnation?" she added for good measure.

"Don't swear," he warned, the words coming out choppy with his uneven gait. He kept running, almost tripping in his haste. "They found Ian Thorne! His pa traded for him, just like he swore he would."

Jenny's eyes went round with amazement. "After all these years!" She crushed her straw bonnet on her head, grabbed up her shoes, and ran to meet her older brother. Meadow grass and wildflowers flattened beneath her bare feet. The hem of her starched cotton day dress turned gray from the rich delta soil, but still she kept running, her heart beating as fast as her legs churned.

Halfway to Sam, her bonnet went sailing and her hair came tumbling free, a wild mass of rich auburn that fell like a sleek pelt to her waist. She grabbed at the trailing bonnet ribbon but kept running until she almost plowed into Sam.

"Whoa," he breathed, catching her upper arms for balance.

"I can't believe they found him! Where?"

Sam was bent at the waist, breathing hard. "They traded somewhere near Santa Fe." Doubled over, he waited for his sister to catch her own breath. "I saw him, Jenny! He ain't Ian no more, he's a Injun."

"Oh." The word was little more than a formation of her mouth. She couldn't picture the boy she remembered from childhood looking any different than the young Southern gentleman that he had been at age twelve. Still was, she guessed, now that they had found him alive.

While everyone had whispered behind their hands and quietly mourned, Ian's father had never given up hope. Jenny knew because Patrick Thorne talked of his son often and lit candles in church and said prayers, and told everyone he knew that he would find Ian one day and bring him home.

Jenny loved Patrick Thorne like kin and was glad he had just proved every one of those gossipy, head-shaking whisperers wrong.

"C'mon," Sam urged. "You gotta see him!"

They cut through the back woods that ran along the

river and joined the two plantations. Past the kitchen gardens and outbuildings they sprinted, darting in and out of the shadows lest they get caught and have to spend precious time explaining why they were running like hoydens. Past camellias and magnolias and Mama's roses, they continued until they reached the heavier, untended forest where they had played with Ian Thorne almost from the time they could walk. They finally slowed when they reached the white split-railed fence surrounding the vast manicured lawn of Thorne Manor.

It was a graceful, inspiring place of tall columns, bricked courtyard, and well-tended grounds. Pride without pompousness imbued every inch.

People were everywhere. Wide-eyed slaves and house servants, horse trainers and stable hands. They all stood by in shock or terror while a young man held everyone at least ten feet back with a wicked-looking dagger.

Jenny climbed over the fence, then stopped, her breath snared in her throat.

He was wild and brown, his moss-green eyes the only link to his lineage. He wore the tailored clothing of a gentleman, but his coat lay on the ground and his shirt was open to his waist, exposing the hard muscles and corded tendons of his sun-bronzed chest. His features were slim and sharp as carved marble.

"He's a savage," Sam whispered with a superiority that Jenny didn't care for. "They had more clothes on him but he got loose and started stripping them off, right in front of everybody."

Jenny saw a waistcoat and cravat piled in a heap on the ground.

"Aaron said Mr. Pat had to keep him tied up the whole trip home. Mr. Pat thought when Ian saw the house, he would remember. But when they untied him, he went berserk. Mr. Pat threw him his Injun stuff to calm him down." Sam shook his head in disbelief. "He got a knife out first thing. Mr. Pat didn't know he had it. He's a savage all right."

Jenny could see that easy enough. His hair was long and straight. It hung halfway down his back and was held back by some kind of leather strap. But his eyes told the real story. Mean, feral eyes that said he would slice anyone who got near.

Shock settled like a stone in Jenny's heart. She turned to Sam, bereaved understanding on her face. "He didn't want to come back."

Sam stiffened up with the arrogant disbelief of one who had been raised to respect and revere his way of life. "How could he not want to come back after living with those heathens? He's just got to get used to things again."

Jenny didn't think so. Ian Thorne looked nothing like she remembered, almost as if Mr. Pat had found the wrong boy. His eyes were hard and uncivilized, yet a definite intelligence lay in their cold depths. His blade moved back and forth, his entire body ready to strike out at the very people who loved him. The injustice of it sparked Jenny's indignation.

For six years Mr. Pat had waited and prayed, sent money and men to find his only son. All these years he had stood constant. Jenny had watched her neighbor keep a flame of hope alive through the death of his beloved wife, past the rumors of war to the actuality of battle. And all for what? So his ungrateful son could come back and mock him? Incensed, she moved away from her brother and walked toward the young warrior.

"Hey, Ian," she called, kind of flirty like her older cousin Camellia often did in mixed company.

His gaze pinned her for a split second, then seared right through. He went back to scanning the crowd.

"Get back, Jenny!" Patrick Thorne warned. "Don't get too close, honey. He's not like you remember."

The anguish in his voice tore at her. "It's all right, Mr. Pat," she called, confident that Ian just needed to recall things a little better. She understood that he'd been away awhile, but this nonsense was eating away at his father.

She strolled closer, a casual, loose-limbed stride. Camellia got whatever she wanted out of boys when she used the same walk and batted her eyelashes a bit. "How you doing, Ian?" she drawled, though there was a sharp edge to her voice. "Why, I wouldn't have recognized you."

"Jenny, get back!" Patrick Thorne's face turned red, his expression desperate. "He doesn't understand you, honey. He's been away too long."

"Course he understands." Jenny moved closer, a warning in her eyes for the stubborn young man. "Don't you, Ian? It's me, Jenny Delaney. We used to sneak down to the river, remember? You and me and Sam." It had been a ritual on Saturdays for the two older boys, with Jenny as a tag-along who threatened to tell if they didn't let her follow.

"Close your ears, Mr. Pat!" she said over her shoulder, then turned back with a smile. "We used to sneak Mama Sassy's pies and take them down there to eat." Closer still she moved, with the impulsive confidence that ruled most of her life and kept her on her mama's bad side. "You remember Mama Sassy's pies?" She had his eye now, though it was obvious he had everyone else in focus too.

"We got caught once and had all our hides tanned and had to go to bed without supper. But we just sneaked right back out. Remember, Ian? We stole on down to the dock and finished off the rest of those blackberry tarts we had pilfered the day before. Mama Sassy never did guess what happened. She blamed old Enis."

She was close enough now to smell the animal fear on his brown body. There was no recognition in his sharp, cold eyes, nothing but an untamed threat. The air was still and humid; a waiting expectancy seemed to hover in the atmosphere. She shuddered with the first hint of uncertainty. She had gotten close, too close. The blood slowly left her face and her throat went dry. "You remember that, don't you, Ian?" she whispered.

His eyes changed in the split second before he lunged, catching her around the shoulders. He crushed her back against his chest and placed the blade at her throat. A string of guttural Comanche flew from his mouth.

His arm was a steel band across her breasts, crushing the air from her. She could feel the knife biting into her neck. More than a warning, it was a lethal promise. Her knees went watery. Her eyes, hopeless and so embarrassed, went to Patrick Thorne.

"Guess you were right, Mr. Pat."

Patrick Thorne raised his palms in supplication. A trickle of blood ran down Jenny Delaney's throat, but the desperation in his son's eyes tore at him just as badly.

"Please, Ian, let her go." Tears threatened to unman him. All these years he'd searched and prayed and kept to his beliefs, only to find his own flesh and blood was someone else now, a young savage who neither needed nor wanted him or the inheritance he'd held intact all these years. "Let her go and we'll take you back, son. We'll get you back to your p-people." He swallowed the hot ball of resentment in his throat. "Ian—"

"No Ian. Thorne!"

The words were harsh, clear, spat through the young warrior's teeth.

"Thorne," Patrick repeated, dying inside. The variation of his son's given name broke his own need and will. He had lost his Ian. His mind knew it, though his heart refused to reconcile the fact. "You are my son," he said in bitter anguish, "whatever your name."

The Comanche began backing away, dragging Jenny with him. Her throat burned but she dared not cry. Fighting back was impossible.

"Wait!" Patrick pleaded. "Thorne, wait!" When the warrior paused, Patrick bade everyone put their weapons down, then ordered them to disperse. Guns and tools followed ropes and chains. The servants began to back away, but the horse trainer stayed on the fringes. "Go on," Patrick commanded him. "Everyone." He held his empty hands up to his son, a show of surrender.

Eyes calculating and suspicious, the Comanche continued backing up again until he was near the woods. A string of foreign words followed, a dire warning.

Patrick looked at him in confusion. "Please, son, we're not going to harm you."

"No son!" the Comanche said clearly.

Jenny had never run so far without stopping. Her lungs heaved. They felt like they would bleed. Her legs and hands had long since started tingling toward numbness. She waited only for her head to do the same. If she fainted, maybe he would leave her behind. She prayed he wouldn't kill her.

A ring of bruises banded her wrist beneath his fingers. Every tug sent fresh pain up her arm. She tried to keep up but her body would no longer obey. She stumbled on a root and went down, then lay there, unable to pull herself up at his relentless tugging. Even the knife waving threateningly before her had no power to move her. She simply could not respond.

She flung her forearm over her eyes. She didn't want to look when he cut her throat, didn't want to see the triumph on his face or her own stupid reflection in his eyes. Her breath rasped in her chest, burning worse than her cut neck.

"Just go ahead and get it over with!" she rasped.

Her clothing clung to her sweat-slick body. The smell of damp earth and summer grass rose from the fecund ground to fill her gasping nostrils. Sunlight filtered through the leaves overhead, making patterns on her closed eyelids. She heard a slithery rustle near a clump of palmetto but still she couldn't move.

When nothing further happened, she opened one eye, then the other. Ian stood still as stone over her, arrested and alert. She caught the sudden glimmer of sunlight off the wicked blade and whimpered low in her throat as it arched down with a soft *whoosh*.

It missed her head by a breath. By the sound of the whipping underbrush, the blade had struck something else though. She rolled to her knees suddenly and stared at the snake severed in half next to the spot where her shoulder had been.

She hung her head, trying not to be ill, but the events of the past half hour were rolling in her belly like curdled milk. She wrapped her arms about her middle and clung, too tired even to retch.

The Comanche scooped up the snake and stuffed it into a pouch, then tried to drag Jenny back to her feet.

"I can't," she said. "I can't go any farther. Just go ahead and kill me."

He looked her over with fierce green eyes, then crouched down in front of her and put the knife at her breast. Her heart slammed against her ribs but she had no energy to fight back. Her chin lifted and her eyes flashed with resentment, but that was the only part of her with enough strength to function.

His eyes narrowed in cunning. One by one he began slicing off the small pearl buttons of her bodice and put them in his pouch. Her dress loosened, then began to gape. Her transparent chemise showed, and her damp flesh beneath. When he reached the fourth button, she rallied and grabbed the gaping fabric in her fist.

"All right!" she cried. "I'll rise!" One hand clutching her bodice, the other grappling with the trunk of a cypress tree for leverage, she pushed to her feet. Her knees were like jelly, and she had no strength to remain standing, much less run again.

He must have known, must have seen it on her face. In a movement too quick for her to counter, he rammed his shoulder into her midriff and hefted her over his back. Like a sack of potatoes, she was carried at a trot along the shallow edges of the riverbank. When the land fell away, he gained dry ground, but most of his time was spent in the shallow depths, where she realized his scent would not be picked up by man or the dogs they would send out to track her.

She closed her eyes in despair and bounced limply over his shoulder. She didn't think of her family, who would be incensed over this latest scrap, or Patrick Thorne, who would feel responsible, but she did wonder what Granny Delaney would have done in a situation like this.

In a fit of exhausted temper, she swiveled around enough to catch his eye. "I'll never forgive you for this, Ian," she said, as if it mattered a whit to the boy she had once loved like a brother.

He only stared back at her, his gaze cold and intractable, not an ounce of regret on his savagely beautiful face.

"This isn't over," she added. "If I get out of this alive, I'll never forgive you."

A woman's manifest destiny is to marry early, and make some man a capital wife and housekeeper.
—*A Proper Wife's Guide to House and Home*

Drivel! Woe to the state of our nation, when such material, and stuff even more flimsy, are to be made the precepts of wives of the rising race, the mothers of the next generation! Into this world of such supreme ignorance, a woman must ascertain with utmost diligence to be smarter, stronger, and more daring. An accomplishment, be warned, men do not appreciate in the least.

—Granny Delaney
Granny's Journal
18 February 1776

Chapter 1

Little Town, 1872
The Territory of New Mexico

JENNIFER DELANEY WAS HOPPING MAD. LITERALLY.

She slapped a battered Stetson against her heavy serge skirt and stomped her foot hard, sending a shock of pain up her leg. It was a tantrum that would have done any one of her second-grade students proud, but on a twenty-three-year-old spinster, in the middle of Main Street in Little Town, it was downright embarrassing.

"Now, Miss Jenny," the sheriff cajoled.

"Don't you 'now Miss Jenny' me, Milton Hardaway!" she growled. "I want to know what this is all about!"

A small crowd began collecting, the silversmith, a banker, the bartender at Whiskey Joe's.

Jenny shoved a paper into the sheriff's chest.

Milton winced. He was an easygoing fellow but not the sort to put up with being molested by a half-pint schoolmarm, in broad daylight, with the town looking on.

"Now, that's enough, Miss Jenny." He rubbed his injured chest in a sullen manner. "That's an official letter of resignation."

"Well, I'm not signing it!" she stated with belligerence. Her chin was stubborn, her eyes ferocious, but inside Jenny was crumbling at the double betrayal. First the turncoat school board, which she had served faithfully for two years, and second Milton himself, for whom she harbored a secret but undying affection.

The sheriff shook his head. "If you don't sign it, Miss Jenny, the school board will fire you. Now, how would that look?" He watched her face turn red and braced himself for the explosion that he could not, as hard as he tried, take too seriously.

Jenny Delaney was about the sweetest, most sincere young woman this side of the Mississippi. Righteous indignation only made her cheeks more rosy, her golden-brown eyes more alive. With her slim figure, healthy complexion, and dark auburn hair, she was the best-looking spinster the territory of New Mexico had ever seen.

And therein lay the problem. Jenny Delaney didn't

look or act like a proper spinster—a fact that made everyone in town insist that she shouldn't be one.

Her nice eyes narrowed a bit more than Milton was used to, and her next words came out considerably louder than he expected.

"Fire me on what grounds?" she bellowed.

He cringed. "That loud mouth might be one!"

He held his hand up when she opened her mouth to protest. She was a bright girl, pretty as a spring daisy and as good as they came. There wasn't a soul in town who wouldn't give everything they owned at least half of the time to help her out.

But Jenny Delaney had a streak of independence a mile long that put her crossways with Little Town's citizens a goodly portion of the other half. She'd been that way forever, to hear her uncle tell it, but ever since Nat Delaney had passed away, the streak seemed worse.

"On what grounds?" she repeated.

In all fairness, the sheriff hated being the one to drop this news on her, but it wasn't like she hadn't caused it. He looked her up and down with disapproval. "You know why."

"Because I kissed that mealy-mouthed tattletale Jimmy Henderson behind the schoolhouse?" She slammed her hat down again. "That's not a crime!"

"Is too, Teach!" Whiskey Joe called from the street. "So is wearin' them ridin' skirts." He spit a stream of brown tobacco juice out the side of his mouth.

"Go on back inside, Joe," the sheriff said over his shoulder. "Miss Jenny's skirts are fine, even if they are a bit unusual." He turned back, his gaze inadvertently making a cursory run over her attire. Slim and shapely, she was a sight for any man's eyes. Jimmy Henderson hadn't had a chance. "You knew the rules when you took the teaching job. No courting, no marrying."

Her eyes narrowed to blazing slits, pretty as agates if one was of a mind to notice, which the sheriff was on occasion, though he was happily engaged to Hannah Thompson. Hannah was a nice temperate woman who knew her manners in public.

Jenny rubbed her throbbing temples. "I was not courting or marrying Jimmy Henderson," she said between gritted teeth.

The sheriff shook his head again. The moment of truth was upon them, and he didn't think Jenny would take kindly to it. "Which is exactly why the school board can't overlook it."

Confusion flashed briefly in her eyes, so much more touching than her spurts of indignation. A man wanted to protect a woman when she looked like that.

Milton guarded himself against it. "You have no excuse for such wanton behavior, Jenny Delaney, and you know it. Now, if you had been caught up in a swoon of love and devotion, they might have turned their heads and got ready for a June wedding, but you had no intentions at all beyond sowing wild oats. Your uncle would roll in his grave at such a show of loose morals."

The mention of her dear departed uncle made her bottom lip quiver. "That's not fair, Milt."

He knew it wasn't, but he needed every weapon he could find where Jenny was concerned. It was just too easy to overlook her rebellion and sink into those generous, honest eyes like the rest of the town did. She was their darling, loved and indulged since her arrival from the war-torn South. But at age twenty-three, they'd had enough of her independent ways.

"Darn it, Jen," he whispered with the intimacy of long friendship, "you could have at least shown some remorse for getting caught. Just a little would have helped."

His familiar use of her name caused Jenny to go soft inside. "Oh, I'm remorseful," she said. "It was the stupidest thing I ever did." She grimaced just thinking about it. Jimmy Henderson's kiss had been wet and slimy and grasping. The man had nearly fallen into a faint when she broke contact.

"But Jimmy's intentions were honorable. He'd marry you tomorrow, if you'd just say the word."

"Me and every other woman he's asked from here to California."

It was no secret that Jimmy was a bit free and excessive in his declaration of love. "Still, you have a legitimate claim."

Jenny's stomach heaved at the thought of marrying Jimmy. He *had* been trying to court her, in a manner of speaking, but he was about as insincere as a truly decent man could be. That day behind the schoolhouse—the last day of the school year and Jenny's birthday to boot—he had been handy and willing and a big mistake.

Jenny's heart sank when she thought of half the town knowing of her behavior, especially the sheriff. It had been a foolish, meaningless thing to do, but she had never dreamed it would cause such upheaval. And the children! The children were about to be stripped from her tutelage because of one reckless moment.

She stirred the dust with her toe. "I just wanted to see what it was like, Sheriff. Just once," she added with the old Southern charm all but gone from her life. "Is that so bad?"

The sheriff wasn't proof against her soulful eyes. A pretty, twenty-three-year-old spinster *should* be able to know what it felt like to be kissed by a man. If he wasn't engaged . . .

Her mouth tightened at his silence. "It's not like I took him to my bed."

A fit of coughing seized the sheriff. He glanced around quickly to see if anyone else had overheard. "Lord have mercy, Jenny! You better quit such talk or you'll be run outta town on a rail!"

She flung her head back and stared skyward, as if seeking divine intervention. "The nearest railroad is Santa Fe." She looked back at Milt. "There has to be something you can do," she pleaded, "something you can say to them. If you're truly my friend, Milt—"

"Don't," he said. He would not be pulled in by her pleading. He had already talked to the school board, just as she had, all to no avail. " 'Bout the only thing they'll listen to is wedding bells."

She gritted her teeth. "I'd rather die." Her hands flew to her slim hips. "So this is it? One kiss and I'm reduced to the equivalent of a floozy, not fit to teach the children?" The betrayal of it washed over her and made her see red. Jimmy Henderson didn't love her any more than any other girl he had courted, yet the town would marry Jenny off to him without a thought. And strong-arm her into doing it by threatening to take away the very thing she loved most!

She turned sharply, grabbed her mare's reins, then slapped them into the sheriff's hand. "Take care of Bulle," she said with high drama. "Since I'm such a loose trollop, accused and condemned without trial, I have to go find another job more appropriate for a fallen woman." That said, she turned on her heel and proceeded to march down Main Street, every bit of ire inside her transferred to her long, ground-eating strides.

She had nice, slender hips that swung like a sassy pendulum in the split skirt, Milton thought, then felt bad for his wayward attention. No one could deny that Jenny Delaney had a good heart and a giving soul. She just had too much spirit to go with them.

She passed the milliner, the apothecary shop, the general store, and still she kept going.

Doc Brown waved at her from the front door of his office, and Walt Henry from the jailhouse. The sheriff watched as Wolf gave her a funny look when she passed the general store without so much as a hello. Where in tarnation was she headed?

If the truth were known, half the men in town were afraid Jenny Delaney was going to turn into one of those high-minded suffragettes and half the women were afraid she wasn't. Both sexes agreed it was past time for her to be married and settled, and the school board, which now had leverage, was determined to see it done the best way they knew how.

The sheriff coaxed Bulle over toward the livery. "Obstinate girl."

Thorne had watched the altercation from the shadows of the stable yard. He was used to seeing the sheriff in action when a fight broke out or when Henry Winchell got a little too drunk or the mayor's wife was upset because the Larkins' pigs were in her vegetable patch again. But he'd never seen anyone end up on the wrong side of the schoolteacher. She was a bold thing, with her chin jutted out and eyes flashing golden-brown fire.

She had always been that way.

A fight broke out in the general store. Willie Joe Turner and Bobby Wright tumbled into the street, swearing and swinging. The sheriff swore beneath his breath and looped the gelding's reins over the hitching post.

Thorne stepped into the sunlight and gave him a look. "You gonna let her keep going?"

Milton glanced back to see that Jenny had passed all the respectable businesses in town and was headed for the seedy end. He cursed a blue streak, took the reins back, and handed them to Thorne. "See to her, would you?" he asked. "I've got to go break up this fight." He took off toward the store.

Thorne, the mare in tow, followed Milton into the street. "I don't think that's wise, Sheriff."

"The hell with wise," Milton said in exasperation. "Just go before she gets herself in worse trouble. Tell her she's made her point and to git on home."

"And if she won't go?"

Willie Joe had grabbed up a branding iron from the back of Bobby's wagon and was about to bash the younger man over the head with it. "Turn her over your knee," the sheriff yelled on the run.

Thorne swung up onto the mare's back and took off. He could see that Jenny had reached the steps of Lucy's Lovely Ladies and was actually going toward the door. He kicked the horse into a gallop. Dust rose beneath the mare's hooves as the road sped away beneath. By the time Thorne reached the stoop, Jenny was pounding at the wooden door. He flung himself from Bulle's back and caught her around the waist just as she was about to knock a second time.

A startled shriek rent the air. She flailed her arms about wildly as she lost her equilibrium, then twisted and dodged until she was put back on her feet.

"What do you think you're doing, Jenny Delaney?"

The voice was deep, not the sheriff's. The arms around her middle were exceptionally strong. Jenny twisted sharply to find herself face to face with Ian Blackwell Thorne. A quiver of unease moved over her.

"Get your hands off me," she said softly. She tried to shrug him off but his hold was unbreakable. "Let me go, Ian. This is none of your concern."

She was the only one left in the world who called him Ian. It put an old familiar wrench in his gut. "The sheriff made it mine." He tightened his hold in warning. "I have specific instructions if you refuse to follow."

Her eyes flashed fury and false bravado. "What are you going to do, Ian, put a blade to my throat again?"

Her chin lifted in haughty arrogance, revealing the thin white scar at her neck, but the effect was spoiled by a hint of unshed tears.

"If I have to," he warned.

He was dressed like any other man in town, gritty from the constant dust-laden wind, but his bearing bore the strong, sure quickness of the savage he had been ten years ago. Jenny broke eye contact first. She'd never been able to reconcile the Ian she had known as a boy to the Comanche who had kept her hostage in the woods for three days before deciding he would return to his father's plantation. He had left her on her own doorstep as if she were nothing, less than a consideration. And she had ignored him in the same manner over the following years as the war consumed the South.

Now Ian, yet another personality, had shown up in Little Town three years ago to take his place as a common citizen, hardworking and seemingly honest, but Jenny didn't fully trust him. The boy she had known was gone and in his place was an enigmatic man she didn't care to know.

The bordello door opened a crack. A tousled, sleepy-eyed matron peeked out. "Why, Mr. Thorne, whatever are you doing here this time of day? You know we don't see customers until dusk without special arrangements."

The schoolteacher stiffened in his arms, and he clenched his teeth. "Mornin', Lucy."

Lucy looked Jenny up and down with feigned surprise. "You can't bring your sweetheart in, deary. She's not one of my girls."

Jenny lunged forward but got nowhere. "I'm applying for a job!" she said over the stranglehold Ian had around her waist.

Lucy rolled her eyes. "That right, sugar?"

"No," Thorne interrupted. "Pay her no mind, she's just overwrought right now. Sorry to trouble you." He began dragging Jenny back down the sidewalk toward her horse.

Lucy leaned out so that her generous endowments almost spilled from her gauzy peignoir. A cloying hint of gardenia drifted on the dry air. "Been awhile, Thorne," she purred. "Come on back later without your little friend."

He said nothing, just kept carrying Jenny bucking and twisting to her horse. Despite a jab to his ribs and several misplaced kicks that came dangerously close to his groin, he got her in the saddle, then swung up behind her. When she tried to squirm back over the side, he grabbed the front of her blouse in a hard fist. "You make one more move," he warned, "and I'll tan your hide good. Sheriff's orders."

She growled something sullen and unladylike beneath her breath. She would have taken off like a shot, but his arms had her penned and his hand was pressed into her midsection. She didn't like one bit the fact that Ian Thorne still had the power to intimidate her a little.

Ten years had passed since she found out that charm and sweet words could not soothe a savage beast. But with his strong arms controlling her horse as easily as he had controlled her that day, it felt more like ten minutes.

The old feelings of fearful insecurity came rushing back like a bad dream.

Her misplaced boldness, her stupidity at attempting to do what none of his family had been able to, still embarrassed her. And she still had the scar on her neck to remind her that it was a wonder she was alive at all.

Her back bumped into his chest and she didn't make any effort to sit up straighter. Let her weight drag him down, make it harder for him to stay in the saddle.

"I can't believe you decided to come back here and settle down," Jenny huffed.

He had been part of Little Town for several years, but it was a complicated subject and one he chose not to discuss.

When he said nothing, she added, "I can't believe you're Jeremiah's daddy!"

"Why?"

"He's so sweet and friendly and *smart*."

That was Jeremiah, all right. The brightest star. The best thing in Thorne's life. The only thing left. "Yep."

That was all, just that one word while he controlled her horse and bore her, against her will, back into the heart of town. "I'm not resigning!" she said mulishly.

He didn't have a clue what she was talking about. "Good."

She swiveled around and tried to face him, but his arms tightened to pin her more firmly to his chest. "You don't agree with everyone else?"

"Depends."

"On what?"

"What you're talking about."

She slumped back in pique and folded her arms over her middle. His chest was solid against her back, the heat of him seeping right through the back of her shirt. Gingerly she straightened back up. He was an uncomfortable man to be around with his dark looks and silent calculations. Although she knew he was a law-abiding citizen and not one to cause trouble in town, she generally stayed out of his way. There was too much between them for her ever to feel comfortable in his presence.

"Never mind. You'll hear soon enough."

Thorne rode right up to the sheriff, delivered Jenny into the dust at the lawman's feet, then swung her horse around toward the livery. The schoolteacher, sassy temper and all, riding up against him for just those few minutes had had an obvious impact on his masculine senses. Ten years certainly did change a girl, and it had changed Jenny Delaney in all the right places.

Milton helped Jenny up. Her eyes were blazing, her fists balled at her sides. But there was also a hint of hopeless tears in her eyes that softened him.

"Jenny . . ."

"I can't lose that job, Milt!" she whispered in desperation. Her eyes held his in silent understanding. Not only would she lose her children, but the ranch would fold without the meager pay she put back into it. "You know I can't."

He did know, which made him all the more determined to stand with the town on this. Her foreman had run off with a saloon girl less than a week past, compounding her already dire problems. She needed a man who not only could keep her in line but one who could work the ranch and keep it from going under. But Milton couldn't find it in himself to hurt her further by saying so.

"Talk to the parents," he said. "They may not feel as strongly about this as the school board."

Jenny shrugged out of his hold. Anger and fear clogged her throat, making her hoarse. "The parents *are* the school board."

"Only six of them." Compassion aside, he regarded her frankly. "If anyone was to ask my opinion, and they will, I'll side with you, at least as far as the resignation is concerned."

Her heart skipped a beat. "Thank you, Milt."

He meant every word. She was Hannah's best friend, *his* friend, and the best sort of person. For all her feckless ways, he'd seen her with the children and found nothing to criticize. She was warm and stern and forgiving. A rare combination among the stiff-necked, hickory-stick-swinging educators he'd grown up with.

Jenny Delaney, the teacher, didn't put up with any foolishness, but she did send boys like Tommy Chancellor out to run off their rambunctiousness when they got scrappy from sitting so long. Tommy's own parents didn't have that much patience. If Milton, who didn't even have any kids, could see her value, maybe a lot of others felt the same way.

"Talk to the parents, Jenny. There's a whole summer ahead of you to convince them."

A small spark of hope ignited within her, replacing the desperation. "All right, Sheriff, I'll try."

• • •

It took Jenny almost three days to get around to every family in Little Town. Halfway through the third day, her stomach was in knots, her hope dwindling fast. Half the parents, stammering and uncomfortable, didn't have much more sympathy than the six school board members. Few wanted their children taught by a woman who had let her morals slip. But oddly enough, all were willing to forgive her if she agreed to marry Jimmy Henderson.

It was a conspiracy at the highest level, and she was not giving in to them.

The other half of the town thought the whole thing was the most ridiculous bit of nonsense they had ever heard, but agreed that rules were rules and she *had* taken the job knowing them. It seemed that they would be pacified as well if she would just marry Jimmy Henderson.

Beneath all the ruckus, no one could really understand why a pretty girl like Jennifer Delaney had let herself go unattached so long. It wasn't as if she were long in the tooth, as Ezra Pollock put it, or lacking in good breeding or dowry. She came from an old distinguished Southern family—her mother had been a Brewton from South Carolina, after all, her father a Delaney. One of *the* Delaneys who had made their fortune in cotton, then lost it during the war.

Jenny had inherited her uncle's horse ranch free of debt. Any number of able-bodied young men would like to get their hands on it. Several had made offers, which Jenny had turned down. Within the social boundaries of a town that lived and died by its hard work, weddings, and births, it just didn't make sense. Given the simple existence of frontier life, *Jenny* didn't make sense.

The diligent parents of Little Town, in the Territory of New Mexico, would see Jennifer Delaney married if it was the last collective thing they did.

Chapter 2

With a sinking heart, Jenny kicked her horse into a faster gait to reach the last parent on her list before sundown.

Thorne.

She felt a little knot of tension crawl up her spine as she steered her horse into the canyon. No one in town called him Ian. In fact, they didn't even know him by his real name. He lived up in a secluded dugout, about as far from civilization as a man could be and still use the local conveniences. He was a loner, the townsfolk said, strange but friendly enough. If they only knew, Jenny thought.

She would never forget the day he had returned with her from the woods. No word, no explanation. He had simply walked back to Thorne Manor as if it were his right, leaving her at the gate of her own plantation weeping in anger and relief as her family had rushed to enfold her.

She went for months without seeing him after that day but she always knew he was there, a mere stone's throw away, and she had steered clear of Thorne Manor. Then the war had come, four years of anguish and despair that had seen the end of Jenny's carefree life.

She and Ian had both lost their families and most of their land as a result of the war. Jenny had been sent west to live with her uncle. Thorne, the only name he would allow anyone to call him, had been her escort.

Mr. Pat, broken from the war and grieving from the recent death of Jenny's father and brother, had cried as he confirmed the simple facts she already knew. There was nothing left for her in Mississippi. Her mother had succumbed to a fever years before, the plantation had been burned to the ground. Her only living relatives were her father's brother, Nathaniel, and a senile aunt, Matilda.

Outside the charred remains of River Run, Patrick Thorne had struck a bargain with his estranged son: Take Jenny west and Thorne could stay there if he wished.

Though he spoke English when he chose and dressed like a white man, Thorne had never really reacclimated to his former life. Sullen and resentful, he had done little more than live off the land the first few months of his return, a silent betrayal that had eaten at his father. Then one day Thorne just walked into the house as if nothing had happened and took his place at the table.

Over the next year he read every book in Thorne Manor library, worked with the horses from dawn to dusk, and learned everything he could about the running of the stables. For another year after that, he traveled extensively, which made Mr. Pat very nervous. But he always returned. On his last visit home, he stayed.

Despite the war moving increasingly closer to Mississippi, despite the great number of horses that continued to be sent to help the cause, it was the happiest Jenny remembered seeing Patrick Thorne. His son was finally home.

Then tragedy struck and shattered all their dreams. Jenny received word that both her father and brother had been killed in battle. Federal troops moved into Mississippi. They burned River Run to the ground and took over Thorne Manor, confiscating the rest of the horses.

Patrick absolved his son of any responsibility for what remained of his inheritance and turned his attention to doing what he could for his best friend's child. He understood, as Jenny did not, that his son could not stay. Patrick asked Thorne to see Jenny safely through the South and on through Indian territory to her uncle's ranch. He then bade his son, the son he had searched for all those years, to stay out West until the war was over.

There was no other choice. Young, strong, and able-bodied, Ian Blackwell Thorne would no longer be allowed to lead an independent existence. Mr. Pat knew his son would have to choose sides if he stayed and fight for the North, which would have been an abomination to the land of his birth, or fight a losing battle for the South. With his world caving in around him, Patrick chose the only thing that made sense to him: secure a safe future for Jenny and his son.

Stealing his own horses in the dead of night, the man now known only as Thorne had taken Jenny on the most grueling, heart-wrenching journey of her life. He'd had no pity for her tears or exhaustion, no sympathy at all that she was leaving behind everything she had ever known. He had a job to do, a promise to keep, and he did it.

In the end it was probably for the best. She'd had little time to think, to mourn, or to wallow in self-pity. Each grueling day was given over to simple survival. When they finally reached the Territory of New Mexico, Jenny felt as if she'd been through the fires of Hell, emerging charred but stronger, purged of the pampered life she'd left behind.

Almost five years from the day he had hauled her into the woods, Thorne left Jenny Delaney in Little Town with her uncle Nat, then disappeared. She remembered praying at night that Thorne had returned to his father, that Mr. Pat was not alone at the plantation he had built for his son. Her prayers had gone unanswered. Thorne showed up in Little Town less than two years later, no explanation, with a baby strapped to his back. A half-breed, some said, but no one knew for sure since the child had fair skin and hair. In fact, no one knew anything at all about the man known only as Thorne, except that he spoke Comanche as fluently as he did English, had a peaceful nature at first glance, and fought dirty as a savage when provoked.

He was accepted over the next few years as a hard-working and honest man, but few could really say they knew him as a friend.

Jenny stayed out of his way.

She reined her horse in when the land rose sharply. This last part of the trail would be tough, but she had no choice. He was a parent like any other and due his own opinion. Still, she'd rather cut her own tongue off than ask for his support.

Not that he'd give it.

She started up the incline on foot, dragging her gelding after her. The path was steep, slippery. She stumbled several times, then gritted her teeth and pressed on. She was here for the children, the students who meant everything to her. And Thorne's son was one of the brightest— which was inspiring, since Jeremiah Thorne was only four years old.

She gripped the base of a scrub oak and pulled herself higher. Although each of the children she taught held a piece of her heart and gave her a reason to go begging on doorsteps, Jeremiah Thorne gave her the biggest reason of all. Deep down in the secret heart of her, he was her baby, the child she might never have. It might have been unprofessional for her to become so attached, but she felt a personal affinity for all her students, and Jeremiah gave her plenty of academic reasons as well.

Astonishingly bright, he was already doing mathematics and reading with the second graders, yet he was so young and still needy in a way the older boys who went home to their mothers every night were not. He crawled into her lap at storytime. He needed every bump and bruise kissed. Blanket clutched in his fist, thumb in his mouth, he still took a nap midday.

Jenny took a deep breath for composure. What would happen to this child if she were replaced with some stern-faced university scholar who had grandiose notions of civilizing the rough West?

The thought was horrifying and gave her the strength to continue on. She wasn't afraid of Ian. At least, she told herself she wasn't. The slight unease in her body was due to the chilling wind moving down from the north. It had a wicked bite that stung her cheeks and nose and made her ears ache. Spring had waned, summer was all but here, yet it seemed to have taken a recess for the time being. Clouds had moved steadily in over the ride out, an ugly gray cloak that didn't bode well for her return trip home.

Jenny tugged on Bulle's reins. "C'mon," she urged, but the horse, unpredictable by nature, was growing even more skittish with the changing weather.

A portion of sandy soil and rock fell away and Jenny slipped. She grappled for a hold on a gnarled stump but went down hard on one knee, wincing as a sharp stone dug into her flesh. Murmuring an epithet beneath her breath, she rose and kept climbing.

Her leg was throbbing unbearably, her mood as foul as the weather when she reached the flat mesa at the front of the old dugout. Cut from the canyon wall, it emerged as part of the land itself, the protruding front finished with stone and adobe masonry. Smoke curled from a chimney, so she knew someone was home, but that was the only sign of life. It was a dismal place, harsh and uninviting. She limped up to the door and rapped. It seemed to take forever for it to open a crack.

A man stood there, tall and imposing. There was no welcome in his eyes.

"Ian—" she began.

"Thorne."

"I know who you are," she returned in a curt tone, then felt bad for alienating him when she needed his help. "Thorne," she conceded. Her knee hurt so badly she wanted to cry. She had to grit her teeth against the pain. "May I come in?"

He didn't budge. He had wrestled for two and a half days with the twisted, unsettling emotions of being close to Jenny Delaney again, and he wasn't in the mood to resurrect them. "If this has something to do with the other day—"

"The school board has asked me to resign."

The door swung open forcefully, and he pulled her inside with a hissed raw profanity. "Imbeciles," he added, and bodily put her in a chair.

With a skewed sort of reasoning, Jenny sensed an ally in the man standing before her with a black scowl on his face. It wasn't his expression, which was hard and cold, and certainly not the rough way he handled her, which had her leg throbbing even worse.

"I'll make coffee," he said.

She nodded like a dimwit and folded her hands in her lap. She felt insignificant in his presence, just as when she was thirteen and held captive in the woods, then at seventeen being bullied across endless miles, pushed until she could go no farther, then forced to go farther still.

He was taller now, even more intimidating, and Jenny knew better than anyone what he was capable of. Her fingers went to the collar of her blouse.

She wished she hadn't come now, wished she had just gone on home to think things through better. But she was fiercely protective of his young son, and the school board's threat had her more frightened than the man who called himself Thorne.

Stiffly, ungraciously, she said, "Thank you for seeing me uninvited."

He glanced back at her over his shoulder, a sardonic lift to his brow. "We don't often stand on ceremony here."

Jenny glanced around for Jeremiah but he was nowhere in sight. "You should know that I'm here to gather support against the school board."

She took a deep breath and began to state her case. "I've been on my own for years, caring for the ranch my uncle left me and teaching Little Town's children. I'm poor at ranching, and no one will say differently, but I'm a good teacher." It was her love, her life, her human contact. And it was all about to end.

The ache in her knee worsened. She felt a little woozy with the pain. The fact that Ian Thorne might be on her side was the only thing keeping her in the dugout. Otherwise, she would have been tearing out of the mountain at breakneck speed and getting herself over to the doc.

She studied her surroundings to get her mind off the pain, but her vision began to blur. The shelter looked as old as the hills it was carved from, but it was tidy. The furnishings were spare and handmade. A sturdy table and two chairs, a bedstead covered with a hand-woven blanket. It was too dark inside for her comfort, a bit like the man at the stove.

"Where's Jeremiah?" she asked.

"Napping."

He didn't turn, didn't acknowledge her at all beyond the clipped answer as he continued to make coffee. Jenny wondered if she'd misread him earlier. She pressed a hand to her throbbing leg, then gasped. It came away bloody.

Thorne turned at the sound to see the schoolteacher's face go white. Her hand was fisted in her lap, and a dark wet stain was spreading on her skirt. He set the coffee down and moved forward. "You hurt or . . . inconvenienced?"

She blushed. "Hurt." She swallowed back a lump of nausea in her throat. The pain was tearing at her now that she knew she was really injured. "I fell on my way up."

There were several ways to handle this, but Thorne wasn't sure which one was best. He could crouch down and flip her skirts over her head, but she was on the verge of fainting anyway, so he thought he'd just wait for that to happen, then do whatever needed to be done. "I'll turn my back while you look at it," he said.

He heard a throaty moan and cursed silently. "You done?" He turned back slowly to find her face whiter than before. "Is it bad?"

She nodded and began to sway.

He gripped her by both arms to keep her upright. "I'm going to look at it."

She got a concerned look on her face for a fleeting second, then nodded and hung her head.

He pushed skirt and petticoat up to midthigh. The gash was just below her knee, ugly and deep. It went all the way to the bone and must have hurt like the devil. "You really did it," he muttered. "It needs stitching."

"No," she rasped, wide-eyed.

He smiled wryly at her graying features. "You won't feel a thing." He caught her as she toppled from the chair and lay her on his bed. She wouldn't stay out long, so he worked fast. He fetched a medicine box, then returned to the bed. After reaching up beneath her skirt, he grabbed both her garter and torn stocking and slid them to her ankle. He then cleaned the wound and began applying a salve that would keep the area somewhat numb.

She mumbled as she came to and tried to sit up. He placed a hand to her midriff. "Keep still."

The command was cold and firm. Jenny lay still. She realized she was on the bed she'd noticed earlier. "How did I get here?"

"You swooned."

An incensed gasp followed. "I would never swoon!"

"Then how did you get here?"

Her chin went up. "I passed out. There is a difference."

He had the urge to chuckle, but her leg was no laughing matter so he contained the emotion. He held up a cup. "Drink this."

She eyed him suspiciously. "What—"

He caught her behind her head with one hand and practically poured the tea down her throat with the other.

She coughed and sputtered and tried to sit up straight, but his hand was there, pressing her back down into the mattress. "Sing to me," he said gently.

"What?" she asked, feeling dazed. She spoke to the back of his head, since he was bent over her leg. His hair was brown but so gilded by the sun it almost appeared golden. It was too long for civil society, making him look like an outlaw, but his hands were gentle. The world was beginning to fade at the edges of her vision.

"The songs you sing to the kids in school. Sing them for me."

Her eyes narrowed, a great feat since everything was murky now. "Why?"

He lifted his head and gave her a direct look. "You'll need to keep your mind off what I'm doing."

Her face blanched again and tears filled her eyes. "What *are* you doing?"

"Sing!"

Her voice was wobbly and weak, but she sang. Her head spun from whatever he had given her to drink and her tongue was sluggish. But trying to remember the words did help keep her mind off other things. There was pain, but it was distant, an irritation that almost felt as if it were happening to someone else. The sharper it grew, the faster she sang. She didn't realize he was done until he began tearing strips of bandaging. She trembled all over in the aftermath.

He held out a kerchief, and she gave him a perplexed look. "For the tears you are not crying," he said dryly.

She grabbed it and pressed it to her eyes. "I didn't swoon."

"Right." He pulled her shoe off and removed the ruined stocking. He decided to forgo the other one. She was trim and shapely, and he must be a lecher to notice how nice her legs looked at a time like this. He pulled her skirt back down, then rose and dragged a chair over. "We need to talk."

She looked at him, though his image seemed to swim a bit. She refused to be intimidated by his stern voice. "That's why I came up here."

Thorne laid the rest of the bandaging aside. Jenny Delaney was pert and pretty, and he'd been much too long without the comforts of a nice woman. Despite Lucy's invitation, he'd never been to the brothel. He couldn't get away for such lurid pleasure with a four-year-old in tow. Although he didn't consider himself to have any moral compunctions *not* to indulge, he just didn't seem inclined to go after overused forbidden fruit.

Jennifer Delaney was a different matter. She was innocent and feisty, and the combination added to prolonged abstinence was twisting his insides into nice tight knots.

He rose quickly. "You've got to keep the leg still or the stitches will tear," he warned.

Jenny's bluster began to waver. She knew what he was saying but didn't want to believe it. She gave him a doubtful look. "I can't leave here yet?"

He nodded.

"Then where will you go?"

He wouldn't look at her. "Nowhere. There's a storm moving in."

She flung her head back against the pillow and covered her face with both hands. "I'm doomed, ruined, a fallen woman!"

Thorne's gaze swung back to her, narrowed and vicious. "I'm not going to touch you."

She slammed her fist down. "I know that, but tell it to *them*. I'm already soiled in their eyes. This will just clinch it. I'll lose my job for certain now."

"Whose eyes?"

"The school board's. That's why I came up here."

He wondered if the drugged tea still had her a bit light-headed. "What did you do?"

Her bottom lip pushed out in a pout. Her vision was still fuzzy and she felt as if she talked to him through a mist. "I kissed Jimmy Henderson. One stupid kiss and they want to brand me as a wanton woman. If I stay here all night, they'll have more than enough ammunition to finish me."

Ah, the strictures of polite society. "Why'd you do it?"

The storm started rattling the windows. Leaves began to swirl like confetti on the air. Jenny groaned and turned her face away. "It was stupid."

"So was coming up here with weather moving in from the north."

"Go away," she mumbled. He backed up and headed for the door. Jenny's eyes went round. "No, wait. I was just—"

He gave her a long-suffering look. "I'm going to see to your horse."

She lay back in his bed, feeling about as skittish as possible with her mind in a cloud. Thorne was too handsome, all sharp features and rugged angles. He was tall and strong with an air of inviolability. If she was going to be fired anyway, she wished she had kissed *him*!

The thought put a little quiver in her belly, and she regretted the shocking notion. She was half in love with the sheriff, despite his engagement to one of the sweetest girls she knew. Milt was a man of honor and upright standing in town. Thorne was a dangerous, unpredictable loner with a savage past. Not only had her morals slipped, so had her mind.

Tears stung behind her eyelids. She couldn't quite credit the fact that she might lose the children. She missed her family so badly she couldn't breathe sometimes, and her students filled the awful emptiness, at least during the daylight hours. If the loneliness crept back each night, it was something she'd grown accustomed to, something that must be endured. At least she had her days to counterbalance it.

Oh, Uncle Nat. She missed him too and had made such a muddle of things since his death. She heard Bulle whinny outside and pushed herself into a sitting position, clenching her teeth against the pain. Ian Thorne was too imposing a man to face flat on her back.

The weather that had been threatening all afternoon

finally moved in with a vengeance. Thunder shook the walls in a sudden rumble, then rolled on down the canyon. The patter of small feet followed.

"Pa!"

Jenny glanced at the four-year-old tearing down a ladder from the loft. "He'll be back in a moment."

Jeremiah stopped dead still and stared, mouth agape. "Miss Jenny?"

She smiled. "Hi, Jeremiah."

He tilted his head to the side. "What are you doing in Pa's bed?"

A blush heated her cheeks. "I was paying a visit to tell him how excellent you're doing in school and I hurt myself."

His mouth formed an "O" of concern. "You all right?"

She smiled and nodded. His *r*s were still immature and sounded like *w*s. "I will be, but I can't move my leg right now or ride my horse home."

He looked at her intently, an expression he often gave to harder work in school. "Are you sad, Miss Jenny?"

She was heartbroken at the thought of not teaching this child any longer. "No, why would you think that?"

"You've been crying. We don't have much here. Your place is lots better."

Perplexed, she studied him. "But you've never been to see me."

"Me and Pa ride there a lot on Sundays. We take a picnic past your house to the stream in the mountain. He says we'll have a place just like that one day."

"Oh." She felt as if she'd been poleaxed. Her ranch

was a good thirty-minute ride away. "Your pa works at the livery, doesn't he?"

"Yes, ma'am." He climbed up in the chair by the bed and swung his feet. "You still look sad, Miss Jenny."

"I just feel so badly about imposing on you and your pa."

"What's 'posing?"

"Oh . . . needing or expecting attention from you. I'm sure your pa has better things to do than nurse a clumsy schoolteacher."

Jeremiah shrugged. "He likes you something fierce."

Jenny's mouth fell open. "Why do you say that?"

" 'Cause when we go by your house, I say to Pa, 'Ain't she pretty?' and he says to me, 'She sure is, Jeremiah.' Then he says *'Don't say ain't!'* just like you do, Miss Jenny."

She smiled, a bit embarrassed, a bit flattered, though she had no delusions about herself. At twenty-three and no prospects she was a spinster, on the shelf by her own hand, without much hope of getting down. But the words still warmed those places inside her that had missed the courting and flirting stripped from her teenage years by the war.

She shifted to better regard Jeremiah from her prone position. "Tell me again why you come by my house."

"Pa likes the horses. He says you have the best stock in the territory, but your place is going down fast since your uncle died."

Anger lit inside Jenny. The place was going down fast because she couldn't work it and teach at the same time, her foreman had just quit, and there was no money to hire on any more help than she already had.

"I suppose your pa could do better?" she asked, then felt mean-spirited for saying it aloud.

"Of course," Jeremiah said matter-of-factly. "The Comanche are great horsemen."

Chapter 3

COMANCHE? IAN BLACKWELL THORNE WAS NO MORE Comanche than she was, Jenny thought, then changed her mind. The savage who had put a knife to her throat ten years ago was everything but a gentleman farmer from the great State of Mississippi.

She had changed as well. Afternoon teas and summer socials were a thing of the past, long dead from a life that had veered off completely. She hardly thought of the old life anymore and missed it even less. It was her family that she longed for, the sense of home and comfort and belonging, not perfumed honeysuckle vines and sipping mint tea on the verandah.

Too restless, too unfit to be a proper lady, Mama used to scold. Jenny missed even that, not the fussing but the care her mother had taken to "raise her properly." She had never really been like her mother, not like her cousin Camellia or her friend Hannah. *A hoyden,* her father had ungraciously called her, but with affection—always with a certain pride and affection in his booming voice. He had taken immense delight in letting her proper mother know he didn't disapprove of Jenny's boyish ways.

She missed that most, the loud, window-rattling roar of his "Jenny girl! Get down here! Got something for you to see!" Her schoolwork would scatter across the polished desk as she raced from the table. Her tutor would roll his eyes and swear beneath his breath in French. It was never anything big, she realized now, never anything so important that it couldn't wait for lessons to be over.

But they had been big surprises to a child. Things to delight in and gasp over: an odd-looking stone, a robin's egg, a scrawny abandoned kitten with its eyes still closed.

Together she and her father had found shelves to display, made beds to warm abandoned pets. Together they had enjoyed the beauty of nature—or its capriciousness. That's why they were human, her father used to say, separate and superior to mother cats who dragged off their young to die. They had a duty to care for creatures who couldn't care for themselves.

The door opened. Jeremiah swung around with an exhaled "Pa!" and rushed into his father's arms. Thorne lifted him high and settled him in the crook of his elbow. "I told Miss Jenny you're a better horseman than she is."

Thorne's eyes widened, then narrowed, shielding his thoughts. "Did you?"

"But she's the best schoolteacher."

"Without parallel." He put his son down and regarded Jenny. "Sorry."

"I didn't take offense," she said. "Fact is I'm terrible with raising horses because I never learned how. Back at River Run, Papa raised cotton. Horses were only a sideline for him." She smiled wistfully. "He and your father could talk for hours about raising and racing them. I was always sent off with the women. Papa didn't want me to 'worry my pretty head' about anything pertaining to business."

She frowned. "I think they wanted to talk about breeding and didn't want me to listen. After I got here, well, Uncle Nat tried, but there wasn't time." She gave a huff of displeasure and plucked at the blanket. "I sure could use some of their knowledge now."

Thorne understood. Learning the intricacies of horse ranching took time, time that Jenny had not had before illness took her uncle. But she was attractive and smart, and had a dowry any man would envy. It didn't make sense that a once-prosperous horse ranch was failing for lack of attention. "Why haven't you married?"

Her chin lifted a notch. She thought everyone in town knew, but apparently this man minded his own business when he went in for work or supplies.

"When Uncle Nat took ill, he couldn't be left alone. I had to care for him. There was no time for the usual socializing, and no one wanted the burden of a wife with an invalid guardian and senile aunt." Her expression hardened. "Anyone who came around after he passed away, I sent packing. If they couldn't help when

Uncle Nat was alive, I wouldn't have them after he was gone."

She looked down, self-conscious and puzzled as she smoothed the folds of her skirt. "Time got away, I guess. The next thing I knew, I was past the age for courting but without the liberties of a widow." Her brow furrowed, as if she had just realized the truth of her own words. "The thing is . . . I don't feel any older. It seems like I just turned around one day and went from eighteen to spinster."

Thorne found no self-pity in her expression, just a baffled embarrassment that she had revealed so much. She might not feel older but she looked it in every way that counted. There was a maturity to her unblemished features, an intelligence that belittled the childishness of a younger woman. Her youth showed through in her exuberance and fire and flawless complexion. But it was her maturity and straightforward candor that sent heat seeping into uncomfortable places in his body. It wasn't her age that had put her on the shelf but her bold manner and fearless acceptance of life, if not its strictures.

While the others had cowered that day a decade ago on his father's plantation, Jenny had marched forward, undaunted by what she saw. She knew only what needed to be done. If reckless and impulsive, she still showed an inordinate amount of bravery, and he had to respect that.

The men of her generation had been reared to respect piety and circumspect behavior in the women they took to wife. They were skittish of women who needed taming.

But Thorne had not been raised since age twelve with

the same social conventions. A woman like Jenny was stirring to a man who had not been near anything like her—had purposefully stayed clear of everyone—in more years than he now cared to remember. Her showing up on his isolated doorstep, with a bad cut on a pair of legs that were much too shapely, didn't help matters any.

He glanced aside to see Jeremiah busy playing with a carved wooden horse, then looked back at Jenny. "Why did you kiss Jimmy Henderson?"

The question threw her, and it took a moment for her to recover. She sent him a self-deprecating smile. "Because I'm an imbecile?"

"Hardly. Why?"

She sighed and looked up at the exposed, rough-timbered roof. "Because it was my twenty-third birthday and I had never been kissed." An unavoidable blush crept up her neck. She turned to look at him, a hint of outrage in her tone. "I wanted to be kissed, just once. Is that so horribly wrong?"

The intimate recesses of his body quickened. Thorne grimaced. "By Jimmy Henderson it is."

A soft trill of laughter escaped Jenny, lighting the dugout. It was an almost physical transformation, Thorne thought, like sun coming from behind a cloud, or day breaking over the horizon.

"I certainly regret it now," she said. Her smile dwindled; the shadows moved back in. She regarded Ian critically, but other than his overlong hair and burnished features, she could see little of the savage left on the surface. He wore rancher's clothing and spoke with a deep, unaccented voice.

But underneath she sensed the renegade still lurked, coiled and ready to spring. A wildness lay behind his eyes, the coy and primitive hunter on the prowl. He was exceedingly handsome on the exterior, smooth but not polished, intelligent but not bookish. Everything in perfect juxtaposition. Yet she sensed danger beneath, an uncivilized nature capable of anything. It distressed her to realize that even after all these years he still had the power to disturb her.

"So," she said, "you agree with the rest of the town?"

He gave her a half smile. "That you are wayward and immoral for indulging in a little wickedness? I'm hardly the hypocrite to cast stones. The others should be careful how they throw them as well." She gave him a look that said she didn't understand, but Thorne wasn't ready to enlighten her to the moral improprieties of certain local citizens unless they pushed her too far.

She was a good teacher and a good person, as far as he could tell. She had fought the town to allow Jeremiah the right to attend school at such a young age, which had enabled Thorne to work at the livery. He'd be hanged if he'd let the judgmental do-gooders in town cast her out like a harlot for one kiss.

"How badly do you want to keep the teaching position?" he asked.

She laced her fingers together in her lap. "I know what I *need* to do. I need to tend the ranch, but I want to teach the children. Besides, I need the money."

"There might be a way for you to do both," he said carefully.

Hopeful, she looked at him. "How?"

Only With You

"You could marry."

She stared at him blankly for a moment, a pretty, perplexed young woman waiting for the words she had heard to change into something her mind could understand and accept. Her mouth dropped open, slowly, as slowly as the confused narrowing of her eyes. "Are you asking for my hand?"

Thorne stared back at her boldly, not a hint of the shock thundering inside him showing on his face. He had not meant himself! He had meant to offer her assistance or advice or an alternative, not a proposal. The soft anticipation on her face made him feel as if he'd been punched in the gut.

He blinked once, deliberately, and forced air into his lungs. "What I mean is, if you marry *someone* the scandal will eventually die down."

She nodded numbly. "Yes. That would do it." She tilted her head to the side and regarded him. "So, are you asking for my hand?"

Thorne checked to make certain Jeremiah was still otherwise occupied. "Not exactly."

"I see. You think I should marry someone, but not you."

He could tell by the fire beneath her calm words that he needed to tread lightly. "I'm not in the market for a wife, but—"

"But you think I should marry Jimmy Henderson." She was seething now, hot as a pot left too long on the stove. "You aren't willing to save poor little Jenny Delaney from spinsterhood but you think someone should!"

"I wasn't thinking anything of the sort!"

"Yes, you were. You're just like all the rest!"

"Fine, then. Marry me. Does that make you feel better?"

They both stopped and stared. He went still, his body awaiting her refusal of the words that had spewed from him without thought or caution. Without permission.

Her jaw dropped. "Marry you?" Her eyes narrowed suddenly and her face flushed dull red. "I'm not a charity case, Ian Thorne! You needn't feel as if you have to martyr yourself to save me from my own misfortune!"

He hooted suddenly with laughter—head thrown back, deep throated and insulting laughter.

Jenny's hackles rose. She tried to get off his bed but the pain in her leg stopped her cold.

Thorne put a restraining hand on her arm. "It's not charity, Miss Jenny. Believe me, you are not a woman who inspires charity in a man. I don't want to get married any more than you do, but now that I think about it, we are each what the other needs."

"I wouldn't need you, Ian Thorne, if you were the last man on earth."

"You have a horse ranch exactly like the one I plan to build, and you need help with it. You like children, of which I have one who is motherless. You are beautiful and smart and unmarried." He bowed from the waist in a show of blatant mockery. "Yes, Miss Jenny, I guess I am willing to be just such a martyr."

Beautiful and smart? She could feel herself wilting, going all silly inside. Her shoulders stiffened instead.

"So, you are offering to marry me just so you can have my ranch."

She made it sound so mercenary, which of course it was. She was an attractive woman, but there wasn't even enough friendship between them to pretend the offer was anything else. Still, he tried to temper his words for her sake. "And a mother for Jeremiah and schoolteacher for the town."

Sarcasm drenched her smile. "When did you—who has never been seen at a council meeting or church picnic—ever care about the town?"

"When they tried to run you off," he said simply. All teasing left his voice and there was no doubt of his sincerity. "Jeremiah is the most important thing in my life. The next teacher might not be so accommodating about taking on a bright boy who is still just a baby."

"I ain't a baby!" came a highly insulted voice.

Their heads turned at once. "Don't say ain't," they said in unison.

They looked back at each other, a new uncomfortable awareness in their eyes. It hadn't been there before, when they were merely teacher and parent, or childhood acquaintances, or even old enemies. It was there now that the words had been said, the offer made. The very idea put a lump in Jenny's throat.

"Jimmy Henderson already asked."

"But you're not marrying Jimmy."

"No." A dull ache started behind her eyes. How had she managed to get herself into such a ridiculous mess? "I'm not marrying anyone." But she wanted to, had pictured a thousand times walking down the aisle with her gallant knight.

"Suit yourself," he said, "but I'm offering a convenient situation for both of us."

"Oh, I see. A marriage of convenience." Her eyes narrowed. "Then I assume you mean to forgo any, uh, conjugal rights in this convenient marriage?"

He met her stare head-on. "I mean nothing of the sort."

She had not expected such a blunt reply. A flush started in the pit of her stomach and spread upward. "Oh." She couldn't quite meet his eyes. "Then I must refuse."

"Coward," he said softly.

Her head jerked up but she had no words to rebut his accusation.

Thorne had known she would refuse, but he was oddly surprised at how disappointed he felt by her predictability. She had fire and energy, and she was anything but a coward in reality.

"You could go back to Thorne Manor," she said. "It still stands."

He shook his head once. End of discussion.

The motion hit her like a betrayal. She, who longed to return, had nothing left. He, whose family home still stood, lived like a hermit in an ancient canyon dugout. "Why?" she accused. "You live here in abject poverty, yet a veritable mansion awaits you in Mississippi. How can you do that to Jeremiah?"

"I don't live in poverty," he said in a dangerously quiet voice. "I live in simplicity. Don't prejudge what you don't understand, Jenny. And don't measure my standards by your own personal sense of necessity. We all have different needs and ambitions and different ways in which we set out to achieve them."

Her face colored hotly. "I'm sorry. That was cruel of me."

He would have agreed had her concern not been solely for Jeremiah. "Just presumptuous," he countered. He should sell Thorne Manor. There was too much past back there, too much sorrow and unanswered guilt for him ever to return. He still couldn't think of his father without remorse. Patrick Thorne had searched for him, loved him without reserve, then allowed him his freedom. He had all but deserted his father and left him to die alone.

He glanced over at Jeremiah. Only now did he understand a father's devotion, the fierce instinct that had driven Patrick Thorne's relentless search all those years. Only now when it was too late. But he couldn't go back, and holding on to nothing, struggling to pay the yearly taxes on a place he would never return to was foolish. Yet he couldn't completely let go.

He regarded Jenny frankly. "Will you marry me or not?"

"I've had plenty of offers," she returned to salvage her pride.

"I'm sure you have."

"Why should I choose you?"

"No reason," he said. "My offer is no different than the others who wanted your ranch. Except," he added seriously, "if I had known that you wanted help, Jenny, I would have offered it when your uncle took ill."

The familiarity of the way he said her name made chills run along her arms. "Why?"

"Because you tried to help me ten years ago."

She smiled without humor. "And I have the scar to prove it."

"I could apologize, but it wouldn't change anything."

"No." She clutched her fingers together to keep from putting them back at her throat. The memory still had the power to rattle her, and his frigid countenance at this moment didn't help any. He'd dragged her from Thorne Manor that day, back into the woods where he'd hidden out until hunger had gotten the better of both of them. His father and the others had let him take her to keep her safe, certain as they were that they could track and find him.

But he had been far superior at hiding his passage, far more experienced. He'd stayed in the woods until he was ready to return.

For three days he'd kept her a prisoner terrorized by hunger and cold, her bodice gaping from where he'd cut her buttons. He'd also cut the hem of her dress and used the strips of fabric to bind her hands and ankles while he hunted for food. At night he'd slept beside her, his arms and legs a prison that had kept her warm but upset, his hands falling to places that had made her ashamed.

She stared at her laced fingers. "Why did you do it?"

He didn't pretend not to understand. "Control. Intimidation," he said flatly. "It was nothing personal."

Her eyes flared. "It was *very* personal!"

He nodded. "For you." He snatched up a blanket from the foot of the bed and spread it over her. "I can't change what was done, Jenny. If it stands between us, it would be best for you not to consider the offer."

"I couldn't possibly consider your offer," she said, but somehow her words lacked conviction to her own ears.

Jeremiah climbed back on the chair beside the bed and regarded both adults. He had jam and crumbs smeared across his chin. "What offer?"

"Go wash," Thorne said.

"What offer?" he repeated, but his father gave him a look that sent him scrambling quickly from the chair.

Thorne regarded Jenny. "You don't have to decide now. I'll help you out at the ranch while you're recovering."

She couldn't accept. She'd practically been paying her foreman on a prayer. Incurring the expense again would be too much. "I can't afford—"

"Room and board for me and Jeremiah. If you decide not to marry me, I'll take a small percentage of the horses as payment after I get the ranch back on its feet."

Jenny bit the inside of her lip. She might be a bit unconventional at times, but no one to her knowledge had ever called her stupid. She couldn't afford to refuse Thorne, and she knew it. With her teaching job uncertain and the ranch going downhill fast, she had no choice but to set aside her pride and take what help she could get. Wrapping herself up in a stiff cloak of dignity, she nodded. "All right, room and board. What percentage?"

"Ten percent of the stock count."

"Ten percent! Have you lost your mind, Ian Thorne? That's robbery!"

"Ten percent."

"Current or future?"

He smiled at her astuteness. If he said current, he had a sure thing. If he gambled on the future, the number could soar or sink, depending on how well he did after he got there.

"Future."

"Deal," she said. She held her breath while she waited for him say something, anything else. But he only nodded, murmured something about firewood, and left the cabin.

Jenny dropped her face into her hands. Her leg was throbbing, she had all but lost her job, her reputation was fully compromised, and Ian Thorne had just asked her to marry him. "I can't believe this."

Jeremiah crept back, all freshly scrubbed, his expression uncertain. "What's the matter, Miss Jenny?"

She looked into his precious gray-green eyes and forced a smile. "Nothing now that you're here, Jeremiah."

The storm tore across the mountain with bared teeth, flinging ice and plunging temperatures. Wind pounded the windows with sleet and debris, moaning like a lost soul. But inside the tiny dugout, safe from the elements, warmth and contentment permeated the air. The cold was there, slipping between old sod blocks and window casings, but it was held at bay by the fire burning in the hearth and the close contact of human bodies.

Wrapped up in blankets, Jenny snuggled close to

Jeremiah on the bed, while Thorne sat near the fireplace. She knew they would have been warmer huddled together, but the thought of him climbing in beside her sent a shiver of uncertainty along her limbs. And a quiver of something else: awareness.

She was terribly aware of how tall he had grown, of the way the gold-tipped ends of his dark hair curled over his shirt collar. Firelight cast intriguing shadows along his strong jaw, an older face, a man's. A masculine scent, so absent from her life since her uncle's death, permeated the close air.

She pulled the covers up tighter under her chin in a protective gesture. He was an alarming man in some respects, certainly an enigmatic one. Though he was helping her now, she still felt the betrayal of that day so long ago, the riot of fear that had caused her to alternate between weeping and begging and cursing him. The knowledge that she had made a fool of herself by assuming he would remember his childhood when she'd strolled forth so boldly.

"*Do* you remember stealing Mama Sassy's pies and swimming down by the river?" she asked. She heard the sharp edge in her own voice. She had never asked, not even over the long journey west, but it seemed important now that he should admit it, that she had not been completely insane that day.

He looked at her, his skin burnished gold in the firelight. His eyes were pale and sharp. "You have a mark on your left thigh, high up. *Real* high up."

Color flooded her face. He had seen that? The birthmark, low on the side of her hip, was a secret embarrassment, a superstitious omen to the mammy who had helped raise her.

Thorne turned back to the fire, a hidden smile on his face. That had shut her up fast. He didn't want to talk about Mama Sassy and the old life he had abandoned, didn't want to remember Sam and Jenny as they had been that fateful spring before his father had taken him west to sell horses to Jenny's uncle Nat.

He'd rather think of that small butterfly-shape mark on her hip. It had meant little to him as a child. The thought of seeing it now, at the top of such long, slender legs, sent an unwelcome kick of lust through him.

He was pragmatic enough to realize that close proximity to any attractive female might cause the same reaction at this point in his life, but it was Jenny who lay in his bed, Jenny whose scent he could smell, Jenny whom he wanted to bury himself in until the crisis of climax took the rest of the capricious world away.

He watched her stroke Jeremiah's hair back from his forehead. The child was snuggled next to her, warm and content in sleep. She had a gentle, natural hand with children, an ease that was becoming to the spirited side of her nature. She would make a fiercely protective mother someday.

Jenny glanced up to find him watching her. "Why did you return to them after you left me here?" she whispered sadly. "Your father must have grieved so."

A muscle twitched in his jaw. "I had a wife."

Her eyes widened. Not once had she considered his feelings or the life he had left behind. Seeing Mr. Pat mourn day after day for his lost son, while the war approached to take the rest of him, there had been no room and no inclination to blame anyone but Ian.

"But they traded you."

"She was the daughter of a white woman, another captive. Had I married a full-blooded Comanche, it might have been different. In any case, they knew I was old enough to come back if I chose."

Jenny glanced at Jeremiah. "Which you did eventually." There was no accusation in her voice now. "Did you tell your father? He would have understood."

He had been eighteen, fearless and frightened and angry at the universe. Twice he'd had his world ripped from beneath him and he hadn't trusted anyone, had resented everyone. He'd spent years in turmoil at the plantation, trying and failing to become the son he had been. Years of wanting to get back at the Comanche for trading him and at his father for losing him the first time. In the end, he had only himself to resent for wasting what time he had left with the man whose biggest crime had been loving him. "I told him."

Relief eased through her for the man she had loved nearly as much as her own father. "That's why he sent you back, isn't it?"

"That and the fact that I would have had to take sides in a war where I had loyalty to neither faction. Also to keep you safe."

"I didn't realize," she began. "What happened to your wife?"

He looked away. "She died in childbirth."

"I'm sorry."

"Don't be," he said, but that was all. He stirred the

fire for a time, then stretched back. "I gave Jeremiah a white man's name and left when he was old enough to travel. I would have returned to River Run, but I found out the news of my father's death from your uncle when I came through here."

Her heart squeezed. She would have given anything for Patrick Thorne to have seen his son again. "Will you return someday?"

"No." His tone was final, leaving no invitation for further questioning. "Try to get some sleep."

"But why—"

His gaze sliced through her, cutting her words in half. Her mouth went dry and her arms tightened around Jeremiah. She remembered that look only too well from before.

The storm moaned against the dugout, trapping her in perfect, unalterable compromise. She'd never get away with this unscathed unless she could sneak back at daylight and swear everyone on the ranch to silence. She blinked back hot tears of resentment and turned her mind to the positive side of this situation. Ian was going to help out at the ranch. Room and board only. It was a miracle, a gift from God, the answer to a prayer.

She sure hoped it would be worth the price of her ruination.

The storm lasted only a few hours. Toward midnight, the stars were bright as ever, glittering off the barren ground. Jenny slid from the comfort of the bed and tested her injured leg. It held her weight if she kept her balance on her left foot and didn't try to move too fast.

Thorne's voice cut the darkness. "You're risking your life over the chance of notoriety."

"Yes." She hobbled toward the door, an excruciating throb setting up in her shin. "I don't expect you to understand."

"That you care more for your reputation than your life? No, I don't understand."

"I could care less about my reputation," she said. "It's my job that I can't lose. If someone finds out about this, I'm doomed."

He rose out of the dark, a tall, shadowy form backlit by the dying embers. He lit a lantern but kept the wick low. Reaching for a heavy wool poncho from a wall peg, he lifted it down, then brought it to her. "Wear this." He settled it over her head, then fetched another for himself. "I'll see you to the border of your property. If you make it that far without passing out, you'll get the rest of the way on your own."

"But Jeremiah—"

"He'll sleep through the night."

She closed her eyes on a prayer. "Thank you, Ian."

"Thorne."

Chapter 4

THE DARK WAS BOTH EXPANSIVE AND OPPRESSIVE. The canyon walls rose high on both sides in some places, falling away to instant death in others. The wind whispered here, lonely, eerie, like the moan of a child forever lost to daylight. Jenny would never have made it back on her own without going through town and risking instant discovery.

She rode sidesaddle in front of Thorne, while her horse followed behind on a lead rope. He could not take the chance, he had said, of her losing her way in the dark, or *not* swooning again.

She had smiled at that against her will.

He was taking her by a back way. Through corridors of canyon walls, across flat mesas, over crumbling, uneven paths between boulders. Even in silence she could feel his reproach in the rigid set of his shoulders against her back. He might think her foolish for wanting to protect what was left of her reputation, but he was a man and therefore exempt from all but the basest behavior. A woman with no family had no one to champion her, no one to turn to in times of trouble. Without a decent reputation, she was doomed to a life of disgrace. In Jenny's case, she would be without the job that supported her.

The wind moaned between the high walls. The scent of spruce and pine left a dry, pungent taste in her mouth. This had been the land of the ancient ones once, a people who worshiped the pagan deities of sun, moon, and rain, the spirits of water and wind. They had built homes among the cliffs and offered sacrifices and grew corn. They had lived and loved among the high homes, gave birth and died.

Then they were gone.

Jenny felt the horse stumble then right itself. She cringed at the jolt but kept silent as they made their way down from a higher grassy plateau onto a narrow ledge. Loose shale scattered over the edge of the trail, showering the canyon below. She swallowed at the amount of time the rock took to hit bottom. One false step and Thorne, the horses, and she would plunge to their doom.

She shivered at the thought and felt Thorne's arms tighten around her.

"Cold?"

"No, just apprehensive. I can't see two yards in front of me."

"The horse is surefooted."

His voice reverberated against her face where she

leaned against him, her cheek bumping rhythmically into his chest. She had little choice in the awkward position, but her strength was waning so she ignored the unease of being so close to a man, especially one she felt uncomfortable around. He wore a poncho similar to the one he had given her, its scent heavy with the daily life of the man who wore it. Horse and dust and hard work permeated the fibers, along with the fainter hint of charred wood from a cook fire. The wool was scratchy against her skin, but warmer than the cold night air.

Her heart sighed. He'd been a friend once. A dear companion. She tried to remember that but there was nothing discernible of the boy left in the man. He was like the people who had lived here before, gone from existence, swallowed up by the constant tide of an ever-changing world. But not forgotten.

She shivered again, though she was insulated against the cold in the heavy woolen poncho and the close heat of Thorne's body. It was more a reaction to the night, the trauma of hurting herself, the uncertainty of her decision to accept Thorne's help. And the relief that she had done so.

Eventually, the ground flattened out into a mesquite trail leading into the scrubland of the foothills, then eventually into the pastureland so necessary for raising livestock. Weary but alert, Jenny straightened.

Thorne pulled her back into the warmth of his chest. "Not yet. I can get you a lot closer without your hired hands being the wiser."

She relaxed against him, grateful for a few more minutes of reprieve.

In daylight, the Delaney ranch rose from the desert like a jeweled decoration, a complement to the land that, at first glance, appeared empty and desolate from desert to mountain. The ranch had been named El Dorado by Nathaniel Delaney, his golden dream, his future carved out of a wasteland. Nat had seen further than the conquistadors who had christened the area *despoblado*. There was abundance here, if one's vision ranged broadly enough, if one looked with the foresight of fearless optimism.

Snowcapped peaks reached into blue heavens. Fresh spring waters cut silvery ribbons through red canyon walls. Rich green meadow grass ripened in springtime amid a flurry of colorful poppy and sunflowers. Slender-leafed yucca and spiny cactus stood in solitary quiet beneath a blazing summer sun.

The house was built of earth-gathered adobe. Formed from the land, the sun-dried bricks seemed to reflect the changing moods of the endless cycle of dawn to dusk. The pinkish glow at sunrise gave way to pale gold by noon. But it was at sunset that El Dorado reigned in all its glory. Burning crimson, it was a tireless sight to those who called it home.

The house was U shape and had been built around a large courtyard, an oasis complete with fruit trees, a bubbling fountain, and flower boxes for seasonal blooms. Huge urns held broad-leafed trees at strategic spots on the shady tiled patio.

The flower boxes were overflowing with desert wildflowers, hardier in the summer heat and chilly nights than the pampered hothouse blooms sent in by train and wagon from back East. In the center stood a fountain of cold, sweet water with a circular pool. It was Jenny's favorite spot to sit and reflect.

Beneath a cold moon, she limped barefoot across the cool tiles. The bubbling water was soothing but she could not stay to listen. She was too exhausted to explain to her housekeeper, Mercedes, why she was coming in after midnight. Hopefully, Aunt Tildy had gone to sleep long before realizing it was past time for Jenny to be back from town.

Her bedroom was at the back of one wing, a restful haven overlooking the fountain and courtyard. The ride out had not been as harrowing as she had expected, but the walk from the stable had just about done her in. Her leg was throbbing again, protesting her foolishness in agonizing pulses.

A crash of copper pans followed by a string of angry Spanish made Jenny wince. *Caught.* She sighed and leaned against the patio wall. Mercedes bustled out from the dining room at the center of the house, wringing one hand in an oversized apron while the other carried a lantern.

"Señorita! At long last, I see you come, and you are sneaking in like a thief. I thought *banditos* got you!"

"A rock got me," Jenny answered tiredly. She pulled the hem of her skirt up. "I had to have my leg stitched, then the storm hit . . ."

"Oh!" Mercedes gasped. Her maternal instincts took

over and all questions ended. She hurried to put her plump shoulder under Jenny's arm. "Come, I will help you to your bed."

Jenny leaned heavily into her housekeeper who smelled of puchero and tortillas. "Is Aunt Tildy asleep?"

"Oh, *sí*. She rambled for hours about the Yankee men coming, then fell asleep in her rocker. I had Luis put her to bed."

Jenny wasn't certain how the slender, fine-boned Spaniard had gotten her aunt from rocker to bed without waking her, but she was grateful that he had managed it. Jenny hobbled beside Mercedes to the multipaned doors leading into her room. There were heavy wooden shutters that could be closed in case of Indian or outlaw attack, but it had been years since such security had been needed.

"Gracias." She sighed as she tumbled into bed.

Mercedes clucked like a hen. "I will get your night clothes, *sí?*"

Jenny sat back up. She would have stayed in her dusty dress had she not been too ashamed for Mercedes to know it. "Yes, thank you." She held up the small leather pouch Thorne had given her. "Can you make this into a tea? It is supposed to help the pain."

"Oh, *sí*," Mercedes agreed. "Right away."

Jenny reached beneath her pillow and pulled out Granny's journal. She read it daily, as one would a book of inspirational scripture, finding humor and strength to combat the oftentimes confusing world around her.

She thought of Ian's stern face, so at odds with his

generous gesture. "I don't like him," she whispered to the well-worn journal. "But I need him."

Saturdays were reserved for every chore Jenny couldn't find time to do during the busy week. But this day, just like the last two, had been set aside for lying about with her leg propped up. Her shin was sore and swollen but better for several days' rest. Thankfully, there seemed to be no infection setting in.

She sat in the shade of the patio, Granny's journal forgotten on her lap. The scent of baking bread drifted on the breeze, along with something spicy. A stew, perhaps, or Mercedes' mixture for filling tamales. Aunt Tildy wandered about, muttering to herself about infiltrators hiding behind bushes. Jenny could hear her beating at the scrubby hedges along the outskirts of the courtyard with a broom handle.

Jenny hadn't been able to grow a decent flower garden in months. Thank goodness Tildy left the vegetables alone, or there would be no yellow corn or red chile peppers hanging to dry outside the kitchen.

"Aunt Tildy," she called.

"One more" came a determined reply.

After several thrashing sounds, a small woman popped around the corner of the patio. She was thin but spry, her dark eyes dancing. "Got 'em!"

Jenny caught her bottom lip between her teeth. Tildy had one leg of a pair of stretched-out pantalets on her head, presumably as a mobcap.

"Aunt Tildy." She sighed.

"Got every last one of 'em!" Tildy boasted.

Broom in hand, she marched up to her niece in a morning dress of fine jaconet muslin, ornamented with rose-colored satin ribbon. The gown was hopelessly outdated and impractical but beautifully fitted to Tildy's slender figure.

"Thought they could get to my husband's gold, but I got to them first. Bernard would be so pleased." She eyed her niece shrewdly, then pointed to her bandaged leg. "Did you take a bullet, girl, or is it a saber wound?"

Jenny glanced down. "A rock, Auntie."

"Damn Yankees," Tildy muttered. "No glory in rock fighting. None at all. They have less manners than a backwater tramp."

Jenny smiled weakly. Arguing was useless. Playing along at least afforded her aunt some comfort from the rest of the confusing world.

"A good sign, though," Tildy said. "It must mean the Yankees are running out of ammunition."

Jenny shrugged. She neither encouraged nor dissuaded Tildy's lapses from reality. Uncle Bernard had been dead for two decades, his gold squandered on riverboats and back-alley crap games long before the Yankees went south. Tildy's senility afforded her some pride from a disastrous marriage to a philandering gambler.

She patted the chair beside her. "Come sit a spell, Auntie," she coaxed.

Tildy took a step forward, then her back went pole straight.

Jenny spotted the rider in the distance. He sat his stallion well, admirably suited to the rocking gait as he approached the ranch from the rear. For two days she'd been watching for him, wondering if he'd changed his mind. Her view was obstructed briefly when he skirted a group of outbuildings. A stable block, corrals and paddocks clustered in one area, while a smokehouse, tannery, smithy, and workshop comprised another.

He reappeared closer to the house, and Jenny quickly tried to circumvent a potentially awkward situation. "Aunt Tildy," she called with forced delight, "the new help is here."

Tildy's gaze sharpened. "Help? What help?"

"For the horses," Jenny said gaily. "Mr. Thorne knows everything about horses."

Tildy's eyes narrowed on the approaching rider. "He a Kentucky man? Can't trust a Kaintuck, Tennessean either. Both states too wishy-washy about where their loyalties lie."

"He's from Mississippi, Auntie. Patrick Thorne's son from Thorne Manor."

In an instant, Tildy's face transformed. "Thorne Manor?" Her eyes were bright, a flush staining her pale cheeks. "Patrick's boy. Are you certain?"

"I'm certain." Jenny watched her aunt closely. Tildy's hand had gone to her hair, patting each wayward strand in place. A dreamy smile clung to her lips. "Do you remember Mr. Pat, Auntie?"

Tildy's shoulders stiffened in offense. "What kind of question is that? Of course I remember Patrick Thorne. Most handsome man I ever met outside of Bernard. A true Southern gentleman. I walked out with him once at Clarissa Westland's coming out. We danced, we talked, we strolled along the verandah—in full view of our chaperones, of course—then Mr. Thorne said to me . . . he said . . ." Her voice faltered. Confusion once again dimmed her lovely eyes. "I walked out with him once. A woman never forgets that."

Jenny swallowed. Her aunt was still so beautiful, her fair skin remarkably unlined for her age. She had a thick head of creamy white hair and the petite, classic features of her grandmother's French ancestry. Growing old for Matilda Delaney Darineau should have meant growing more regal, but her ill-fated marriage followed by the war had damaged her mind.

The combination had stolen the belle of the ball, a Delaney from Mississippi, no less, and left a sadly confused matron in its wake.

Jenny reached over and slid the pantalet from Tildy's head. Her aunt's hand went up automatically. "It needs repairing," Jenny explained. "I'll have Mercedes fetch another."

"My best spoon bonnet," Tildy demanded, "the one with the velvet ribbon for Patrick Thorne's son."

The bonnet was outdated as well but would make her aunt feel suitably dressed. Jenny waved until she caught Mercedes' attention.

As soon as the housekeeper stepped out onto the patio, Tildy stood. "Mr. Thorne approaches, as you can see. I daresay he's come to court our Jenny. Please have our best guest room prepared."

"*Sí*, señora." Mercedes nodded but glanced over at Jenny for instructions. Every male on horseback was either a Yankee spy or a candidate for the señorita's hand.

Jenny shook her head. "He's come to work," she said softly. "Please fetch Aunt's best spoon bonnet."

Mercedes nodded. "And the room?"

"The guest room is fine. It's large and his son can have the one next to it." In any case, nothing else would satisfy her aunt, and they both knew it.

Thorne's hands tightened on the reins as he neared El Dorado ranch. Jeremiah squirmed in his seat with excitement. "Oh, Pa!" He gasped. "It's even prettier close up."

Stunning, Thorne thought with a pang of envy so deep it slowed him for a moment. He quickly tamped it down. He did not regret his years with the Comanche. They had been strong years that had taken a pampered boy and shaped him into a more realistic man. But it was not the life he wanted for his son, a life doomed every year by the ever-increasing expansion west, a people destined for extinction or the reservation as a growing country continued on its westward path.

Neither did he want the legacy of Thorne Manor for Jeremiah, an empire built and maintained on the backs of slave labor.

He slowed his horse to a walk and drank in the beauty of El Dorado. *This* was what he wanted for Jeremiah. A life beyond, set apart, created from the beauty of the land. A world where honor lay in honest hard work, prosperity in purpose. A man made his own way here, building a kingdom to hand down for generations.

He saw Jenny in the courtyard out back, but out of respect he steered his horse around to the front entrance.

An elderly woman came bustling from the house, waving a lace hanky. She was vaguely familiar, but the recollection was so far back in his memory he could not recall it. A Spanish woman ran fast behind her.

"Mr. Thorne," the petite woman called. "How good of you to come! We're so thrilled to have you visit us way out here." She paused to stare blankly at the child riding in front of him, then seemed to collect herself. "A war orphan, no doubt. How dear of you to bring the tyke. You must come inside and tell us everything. We've been away so long, you know, and news is so sketchy now that the Yankees have the railroads cut off."

The Spanish woman hurried forward, a telling grimace on her face. She tapped her temple discreetly. "Señor, you must excuse Señora Darineau."

He nodded almost imperceptibly.

"You may leave your horse here. If you go straight through these doors, you will find Miss Jenny waiting out back." Mercedes took Tildy gently by the shoulders. "Come, Señora Darineau, we must collect refreshments for the gentleman."

Tildy smiled. "We'll only be a moment, Mr. Thorne. Do make yourself at home."

Thorne tipped his hat to the elderly woman and the housekeeper, then dismounted and looped the reins through an iron hitching post.

"Pa . . ." Jeremiah began.

"She has grown old, not just in her body," Thorne

explained. "She's a little weak in her mind." He helped his son down. "Treat her with respect."

"Yes, Pa."

They entered the cool interior of the sprawling one-story house. The front room was large and open, extending all the way to the back. The walls were pristine white, the floors polished hardwood. Handwoven rugs were scattered about in small, comfortable groupings. A formal dining space and several sitting areas comprised the large front room and base of the U. French doors in the back opened onto the patio and allowed the stunning beauty of the view to come inside.

Thorne took Jeremiah by the hand and led him out back.

Jenny sat on a cushioned rocker of New Mexico yellow pine, a picture of prim composure beneath the shade of a potted palm. She looked the teacher here, modest and fetching in a soft brown skirt and high-necked white blouse with a cameo pinned at her throat. The only incongruence was the sight of her leg propped on a low table stacked with pillows. The awkward fall of her skirt had necessitated covering her bare feet and ankles with a light blanket that would be suffocating in another few hours.

"Miss Jenny." Thorne tipped his hat in deference.

"Mr. Thorne. Jeremiah," she acknowledged. "Please forgive me for not getting up."

Jeremiah hurried over to his teacher. "How is your hurt leg, Miss Jenny?"

"So much better, thank you." She smiled and held out her hand to the child. He took it and moved close to her side, a gesture he was accustomed to from her classroom manner. She always gathered the children about her. Whether age six or sixteen, they seemed to respond better when they were close and had her full attention. "Have you come to keep me company, Jeremiah?"

His eyes lit up. "Pa says we've come to live here, to help you with the horses."

"Oh, how wonderful!" she returned, as if surprised. "Surely I'll have the best horse ranch in all of the New Mexico territory now."

He grinned from ear to ear. "Yep. The best one."

Aunt Tildy hurried out, a tray of tall drinks in her hands, followed by Mercedes with another of pastries. "Here, Mr. Thorne, do sit down." She beamed at him. "You must be exhausted from your travels."

Thorne eased into a seat, glancing over at Jenny as he did so for his cue.

"Mr. Thorne has not traveled all that far," Jenny stated. "He's been right here in Little Town, Auntie."

Tildy glanced over at her niece, a suspicious, narrow-eyed look. "Really." Her steely gaze swung back to Thorne. "Just how long, Mr. Thorne, have you and Jenny been seeing each other in secret?"

Jenny's face went red.

Thorne eyed the cagey old lady. "Excuse me?"

"It's obvious you've been carrying on for a while."

"Madame," he said with grave insult, "I assure you nothing untoward has occurred between your niece and myself. If, however, our acquaintance distresses you, it is a subject better taken up with General Lee. I am certainly not at liberty to undermine the security of our boys in gray. I'm sure you understand."

Tildy's hand went to her heart with pride. "Perfectly, young man."

Jenny rolled her eyes. Thorne's allusion that Jenny herself might be involved in Confederate spying would only hasten the demise of Tildy's unraveling sanity. "The war is over, Auntie—"

"Nonsense! I'll not hear such treasonous talk again. Mr. Thorne, won't you sit down?"

Jeremiah shifted closer to Jenny. His expression was confused but he kept silent. Jenny patted his hand in reassurance. "Would you like a sweet?"

He nodded but wouldn't move closer to the strange woman, even for a pastry. Tildy fluttered about, making certain Thorne was comfortable. She asked innumerable questions about troop movements in the South, which Thorne answered vaguely enough to satisfy her thirst for information. Jenny had Mercedes bring the tray close enough for Jeremiah to select several small cakes.

Like a princess holding court, Tildy finally sat and spread her voluminous skirts about her. Her hoops had long since been put away and the excess material of her gown pooled upon the cool tiles in a froth of jaconet muslin. "So, Mr. Thorne," she said importantly, "you have come to court our Jenny."

Thorne's mouth opened, then closed. He looked sharply at Jenny.

She shook her head briefly, took a deep breath, then began. "Aunt Tildy, Mr. Thorne has come to help with the horses."

"Of course he has," she stated as if Jenny were daft. "If he wishes to take over your uncle's work after the wedding, he must learn the way of things out here." She flushed suddenly, and her hand went to her breast. "Oh my. Or are you thinking about taking our Jenny back south to your father's home?" She half rose from her seat, flustered and out of sorts. "I should have realized—"

"No," Thorne said firmly. "Never fear, Mrs. Darineau. We are staying right here."

Tildy relaxed back into her seat with relief. "How marvelous, sir. How thankful I am that I shall not be left alone in this wilderness." Her voice lowered. "There are heathens here, you know. Head-scalping, Christian-hating, women-molesting Injuns."

Jenny swallowed back a groan.

Thorne bit down on the inside of his jaw. "I'll protect you, ma'am."

Tildy's fingers went to her lips. "I knew you would, sir. I just knew you would."

"Women-molesting?" Thorne asked later, after Tildy Darineau had retired for a rest.

Jenny grimaced. "You can see she is not exactly right in the head."

"But even for the infirm," he said, "there is usually a basis for their fears or anxieties."

"Not in this case," Jenny snapped. Or if there was it stemmed back to those three days Jenny had been held prisoner by Thorne, then returned home with the buttons on her bodice gone and the hem ripped to shreds. Everyone in both families had maintained a strict silence over it, compounding Jenny's sense of guilt.

Her mama had asked if Jenny was all right, but she had not really wanted to know, had desperately wanted for her thirteen-year-old daughter to convince her that everything was fine. Which was exactly what Jenny had done, then tried not to resent it. When her mother had died of yellow fever the next summer, Jenny was forever grateful that her mother's last year had been fairly peaceful.

She shook off the mild hostility that still seemed to linger at times and faced Thorne. "I have asked Mercedes' husband Luis to gather the few men working here to meet you at dinner. We eat at eight. You and Jeremiah can spend the rest of the week settling in, getting to know the house and the ranch. Please feel free to wander at your leisure."

He had been subtly, if politely, dismissed.

Chapter 5

Thorne stood at the tall, multipaned doors leading out to the plaza. The Sangre de Cristo Mountains rose in the north, walling off a portion of the valley. Antelope and elk stole down from the cooler heights for easy grazing. Mule deer roamed among the pine and spruce trees. So many species of birds flocked to the pinyon and evergreen it was impossible to count their numbers. The whisper of them all floated on the breeze, an indistinguishable song of incredible harmony.

The guest room, as Tildy had termed it, turned out to be a living area as big as his canyon dugout. It had a large open bedroom painted in pale sand and furnished with a bedstead, wardrobe, and night tables of yellow pine. The carved wood was warm yet rustic, an attribute of a land both harsh and beautiful. An arched entry led into a sitting area that included a sofa, two side chairs, and a bookcase filled with classical literature. There was also a table for private dining or cards.

Thorne put away his few possessions in a smaller adjoining room that served as bath and dressing closet.

Jeremiah had been given his own room, but Thorne suspected it would take time for his son to grow accustomed to having such a large space for sleeping. Jeremiah had played there for an hour, delighted with the comfortable arrangements, but once tired he climbed into his father's big bed to rest.

Thorne glanced over at his sleeping son. His arms were curled around an old corn-husk doll that had been made by his maternal grandmother. He was a precocious child, studious and inquisitive beyond his years, but still just a child in need of protection and comfort. Thorne would have this abundance for him, this stability.

Though wealth by the white man's standard was unimportant to him, he knew the value of its security. The world was changing, expanding. The Comanche were being scattered like the wild horses that roamed the cold lands to the north. Thorne had made his own way, apart from the sometimes cruel life of the Comanche, apart from the destruction of the once-gracious South.

He belonged to neither. Bound to no race or culture or creed, he should have been content to remain in exile among the voices of the ancient ones. But a restlessness had come upon him the past few years. The need to be more, do more. A desperate drive to be a worthwhile man in a fallible world. It would be the legacy he would leave his son, the only real thing in a temporal existence.

Love did not last. The communion between a man and woman faded after the first riotous bloom of desire, but the knowledge and care one gave a child lasted to be handed down and passed on to the next generation.

He had raised Jeremiah separate, reared him isolated from friend and foe, a mistake perhaps of Thorne's own need to come to terms with and sort out the confusion of his life. His intent had been to find the right way for his son. Not society's way, with its prejudices and judgments, but Jeremiah's own life path. Something that would endure.

But there was no right way, he discovered. There were only people with differences too great to come together and choices to be made from knowledge gained over the years. He could only do his best to provide an acceptable road for his son to travel and, in time, release Jeremiah to choose his own way.

He pressed his palm against the glass. The panes were cool. The terra-cotta plaza caught the morning sun and remained relatively temperate in the afternoon shade while rising temperatures blistered the land in front of the ranch. The man-made fountain bubbled sweetly, beckoning. Thorne slipped from his bedroom to sit in the shade beside a slender-leafed yucca.

The restless wanting moved over him again, the unsettled yearning for this life. He did not care to feel it, or to admit that he had thrown away an even greater luxury at Thorne Manor. After his years with the Comanche, it had seemed too much a pampered life built on man's unending quest for greatness and esteem. Now he understood it. He clearly understood his father's need to build and leave a legacy for his son.

The scent of pine drifted down from higher elevations, clean and bold as the mountains themselves. He yearned to embrace them fully, to soar like the hawk over crags and peaks rather than merely survive on the fringes.

"What do you see?"

He had heard her approach, had felt her hesitation while she decided whether to stay or go. He rose to acknowledge Jenny.

"What do you see," she repeated, "when you look out there?"

He turned back to the Sangre de Cristo Mountains. "Harsh freedom. A price paid in flesh for the liberty of touching such beauty." He glanced back at her. "What do you see?"

"I'm not certain," she said quietly. But her eyes were on him, not the mountains. "Would you like to go out to the stables now?"

One dark eyebrow rose. "At siesta?"

She smiled. "You won't disturb them."

He shook his head. "I would rather wait for you to introduce me."

She knew there was an advantage to establishing the hierarchy right off, but she wasn't certain when her leg would allow the trek. She needed him to take control of the ranch as soon as possible. With school out for the summer, she had only until the fall to see if this arrangement would work. God and the school board willing, she would be teaching again by then. Her stomach did a nervous flip at the thought, and she took a deep breath to settle it. She would not let herself think otherwise, would not allow for the possibility that the school board would fire her and find another teacher.

She eased into a chair across from him. "I'll introduce you at dinner. Everyone comes to the house to eat."

He nodded, then moved a small table over for her. "Here, prop your foot up." He tried to ignore the awkward fall of her skirt when she did as he bade, tried to ignore the shadowy glimpse of the underside of her raised thigh, the inside knee and calf of her other leg. From his vantage point, her skirt draped like a tent, an open invitation for viewing. Her skin was fair, white as the milky surface of a pearl. She wore neither stockings nor petticoats to obstruct the view.

Jenny pulled and tugged at the fabric of her skirt, self-conscious, and finally eased her foot back off the table.

Thorne scooted his chair over beside hers. "Let's pretend I didn't see what I just saw," he said. He reached down, took Jenny's foot, and put it back on the table. "How many people do you have working here?"

Flustered, she responded in a sharp voice, "If you were a gentleman, you would not have mentioned seeing whatever you saw!"

He looked her dead in the eye. "I am not a gentleman, Jenny. You, more than anyone, should know that." He sent her a wry grin. "If you were a lady, you would not have left off your stockings and petticoat."

Her face burned. "But they were so heavy on the stitches and uncomfort—"

He held a hand up to stave off her excuses. "If I were

a woman, I wouldn't wear them to begin with. They are hot, stupid contraptions invented by idiots."

Her eyes narrowed meanly. "What is your point, Mr. Thorne?"

"The point is," he said, "you don't have to apologize *to anyone* for leaving off whatever clothing you wish, and I won't apologize for seeing a bit of skin." Her mouth opened in rebuttal, but he continued, "And you shouldn't have to apologize for kissing Jimmy Henderson."

He stole her thunder with his last statement. "Tell that to the town."

"They wouldn't listen."

"I know." She plucked at the fabric of her skirt, then rested her head against the slatted back of her chair.

"We all do things we regret. We all make mistakes."

"What do you regret?" she asked.

He shrugged. "Not seeing more of your legs." Her face turned so red, he thought she might explode. He smiled to ward off any recrimination. "I regret that we, as supposedly civilized human beings, can't be more honest with each other. That we must play polite games and pretend things we don't believe and act in ways contrary to our nature."

She wasn't certain where this embarrassing conversation was leading, but he had an excruciatingly valid point that took the starch out of her. She put her face in her hands. "Why *did* I kiss Jimmy Henderson?"

"Why not?"

She shook her head. "Because it *wasn't* honest. He's an irritating man, but it was unfair of me to use him that way. I don't feel anything for Jimmy Henderson; I barely even like him. It was cruel."

Thorne began to understand clearly. He pulled her hands from her face. "Then who *did* you want to kiss?"

Her gasp was audible. Her eyes spoke volumes. Longing, uncertainty, and denial flooded her expression. Everything was there, plainly written.

"No one," she said.

"At least be honest with yourself," he said in mild rebuke.

"I am," she expounded, but they both knew differently. She looked away, angry, but with nowhere to vent her frustration. "If I didn't need your help so badly, I would throw you off the ranch for impertinence."

"Honesty, not impertinence," he countered.

"I don't want to talk about this."

"Fine. Let's talk about the ranch. How many hands do you have working here now?"

"We have four people here full-time," she said hurriedly, thankful for the change in subject. "Mercedes is the cook and housekeeper, her husband, Luis, mostly takes care of the grounds and any repairs around the ranch, though he is willing to help out wherever needed." She smiled wryly. "He is afraid of horses."

Thorne frowned. Two workers on a horse ranch payroll who had nothing to do with horses. Mercedes fed the hands and was therefore more valuable than her husband, but Thorne could tell by Jenny's tone that there would be no discussion of replacing Luis. He liked immensely the fact that she was human first, ranch owner second. Little good it did her financially.

"Barkley is a cowboy who got his experience in catching and taming Wyoming mustangs. Cortez is Luis's friend. I suspect he was once an outlaw, but it has never come out in the open. My uncle trusted him and so do I. He knows horses and is an excellent blacksmith."

There should have been a small army working at El Dorado. Nat Delaney had acquired a vast amount of land and had raised a sizable herd. There were facilities to support a fortress, which the ranch probably had been at one time in order to protect it from the Indians and Comancheros. The stock count had been high in the last decade, but the number of horses had dwindled to an alarming few, considering how many a ranch the size of El Dorado could maintain.

With wise management and even harder work, it could be prosperous again. Accepting Thorne for room and board had been a smart move on Jenny's part. He hoped making her the offer would prove to be a smart move on his.

Jenny glanced down at her hands. "My uncle worked from dawn to dusk. He knew and loved everything about horses. Things began to deteriorate when he took ill."

"El Dorado can be a substantial ranch again."

She looked up, hesitant but hopeful. "How?"

"The same hard work and better management of the help you do have."

"Luis—" she began defensively.

"Luis," he interrupted, "can be better used where he

is not afraid. He doesn't need to rope or ride to be useful."

Her bank account was as slim as her knowledge. She took a deep breath. "How many more do we need?"

"It's hard to say until I've had a look at the herd."

"Guess."

"With a little restructuring and occasional extra help, we'll get by for a while, at least until the numbers begin to build up again."

She stared straight ahead, afraid to read anything in his eyes. "Are you sure?" she whispered.

"No."

She took a deep breath. "Honesty again?"

"Should I lie?"

"No." She pushed up gingerly from the chair. Thorne rose at once and took her arm. She leaned against him, testing her weight on her injured leg. "I need to go into town for supplies. I would appreciate it if you would go with me. I'll make arrangements for Blake's General Store to extend you credit under the ranch account."

"Luis as well."

She smiled. The thought of the ranch wasting away had eaten at her for a year. The relief of having knowledgeable help was almost overwhelming, even if the help was Ian Thorne. "Mercedes and Luis are already on the account. I do use him for more than tending flowers."

"Good." He helped her toward the door. "The trip into town can wait until tomorrow."

"No, I'm fine as long as I don't put any weight on my leg."

He was practically holding her up, which might be unimportant at the ranch, but it would cause talk in town. Just like her impetuous kiss with Jimmy Henderson, she seemed to have no natural instincts to defend herself against social blunders. And yet she kept him to the strictest requirements of gentlemanly behavior. It was an excuse, he realized, a barrier separating him for past liberties when she was thirteen and one more recently.

"If I have to carry you," he said dryly, "there'll be talk."

"There's *always* talk," she countered, "but if you're that worried about your reputation, I'll wait a few days."

A grin tugged at his mouth. His eyes narrowed lazily. "You are as disrespectful of normal conventions as I am."

"Hardly," she said. "I just hate stupid, unspoken rules and mean-spirited gossip. You looking up my skirt is another matter entirely!" Embarrassed at the outburst, she clamped her mouth shut.

Thorne couldn't decide if he needed to protect her or indulge her. Just her reference to him seeing her bare legs sent a little nudge of lust to conspicuous places.

Jenny tried to take a step but faltered.

Without thought, Thorne swept her up before she fell on the hard stone.

Face to face, Jenny discovered Thorne's eyes were an intriguing shade of gray-green, a dusty moss color fringed with heavy dark lashes that should have appeared feminine but didn't. He had a fine, strong jaw and nice skin. "My leg got stiff," she said inanely.

For two unacceptable heartbeats he stared back into

her large eyes. They were golden brown, the eyes of a startled doe caught in quivering uncertainty. Her skin was fair but not wan. A light spatter of freckles covered her nose. If he leaned forward, just the smallest distance, his mouth would cover hers. For all his talk earlier and platitudes of honesty, he retreated at once behind the stiff formality of polite concern.

He lowered her back into the chair, then knelt to one knee as he took her ankle in his hand. "You need to exercise the leg but from a resting position." He lifted her leg slightly, then tucked his other hand under her thigh. "Like this." He worked her leg carefully, bending it at the knee, then straightening it. After several repetitions, he slid his hands free. "You try it, using your own muscles, but don't stretch too far."

She was flustered and didn't know why. His hand under her thigh had been separated by a thick layer of fabric. The strong fingers around her ankle had been strictly impersonal. She felt like a silly young girl. She focused all of her attention away from him and onto her shin. "All right."

She moved her leg several times until fatigue made it start aching. "How many times?"

"Don't push it," he warned. "You'll only make it swell."

She propped her foot on the small table, unnerved and a bit resentful. "You make me uncomfortable, Ian."

She did the same for him but in a much different way. "Thorne," he reminded her.

"And you do it on purpose, I think."

Did he? He looked at her, at a safer distance now than when he held her. "Perhaps."

Her brow knit. "We have such an unlikely past. I just don't know if this can work." She stared back at him, determined, and just a bit rebellious. *"Ian."*

They were at an impasse. Two wills colliding over nothing and everything. "Thorne," he repeated for the sake of argument.

"Ian Blackwell Thorne," she returned. "A Mississippi Thorne, from a long line of—"

He rose from the chair suddenly and headed for his room and the solitude of Jeremiah's unconditional acceptance. "The boy from Mississippi is dead," he said in parting. "Get used to it, Jenny."

She whipped around to deliver the last volley. "Coward! I'll resurrect him, Ian. *You* get used to it!"

Two days of semiavoiding each other had worn on Jenny. She missed their sparring, the intellectual warfare of his rebuttal without censure. Without Thorne near enough to vent her irritation upon, her exasperation had bottled up inside her and was ready to explode. She had sat in the patio each day, begging for a confrontation. He had made it a point to be absent when she was about, so she was wholly unprepared when he stepped from his room and walked toward her.

"Good morning, Ian," she said with a bit of hauteur.

"Miss Jenny," he returned. Without warning, he knelt beside her chair and grabbed her ankle.

She jerked, but before she could utter much more

than a protest, he pushed her skirt up to midthigh. Sputtering, she tried to push it back down.

He held fast. "I need to take the stitches out."

Her fury dwindled slightly at such an altruistic reason for having his hands on her bare flesh. "You could have warned me."

He looked her in the eye. "What other reason would I have for putting my hands under your skirts?"

She blushed crimson. "None, of course."

"Then why did I need to warn you?"

He had her too disconcerted for verbal combat. She folded her arms over her middle and gave him a truly concerned look. "Is this going to hurt?"

"Not as much as putting them in did."

She closed her eyes. "Great."

His hands were gentle and quick. A snip, a tug, then he was exercising her leg as he had before, but this time he watched the skin around the wound stretch and retract. His actions were completely clinical, no more personal than Doc Brown would be when checking her for a sore throat. But, of course, he wasn't a doctor, and no man—not even Doc Brown—had ever seen her bare legs. When he was done, she pushed her skirts back down.

"Keep an eye on it," he warned.

She nodded, self-conscious, then rose to test her leg. She didn't know if it truly felt better or if the removal of the stitches just made her think it was improved. Either way, she found that she moved more freely and with less pain. She had been taking short walks for several days, but she wanted to stretch the distance now. "Would you like to go out to the stables?"

Thorne nodded. "Do you mind if Jeremiah comes?"

Surprised, she looked up at him. "Have I ever given you the impression that Jeremiah is in any way a burden or unwelcome?"

He gave her a wry half smile. "In this situation, you are not his teacher but my boss."

"Your boss." Her chin lifted a notch and she smiled. "I think I'm going to like having you at *my* mercy for a change."

An unruly thought entered his head for a salacious moment. He could picture them both drenched in passion, her head thrown back, making breathless demands, truly having him at her mercy. Thorne dismissed the image with effort. "I'd like to take stock of the herd as well."

"Then let's get started."

Out from beneath the cool protection of the plaza, the sun was a blazing fireball, beating down upon their heads and shoulders with relentless fury. The dry air helped temper the inferno somewhat, though Jenny thought fondly of raging thunderstorms at such moments.

She wore a skirt of durable cotton and a Mexican-style blouse with gathers at the scooped neck and sleeves. A broad-brimmed straw bonnet protected her face. Her stride was conservative yet confident, a woman crossing familiar ground. Jeremiah was at her side, chattering like a magpie.

Thorne noticed that she never once showed irritation

or indifference but listened intently and respectfully to his son's talk, no matter how puerile the topic.

Of all the unlikely causes of pure, undiluted lust, that was the most unnerving way for it to penetrate his defenses, to leave a direct and permanent impression on his soul. Thorne almost reeled from the surge of heat that rushed through him, a hot flash fire of desire that died down almost as quickly as it hit but left a lingering slow burn behind.

It was base and ridiculous. The reactions of an adolescent boy. And he wasn't a callow youth with only night dreams of how things might be. He was a man with full knowledge of how it was between a man and a woman.

Jenny's easy manner with a little boy who all but worshiped her, her intense concentration as she listened to every childish word, created a swift and powerful upheaval in Thorne's blood pressure.

He hadn't felt this savage since the blood-rush of his first kill. Like a trophy, he had attempted to sling the huge white-tailed doe over his shoulder while the braves commended him on his skill and prowess.

He had been fourteen. Respect for the life sacrificed had been the last thing on his mind while his blood raged hot with triumph. He had felt strong, superior, filled with his own self-importance. But when they strung the doe up and slid the blade along her belly to gut her, a small fawn slid to the ground. Slippery and much too young, she lived only long enough to bleat in whimpering horror at her cold, untimely entrance into the world.

Her birth and death had changed Thorne profoundly.

Savage triumph had changed to horror, overweening pride to guilty remorse. Blinded by the flood of emotions, he had fled the woods to weep like a baby. Eventually his emotions settled down and he found the necessary balance for survival. He killed for food; he played games for sport. He never mistook the two again.

To feel that same savage bloodlust now, to be filled with its unruly energy and stealthy ambition was intolerable.

She was just a woman, a slender hot-headed spinster who treated him like a renegade, when her own actions were hardly above reproach. Just whom had she wanted to kiss that day she kissed Jimmy Henderson? He tossed the curiosity aside.

It was her connection to the horse ranch, he reasoned, that caused the sudden, harsh desire. He wanted the ranch more than his next breath, more than anything except his own son. Since Jenny was El Dorado, it stood to reason that his feelings would extend to encompass them both.

He told himself that all the way to the stable block, while her hips swung from side to side in a tempting glide that kept his eyes roaming back for one more look.

Jenny led the way over to the longest shelter. Stepping into the cool interior, she was assailed by the smell of hay and manure, grain and horseflesh. Though Thorne did not touch her, she could feel his presence behind her, almost a silent command. She had never been so overtaken by the compelling urge to turn. She pivoted. Unaccustomed to the dim light, she found he was merely a shadow, a black silhouette against the dusty light filtering in, tall and formidable.

"Well . . . this is it." She swallowed, dreading his reaction. "Do you want to continue?"

Thorne looked at the long row of empty stalls. The building itself was in need of repair, a costly endeavor given its nearly empty state. The amount of work would be enormous, the personal investment incalculable. His gaze slid across his son, then to Jenny. "I'm sure."

Chapter 6

Jenny checked her list one last time, then tucked it into her jacket pocket for safekeeping as the wagon bounced over the rutted road.

Blake's General Store sat smack in the middle of Main Street. George Wolfratshausen Blake, or Wolf as he was called, had been a trapper and guide back in his youth, bent on making his fortune in the new land west of the Red River, but an accident during a flash flood had felled Wolf and forced him to convalesce in a tent late one spring. That tent had turned into a rough-timbered shack, which had eventually turned into the large wood-and-adobe general store.

A town was soon born up around it, a wee little town, as Wolf was fond of saying, then officially Little Town in the New Mexico Territory.

When they reached Blake's General Store, Thorne set

the wagon brake, then swung down to help Jenny. Unaware of any change in the status quo, Jeremiah launched himself into his father's uplifted arms. Jenny might have hopped down on her own, but her leg prevented any sudden movement. Hiding a smile, she sat still while Thorne corrected his son's manners, then allowed both gentlemen to help her alight.

Jeremiah skipped ahead. Town was an adventure, a special treat, just like school had been all year. "C'mon, Miss Jenny," he called. "Mr. Blake has books and licorice inside."

Jeremiah's two favorite things, she had learned. She made her way slowly toward him. "And peppermints," she added with a twinkle. She held out her hand for him and they entered the store with bright eyes and sly grins as they headed for the glass containers lining the long counter.

Barrels full of crackers and meal were grouped alongside tangy-smelling pickle tubs. Sacks of dried beans and flour were stacked near the leather goods. The stronger odors of onion, garlic, and basil permeated one corner.

"Miss Jenny," Wolf Blake greeted, "and little Jeremiah. How are teacher and student today?"

"Miss Jenny gots a hurt leg," Jeremiah said.

Jenny, who didn't want the town knowing Thorne had put the stitches in, rushed ahead. "I'm fine, just a scrape." She pulled the list from her pocket and handed it to Wolf.

He was a robust man with beefy arms and a thick neck, just right for hauling out large sacks of flour and other heavy supplies. He had an accent that Jenny thought sounded faintly German. His manner was friendly to a point. He didn't put up with stealing, spitting, or swearing in his store, or any other foolishness he deemed inappropriate, like fighting. Any culprit who crossed him got booted out by the seat of his pants, hence Willie Joe Turner and Bobby Wright ending up in the street the day Jenny had taken off to Lucy's.

That had been a brilliant embarrassment on her part. But she'd had to do something to get through to Milton Hardaway.

Had to do something *outrageous* to get his attention. The guilty thought tumbled into her head, as sneaky and unwelcome as rustlers on a cattle ranch. She denied it immediately. If that *had* been her reason, she wouldn't admit it, even to herself. The sheriff was engaged to her best friend, and she'd never do anything to interfere with their future happiness. If Milt loved Hannah, that's whom he should marry. If it broke Jenny's heart a little every time she thought about it, well, that was just something she would have to learn to live with.

Jeremiah tugged on her hand. She looked down to find him standing on tiptoe, staring with delight at the different flavors of licorice. She smiled. "How about one of each?"

His eyes brightened. "I gotta ask Pa." He took off like a shot.

"So," Wolf commented. "You have some help finally?"

"Yes, finally," she agreed. News traveled so fast in town it made her head spin.

She gave no further details. Wolf was as gossipy as any

old biddy, and he had a way of getting around to the truth without one seeing him coming. She tapped the list on his countertop.

"I need these things loaded into the back of the wagon, please. I also want to add Ian to my account."

His bushy brows rose. "Ian?"

"Mr. Thorne."

"Ah, Mr. Thorne. I heard he gave notice at the livery. Phil will miss him. Says Thorne knows more about horses than Phil himself. You got yourself a bargain, I hope?"

"I hope," Jenny echoed. "Some licorice, if you please. A handful should do."

Wolf wrapped the sweets in paper. "I heard there was a problem with the school board."

She took a deep breath and plowed straight ahead in defensive rebellion. "I kissed Jimmy Henderson. They want me to resign."

His eyes twinkled. "Or marry Jimmy." Wolf was a widower twice over and newly remarried. "Such nonsense they are going on about over a simple kiss!" All his children were grown, so he had no call to protest on her behalf, but he had an interest in each member of town. "You stay strong, Miss Jenny. Don't let them bully you."

She gave him a grateful look. "I won't, Wolf."

He leaned forward, conspiratorial. "Everyone that comes in, I give a piece of my mind on the foolish matter. By the end of summer, they will wish they never brought it up."

Since everyone *had* to come to Blake's General Store for supplies, Wolf's influence in town was considerable.

"Thank you, Mr. Wolf. I mean it."

"I know you do, Jenny." He winked. "The boy is back with a big smile. His papa must have said yes to the licorice."

Jeremiah was fairly beaming. He pulled a coin from his pocket and put it on the counter. Jenny slid the coin back to him. "My treat," she said. "You may pay next time."

His brow furrowed. He darted off again, only to return within a minute, breathless. "Pa says for me to pay."

Jenny wasn't about to get into a scuffle with Thorne in front of Jeremiah or the store proprietor. "That's fine," she said. "Double my order, Mr. Blake, then tend to Jeremiah."

Wolf knew where this was leading right off. He hid a grin as he stuffed another paper full of licorice, then handed it to the schoolteacher. "The boy will enjoy these later," he commented idly.

Jenny snatched the candy, then turned away, chagrined at being so obvious. "Put it on my account, please."

She limped outside to wait for the rest of her order to be filled. She could not in good conscience comprehend why she had wanted to thwart Thorne by purchasing candy for Jeremiah that Thorne wanted to purchase himself. It didn't make sense that she would purposefully try to anger or alienate him, when he just might be the solution to one of her two biggest problems.

Her leg ached and she eased over to a bench beneath the shady overhang. The spot was usually reserved for elderly patrons who liked to gather and discuss the ills and triumphs of a town barely more than a dot on the territory map. But today the seat was empty, Main Street nearly deserted. Nearly, but not completely.

Her heart gave a painful thump when she caught sight of Milton Hardaway strolling with Hannah Thompson on his arm.

Absently Jenny brushed at a stray curl that had slipped from her bonnet and tried to ignore the fact that she had not put on stockings, even though she had suffered to add a petticoat before she left the ranch. Not that Milt would notice. He had eyes only for Hannah. The couple had been engaged for nearly a year and would be married at the end of summer.

Jenny admitted to flights of fancy sometimes that involved Milt jilting Hannah due to his undying love for Jenny, or Hannah finding out about Milt's deep dark secret—said secret never being fully explained even in Jenny's imagination—and jilting *him*. At which point Jenny was ready to accept him for who he was. Milt would then marry her when he realized it was really Jenny he had loved all along.

Her daydreams never amounted to much more than a heavy dose of guilt. Jenny loved Hannah like a sister and had trouble betraying her friend, even in her imagination.

"Jenny!" Hannah called, waving a lace kerchief.

Jenny forced a smile and waved back. Her friend was always so proper, so perfectly dressed and coiffed. Hannah would never have been caught in town without a petticoat or missing her bonnet. Hannah would never have run off to Lucy's, even if it was just for show.

Jenny pulled her skirt securely over her ankles. Hannah would never—not with *five hundred* stitches in her leg—be caught in town without her stockings.

Hannah left Milt's side with a promise to return shortly. Milt, having been subjected to the women's "short" visits, tipped his hat to Jenny, then sauntered inside the general store.

In a swirl of powdery scent and violet-sprigged muslin, Hannah floated down beside Jenny on the bench, her blue eyes bright. "Can you believe August is almost here?"

Jenny didn't want to think about it.

"My gown won't be in for three weeks! I am simply breathless over the delay."

Hannah was breathless over everything; it was part of her appeal. She had that airy, helpless quality that men seemed to find so endearing. Not that Hannah actually was helpless, quite the contrary. She could cook, sew, sketch, and play twelve different concertos without once looking at her sheet music. She was also quick with sums and kept meticulous household records for her mother, who couldn't be bothered with such tedium, and updated her father's business accounts on a regular basis.

If Hannah had been just a little dither-headed, Jenny might have found room to resent her, but Hannah worked hard to be as proper in manner and efficient in housework as a young lady should be.

Jenny always felt quite diminished in her friend's presence. Though not by Hannah's hand, of course, that would have made her a less than perfect friend. No, Hannah the Magnificent was also the best of confidantes, never once divulging a secret. Jenny propped her chin in her hand, determined to be the best of friends in return.

"So, how are you, Hannah?"

"Anxious and excited," she answered, the evidence of both reflected in her voice. "How are you, Jennifer? I heard about that nasty business with Jimmy Henderson. Not your wisest decision to date, dear."

"Not my worst either," Jenny retaliated.

"No," Hannah agreed. "That award would have to go to your excursion to Lucy's."

"Milt is a tattletale."

Hannah smiled, then whispered, "That was so daring of you, Jennifer!"

"It was foolish." Jenny knew Hannah would never have done such an impulsive thing. She leveled her friend with a meaningful look. "Did you kiss Milton before you became engaged?"

Hannah's eyes widened for the briefest second, then went vague. She folded her gloved hands carefully in her lap. "A lady does not—"

"Did you?"

"No," she hedged, "not exactly."

"How can you 'not exactly' kiss?"

"I allowed Milton to hold my hand and press a kiss to my cheek. As for anything more earnest *before* we were engaged, no." She leaned in close and whispered shockingly, "But I thought about it."

Jenny sighed. "I knew it."

"Oh, I'm not like you." Hannah moaned. "I can't do

things without planning them out, weighing the consequences. I wish I were more spontaneous!"

Jenny stared at Hannah as if she'd sprouted horns. Dear Hannah who freely gave so much of her time to help Jenny by grading mountains of school papers. Hannah who took baskets of food and books to those shut in during the worst of winter. Hannah who had sat with Jenny for days after Uncle Nat's death and cried just as hard when they packed away his personal belongings. Hannah was everything she needed to be. Even the thought that she wanted to be more like Jenny was ridiculous.

"Are you daft?" Jenny asked softly.

Hannah grabbed Jenny's hand. "You are so brave, Jennifer. I am such a coward, afraid of everything! If the town spoke of me the way they do you, I would wither up and die."

Jenny rolled her eyes. "Thank you, Hannah. What are they saying now?"

"Nothing new. Everyone adores you, of course. They just don't understand you."

Jenny didn't understand herself. "What do you think, Hannah?"

"Me?" Hannah's perfect, unfreckled nose rose a notch and she pinned Jenny with an unblinking stare. "I wish I *were* you. There, I've said it, and I won't take it back!"

Jenny smiled. "No one heard you, Hannah; you won't have to take it back."

Hannah's sigh of relief was audible. She squeezed

Jenny's hand. "I told Papa to go to the members of the school board and tell them they are being ridiculous."

Jenny squeezed back, grateful. "Will it do any good, do you think?"

Hannah grimaced. "I don't know, Jennifer. Jimmy Henderson"—she shuddered delicately—"that does show a terrible lack of judgment."

Jenny couldn't help but smile. Poor Jimmy. "He's not so bad, Hannah, just so . . . eager."

Hannah cut her friend a sharp glance. "We'll call him young. Youth covers a multitude of inadequacies. And we had better attach the word persistent. He pursues every available female with the persistence of a dog after a bone." She fanned her face with the kerchief she had already monogrammed with her intended groom's initials. "He has asked every girl in town to marry him at least twice. The elders are as eager to get him married off as they are you, Jennifer."

Jenny dropped her face into her hands. "It's a conspiracy! I've become a scapegoat, the lamb led to slaughter—"

"In a manner of speaking," Hannah interrupted, "but it is undignified to liken oneself to animals. I see that it upsets you, so let's discuss other things before you develop worry wrinkles."

Heaven forbid, Jenny thought.

They dropped the conversation and turned to polite pleasantries and other nonsensical matters, moving on to fashion plates and creams. Jenny smiled and nodded at Hannah's sage authority. They were the same things her mother had found so fascinating to discuss at length.

Jenny hadn't been interested then, and she was even less interested now that she didn't have an ounce of free time to commit to the ladies' toiletries necessary for perfect skin and hair and good health. Her nose was hopelessly freckled, despite the cucumber lotion Hannah was certain Jenny used daily, and her hair could use a good vinegar rinse to bring out the red highlights.

"Or maybe egg whites!" Hannah stated. She snagged one of Jenny's soft brown curls and examined it. "Four egg whites beaten to a froth. We'll rub them thoroughly into your scalp and leave them to dry. Then we'll wash it out with equal parts rum and rosewater. It's the best brightener I've ever used."

Jenny groaned. "Hannah!"

Wide-eyed, Hannah stopped, then answered, "Yes?"

"I don't want egg whites in my hair."

Hannah folded her hands primly in her lap. "All right, then. Be dull as dishwater."

Whatever else Jenny wanted to say got tangled up in what she didn't, but it was the last thought that came blurting out. "Do you really want to get married?"

Hannah blinked. "Well, of course. I mean, why wouldn't I?" Suddenly she looked nonplussed. She snapped open the ivory-handled fan at her wrist and began fanning her face vigorously. "What a thing to ask, Jennifer."

Jenny had lost her mind. There was no other excuse for it. "I just wondered," she continued lamely, "if you ever have doubts or concerns. You hardly mentioned Milt once this afternoon."

"Oohh," Hannah drawled sagely, as if Jenny's meaning had just dawned on her. "You want to know if I'm concerned about *that*. The, uh, husband-and-wife relationship."

Jenny hadn't meant *that* at all. She meant the lifelong, forever-after, until-death-do-you-part relationship. "No, I—"

"It's all right." Hannah patted an imaginary curl in place, a telling sign that she was just a touch uncomfortable. "I have given it some thought—Mama says I'm wicked for doing so, but I don't care—you know how I hate loose ends. Anyway, I think *that* is a wifely duty for the purpose of procreation and it must be performed no matter how disgusting or inconvenient it sounds." Her delicate brow knit suddenly and she looked quite baffled. "I admitted such to Milton and he snickered."

Jenny's eyes widened. "You talked about that with Milt?"

Hannah's posture-perfect back straightened even further. "Not in so many indelicate words, Jennifer, but in a roundabout way. And I am not ashamed. It is my opinion that a husband and wife should be able to discuss any subject, no matter how direct or crude." Her shoulders sagged for a brief second in insecurity. "He snickered, Jennifer. What do you suppose that means?"

Jenny didn't have a clue. "Did you ask him?"

"Well, yes, but he just kissed me on the mouth, *hard*, and said 'Whatever you say, darling.'"

Jenny's knees went watery just thinking about it. She had never pictured Milt kissing her on the mouth. She had imagined him kissing her hand, her cheek, saying endearing things by starlight. But she had never pictured him doing anything *hard*. It sounded so rough and adventurous, it made the hairs on the back of her neck stand up.

She smiled weakly. Mooning over her best friend's husband-to-be was just plain sinful, and she was determined to stop it. "I'm certain he didn't mean anything by the snicker."

Hannah didn't look convinced. "But how would I know? I mean, how do we, as enlightened but unmarried young women, know anything? It's not as if the two of us can take a poll on Main Street about the intimacies of the marriage bed."

"Certainly not," Jenny agreed.

"And Mama won't even discuss it." Hannah leaned in close, her eyes cunning. "I have given this some thought and have come up with only one solution. You must ask Aunt Tildy."

Jenny was horrified. "No!"

"I know she is a bit befuddled, but I'm desperate! Mama keeps spouting things like 'What you need to know, your husband will teach you.' You know how I like things tidy and well ordered, Jennifer. What if I do something wrong when it comes time for that?"

"You won't—"

"Fiddle! How many stitches did you have to rip out the first time you learned to embroider?"

Jenny's sewing skills didn't bear discussing. "Hannah . . ."

"See? A thing isn't done well without knowledge or practice. Since practice is not a consideration, I need knowledge. I warn you, I will be a bundle of nerves until I have the answers!" She turned her most effective, pleading look on Jenny. "Aunt Tildy has been married. She would know the exact way of things."

"You're not a henwit, Hannah. You can figure this out."

"Yes, I am," she said, "and so are you where things of the flesh are concerned." Her eyes narrowed on her friend. "You only *think* you are enlightened, but have you ever actually lain with a man?"

"Of course not!"

"See?" Hannah leaned closer. "Have you ever *watched* two people engaged in carnal knowledge of each other?"

"Hannah!"

"You don't know any more than I do, Jennifer, so that makes you equally ignorant."

"Well, I must have a better imagination," she defended.

"That's all well and good for someone determined to remain a spinster," Hannah said stiffly, "but your imagination won't do me a speck of good on my wedding night."

Offended, Jenny sat back in a huff. "I'm not determined to remain a spinster. I just haven't found the right man." Rather, her friend had found him first.

"Forgive me," Hannah said, contrite. "This whole thing just has me so edgy." She whispered shockingly, "I ordered a book written by a doctor. He says that husbands, as is so often the case in their eagerness, should be ever so careful not to *abuse* their wives' tender sensibilities and persons upon the marriage bed, so as not to cause undue bruising and abrasion, which could result in a lasting revulsion in her toward her husband."

She took a deep breath for composure. "Now, I ask you, Jennifer, does that clear anything up? No, it only confounds me with more worries. I'm certain if I had straightforward answers to my questions, I would settle down." Her expression turned pleading. "Jennif—"

"No." Jenny would never open up such a volatile conversation with Aunt Tildy, who just might repeat every word at the most unfortunate moment.

"Please."

"Hannah."

"I graded over a thousand papers for you last year alone."

Hannah had never fought dirty before. Jenny was impressed. "Aunt Tildy is out of the question, but I might *consider* broaching the subject with Mercedes, especially with the legitimate excuse that it is your request. What *exactly* do you want to know?"

Hannah looked around cautiously to see that no one was eavesdropping, then said bluntly, "Everything."

Everything wound its insidious self through Jenny's mind all the way home. She pictured Milt and Hannah doing things she wasn't even certain existed—or not the way they appeared in her mind. Then the picture changed and Milt was trying to do the same things to Jenny, who slapped his groping hands to prove she wasn't that sort, then allowed him a kiss on the cheek to make up.

Even Jeremiah's distracting chatter wasn't enough to keep her from the inappropriate thoughts. They kept cropping up in her mind, libidinous ideas and mental pictures of half-naked men and women in compromising embraces.

Lost in lewd rumination, Jenny almost toppled overboard when the wagon hit a rut. She grabbed onto the sideboard at the same moment Thorne grabbed onto her. His fingers bit into her forearm. She gasped at the pain. There would be a ring of bruises by morning, but she was grateful for his quick reflexes.

As soon as he was certain she was safe, he let go. "You all right?"

"Yes," she said, disgusted with herself. "Sorry, I wasn't paying attention."

Hannah had asked a ridiculous thing of her. Jenny had let it so preoccupy her mind she had almost lost her life. She would never get up the courage to ask Mercedes such personal questions, and she certainly couldn't ask Aunt Tildy. She glanced over at Thorne. He had been married. He would know every little sordid detail about every wicked question Hannah had.

"What?"

Jenny jumped at his dark voice. "What?"

"What are you thinking?"

She swallowed a huge lump of guilt. "Why?"

"Because you're looking at me as if I hit that rut on purpose."

Jenny hadn't realized she was staring at Thorne at all, much less with such an incriminating expression. She bit down on her bottom lip, abashed. "No. I wasn't thinking anything. Really—" Her father had always known when she was lying by how she rambled over excuses. "Why wouldn't you let me pay for Jeremiah's candy?"

Thorne blinked at her skewed switch in topics. "He needs to learn the value of money."

She turned back toward the road, her sight fixed straight ahead on the glorious sunset. "Well, I see. Fine, then."

"Anything else?"

Jenny shook her head too quickly. "No, nothing."

"You sure?"

If he only knew.

The sky was dark, hardly a star twinkled overhead. Jenny sat on the patio and stirred the water in the fountain with just her fingertips. The stone was still warm from the day's heat, soothing in the cool night air.

She hadn't been able to get Hannah's request out of her mind, had become fixated actually on the idea of what two married people did in their beds at night.

She knew how animals went about their business, but she could hardly picture Hannah and Milt in such an unwieldy position. A small giggle escaped her at the very idea of perfect Hannah trying to do it like the horses . . . perfectly. She clamped her hand over her mouth. She couldn't even *think* about it without getting embarrassed. How in the world was she supposed to talk about it?

The moon slid from behind a cloud, illuminating the courtyard in spare cold light. The fountain shimmered, a silvery waterfall disappearing into a black pool. She stirred the surface again and watched the night reflect in glimmers off the ripples.

A coyote howled in the distance, a lonely sound answered only by the wind, then a deep masculine voice.

"Do you mind?"

Jenny jerked around to find Thorne standing behind her holding up a pouch of tobacco. Her hand went to her careening heart. "You startled me."

"Sorry. I wasn't trying to sneak up on you."

Maybe not, but he moved like a huge cat, all silent power and fluid grace. "I was lost in thought."

He held up the pouch. "May I?"

"Yes, certainly." She scooted over, an invitation for him to sit beside her on the rim of the fountain if he liked. In order for them to work together on a daily basis, she needed to form a rapport that did not involve past grievances and insecurity. She needed to rebuild the trust they had shared when very young. And if she was honest with herself, she would admit that she desperately needed a friend, someone of her own generation to converse with from time to time.

He propped one hip on the stone edge and began to roll the tobacco in paper. His fingers were long and dexterous. He had strong, handsome hands, she noticed, a working man's hands. As soon as he put the cigarette to his mouth, Jenny took one of his hands and turned it over. He gave her a strange look but didn't flinch from her scrutiny. She ran her fingers along the calluses on his palm.

She smiled with approval and looked up at him. "Soft hands would never do out here."

In a reflex too quick for her to catch, he flipped his hand over and took her wrist, then turned her own palm up. He ran one finger along her life line, then down each finger. "A teacher's hands. You would be bloody in half a day."

The contact sent goose flesh along her arms. Surprised, she slid her hand from beneath his and went back to stirring the water in the pool. "It happens every year. I'll toughen up before summer's out." She heard the flare of a match, smelled the tangy scent of sulfur, then the richer flavor of tobacco. "What was your life like with the Comanche?" she asked.

"Why do you want to know?"

She shrugged. "If we're going to work together, I'd like to know more about you."

"It was hard. Successful."

She wasn't sure what that meant. "And your wife? What was she like?"

"Beautiful." The tip of the cigarette flared in the darkness. "Unhappy."

Jenny glanced at him sharply. "What do you mean?"

"She was the daughter of a white slave. Her mother was already pregnant when captured. Allissa was born and raised among the Comanche. Everything she knew was Comanche. When she was given to me at age fifteen, she resented it. She wanted a Comanche brave, not a white man, but because her mother was a slave, she wasn't given a choice."

"Were you a slave?"

"No. I had been adopted and raised like a real son. Because I chose her, she was given to me. She was lucky to have been chosen and knew it, but that didn't change her secret desires."

Jenny knew all about secret desires. "So, she resented you?"

"She didn't bring shame on herself by being an improper wife."

"But she didn't love you."

"No."

Jenny looked down. He spoke so frankly, as if there were no love on his part either for the woman who had borne his son. "Did you care for her?"

He made a short sound that might pass for a laugh. "Of course. She was beautiful. I was young. I wanted to believe that she would love me because I willed it."

"But it doesn't happen that way." Jenny knew from experience.

"No. Love is not something that can be conjured or captured at will." It came like a flash fire of lightning, searing the body and soul, then eventually faded to cold dead ash. "I think she was secretly relieved when I was traded back to my father. She tried to keep it hidden, but I knew. I suppose that's why I stayed away so long. Maybe I thought to punish her. There were . . . parts of the marriage that were good, things I knew she would miss. Perhaps I thought she would miss me as well." The cigarette tip glowed again, then receded. "She was horrified when I returned. She had already chosen another husband, and they were to marry soon. She was honor-bound to return to me, however."

He crushed the cigarette beneath his heel, and Jenny wondered how many memories he endeavored to stamp out with it.

"How awful for both of you."

"She could no longer hide her feelings, and we grew to resent each other. She died giving birth to Jeremiah, releasing us both."

"You make it sound as if she died on purpose," Jenny said, both appalled and sympathetic.

His smile flashed white in the moonlight, joyless and predatory. "Sometimes I wonder."

It was a terrible thing to say, a worse thing to feel. "I'm so sorry."

"Don't be, at least not for me. By the time she died, the only feeling I had left was resigned tolerance. Even that would have faded with time. She gave me Jeremiah, and I can never regret that."

She wondered how a child could have been conceived out of such resentment. "Ian—"

He flung his head back and stared up at the stars. "I won't even bother to correct you." He sighed.

"Thorne is not your name," she returned.

"It is," he countered. In many more ways than he could explain or she could comprehend. It was the merging of two different people and places in time into the man he had become.

Chapter 7

Jenny could not fathom her dream of marrying Milt turning into such a nightmare after years spent together. She pictured a nice, tidy house with several children playing in the yard. She saw herself greeting Milt at the end of a hard day, a friendly smile on her face and a plate of food warming on the stove.

Night cloaked the patio and offered an odd intimacy. "Do you miss her at all, even a little?" Jenny pressed.

"No."

The word was so cold it made her skin crawl. "Well, that was brutally honest."

"Merely the truth."

"Honesty . . . truth. They are the same thing."

"Sometimes." He said nothing more, and Jenny wondered at his reticence. The mountains rose starkly in the distance, black as the night, the cry of the wolf and the coyote their inharmonious nightsong. The temperature dropped in the evenings and a chill now invaded the air, crisp and dry and heavy with the scent of resin.

Jenny ran her finger along the stone lip of the fountain, lonely for the days of her childhood and the closeness of a family she had taken for granted. "I should hope that if I ever died in childbirth, I would be missed."

"You would be."

It was simply said, yet there was an undercurrent, a forwardness, that was as welcome as it was unnerving. Jenny looked at him. "Is that honesty or truth?"

"Both."

"What's the difference?"

"The truth is that Ian is my given name, but in all honesty Thorne is what I go by now."

She smiled at the verbal jab. "Point taken."

The moon cast cold, pale light over his angular features. He was a handsome man, compelling in ways hard to define. She had found it advantageous to study and distinguish her students in order to best meet their individual learning needs. But she had not been able to fully define Thorne. He was complacent one moment, coldly distant the next, friendly when it suited him. His manner was wholly foreign to Jenny, and she found that she could not catalogue or characterize him. For all his blunt, open attitude at times, he was still an enigma.

The breeze stirred the hair at her nape and sent chills down her spine. The night was a screen, allowing them a privacy not possible in daylight. An owl hooted in the distance, an eerie sound followed by its mate's answering call. Marauding Indians used the sounds of nature to signal each other, and Jenny had learned early upon her arrival west to listen for the differences in friend or foe.

There had been no attacks on the ranch for years, but still her guard was raised by even the most innocent noise. A coyote howled again, sending another rash of chills along her arms. She pulled her shawl more tightly around her shoulders. It was a night for secrets, for honesty, perhaps even a small liberty. Hannah's request crept into Jenny's thoughts again, insidious as a snake, always hiding on the fringes ready to strike. She admitted that her own avid interest had a lot to do with her willingness to be an accomplice.

She studied Thorne and wondered how he would react to such an intimate topic. "If I asked you a personal question," she began, "would you answer me, no matter how improper?"

She caught a change in his expression, a hesitation, then reluctance.

"How personal?"

"Not terribly *personal*"—the very thought made her blush, and she was thankful for the gentle subtlety of darkness—"but unconventional, out of the ordinary, sort of educational." She quit rambling and came to the point. "What exactly does a married couple do in the marriage bed?"

If she had fired a Colt repeating rifle between his eyes, he would not have been more shocked.

He reared back and stared at her. *"What?"* The question came out in a near shout that echoed across the patio.

Abashed, Jenny faced him with all the hauteur she could dredge up to cover the obvious breakdown of her moral and mental faculties. She hadn't meant to ask the question quite so bluntly, especially of him, but there was no backing out now. "The details, I mean. You were spouting honesty. Be honest."

"No!"

"Why not?"

Because she had caught him off guard, had sent a boulder-size shock wave ricocheting through him. He was still reeling from the impact. "Just because."

Her chin set stubbornly. "Because why?"

He leveled her with a look. "Because it's not my place to explain the ways of a man and woman to you."

"It's not *anyone's* place!" she fired back in resentment. "No one wants to tell an unmarried girl what happens."

"You own a horse ranch, Jenny. You can't convince me that you don't already have some pretty good ideas of what goes on."

"I do," she said, "but that doesn't mean I have it all sorted out, step by step, exactly as it should be done."

He leveled her with an accusing stare. "And why would you need to?"

"I don't. It's a matter of education." She felt guilty and out of sorts but refused to back down at his tone. "I promised a friend I would find out, but I'm beginning to think there is a reason women are kept so ignorant. Is it so *bad* that men don't want us to know everything ahead of time? If it is such a part of instinct and nature, why do parents shy away from even the most basic discussion?"

She was on a crusade now, all her pent-up frustrations

with the world pouring out on one unsuspecting man. "Is it so *terrible* that men purposefully try to keep women uninformed until its too late? Is it so *horrible*—"

"No." Thorne smiled suddenly. It was a wolf's smile, cunning and intense. He leaned forward, his own expression full of secrets.

Her feistiness began to dwindle at the strange look in his eyes, but she had come too far to back down now. "Then why?"

His eyes were cold and bright as the moonlight. "Are you sure you want to know?"

She swallowed hard. "Yes."

His voice went low, almost purring. "No one tells unmarried women because it makes them want to *do it*."

She jerked back. "It does not!"

His laughter was so insulting, Jenny wanted to slap him. She stiffened in indignation, a mass of wounded feelings and irate embarrassment. "Fine, don't tell me. I didn't want to know anyway. Like I said, I was asking for someone else."

Sure she was. Reaching over, he tweaked a curl by her temple, as if she were a child. "Come back and ask me when you want to know for yourself."

Her gaze narrowed suspiciously on him. "Why? Would you tell me then?"

He rose from the fountain, uncomfortable with the motives behind this brazen conversation. "No," he said as he walked out of reach. "But I might show you."

"Show me?" she whispered in confusion, then the impact of his words flooded her. "Faint-hearted craven!" she called to his retreating back.

Thorne stopped in midstride. He couldn't believe she hadn't dropped the conversation at his parting shot. It had been intended to alarm her into silence, thus ending a discussion so provoking it had him suddenly and inappropriately as randy as a penned stallion. He turned slowly. "Craven?"

"Yes," she accused. "I think men feel superior when they can keep women ignorant."

"Really." He strolled back swiftly to within inches of her earnest face. "I'm not opposed to giving you every little juicy detail your heart desires, Jennifer Delaney. Just how much do you want to know?"

She wasn't quite as certain now that they were eye to eye. "Everything," she murmured.

"Everything," he echoed. "Just how much do you already know?"

Jenny's mouth went dry. She hadn't planned on taking part in the discussion or having to detail her own limited knowledge. The request put a decidedly uncomfortable twist on the situation. "I know . . . things."

He leaned one hip against the edge of the fountain and took the pouch of tobacco from his pocket. "What things?" he asked, idly rolling a cigarette. Smoke curled skyward when he lit it. The tip glowed red as a beacon, as red as Jenny's cheeks.

"I know about the horses, obviously, but nature takes care of that. My *friend* wants to know if humans have the same instincts."

He took another pull on the cigarette. "What happens if my explanation offends your sensibilities? I don't want to take the chance of losing my job and Jeremiah's future."

Her mouth dropped. "I would never . . . your job is not in jeopardy."

"Nice words, Miss Jenny, but how do I know I'm not about to risk getting booted out of here?"

She flung him a sarcastic look. "Don't you think offering to *show* me earlier would have accomplished that?"

"I assumed you knew that was a joke." *Sort of.* Damn if the thought hadn't taken root right down in the most influential parts of his body.

"Oh, well, of course. A joke." Her back straightened and she got that starchy teacher's pose. "I knew you were joshing me."

He detected a hint of pique in her tone and just a bit of disappointment. Interesting. And worth teasing a little more if he were a very foolish man. "I'll make a deal with you," he offered, *foolishly.* "If you still want to know all the sordid details after I've been here a little longer, I'll tell you."

"Sordid?" That put a bawdy picture in her mind. Her fingers curled over the edge of the fountain. "What do you mean by sordid?"

Oh, Miss Jenny, you are a bushel basket full of wanton nosiness. "Not sordid, perhaps. Maybe . . . naughty."

"Naughty." Her mouth formed the word but no sound came out. She ran her tongue over her bottom lip and tried to swallow. "What exactly do you mean by . . . naughty?"

"Not vulgar," he hastened to assure her.

"No, of course not." Her face was hot, the hair on her arms standing up.

"Just . . . naughty. You know."

"I am certain that I do not know," she said primly. "That is the purpose for this whole conversation."

"But why do you *want* to know?" he countered.

"It's not me," she said quickly. "I told you that. It's for my friend who's about to be married. She's the one who wants to know the details."

"Oh, Hannah Thompson. The sheriff's intended."

Jenny's face blanched. "How did you know?"

"Only Hannah would want the whole thing laid out in perfect detail."

Jenny got a concerned look. "You won't mention this to anyone, will you?"

"Why doesn't she ask Milton herself?"

"She tried, but all Milt did was snicker."

Thorne grinned. He could imagine Milt snickering all the way to his overheated toes. With the wedding still more than a month away, old Milt was probably doing everything he could to stay away from the subject. "So, you'll ask for Hannah but you don't want to know for yourself?"

Her chin rose. "I admit to a certain curiosity."

"I see."

"So, you will tell me?"

He shrugged. "I've never been one to stand in the way of a person's education."

She felt heat creep up her neck. Now that the fight was over, she was feeling a bit sheepish. "When?"

He shifted to his feet and crushed the cigarette beneath his heel. "Study the horses for a while, Jenny, then—"

She rose with him. "I *know* that horses are different from people."

It was obvious that she badly wanted him to convince her. "Really?" he asked in abject innocence.

She pressed her lips together. "Yes."

But there was just that hint of troubling doubt in her expression. "Well, if you're so sure . . ."

"When?" she ground out.

"Soon," he said.

Soon.

It had been Thorne's last word before disappearing into his bedroom. Jenny could hardly follow him. She lay in her own bed, unable to sleep, visions of him running through her head. Not Thorne as he looked now but as he had looked the day he captured her. Brown and lean and wild. An earthy beauty draped in gentleman's clothing that had been terrifying. She still saw that look in his eyes at times, the uncivilized warrior robed out in refinement, a mask of his true intentions.

What *were* his true intentions?

He had asked her to marry him, but it had been a halfhearted offer at best. He only wanted what the others did: her land and her horses.

When would she find someone who wanted *her*?

She flipped over onto her stomach and buried her face in her pillow. The truth was glaringly painful. She would find someone who wanted her when she quit behaving like a hoyden, when she quit doing wholly improper things like kissing Jimmy Henderson and marching off to Lucy's.

She rolled onto her back. She might find someone interested in her when she quit asking men to tell her about the details of the marriage bed.

The very idea sent a quiver of shame shimmying up her spine. Animals operated out of instinct. They gave little thought to their choice of mate beyond the process of procreation. Apparently humans did too, since Thorne had a child with a woman who had resented him, in a marriage that had grown bitter.

She couldn't imagine it. Couldn't imagine giving herself to a man where love did not exist. But maybe men were different. She knew they didn't have to love a woman to bed her. Lucy's was evidence of that. But Jenny had never really *seen* anyone go there, save the strangers passing through town, who cared nothing for their reputations. She didn't know which local men kept the place prosperous.

Thorne had been there.

She remembered Lucy's familiarity with him, the way she'd called him Mr. Thorne and told him to come back. A streak of indignation shot through Jenny mixed with morbid curiosity. She had no basis for it, no business feeling it. But she sure couldn't deny it. What did Thorne or any man do when he went to Lucy's? What was it about the coarse, painted women that enticed men to risk local censure if caught in such a place? She flipped back onto her stomach. She wished she wasn't so curious about such sinful ideas.

Only With You

• • •

Jenny leaned against the corral fence and watched Thorne work with a stunning white stallion. His name was Emperor and he had a large regal head, strong neck, and compact body. Jenny never tired of watching the stallion move. Emperor was a Lipizzan, a breed developed from Arabians and Andalusians by Emperor Maximilian II of Austria. Though the breed matured late, they were long-lived, still active in their twenties.

For all his beauty and exquisite maneuvering, Emperor was a vanity. Uncle Nat had seen him as a colt in a traveling circus and purchased him on the spot. Normally used as parade and show horses, Lipizzans had the build and temperament that enabled them to excel at the difficult and complicated maneuvers of dressage. Emperor would have made an excellent farm horse, but Uncle Nat had never wanted to use him that way.

Jenny wondered what Thorne's opinion would be. He had a gentle, steady manner and a commanding voice not easily ignored. He was patient yet firm and tireless with the exacting task of profiling each horse for its worth. She had been watching for a quarter hour, and not once had he deviated from the same tedious routine. Jenny slipped her leather gloves from her pocket and pulled them back on her hands. She needed to get back to the stalls, but it was a pleasure watching Thorne work.

She rested her booted foot on the lowest rail. She wore a heavy cotton shirt with an open collar and a full skirt. Beneath, she wore denim pants for ease of movement. Men's clothes, Mercedes always scolded. Work clothes, Jenny forever corrected. If the idea hadn't been so scandalous, she would have done away with the overskirt. She couldn't move as freely in women's clothing, couldn't work like a man in a girl's dress. It was as simple and as unorthodox as that.

Thorne put the horse through a few more paces, then handed the rope over to Cortez, who acted as both ranchhand and blacksmith. "Take him on in," he said, then stood, hands on his hips a moment, pondering.

Jenny pulled herself up to sit on the top rail of the fence. "What do you think?"

Thorne turned. "He's so beautiful."

"But useless?"

He shook his head as he approached, formulating his words carefully. "Not useless, just not used productively."

"I know." She took his measure, from the toes of his scruffed leather boots to the bandanna tied at his throat. The sun approached the zenith, baking everything in the open, but he looked cool and composed beneath the burning rays. He had broad shoulders and a muscular build. A bit taller than Milton, he was lean without being rangy and personified the typical tough, land-hardened cowboy. Except that he was much more handsome than most of the weather-worn cowpokes she knew, and better educated as well.

To her lovestruck mind, no one was more handsome than Milt, with his sandy hair and sturdy build. Though seven years as the town sheriff had scored grooves in his cheeks, he was still a young-looking man at thirty-two. No, there was no one more handsome than Milt, but Thorne was a close second. Tall and strong, he carried himself with a confidence that inspired respect. She just hoped he was strong enough to carry the weight of miracles needed to get the ranch prosperous again.

She turned back to the task at hand. "I can't sell Emperor."

He pulled the brown felt Stetson from his head and ran his fingers through his hair. "I was afraid you would say that. He would bring a fair price."

"I'm not opposed to using him for harness or farmwork."

He put the hat back on. "That's something, at least."

"Have you had a chance to look at Turk?"

Thorne gave her a guarded look. Cortez had already told him that Turk had been named for his breed ancestor the Byerly Turk, an imported stallion and ancestor of Herod. The entire breed of Thoroughbreds could be traced back to only three horses: Herod, Eclipse, and Matchem. Turk was, without a doubt, one of the most beautiful Thoroughbreds he'd ever seen.

"Yes, I've seen Turk and Herod, and a number of others with impeccable bloodlines. What was your uncle thinking?"

Jenny hopped down from the fence and began to stroll toward the far paddock. "He wanted everything."

"He got everything." Thorne followed, watching the intriguing sway of her hips, distracted by what looked like copper rivets showing through the fabric of her skirt.

"He tried," Jenny said. Her uncle had purchased Thoroughbreds, Morgans, Shetlands, Arabians, quarter horses, Appaloosas, pintos, and the list went on. The only thing he had not done was stick to one breed or even one type.

She watched the horses run in the far corral, then kicked the dust with the toe of her boot. "What do you suggest?"

"How many are you attached to?"

She looked up at him with the largest, most innocent brown eyes he had ever seen. "I named every one."

He flung his head back and groaned. "You couldn't possibly! There are hundreds of horses out there. At least fifteen different breeds."

She smiled, a little encouraged. "I only named the tame ones."

"The most marketable ones, you mean."

Her face fell. "I guess you could look at it that way."

He pulled his hat from his head and ran his fingers through his hair again, agitated, confounded. "What was your uncle trying to accomplish? What was his goal?"

"I think he wanted to breed racers."

Thorne let the word ferment for a moment, then his face transformed. As if a match had suddenly been struck to dispel the darkness, his eyes lit with sharp clarity. "Not breed them," he said, "*race* them."

He slapped the Stetson against his thigh, then slammed it back on his head. He then picked Jenny up by the arms and kissed her smack on the mouth. "Race them!" With something that sounded like a growl of satisfaction, he put her back down, then headed for the ranch house.

Jenny was left standing in the middle of the corral, staring after him, her lips on fire.

Only With You

• • •

Her composure regained, Jenny found Thorne poring over ledgers in Uncle Nat's office. She walked in casually enough but kept her distance.

"What are you doing?"

He glanced up, then back down. "Saratoga Springs, New York."

Call her obtuse, but she did not see the connection. "What about it?"

"The track at the foot of the Adirondack Mountains opened in 1863."

"I'm certain all the fashionable people are seen there."

He looked back up then and focused on her, as if really seeing her for the first time since he'd left the corral. "It's a track for racing horses. Not only that, but the first Kentucky Derby last year was a huge success."

"The what?"

"We're going to save the ranch by building a racetrack. We'll breed and race Thoroughbreds and quarter horses."

He was mad. "In the New Mexico Territory?"

"Why not?"

"It's hardly New York," she said dubiously.

"Exactly." There was a fever in his eyes, a passion she had never seen. He was neither cool nor composed. He was on fire. "We'll fulfill the army contracts your uncle negotiated with wild mustangs from the hills and some of the mixed stock here. But with the Thoroughbreds and quarter horses, we'll breed racing stock year round and offer it for sale."

"I still don't see——"

"And one month a year, only one, we'll offer racing. People will come, Jenny. There is so little entertainment in this part of the country, we won't be able to keep them away."

She felt breathless suddenly, feeding on his excitement. "How?"

He came around the desk, a man with purpose in each stride. "We'll build a track, send out advertisements to every city and settlement within two hundred miles, maybe more. They'll come for the racing, but they'll buy Thoroughbreds when they see the superior stock your uncle has raised. When they return, others will want the horseflesh we raise here."

He grabbed her by the upper arms, and she pulled back. "Are you going to kiss me again?"

He smiled, the predator again, the light of conquest in his eyes. "Maybe," he said softly.

She'd already gotten herself in trouble for improper behavior once this year; she wasn't about to go for twice. "Don't."

"Can't you see it?" he asked with a compelling air of energy that threatened to pull her in. "The crowds, the buyers, the betting."

She could. His enthusiasm was like hot coals under her feet. She wanted to dance and shout and run in circles, but was such an endeavor possible? "I can see it," she breathed, "but it scares me."

"Don't be afraid," he urged. "Not you, Jenny."

No, not her. Not Jenny Delaney who kissed men behind schoolhouses and marched up to brothels and asked for details about the marriage bed.

But she was.

Chapter 8

For two weeks Thorne worked with the horses in the morning, pored over the documents and contracts in Nathaniel Delaney's office in the early afternoon, then returned to the horses in the evening. Aside from shoeing and grooming, there were stalls to rake, fences to repair, strays to round up. A never-ceasing cycle of both backbreaking and rewarding work that callused the hands but cleansed the mind.

For two weeks Jenny watched Thorne with a sort of terrified fascination. She was excited; she was afraid. She felt herself losing control of the ranch, yet there was freedom in turning the day-to-day operations over to a man with the know-how and imagination to succeed.

Uncle Nat had been like that, full of vision and determination. Jenny had not realized until this week how much she missed his enthusiasm, how vital his exuberance was to her own sense of well-being.

She answered Thorne's questions as best she could, but she had not been involved in the daily operations or the future plans of El Dorado. In keeping with her upbringing at River Run, Uncle Nat had turned over management of the domestic duties to her and handled the rest himself. She felt ignorant now, completely inept at answering Thorne's many questions and concerns.

A part of her wanted to run the other way when he approached with a problem. Another part of her, she hoped the best part of her, wanted to learn everything possible so she would never feel adrift again when it came time to make important decisions.

With a vigor she found exhilarating, she began to follow the same sort of daily routine as Thorne. She worked out in the stables in the morning, then returned to the house midday to work on lesson plans for the next school term. She would not allow herself to think that the school board would follow through with their threat and replace her if she didn't marry Jimmy. She could not bear it.

But always the fear of it rested in the back of her mind, a gnawing away of her optimism that she tried violently to shove aside but never fully succeeded. The children depended on her. She had already lost Paul Anderson, a sullen boy with a worthless father. Nothing she had done had been enough to help him, and he had run off weeks before school was out. She felt the weight of that failure as deeply as she felt fear for the other children. What would happen to Tommy Chancellor,

Jilly Perkins, and Billy Masterson if the school board replaced her?

To soothe herself, she sought out Jeremiah often and played learning games with him, continually amazed by his quick mind and easy grasp of almost any elementary concept. His ability to comprehend even abstract ideas was astonishing. But for all his educational prowess, he was still just a four-year-old boy, in need of affection and security and play.

Jenny set aside the yearly planning calendar she had been sketching. She was becoming uncommonly attached to Jeremiah. It was more than student-teacher fondness, more than anything she had ever felt. He filled an empty place inside her, a spot she hadn't even known was vacant. A void, she realized, she'd been trying to fill for years with other women's children.

She rose abruptly from her desk, uneasy with the revelation. Over the past two years she had ridden each day to the schoolhouse searching for completeness, for the family lost to her in the war, for the family that would never be in the future of a spinster. Even knowing this, she had not guarded her heart where Jeremiah was concerned. Now her concern for him as a student had become entangled with her greater affection for him as a child.

She knew she must start taking pains to protect herself against the inevitable hurt that would come when he left. Thorne would not stay at El Dorado forever. Since coming to the ranch he had shown another side of his personality, a farsighted and ambitious nature at odds with the man Jenny had gone to visit in the dugout.

Thorne would not be anyone's ranch hand for the rest of his life. When he left with the ten percent stock profit they had agreed upon, he would go to build his own ranch. And he would take his precious child with him.

Jenny would endure, as she had with all the other losses in her life. If not with the dignified acceptance bred into a true lady, then with the resigned fighting spirit that had gotten her through the rest. She would stomp and curse fate and rail at God, and then she would go on. Lonely. So lonely.

Empty nights loomed before her, nights she would lie awake thinking of those she missed, but she would not dwell on them in a maudlin way. The only alternative was never to have known them at all, and that was intolerable. She often pictured herself, a handful of children in tow, greeting Milt at the end of a hard day. He always had a fond smile for her, a husband's unswerving affection for the children. Their love would conquer all the rigors and hardships of ranch life; no strife would touch their door.

She frowned, wondering why Thorne had not found the same love with his wife, why her own parents had been little more than polite strangers. In her dreams, life was good and rich and fulfilling. In reality, she knew too few couples who typified that ideal, but she would not wed until she found the knight who could slay the dragons of genteel indifference and marital tolerance. She wanted nothing less than undying love.

She rose from her desk and stretched, then pressed her fists into the small of her back. Her sore muscles complained at the extra stable work she was taking on but it was a good pain, the result of long, hard hours and accomplishment. Mucking out stalls might not be the most dignified task for the owner of a large horse ranch, but it was a vital way Jenny could contribute until she learned more.

She heard a sound just outside her office. "Jeremiah?" she called.

He rounded the corner with a running skid that almost sent him into a table. Scrambling to right himself, he beamed up at her. "Yes, Miss Jenny?"

Her heart squeezed, and she couldn't hold back a smile at the fact that he had been waiting close by for her to finish her work. "Do you want to go see Bulle?"

He nodded eagerly. "May I ride her?"

"We'll see what your father says."

His bottom lip poked out. "He'll say 'As soon as I finish my work.' But he won't get done till dark time."

The imitation of the man, given in a child's voice, had Jenny smiling. "I'll see what I can do," she said.

Hand in hand, they strolled from the ranch house as companions, trying to fill with each other the needy gaps in their lives. For Jeremiah, it was the soft feminine touch lost to him in infancy. For Jenny, it was the commitment and companionship of a son. Even knowing this, she was unprepared for the way it struck her full force. She started to pull her hand away, but when Jeremiah's fingers tightened, she found she could do nothing but squeeze back in reassurance. Protecting herself was going to be much more difficult than she had anticipated.

Aunt Tildy was pruning flowers in a corner of the

patio, humming an old tune from her debutante days. She looked up when they approached.

"Mustn't let this ivy take over, dearest. It will choke the irises."

There wasn't an iris in the pot. Jenny smiled softly and touched her aunt's arm to determine whether Tildy was doing too much. The older woman's skin was moist but not flushed. "Don't get overwarm," Jenny warned. She leaned forward to look into the now-denuded pot. "We could try roses if we can obtain cuttings from Mrs. Larkin."

"A disagreeable woman," Tildy stated, "but I might be persuaded to accept a cup of tea in her company if she brings cuttings."

"Aunt," Jenny chided, "that's just a bit mercenary, don't you think?"

"I suppose," Tildy agreed, "but her husband is a Yankee spy, so I don't feel a bit bad about it. He's selling guns to the Mexicans, you know."

Tildy didn't need a reason to come up with such an outrageous assumption, so Jenny let it pass. She'd long ago quit trying to talk her aunt out of her unreasonable suspicions. "Jeremiah and I are going to see the horses. Would you like to come?"

Tildy shook her head. "I've important letters to write as soon as I finish getting rid of this ivy. It has choked the irises, you know."

Taking a deep breath, Jenny nodded and took Jeremiah's hand once again. They headed for the paddocks in the stable block. Although the sun had begun its evening descent, the day's heat still smothered the land like a wool blanket and shimmered on the horizon. One of the hands rode in the distance, bringing in horses to stable for the night. The wind was sweet and soft, the rhythmic sounds of a ringing anvil the only noise breaking the afternoon quiet.

"Cortez is making shoes," Jeremiah said.

"Shoes?"

"For the horses' feet."

Jenny nodded. "For their hooves. Yes, he is." She waved as they passed the blacksmith section of the stable block. "May I get you some water?" Jenny called over the noise.

Cortez looked up, then shook his head. "I will only be a moment longer, señorita. This shoe could not wait. I won't do more until evening when the temperature is cooler."

She nodded, then led Jeremiah over to Bulle's stall. "Here we go." She picked the boy up so he could get a better look.

Bulle was a hardy bay, with a long head, flat shoulders, and sloping rump. She whinnied when Jenny spoke and stuck her head over the stall door to be stroked. Jenny moved Jeremiah close so he could reach the horse's nose.

"She likes her forelock scratched," she encouraged.

Jeremiah ran his hand gently up and down the horse's long forehead. "Can I sit on her back?"

"Let's wait for your father." She didn't want to admit, even to a four-year-old, that she had never saddled a horse, that the men on the ranch always had done it for her. Though it certainly was not uncommon for a lady to expect to have the service performed for her, it was not Jenny's way to have others do work that she was capable of doing herself when their own schedules were so busy. It was downright embarrassing to realize that this child probably knew more than she did about the whole process.

"Jeremiah," she asked idly, "do you know how to saddle a horse?"

He looked at her as if she were being silly. "Everybody knows that."

Not everybody, she thought. "Can you show me?"

"I ain't strong enough."

"Don't say ain't," she corrected, then added casually, "I don't mean show me. I mean tell me."

Jeremiah smiled. "Like a spelling bee?"

"Maybe," she hedged, hoping he would elaborate.

"Even though *you* know the word, you still want *me* to spell it."

She looked away from his sincere expression. "Exactly."

"Well, first—"

"First," echoed a masculine voice behind them, "you admit you don't know how."

Jenny spun around. Thorne was little more than a tall black silhouette against the molten glow of a setting sun at the paddock entrance.

"Pa!" Jeremiah called with delight. "Can I ride Bulle?"

Thorne strolled forward, noting several things at once. The faint blush on Jenny's cheeks and the way her eyes wouldn't meet his when she was normally so bold. She could sit in a moonlit plaza and ask him about sex, but it embarrassed her that she couldn't saddle a horse. He paused, stymied by the incongruence, then continued on as if it were nothing out of the ordinary.

"Come on. I'll show you how, then we'll take Jeremiah for a ride."

She turned away too quickly and headed for the tack room. Her heart banged against her ribs, making her embarrassment keener. She didn't know why she felt so ashamed, but she did. Not ashamed that she didn't know how to saddle a horse but that she had never learned, that Thorne would know she had let others do the work for her. She pushed through the tack room door and began pulling a western saddle off the rack one-handed.

Thorne put a restraining hand on her shoulder. "Wait." He pulled Jeremiah from her arms, then tried to turn her but she stayed planted, hands gripping the saddle, stubborn for no reason. "It's not important, Jenny."

Hectic color burned her cheeks. "Yes, it is," she whispered. "I own a horse ranch. The men work so hard here, yet I'm about as useless as . . . as . . . I can't think of anything useless enough." His fingers tightened on her shoulders, his grip warm and solid as a harness left out in the sun. She relaxed her hold and allowed herself to be turned until she stood facing him, her backside pressed into the saddle.

"You're not useless," he said. "You muck out stalls, fill grain buckets, and lay down hay like a pro."

She rolled her eyes but wouldn't fully meet his gaze. "Let's get this over with."

His hands drifted from her shoulders, leaving her oddly bereft. She was unaccustomed to the casualness of a man's touch. In one way, it was pleasing. There was a warm fellowship in conversing with another human being on such a personal level. But in another way, she was disturbed by the intimacy of such close proximity. A silly giddiness washed over her at his nearness and attention. It was juvenile and irrational and not at all her. As with Jeremiah, her emotions seemed to get tangled up in what she felt and what she wanted. Was Ian Blackwell Thorne a hired hand or a friend? Was it possible for him to be neither and both?

"Start with a blanket," he said, retrieving one, then putting it in her arms. "Then a bridle." Leather straps and iron buckles piled atop the blanket. "Then the saddle—"

"Wait!"

She couldn't carry it all, and he knew it, which was evident in his dry smile when he turned. "No one can do everything, Jenny. We all need help now and then."

"I know that," she responded. "It's the fact that I never learned that bothers me."

"That's just the teacher in you. Women rarely saddle their own horses if there's a man around. You're just stubbornly independent."

She sent him a chagrined smile. "You flatter me."

His voice lowered for her ears only. "You seem to want to know a lot of things, even some you don't need to know."

She refused to let him bait her about passing along Hannah's request. "Exactly," she returned just as quietly, "and you're just the man who's going to teach me."

She had no idea how provocative her statement was

or how it heated Thorne's blood. She stood before him, trim and pretty as a picture, her golden-brown eyes impish. He'd like nothing better than to expand her education to the fullest. She compelled him in ways too complex to understand. He knew better than to tamper with physical urges, but baiting and titillating Jenny had a way of turning plain days into interesting challenges. He suspected that, for whatever reason, she had decided he was safe and she could indulge her thirst for forbidden knowledge.

But he had discovered something significant within a few days of his arrival. He wasn't exactly safe where Jenny Delaney was concerned. And neither was she.

"I'll carry the saddle for you," he said too quickly, then led the way back to Bulle's stall.

For the next thirty minutes, Thorne proceeded to show Jenny the correct way to saddle a horse, then had her try it several times. By the time they were done, her arms burned from the strain, but accomplishment was its own reward. She would never again have to wait for one of the men to do the job for her.

She checked the girth one last time, then turned around and smiled at Jeremiah. "You sure are a good teacher."

Beaming, Jeremiah shook his head. "Pa did it, Miss Jenny, you know that."

She looked up. "You sure are a good teacher, Ian—"

"Thorne," he reminded.

She laughed, invigorated by accomplishment. "I'll never call you that name."

His eyes held a strange, quiet confidence. "Yes, you will," he said simply.

Jeremiah tugged on his pant leg. "Can we ride now?"

Thorne checked the position of the sun, then studied his son. "It's getting too late to go far. How about a ride in the corral this evening, then a long ride tomorrow?"

Jeremiah's face fell. "A long time in the corral?"

"Twenty minutes."

His small chin jutted out. "A long time tomorrow?"

Thorne nodded. "A very long time tomorrow."

The aroma of Mercedes' cooking greeted them as soon as they entered the house. The meat and spices of her Mexican dishes mingled with the ordinary scents of home: starchy clothes on the line, soap from the kitchen sink, candle wax and lantern oil. Jenny inhaled the rightness of it and washed up, then set the table with colorful, hand-crafted pottery. Though not the delicate bone china her mother had prized back at River Run, the earthen plates, bowls, and cups were perfect in the rustic setting.

Tortillas de maiz and spicy enchiladas filled a serving platter, followed by a pot of beans, another of seasoned rice, and a bowl of succulent fruit. Dinners, except on Sunday and those served for special guests, were casual affairs and set out on a sideboard, where each diner filled his own plate.

Tildy fluttered around, as she had every night since Thorne's arrival, wearing her best dress and touching up her cheeks with rouge.

When nearly everyone was seated at the table, she smiled shyly at Jenny, then reached over to pat Thorne's hand. "Have you all set a date yet?"

Jenny ground her back molars. "Aunt Tildy—"

"Not yet," Thorne intervened smoothly. "What with everything still so unstable."

Tildy nodded sagely. "Still, it won't do to drag it out too long. People will talk."

"Ian *works* here, Auntie," Jenny reminded.

"Well, of course he does. I'm not daft, Jennifer, or blind. Can't allow a lazy man to come courting, can I? Your father would have apoplexy. It's not as if he doesn't have enough to worry about these days, and your mother too, trying to hold that plantation together with the Yankees practically at their doorstep."

Jenny sighed. It was one of Tildy's bad nights, where she thought everyone was still alive and fighting a winning battle for Southern independence. There was no use arguing or upsetting her, but her insinuations about marriage to Thorne were embarrassing.

"Can we discuss something else?"

Tildy's chin went up in a haughty miff. "Of course, dear. If your future is so unimportant to you, I daresay it is no concern of mine." She looked down her patrician nose at her niece. "Aunt Clarice sent her husband out for supplies one day. He never returned."

Jenny blinked. "Your point being?" she asked politely.

"At least Aunt Clarice had a husband."

Jenny closed her eyes briefly. "A husband who abandons his wife is better than no husband at all?"

"If the shoe fits, dear."

Jenny hid a smile. Tildy was, indeed, in unmatched form tonight. When Great-Aunt Clarice had divorced her feckless husband, it had caused a greater scandal than his running off. Her name was hardly mentioned above a whisper until her death.

Thorne looked at Matilda Darineau. "I would never run off," he said seriously.

"Of course not, dear sir." Tildy sent Jenny a superior look.

Exasperated, Jenny looked at Thorne and mouthed silently, "Don't encourage her."

He leaned in close, intimate. "Well, I wouldn't. I could never leave you, Miss Jenny."

To say that his words, however joking, were not flattering would have been a lie. Jenny could not recall that she had been flirted with much since leaving Mississippi. It felt good, sweet like dessert, but it was also uncomfortably foreign, a bit like Mercedes' cooking when Jenny first arrived. The strange new dishes smelled delicious but tasted odd on the palate.

Looking shined up and slicked down, Cortez and Barkley made a brief appearance to report the day's work. They both declined dinner, then headed for town. It was Saturday night. "A night for romping for a single fellow," Uncle Nat used to say.

Jenny had always wondered why single women were supposed to sit home and stitch pillowcases for their hope chests while single men were allowed out to "sow wild oats." It irritated her sense of justice that men were not held to the same boring conventions. What about wild oats for women? She certainly couldn't see any excitement in going into a smoky saloon to play cards with a bunch of foul-mouthed men, while scantily dressed women danced and served liquor.

But an evening at the opera, which would have been acceptable for a woman with an escort, just didn't seem daring enough to count as wild oats.

She glanced at Thorne over the rim of her glass, a sly sparkle beneath her seemingly innocent gaze. "How do unmarried women sow wild oats?" she asked.

He coughed as his sip of water went down the wrong way. Here we go again, he thought. "Pardon?"

Her brown eyes were intense. "A single man goes out for a night on the town, gets liquored up and no telling what else. How does a single woman sow wild oats?"

He put his fork carefully beside his plate. "A woman doesn't have wild oats that need sowing."

"I *knew* you'd say that!" Jenny sat back in a healthy pique. "How can a man need oat sowing but not a woman?"

A smile tugged at his handsome mouth. Darn her and her meddlesome mind. She had a point, but he wasn't going to rise to the bait. "Because women are far superior to men. Men are weak and will-less."

Jenny rolled her eyes. "Preserve me from patronizing rhetoric."

"Oh, no, señorita," Mercedes chimed in, smiling. "It is true! Women are far superior to men, just ask my Luis."

Luis shook his head. "Oh, no. I will not argue with such a statement and get myself into trouble." He sent Thorne a pleading look. "Tomorrow is the Lord's day. I went to confession only last week. Please, let us drop this talk so I do not have to go again so soon for lying."

Gentle laughter rippled around the table.

The warmth of friends and the camaraderie of family, the satisfaction of a good meal at the end of a hard day. It was everything Thorne wanted for Jeremiah, perhaps for himself as well, but none of it was his for the taking.

And the price of purchase was too high. He could not see himself courting and marrying another woman. Although he had made Jenny the proposal out of convenience to both of them, he had been relieved when she refused. He wouldn't mind a woman's warm body next to his in the night, but daylight came all too quickly and inevitably. All of his emotional investments were reserved for his son. Marital love was fickle as a woman, burning hot in the first rush of attraction, then growing cold as dead ash later.

Physical needs compelled a man and woman together, but only children kept them united. Sometimes not even then. He'd seen it all too often, had experienced firsthand the irritation and resentment that slowly followed the cooling of desire. Not a swift betrayal but a slow, painful process that drained a man until he hated even the sunrise on his wife's face. Until avoidance became a crucial part of every day.

He studied Mercedes and Luis. Perhaps friendship was the key to comfortable longevity. To find the respect and friendship that the couple had built together was rare and important, much more important than believing in the mad, volatile excitement of lust that people mistook for love.

Watching Jenny's earnest expression, he suspected she still believed in poetic and idealistic love, but he knew that fallible emotion actually was made of strong, healthy lust and a quick-burning fuse.

"Are wild oats like wild strawberries?" Jeremiah asked, confused. "Pretty to look at but you can't eat them?"

"Exactly," Thorne answered. "Neither one is any good for you."

"Will wild oats make you sick?"

"If you sow too many," Thorne said. "Finish your dinner," he added before his son asked for more explanation than he was willing to give a four-year-old.

Jenny regarded Thorne frankly. "Did *you* ever sow wild oats?"

His lids lowered over hooded eyes. "Maybe once or twice." He reached for the tortilla on his plate and filled it with chorizo picante. The sauce was hot and burned his mouth, but it felt good. Like watching Jenny's curious mind churn over subjects that polite, self-respecting young women weren't supposed to think about.

"I sowed wild oats once."

All eyes turned to Tildy, who had been quietly munching an apple. Jenny cringed, wondering what her unpredictable aunt would say now.

"It was back in '46," Tildy continued between bites. "Bernard was off doing business and I was beside myself with loneliness. Marleen Charles—you remember, Jenny, she was one of the Virginia Charleses—got ahold of a jar of elderberry wine. Her beau had run off with a floozy from Memphis and she was feeling right low. We sat out in the gazebo by the river and drank the whole jar." She smiled, remembering. "We were tipsy as two tadpoles. We stripped right down to our skivvies and swam in the river."

She began fanning her face as if the embarrassment was still fresh upon her. "The next thing we knew, Dixson James, a rogue and a scoundrel if there ever was one, stole our gowns and petticoats and hung them on the front gate of River Run. That was the very day that the Reverend Patterson chose to pay us a visit. There we were, two grown women, laughing like banshees and running from bush to bush, dressed in nothing but our unmentionables. I was never quite able to hold my head up in polite society again."

Jenny had no idea if the story was true or part of Tildy's unreliable but vivid imagination. "What happened to Maureen?"

"She married that no-good Dixson James and had eight children." She shook her head. "You just never know what impresses a girl's heart."

Jenny knew what impressed her own. A tall, handsome sheriff with a genuine concern for the citizens of his town. A hardworking man who always put the needs of others above his own. A trustworthy man who was engaged to her very respectable best friend.

She pushed the rice around on her plate and tried to think of more pleasant thoughts. She glanced up at Jeremiah. "What plans do you have for tomorrow?"

"Me and Pa are riding up into the mountains. Do you wanna come?"

Jenny smiled to soften her refusal. "Thank you, but I'm sure your pa wants a day with you all to himself."

Jeremiah looked over to see if that was true. "Miss Jenny can come, can't she, Pa?"

Thorne shrugged. Though he had been looking forward to a quiet day with Jeremiah, with no interference or interruptions from the outside world, Jenny's company wouldn't be unwelcome. "We'll take a picnic up to the stream." He turned to the others sitting at the table. "You are all welcome to come along."

Tildy looked quite perplexed. "Oh, I just couldn't, but you young people go ahead."

Jenny looked at Thorne. "I should stay here." In truth she really wanted to go. It was too dangerous to ride into the mountains alone, but their majesty and serenity always beckoned to her. On rare occasions she had accompanied Milt and Hannah on Sunday excursions, but she felt too much the outsider there. She didn't want Thorne to feel he had to allow her to tag along on his only day off.

Thorne shook his head. "You are welcome to come, Miss Jenny."

"Go," Mercedes coaxed. "Have fun. Luis and I will stay here with Señora Darineau as soon as Mass is over."

"But you usually visit with your daughter and son-in-law," Jenny began.

"I will invite them here," Mercedes said. "If that is all right with you."

"Of course, but—"

"It is settled then." Mercedes beamed. "You will have a nice day for yourself, *sí*?"

"*Sí,*" Jenny echoed, feeling as if she'd been manipulated somehow into doing exactly what she wanted to do.

She slipped out onto the patio when she noticed the tip of Thorne's cigarette flare in the darkness. "I won't disturb you," she said. "I just wanted to speak with you a moment."

"You aren't disturbing me," he said, "but I'm not answering any sex questions tonight."

She almost strangled on a laugh. "It's not that." Well, maybe it was a little but she wasn't going to forewarn him.

The night was expansive. A billion stars shone overhead, so vast it was hard to comprehend the complexity of the universe. Coyotes howled at the moon, a lonely sound that never failed to make Jenny glad she shared the ranch with others.

"Are we back to wild oats?" Thorne asked.

"No," she said. "I'll pry that out of you later."

Later. She could pry more than words out of him, if she were so inclined. She was bold, yet too innocent to understand that gritty love talk made for a very real physical inconvenience.

"I just wanted you to know that I can bow out of tomorrow, if you want to be alone with your son."

Jeremiah would be hurt, so there was no question of Thorne reneging when there was no valid reason for it. Except that continued close proximity to Jenny had begun to cause a constant upheaval in his pulse rate. He might have laughed at his callow reaction, but there was nothing humorous about existing in what seemed to becoming a perpetual state of arousal. He supposed it was normal after years of infrequent female companionship, but it was no less tolerable.

There was a savage place within him that had nothing to do with his years spent with the Comanche, though those years had enhanced it to a keener edge he kept controlled with restraint. Shaken down to the bare elements of his core being, he could be as aggressive as a jungle animal, as stealthy as a night prowler. He needed to make certain he didn't unleash that instinct on Jenny.

"Jeremiah wants you to come," he said.

"And you?"

He grinned coldly.

Jenny glimpsed the predator again, a rare sight but one that never failed to unnerve her a small bit. "What about you?" she repeated.

"I want you too," he said.

Something about his tone made her slightly uneasy. She pushed the feeling aside, in favor of the real reason she had sought him out. "About our earlier discussion." His pale eyes were mysterious in the dark, probing. She shuddered suddenly, as if a chill wind moved over her. Perhaps this wasn't such a good idea, but she hated retreat, especially in the face of his subtle intimidation.

Thorne wouldn't have this talk with her, wouldn't satisfy her curiosity with words. If he ever let her know the reality of a man and woman coming together, it would be with his body, not words. He moved closer, a beast on the prowl.

She backed up a step, then stopped herself. She was not afraid of him. "About Hannah's request—"

"*Jenny's* request."

She shook her head. A dryness had set up in her tight throat. He was so close now she could smell the tobacco smoke on his clothing along with a faint musky leather scent. Her heart rate stumbled, and a dull blush spread up her cheeks. Thankfully he wouldn't notice it in the dark.

He advanced until he hovered over her, his arms sliding around to either side of her hips. He would put a stop to this discussion before it went any further. He planted his hands on the edge of the fountain, hemming her in. The pulse in the hollow of her throat began throbbing anxiously. Good.

"You want to know what happens between a man and woman," he said in a dark voice.

She nodded mutely, but she wasn't quite so certain anymore. His closeness concerned her, no matter how she tried to deny it.

"What if I told you," Thorne began in a deep raspy tone, the whisper of bad secrets, "that all I can think about since you brought the subject up are the details of lovemaking, of the way a man and woman come together in perfect ecstasy, uniting their bodies in a primeval rhythm that beats like the blood in their veins, beats like the fast and furious pace of fulfillment?" She gazed up at him, her breath caught in her chest. "What if I told you that when I see these people locked together, I see you and me, Jenny?"

Her eyes flared briefly; lightning speared her insides.

"I didn't mean . . . I thought you would tell me about your wife. It's not me who wants to know but Hannah."

"It's you," he said quietly. "And now it's me too."

"You?" she squeaked.

"I want to know as much about making love as you do. I want to know how it is to make love with you."

"Oh." With a jolt, she darted suddenly beneath his arm and sprinted for her room. She knew in an instant he followed. She could hear the beat of his boots on the tiles, gaining ground much faster than she did. He caught her just as she reached for her door.

His arms went under her breasts, pinning her to his chest. His breath stirred the hair at her temples. "Do you still want to know everything?"

She heard the unmistakable humor in his voice and knew she'd been had. Embarrassment pooled in her belly. She pinched his forearm *hard*. "You've had your fun, Ian, now let me go."

"Thorne," he insisted. "Say it."

"No."

"I thought you wanted to talk."

She realized what he was doing. In an effort to avoid her probing questions, he was being bold and outrageous to drive her away. The conniving cur! A secret smile lit her face. "I do want to talk," she said in sweet innocence. Her finger ran up and down his arm, a lazy, flirtatious motion. "And maybe you could show me just a *little* of what you've been thinking about. Just enough so I could get a fair idea of what really goes on."

He jerked suddenly and let her go. The joke had

turned on him and his overheated body. His dreams would be full of her tonight, erotic images that would linger into the daylight hours along with the raw, edgy effects of unfulfilled desire. "Damn you, Jenny," he huffed.

"Ha!" she taunted, spinning to face him. "You can dole it out but can't tolerate it flung back at you!"

A devilish smile lit his eyes. She was a worthy opponent but not experienced enough to spar with him. He took her by the upper arms and pulled her close. "Listen, little girl. I can handle anything you're doling out."

"I'm not a little gi—" she began before his mouth crashed down on hers.

Chapter 9

If she'd been capable of slapping him, she would have. As it was, Jenny's hands were pinned at her sides while her mouth was marauded by Ian's punishing kiss. He was so tall against her slight frame, overpowering in presence and intent. The harsh metal of his belt buckle bit into her middle and his arms felt like iron bands around hers, his hand warm and strong on her lower back. There was nothing kind or loving in the kiss. His mouth devoured, consumed hers in a mind-robbing conflagration of heat and purpose.

Never had she imagined a kiss like this: hot and gritty, his lips abrasive against her tender flesh. The scent of tobacco and night air clung to him, but she tasted heat and raw desire. He seemed to pull strength from her limbs, exhausting her resources for fighting back, stripping away the niceties of a secret stolen moment and turning it into a barrage of fire and carnage. A sound of protest rose in her throat, and he stole it with the pressure of his mouth, the slick insidious movements of his lips.

She strained away, but he followed, bending deeper into her, his fingers clenching in the fabric of her dress. Those strong fingers stroked and explored, his thumbs digging into her hips as if he would hold her by force. He need not have bothered. She was rooted to the spot, her entire being stricken to stone at his unseemly behavior. His fingers searched briefly over her waist and hips, making her squirm and exhale muted sounds of protest.

Then suddenly his hands were gone.

"Have you got pants on underneath this skirt?" he asked hoarsely in surprise.

Though only seconds long, the kiss had seemed endless in intensity. Jenny stared at him a stunned second, then regained her breath and spun away. "How dare you take such liberties?" Her mouth was on fire, swollen. She pressed the back of her hand to her lips.

The light of vengeance glowed in his eyes. "Never think that I can't do exactly what I want, when I want," he said. "Never think that you'll stop me with words or tricks." He balled his hands into fists to keep from reaching for her again. "You tread on dangerous ground here, Jenny. Not just with me but with any man. It's the old adage. If you play with fire, you will get burned."

"I'll remember," she said coldly. "You ever kiss me like that again and you'll be the one who gets burned, because I'll fire you."

He smiled coldly. "What about the ranch?"

"The ranch can go to the devil!" She spun on her heel and would have fled through her bedroom door, but he grabbed the tail of her skirt and tugged until she was brought up short. His eyes lit with sardonic humor as they raked her. "You do have pants on underneath. How . . . unconventional."

She snatched her skirt out of his hand and darted for her room. She fell back against the door, her heart pounding, her chest constricted by what had just happened. Jimmy Henderson's kiss had been nothing like that. She tried to picture Milt in the same heated response, but she knew he was too much of a gentleman ever to be so bold and uncivilized.

Her hands were shaking as she went through the mundane chores of readying herself for bed. She washed her face, cleaned her teeth, and changed into her nightgown. Her hands were still trembling when she knelt to say her prayers. She was hard put not to ask God to inflict all sorts of revenge upon Ian Thorne.

As her fury began to settle, the reality of her situation began to seep past her enraged feelings. She hadn't meant it about the ranch. Though she didn't deserve his crude, heartless treatment, she wasn't going to fire him for taking a liberty. She needed his experience and ambition to get the ranch prosperous again, and she wasn't going to force the one person who could help her off El Dorado.

She climbed into bed and pulled the covers to her chin. She'd just stay out of his way, keep as far from him as was reasonable.

She was about to turn down her lamp when she heard a light rap on the outside door. Her heart paused, then beat unevenly. It had to be Thorne. No one else would have approached her room from that entrance. Her emotions vacillated between anger and concern. As angry as she was with him, she was more afraid he was going to quit and leave her in the same desperate situation she had been in before he arrived. Perhaps if she pretended sleep, he would go back to his room and rethink his resignation.

The knock came again, louder.

She flinched and pulled the covers over her head. If she refused to talk to him, he couldn't resign. The knock came again, even more insistent. She gave up, crawled from the bed, then padded over to the door barefoot until she could make out a large outline against the rising moon. Taking a deep breath, she pulled the drape aside and peered closer.

Ian stood outside, a glowing cigarette in his hand. Her heart made a sickening plunge while she tried to decide what to do. If she ignored him, he just might ride off without even saying good-bye. She opened the door a crack.

"Can you come out?" he asked.

"I have on my nightclothes."

Impatient, he sighed. "Get a robe, please. I need to talk to you."

Irritated and afraid, Jenny donned her robe. She was so disgusted with him, she wanted to punch him in the nose, but deep inside she was still more fearful he was going to leave her stranded. She almost wanted to beg his forgiveness and promise she would never ask another lurid question, but she had been wronged, and she had too much pride to let it go.

She walked outside stiffly.

He stood before her, trying to ignore the way the moonlight washed her hair into pale shades of reflected light, the way her thin gown and robe hid little of her figure beneath. Her shoulders were stiff, her jaw set, the perfect picture of an outraged spinster. Except for the nightgown. He had the mad urge to spin her in front of a full-length mirror and show her how ridiculous she looked all stiff and starchy when wearing such delicate attire.

"I came to apologize," he said. "I don't know what came over me." Actually, he knew exactly what had come over him but didn't think it prudent to admit it. *She* had come over him and through him, crawling right inside to overwhelm his male senses. The thought of kissing her lingered still. The memory of her soft, lush mouth, the small perfect way she fit against him. But none of that was excuse for his rash behavior on someone so unsuspecting. "I won't do it again."

She sighed, so relieved she wanted to wilt into the nearest chair. "I'm sorry too." Uncomfortable, she turned and tried to return inside but he reached out and took her arm. She stopped immediately.

"Jenny, listen."

His features were harsh but honest, his hold painlessly restrictive. "My actions were unforgivable. Like I said, I don't know what came over me. One moment I was teasing you, the next I felt I had some point to prove.

You have every right to throw me off the ranch, but since you haven't, I want you to know that I'll do everything I can to make it up to you."

Relief poured through her. Not just because he was staying but because he admitted the mistake and was sorry for it.

She nodded, finding safety in a certain aloof and polite manner. "Maybe I shouldn't have been so persistent."

He shattered her defenses as he took her chin in his hand, forcing her to face him. "Don't you dare blame yourself for my ignoble actions. No matter how many questions you ask or how frustrated I get with your prying, I had no right to take my frustrations out on you."

She wouldn't meet his eyes, her gaze going past him to the dark sky. "I'm just relieved you're not giving notice."

He could tell she didn't understand why her questions had caused such an upheaval in him. "Look, Jenny, you are a beautiful woman. When a man starts talking about such things, it makes him . . . restless."

Restless? But that's how *she* felt. Like everything inside her wanted out. She still didn't see what that had to do with his behavior. "I would like to understand," she said, then shrugged, "but I don't."

He ran his fingers through his hair, an action she was beginning to recognize as agitation.

"Do I have to define restless, Jenny?"

"I know what the word means," she said. "I just don't know why it made you so mean."

"I wasn't being mean," he countered, "I was acting on impulse. Badly, I'll admit, and foolishly."

"But *why*?"

He shoved his hands in his pockets. "Have you ever watched a stallion who can't get to a mare?"

Her eyes widened, then she looked away. "I hardly see what that has to do with anything."

"You know how he kicks and stomps and acts a fool?"

She didn't like the correlation. It was too blunt, too personal after what had just happened. "You are not a stallion—" she began.

"And you're not a mare," he finished, "but I have animal instincts, Jenny, just like you do."

"I do not!"

He smiled without humor, then pushed off the wall to tower over her. "Yes, you do."

The friendship that had been reestablishing between them was dwindling fast, swept away in a moment of unruly temper and discomfiture. An awkward mistrust lay like a barrier now, an edgy awareness more tangible and unsettling than the bond of their early childhood or the newfound work connection.

Jenny thought she had gotten past what had happened when they were teenagers, but it wasn't so. All the old fears had come rushing back with his kiss, with new ones now to compound her misgivings.

"You can accept the fact that there is something very elemental going on between us, or you can deny it."

" 'Elemental,' " she echoed uncomfortably. Her mind

turned over the word, not liking the implications. Her brow knit in consternation. "I'd rather deny it."

"Fine, but it's always been there. Deny that too, if it makes you feel better." He turned and headed for his room. Halfway there he paused to look back at her. "Good night, Miss Delaney," he said formally.

She stirred the sand that constantly blew across the patio with the toe of her slipper. "Good night, Ian," she whispered, but she would never again mistake Ian, her girlhood companion, for Thorne the man.

Thorne was surprised at breakfast when Jenny told his son that she was still going on the picnic with them. After last night, he thought she would keep her distance, and in some ways she did. Her manner was cool at the table but not unfriendly, a reserved formality that she fooled herself into thinking would change the physical tug afflicting them both.

He put his coffee cup down. He had realized over the long, sleepless night that he wanted Jennifer Delaney in the most base way. The fact that he couldn't have her didn't change the wanting, it just made it keener. "I'll drive you and Aunt Tildy to church."

Jenny looked at him as if he'd offered to put arsenic in her coffee. "Why?"

He gave her a condescending look. "I don't have ulterior motives, Miss Delaney. What with Cortez and Barkley sleeping off a good drunk, I thought you might need help driving the team."

"I see." She stirred the eggs on her plate. "Will you be staying for the service?"

"Uh, no."

She smiled in spite of herself. "It's not that bad, Ian; you really should for Jeremiah's sake. The circuit rider only comes through once a month. Until we get a preacher of our own, you won't even have to go regularly."

He'd rather have a tooth pulled. "Let me think about it."

Jeremiah bounced in his chair. "Yes, Pa, let's go to church with Miss Jenny."

"Dear me," Tildy gently scolded. "Don't tell me you have been neglecting this precious young man's spiritual education."

Thorne hadn't been to church since he'd lived with his father, but he knew it was past time for Jeremiah to be learning more than the nightly prayers they said together. Church was not only the moral conscience of a town, it was also part of the social structure and a vital meeting place for any man who planned to do business with others in the community.

He didn't relish sitting through a boring Sunday sermon, but he had known for some time that he had to get back to it. If he planned to make a place for his son within the framework of society, he had to accept certain obligations that went along with it. It had been convenient to put Sunday services off for only so long.

The church was a modest clapboard building at the edge of town. The small steeple housed a bell donated by Wolf that rung out boldly as their wagon rambled down Main Street. A crowd milled about in their Sunday finest, smiling because the day was glorious and meeting only once a month made Sundays that much more special. A picnic would follow the service, and the smell of sweet pies and succulent meats rose from baskets sitting in the backs of hitched wagons.

Jenny didn't know how in the world she had overlooked the fact that Aunt Tildy would have a heyday with Thorne along. Not two seconds after their feet hit the ground, Matilda Darineau was announcing Jenny's upcoming nuptials to the entire congregation.

Jenny just glued a smile on her face and tried to make light of it all. The fact that Tildy also introduced Jeremiah as a war orphan helped keep the gossip to a minimum.

Hannah, wearing a new gown from her recent trip to Santa Fe, hurried over. She was a vision in blue and white striped silk, sporting a dashing new parasol that complemented her gown and bonnet. Twirling like a schoolgirl, she smiled. "What do you think?"

"Lovely," Jenny said, envious. "I wish I had three."

Hannah made a face at her but smiled. "You could, but you choose to wear only the most primitive of gowns."

"The most serviceable," Jenny corrected.

Hannah looked contrite. "I bought only two like this. The others are more suited to our rugged climate. In any case, I was able to check on the progress of your ensemble for the wedding. Everything is complete and should be arriving in two weeks." She clasped her hands together blissfully. "Isn't it just wonderful, Jennifer?"

"I'm so happy I could cry," Jenny answered, more or less truthfully. She turned to introduce Ian. "Are you acquainted with—"

"Mr. Thorne, of course." Hannah held out her hand. "How good to see you at church." Her eyes sparkled with merriment. "Congratulations on your upcoming marriage."

"I see you've spoken to Mrs. Darineau," he said in a cordial tone. Like Jenny, he found unconcern to be the best line of defense. "I'm just helping Miss Delaney out at the ranch."

"How kind of you," Hannah said sincerely.

"And this is Jeremiah," Jenny added, "his son."

Hannah's face softened. She bent to accommodate Jeremiah's slight height. "Hello, young man. I've heard so much about you from Miss Jennifer. Am I to understand that you are now residing at El Dorado?"

His brow creased in uncertainty. "I live at Miss Jenny's house."

"A wonderful place to live," she said. "How do you like it?"

"I like it just fine," he answered. "Lots better than my house." He began to squirm. "But I don't like these itchy church clothes."

"They do take some getting used to," Hannah sympathized. "However, you look quite dashing in them."

"That's what Miss Jenny said," he admitted, "but they still itch like the dickens."

Hannah regarded Jenny. "I'll send over my best

receipt for softening your wash water." She turned back to Jeremiah. "Would you care to come to my house this afternoon? You can play with my little brother Tad, while Miss Jennifer and I visit."

Jeremiah looked at his father, then Jenny. He knew Tad from school and liked him, but he didn't want to miss their day on the mountain.

"Jennifer, say you will," Hannah pleaded. "You must come over after the church social. Mr. Thorne can keep Milton occupied while Mother and I show you my trousseau. We were able to purchase almost everything this past week."

Jenny couldn't think of anything more dispiriting than looking at the beautiful clothes Hannah had bought for her life with Milt. "I'm sorry, Hannah. I can't today, but I promise I'll come by midweek." Jenny turned to Jeremiah. "See if you can find Aunt Tildy and we'll go inside."

"I'll help," Thorne offered quickly, and escaped with his son.

As soon as they were gone, Hannah studied Jenny with idle interest. "Jeremiah is a beautiful child," she said, fiddling with the lace at her cuff. "And his father is quite handsome as well."

"Don't even think it," Jenny warned. "I've hired him to do a job. Quit matchmaking."

"I'm not." Hannah pouted but with a devilish gleam in her eye. "The thought is not without merit, though."

"The thought is ridiculous," Jenny said. She slipped her arm through Hannah's and led her toward the church. "Now, tell me about everything you saw in Santa Fe."

"Oh, it was marvelous!" Hannah began to embark on an exhaustive outline of her entire week's shopping spree and entertainment. Hannah's exuberance was refreshing, reminding Jenny of the sweet days at River Run when refinement was a way of life, not a luxury. No matter how rough the West, women like Hannah contributed a gentility that reminded one that a softness could exist beneath even the most leathery exterior and its value in keeping life civil was priceless.

"Would you go with me next time?" Hannah asked.

"I'll try," Jenny agreed, but meant it in wish only. She couldn't leave Thorne with the exhausting ranch work to gallivant to Santa Fe on a whim.

The church was crowded. The front pews were taken, so Jenny scooted into the space Thorne and Aunt Tildy had reserved for her near the back. Jeremiah was already fidgeting in his "itchy" clothes, and Jenny knew the stuffy heat emanating from so many close bodies would make it worse. She broke off a small chunk of peppermint candy in her reticule, then slipped it into his hand.

Thorne eyed the conspiracy taking place and smiled secretly. Jenny was a good woman, as soft-hearted as they came. Too bad the town matriarchs were tired of looking past her little rebellions.

Hushed anticipation fell across the congregation when the circuit rider took the pulpit. He was a young handsome man with bright, intelligent eyes and a kind smile. Too handsome, was the consensus of the ladies' quilting circle, to still be single.

She rode well. For all her inefficiency in rigging out a horse, Jenny Delaney certainly knew how to sit one. Thorne watched her with the astute eyes of a horseman, then the possessive eyes of a man. Her slender bottom rose and fell in a natural rhythm with the horse's gait. Her back was straight, her hands comfortable on the reins. She rode with grace and ease, and a natural elegance that made him think of other ways a woman could ride that had nothing to do with horses.

His heated thoughts gave way to an uncomfortable ride on his own saddle and just the slightest guilt that less than an hour after leaving a church service, he was having very carnal thoughts about his boss.

He shifted Jeremiah in front of him and diverted his wayward imagination by instructing his son on the varied plants and wildlife they passed along way. Although Jeremiah rode a horse well within the confines of the fence, Thorne was not yet willing to allow his son the freedom and the dangers of the range.

They left the stables behind and headed for the evergreen forest in the distance. Pine resin filled their senses with the clean, green scent of nature. They traveled through a patch of desert scrub, picking their way through sagebrush, cacti, and creosote bushes, mindful of the rattlesnakes and scorpions that liked to hide in the dry areas. The fragrance of spruce grew thicker as they reached an open glade.

Slowing, they took in the beauty around them and let the horses graze the thicker grass in the valley. The trees grew denser ahead, their branches heavy with late foliage.

A stream meandered through the pasture, a mere trickle of water running over a sandy bottom through grass and forest. Though narrow at times, it was more predictable than the dangerous arroyos that flooded unexpectedly in heavy rains. They followed the stream into the mountains, climbing higher among the Douglas fir and ponderosa pine. The air was crisp and cool, so refreshing Jenny wanted to take it deep into her lungs.

She loved it here, loved the smell and taste of the air, the feel of its crisp bite on her cheeks. The stream expanded as they rode deeper into the mountains. The canyon walls rose around them and the grade became steeper, the climb harder, but the horses were well trained and used to the terrain.

Keeping their pace slow but steady, they absorbed the changing beauty of the land. The canyon grew wider and flat; the stream became a silver slice of heaven that picked up depth and speed as it tumbled over rocks. Through strands of cottonwood and dogwood, it glistened, echoing a mountain song along the high walls until finally ending far up ahead in a raging froth of white rapids at the base of a sheer cliff.

The waterfall was awe-inspiring. Mist rose like faint clouds, spilling droplets of moisture onto a dewy profusion of wildflowers that grew during a short blooming season at this elevation. The burst of color and the thunder of rapids never failed to take Jenny's breath. She was awed by the power, humbled by the grace. Delicate flowers peeked between cracks of huge boulders, small reptiles slithered like kings into the holes of their many-roomed castles.

They watched the waterfall for a while, then tracked back to a tamer spot midway where the wild mountain waters were gentler and deep enough to wade into. Among the rock walls and glistening boulders, Jenny had spent many a wistful hour dreaming of swimming beneath the clear water, darting like cutthroat trout from rock to rock.

It was one of the things she missed most about plantation life: the safety of her own land, the security of being able to romp unfettered over forest and field, to swim in a river inlet without fearing for her life.

Uncle Nat had never let her ride out here alone, and for good reason. Danger lurked everywhere, in the form of man and beast and unpredictable elements. Bands of outlaws and marauding Indians still roamed the territory, wild animals hunted easy prey. The mountains were full of black bear, wildcats, and wolves. But it was man that she feared most. Groups of Apache and Comanche still lay in wait for unsuspecting settlers.

She glanced over at Ian and wondered what he felt. Did he fear attack, or would he be protected by his past association? Within the Indian culture, did brother turn against brother, as the North and South had done, or did a bond of loyalty exist that was stronger than blood?

Dismounting, she looped Bulle's reins over the low branch of a cottonwood at the very edge of the stream so the mare could drink. She pulled a lunch basket from her saddle and bade Jeremiah pick a spot in the shade. He chose a flat area of ground where the nearby stream was shallow and clear, flowing over a rocky bottom. As soon as Jenny laid the blanket out, he plopped down and began removing his shoes.

"Are you gonna swim, Miss Jenny?"

Startled, she looked at him. "Are you?"

"Course." He smiled up at her, all bright-eyed and unself-conscious as he began to strip his pants off.

"Whoa!" Thorne called, and scooped his son up before his trousers went down. "Jeremiah," he began seriously, fighting a smile, "you can't undress in front of Miss Jenny."

His small brow furrowed. "Why?"

"It's not good manners."

"Then how am I gonna swim?"

"Well, I guess you're not."

Jeremiah's mouth trembled, tears pooled in his eyes. "Not swim?" His gaze swung to his teacher, as if she could rectify the situation. "Miss Jenny, tell Pa I can swim."

Jenny looked at Ian, her heart annihilated by Jeremiah's plea. "Let him," she begged. "What harm can it do?"

Thorne saw it then, a longing in Jenny's own eyes, and he remembered the many stolen hours they had spent as children on the banks of the Mississippi. His gaze was direct and unflinching. "You could swim too."

Her cheeks flushed. "I couldn't."

"I'll turn my back, keep watch for you."

Oh, what a wretched man to suggest it! She glanced at the water with longing, then back at Ian. "I couldn't."

He shrugged. "Suit yourself." He placed Jeremiah on the blanket, then sat beside him and whispered, "Leave your drawers on."

Jeremiah gave his father a dubious look but did as he was told. Within half a minute, he was splashing in the shallows, his laughter ringing like music. "C'mon, Pa!"

Jenny glanced sideways at Ian to see what he would do. Obviously, this was something father and son did comfortably when alone. A smile tipped the corner of her mouth. "Go ahead," she said. "I'll turn my back and keep watch."

He stood up. "No need."

Jenny's face heated up as his hands went to the buttons on his pants. "Wait!"

He looked down at her, his movements arrested.

"I . . . it was a joke."

"I see." He sat back down.

The sun beating down on them made her cheeks even warmer. She'd left off her bonnet and now wished she hadn't so she could hide beneath it. She plucked at the luncheon basket. "Would you have really . . . I mean, with me here and all?"

"Yeah. Why not?"

Her mouth dropped open. " 'Why not?' How can you say 'why not?' "

"Why," he articulated carefully, "not?" He lay back on the blanket at an angle where he could look at Jenny and watch Jeremiah at the same time. "We swam in our skivvies as children. It's not like we have anything each of us hasn't already seen."

"But we were children!"

"And we would have had our hides tanned if we'd been caught."

"So?"

"So, now we are adults. Why can't we enjoy the same things?"

It's just not proper! floated through her head, sounding too much like her mother's voice. "Because we've changed."

"Our bodies have changed. Our desires have not." Which wasn't exactly true. His desires, at least around Jenny, had changed drastically.

Her voice rang with frustration. "You know it would be wrong."

"Why? Because someone else says it is?"

His eyes were on her, probing and intense, penetrating her proper teacher's morality down to her inquisitive soul, to the part that had romped and dared and dreamed as a child, the part that couldn't be so far gone from the woman. He knew her, knew the young, capricious Jenny. She still wanted to explore and partake and indulge in all that life had to offer. But Jenny the spinster and teacher had rules to restrict her life.

"Why is it wrong?"

"Just because it is," she said without much conviction. The school board members would have a fit to know she had accompanied Ian unchaperoned. To swim in her skivvies would be the kiss of death.

"No, just because it makes you uncomfortable to think about someone finding out. What if I could promise you, beyond a shadow of a doubt, that no one would ever be the wiser. What then?"

He was the devil. Temptation itself. She would swim in a second, less than a second, if she knew no repercussions would be forthcoming. The very idea that she was such a hypocrite made her unhappy with herself.

"Nothing then," she said, angry because he made her think things she didn't want to think, made her feel things she didn't think she should be feeling at her age. She rose from the blanket and moved to sit on a boulder beside the water. Jeremiah was happily wading among the rocks, kicking up splash after splash of crystal-cold water.

She wanted to be right there with him.

Jeremiah slipped suddenly and fell to his backside. A moment of startled betrayal crossed his face as the chilly water soaked him to the chest. He didn't know whether to laugh or cry, to be offended or excited. Jenny leaned forward, ready with comfort or teasing, whatever he needed to get through the shock.

A trout swam by, catching his attention, and the moment of uncertainty was forgotten. His features transformed into childish delight as he scrambled up again and chased the fish.

Jenny sat back and tried to relax, but the picture of her and Ian swimming in their undergarments kept running through her mind. Only the images were not of Ian as a boy but Ian as a grown man, tall and fit and dark, his eyes coaxing roguishly, his smile daring. She tried to replace the vision with Milt, but she'd never even seen the sheriff with his coat off, so the fantasy was murky.

Oh, Milt! Any outrageous thing he felt inclined to do for the rest of his life would be done with Hannah.

"Miss Jen-ny."

She heard the drawn-out teasing in a very masculine voice. "I'm not speaking to you, Ian," she said in her haughtiest tone.

"A nice cool dip sure would take the heat out of the day. Make lunch a lot more satisfying too."

She refused to look back at him. The fact that he knew just how badly she wanted to shuck her clothes and dive right in made her surly. For all her unconventional ways, she wasn't that far gone in impropriety and she resented the fact that he thought she might be. One stupid kiss with Jimmy Henderson and she was branded for life.

But that still didn't stop the yearning. She sighed as she stared at the water, crystal clear and so cold it would steal her breath. She could taste it, feel it.

She reached down suddenly and tugged her boots off, then rolled her stocking down. By golly, if she couldn't swim in the water, she would at least test it. Hiking her skirts up, she strolled into the shallows, then waded deeper.

The stream was formed by the runoff from snowpacks higher in the mountains. She gasped at the frigid temperature, pausing to grow accustomed to it, then smiled at the utter delight of Jeremiah's call.

"Come deeper, Miss Jenny!"

"I can't," she called back, "but you go ahead. I'll watch."

He scrambled up onto a low flat rock, then jumped back in. Several times he repeated the game, growing a little braver, leaping a little further each round.

"Be careful—" Jenny began.

Without warning, she was swept up from behind. Ian's arms were tight around her waist, his chest pressed to her back. "Don't turn around."

Her heartbeat accelerated at the warning sound in his voice. "Why not?"

"You'll be embarrassed." He carried her out a little ways and put her on a wide flat rock, facing the opposite way. "Give me a few seconds to get into deeper water."

Her back stiffened. She put her hand on his forearm, then ran her fingers all the way up to his shoulder. Bare! He was bare as a newborn, bare as a man who had doffed his clothes and was going for a swim. After making such a show with Jeremiah earlier, he'd taken liberties himself.

"Darn you!" She swallowed. "How much did you take off?"

"Enough," he warned.

No doubt he had hardly a stitch on, and she was going to be left sitting on a rock in the hot sun with her moral conscience for company while he and his son had fun. "I hate you, Ian."

"Thorne."

"I hate both of you."

Silent laughter moved his chest against her back.

"What kind of example are you setting for your son?" she demanded prudishly.

A terrible one probably, but he didn't care. Swimming was a harmless, enriching part of nature that deserved to be enjoyed. "You could come too. No one would know except Jeremiah, and I can swear him to secrecy."

"I loathe you."

"Only because you want this so badly."

"Just leave me on my rock. I'll sit in the sun like a salamander and bake myself insensible."

His laughter came again, deep and taunting against her ear. "Whatever you say, Miss Jenny."

He began to drift back from her. "Count to ten before you open your eyes."

The knowledge that he was heading for deeper water so she wouldn't see anything offensive had an odd effect on her nervous system. Goose bumps crawled up her arms, yet her cheeks flushed as if overhot. She should not put up with such outrageous flouting of decency. She should jump on her horse immediately and ride hell for leather back to the ranch. She should fire him.

She buried her face in her hands. "One, two, three, four . . ."

> Cockroaches, mosquitoes and men!
> What was the good Lord thinking?
>
> —Granny Delaney
> Granny's Journal
> 17 March 1778

Chapter 10

Jenny peeked up over her fingers at the count of nine. Thorne swam in deeper water, only his head and bronzed shoulders visible. Jeremiah was still jumping off the rock. She dangled her toes in the water, disgruntled, feeling about as sorry for herself as it was possible to feel on such a glorious day.

The sun was a bright, white blessing in the azure sky. A hawk soared overhead, dipping on the breeze in search of a meal. Its shadow moved silently over the land, passing briefly over the water and the two swimmers.

Jenny watched Thorne. He was unconventional, but she suspected that if Milt were here he'd be doing the same thing. He probably wouldn't have chanced it with a woman around, but Milt would have done it on the sly. He had a way about him that Jenny called lazy-brazen.

He was good for any safe foolishness, he just went about his own easygoing way of doing it.

She propped her chin on her knees. Why should men have all the fun?

With a very unladylike epithet, she flung herself from her perch and walked straight into the stream. Cold water soaked her ankles, then calves, then thighs. Deeper she traveled until she was floating, clothes and all, treading to keep her head abovewater in the sodden garments.

Jeremiah squealed with delight. "You gots your clothes all wet, Miss Jenny!"

She laughed and swam toward him, coming upon more shallow ground until her knees scraped the sandy bottom. She sat, fully dressed and happy as a toad, while water soaked every inch of her. Jeremiah splashed over and climbed onto her lap, as unabashed in his youth as she wanted to be in her maturity.

"I gots a cut." He pouted, holding his finger up.

"Oh," she returned with concern. "Let me kiss it and make it better." She smacked the small scrape loudly, which made Jeremiah giggle.

"Pa says kisses don't really heal cuts. It just makes them feel better."

The water permeated her skirt and blouse. It was the oddest sensation of cold and warm, a touch of restrained freedom. She remembered swimming as a child, the joy and sense of wonder. "Well, there is something very good to be said for feeling better," she announced. She stretched back, hands behind her head, and rested against the rock. Jeremiah bounced on her lap, raucous and undignified and wonderful.

The hawk circled back, sending shadows skimming again across the surface of the water. Jeremiah smiled and pointed, then immediately was diverted by a rabbit rushing past their picnic blanket.

For twenty minutes, he laughed and splashed and pointed out every bit of wildlife that came to explore the rowdy humans. Then, without warning, he yawned hugely, leaned forward, and laid his head on Jenny's breast. He popped his thumb in his mouth, his eyes drowsy, his body growing limp.

"Are you going to sleep?" she whispered.

"Just resting," he mumbled.

But his arms and legs were like noodles, his eyelids too heavy to keep open. Jenny reached up and ran her fingers through the damp ends of his hair. Baby-fine curls wrapped around her fingers and clung. It was a special moment, one never possible as pupil and teacher, a moment made even more extraordinary by the bond that had been growing stronger between them. Immersed in the security of each other's trust, needs were met, empty spaces filled with the sweet, honeyed warmth of human contact.

A powerful sense of contentment flooded Jenny. She'd not felt the likes since she was a girl, since the day Ian Blackwell Thorne had taken her hostage. The decline of the South had begun in earnest about that time, and she had always melded the two occurrences into the same thing—one horrible summer that had eventually stripped her of everything she knew and loved. It was important somehow that such a remarkable sense of well-being could banish those dark years, if even for only a moment. More remarkable still that the feelings were inspired by Ian Thorne's child.

She stroked Jeremiah's cheek, running her fingers over the fine textures of youth. His skin was warm and resilient beneath her finger, soft as down. His face burrowed deeper, fighting sleep, losing. His thumb slid from his mouth and his arms hung slack.

They would both grow chilled if they stayed inactive in the water, but it felt so good to simply hold him. To pretend that he was hers.

The thought gave her a jolt but she didn't allow it to shadow her enjoyment. He was hers. He was her pupil, her friend, her guest. The tears stinging her eyes had nothing to do with the fact that for everything Jeremiah was, he was not her son.

Thorne treaded water in the deepest part of the stream. He had been watching the attachment between Jenny and Jeremiah take hold over the past few weeks. Had this been a perfect world, their affection would have been perfect timing in a perfect place to fill in the missing places of his son's life. But fate and fortune were not driven by perfection; rather, they played out sometimes in unmanaged and unwanted directions.

He did not believe in destiny. He believed in hard work, dedication, and ambition. Luck was a lady of loose morals, never to be trusted. He trusted only himself and believed his future would be shaped by his own hand, by the hard work and perseverance he put into it, and by his agile ability to stay quick and sharp when danger approached.

Ambition had taken him to El Dorado ranch, and he didn't want Jeremiah hurt in the process. Jenny would never be his son's mother, and Thorne didn't want their unguarded and growing affection to make things more difficult for Jeremiah when it came time to leave.

He didn't want it to be difficult for himself either. Other than his inconvenient attraction to her, she was a comfortable person to be around. Smart and friendly, she tackled problems head-on and didn't shy from circumstances that would make other women swoon. He liked her verve and the sort of gentle-toughness that it took to live in this land. He just might miss her when he left, but they could remain friends if he managed to keep his hands to himself.

For Jeremiah it might be different. Thorne wasn't certain his son would understand why they couldn't live with Miss Jenny anymore.

He swam nearer, knowing it would spook her. But upon closer inspection he was forced to draw up short at the sight of her. Her wet blouse clung to her. Of thin cotton, it became transparent when soaked, outlining every inch of her shape and the lawn chemise beneath. Though not full figured, she was very nicely rounded in all the places a woman should be.

Thorne paused halfway and let the cold stream counter his physical reaction to the sudden sight of Jenny Delaney in all her sodden glory. Her face was rapt with delight as she stroked his son's hair back from his face, her eyes glowing. Her hair was pulled back and secured in a prim knot at her nape, but Thorne wondered what it would look like down, wet as her blouse, floating atop the gentle current. He wondered how it would feel in his hands.

He took a deep breath and sank beneath the surface of the water. He was in heat. There was no other word to describe the crafty desire that crept up and took his body with shocking swiftness, the need that demanded he abandon rational thought and satisfy his physical craving. Resurfacing, he watched Jenny stretch back, arms lifted to the sun. He could picture them lifted to him, warm and welcoming, molten passion in her eyes.

He shivered suddenly in the cold stream and banished the vision. He had been so long without a woman, he was having delusions. Disgusted, he got himself back under control and swam to work off the pent-up energy. Reaching waist-deep water, he called to his son.

Jeremiah shifted, his subconscious answering but his body too tired to respond. Thorne called again.

Jenny shook Jeremiah lightly. He sat up, eyes half closed, head tilted back. His skin was cold. Jenny rubbed his arms briskly to bring back some heat. "Wake up, Jeremiah, your pa is calling."

He swiveled around on her lap. "Yeah, Pa?"

"Do you want to swim out deeper for a little while?"

Jeremiah shook his head, then plopped his face back down on Jenny's chest. Smiling, she pushed him back up. "You're going to get cold, honey, if you don't keep active."

Jeremiah looked at her. "Do you want to swim, Miss Jenny?"

Oh, to be suspended like a bird in flight, to feel nothing but water surrounding her on all sides, to dive beneath the surface and hear little but the hum of nature and the beat of her own pulse in her ears! More than any other nonfamily element of her former life, she missed swimming the most.

Reviving somewhat, Jeremiah rocked on her lap. "Do you want to?"

Jenny looked over at Thorne. His eyes were dark, their color indistinguishable from this distance. There was no welcome in those eyes. Even around a man who had so little respect for proper behavior that he would strip his clothes off in the presence of a lady, there were apparently boundaries that should not be crossed.

"No," she said. "You go ahead."

"C'mon, Miss Jenny," he pleaded.

"Not today," she temporized. "Hurry before your pa changes his mind."

The urgency of her tone sent him scrambling from her lap. He splashed in the shallows until the water reached his chest, then swam the rest of the way into his father's arms. Jenny sat back against the rock, feeling sorry for herself again. Thorne had tried to coax her to swim earlier; now everything about his expression held her back.

She pushed off the rock and swam in the opposite direction. If he didn't want her near him, she would happily swim elsewhere. The current picked up speed and depth as she got farther away. It dragged at her heavy skirts and made floating a chore. She tried treading water but found herself constantly swimming back to maintain her position. She knew better than to test her limits further in the restrictive clothing. To defy etiquette was one thing. To risk her life was quite another.

In a pique, she struggled back upstream toward their blanket and waded out of the water. The sun beat down on her head and shoulders, warming her skin and the clothes plastered to her body. She couldn't blame Thorne and Jeremiah for the conventions that didn't allow men and women to swim together, but that didn't stop her own wish that things were different.

She checked on the horses, then fetched the picnic basket and set everything out on the thick blanket beneath the shade. Once she was dry, the spot would be refreshing, but now it was too cool. She found an outcropping of rock, shiny in the sun's reflection and brimming with the day's heat. She went there to dry out.

Her clothes felt clammy on her skin, too tight in some places, too loose in others. Though the wet fabric felt comfortable now in the blazing afternoon sun, she would become chilled if they waited too long to start riding back. Temperatures dropped swiftly once twilight approached.

She made herself comfortable and must have dozed. When she opened her eyes, she felt a presence. Glancing up, she found Jeremiah staring intently down at her. His hair was combed and he had on dry clothing. She smiled. "I didn't hear you get out of the water."

His gaze narrowed to someplace below her chin. "How come girls have ribbons in their underwear?"

Jenny's gaze flew down to her blouse. Her chemise was visible beneath the damp fabric, along with the pink ribbon that threaded the scooped neckline. Her hands shot up to cover her chest and her cheeks went red as ripe cherries.

"Yeah," came Thorne's deep voice. "How come?"

Her eyes met his, startled and embarrassed.

Thorne scooped his son up and whispered loudly, "You don't ask a lady about her underwear. It's not good manners." He flipped his son upside down to divert his attention and, amid squeals of delight, carried him over to the blanket. "Chicken or beef jerky?"

"Chicken and cake!" he answered. "C'mon, Miss Jenny."

Jenny was frozen. If *she* could see straight through her blouse, then Thorne could see straight through her blouse. *Had* seen straight through her blouse! Humiliation flooded her, a feeling compounded by the offer of a man's shirt, Thorne's shirt, now being dangled before her eyes. It was wrinkled and smelled like saddle leather. She snatched it out of Thorne's hand and turned her back to put it on.

His hands went to her shoulders. "Wait," he said with some irritation. "Go behind that copse of trees and change. You can lay your blouse out to dry and no one will be the wiser. There's not much you can do about your skirt, but it won't be as obvious."

She nodded and headed for the thicker stand of trees. He regarded her critically when she reemerged. The hem of his shirt reached halfway down her wet skirt, the arms reached her knees. Her cheeks were still a bit flushed, but she seemed to have composed herself. Once she sat down, he took her sleeve and began folding back the cuff to a reasonable length. "I must say," he commented idly, "I've never seen this old shirt look so good."

She swung away from him and grabbed for the lunch basket. "I must say," she mimicked, "I've never been so embarrassed in my life."

His laugh was low and restrained. "Can't say as I regret that."

She swung back, a chicken leg clutched in her fist. "What is that supposed to mean?"

He shrugged. "I love pretty things. That pink ribbon, well, it was one of the prettiest I've ever seen."

"Oh!" It was all she could manage, just one burst of outrage with Jeremiah sitting so close and taking everything in. "A gentleman would not have looked," she said between her teeth.

His grin narrowed cynically. "He would have looked," he corrected. "He just wouldn't have admitted it."

As if he'd not been in the water at all, he was fully dressed in conservative ranch clothing, his wet hair slicked back, but there was a wicked gleam in his eye. "And you are no gentleman," she accused.

"Not even close. But you know that."

Shadows fell over them, so quickly Jenny looked up expecting to see a low-flying hawk. Her breath lodged in her throat. They had been surrounded by several men.

Thorne didn't move. He never even looked over to acknowledge them. But his body was tense, ready to spring. He said something ominous in a language Jenny assumed was Comanche.

They answered him in Spanish, cocksure voices that held a taunting edge. Without warning, Thorne rolled to his belly, a pistol in hand. The shot that accompanied the motion knocked one Comanchero off his feet. The outlaw screeched, clutching his shoulder, but did nothing more than writhe on the ground. The pistol leveled on the next outlaw. Thorne fired off more Spanish, a taunt of his own.

Jenny had begun to shake as the reality of their situation set in. Her face went white when she saw who stood over them. They faced a filthy group of bandits made up of two Comancheros, an Indian, and a white boy who didn't look old enough to be out of the schoolroom. Paul Anderson, her former student, a good boy gone so very bad. Her heart lodged in her throat. She croaked out a whispered "Paul."

He gave her no more than a scathing glance, and she knew better than to alert the others to the fact that they knew each other. The outlaws all had guns pointed in her direction.

Their eyes were hot and feral, but their look was nothing compared to Thorne's. His gaze was cold and composed, his hands steady. If he breathed, Jenny could not tell.

The man on the ground groaned, gripping his chest. Blood spread through his fingers and soaked his shirt. Thorne looked in his direction and muttered an alternative in Spanish. Jenny understood enough of the language to loosely translate Thorne's warning that the men could take their friend and get him some medical help or stay and take their chances.

They backed away slowly, never lowering their pistols, until they reached the man on the ground. Without ceremony, they hoisted him over the back of his horse and rode out, shouting a promise of revenge in parting.

Jenny crawled clumsily across the blanket and pulled Jeremiah into her arms. She buried her face in his neck, feeling like she wanted to cry and laugh at the same time. Tremors of shock and grief racked her in the aftermath.

The boy squirmed at her tight hold. "You're squishing me, Miss Jenny!"

She couldn't let go. She relaxed her arms a bit so he wouldn't feel so strangled, but she couldn't seem to let go.

Thorne gathered up the picnic supplies and repacked the horses. "Let's go," he called tersely. "If their leader doesn't make it, they'll be back sooner than we need."

That the bandits definitely would be back was evident in his tone. Jenny shivered and rose quickly to her feet, pulling Jeremiah with her. Her knees felt like jelly. "Who are they?"

"The Indian is an Apache, one of Goyathlay's followers who have moved to Mexico since the government put Apaches on the White Mountain Reservation in Arizona. The rest are Comancheros, half-breed outlaws who exist between the Indian, Mexican, and white man's world. They trade with all but have loyalty to none."

And the boy was Paul Anderson, her biggest failure.

She stared at the spot where the men had been. "Trade what?"

Thorne shrugged. "Whatever anyone needs. They supply the Comanche and Apache with liquor and guns."

"Guns! Who supplies them?"

"Anyone who wants to keep things stirred up. Rebel supporters who aren't convinced the war is over. French and Mexican supporters who want to establish their own republic in the territory. The list is endless, but those are the main problems."

Though the surroundings were once again peaceful, the picnic was spoiled. Her hands trembling, Jenny began to roll up the blanket. "They are insane."

"Worse," Thorne said grimly. He kept his gaze trained on the distance. "Plenty of them are cunning and organized. They've managed to keep the federal troops riding from crisis to crisis, thus weakening the troops' overall effectiveness. Now with Goyathlay, or Geronimo as he is called, in Mexico, I suspect the unrest will grow worse."

Jenny looked up. "Here? What could they want with us?"

Thorne shook his head. "Vengeance first."

Chapter 11

After a restless night dreaming of Paul Anderson's young face amid hardened bandits, Jenny rose with a sense of impending doom. Her eyes were puffy and gritty from lack of sleep. The last thing she needed was a visitor, but that was exactly what she got when Milt and Hannah rode up at half-past eight.

Hannah eyed her friend with open concern. "You look like the wash-up from a shipwreck, Jennifer. Are you ill?"

Jenny tried to ignore the fresh appearance of Hannah's mint-green striped skirt and smart jacket. Instead, she looked at Milt. "We were attacked by Comancheros yesterday."

"Jennifer, no!" Hannah's hand went to her heart. "Are you all right? Are you—"

"I'm fine," Jenny said, raising her hand to ward off

any unnecessary drama. "A bit shaken but fine." She glanced at Milt. "I was going to have Ian ride in today so you could file a report, but now that you're here . . ." She paused. "Why *are* you here?"

Hannah stepped forward and put her hand on Jenny's arm. "The school board has called a town meeting," she said in sympathy. "We thought you should know."

Jenny closed her eyes briefly. "When?"

"Day after tomorrow at the courthouse."

So, they would put her on trial. Panic erupted inside her, a clawing mass of nerves and fear that centered in the pit of her stomach. She seemed to have no control over it, no defense against it. She told herself she had to be strong, to stand firm in her convictions that she'd done nothing so terribly wrong, but the fear of losing her job drained her energy and initiative. She nodded woodenly at Hannah and stepped back. "Come on in. I'll make coffee."

"Hey, Miss Jen—" Jeremiah skidded to a halt in front of the sheriff and Miss Hannah. "Oh, sorry."

Jenny's expression softened. She smiled, then scooped him up for a good-morning hug, which he reciprocated with a loud, smacking kiss. Hannah and Milt exchanged glances at the obvious morning ritual.

"Hello, Jeremiah," Hannah said.

His arms tightened around Jenny's neck but he smiled hugely. "Hello, Miss Hannah. How's Tad?"

"Tad is just fine, thank you. I'll tell him you asked."

Jeremiah leaned close and whispered in Jenny's ear, "She's pretty, Miss Jenny, and she smells good."

Jenny bit off a sudden laugh. She didn't want to

embarrass Jeremiah or encourage him. "Go find your pa. Tell him the sheriff's here to talk about those mean bandits."

"Hold up, partner," Milt said. He turned to the two women. "I'll go with him," he said. "No sense in Thorne having to come inside." He picked up Jeremiah and settled him on his shoulders. "Lead the way, partner."

Thorne came in through the kitchen door, surprised to see the sheriff with Jeremiah. "Milton," he acknowledged. "Miss Hannah."

The sheriff nodded. "Thorne. Need a word with you, if you've got a minute."

Thorne nodded, then turned to Jenny and stopped dead still. It was less than a glance, but he caught something in her eyes, a lingering, shuddered look she passed over Milton, then covered by busying herself making coffee. Well, hell.

The sheriff headed toward the door. "Don't want to keep you from your work. I'll just follow you back out."

Thorne sent Jenny one last look, then led the way.

As soon as the men left, Hannah looked at Jenny. "Jeremiah's a darling child. Very bright."

Jenny nodded. "Wise beyond his years."

Hannah pulled her lace gloves off. "You seem uncommonly attached to him."

"I don't deny it."

Too innocent, Hannah probed. "What about his father?"

"I'm sure he's attached to Jeremiah too."

Hannah slapped her gloves down on the table. "You know what I mean, Jennifer."

Jenny's jaw tightened. "I haven't a clue."

"Haven't you?" Hannah rose from the table and lazily strolled into Jenny's kitchen. She took two mugs from the cupboard. "He's poor as a church mouse but handsome as sin."

"Really. I was unaware that you had noticed." Jenny's eyebrows rose. "Just how handsome is sin, Hannah?"

Hannah glanced back over her shoulder, her eyes twinkling. "Very handsome," she said seriously. "Handsome enough to cause a girl lots of trouble if the girl isn't careful."

"I'm very careful," Jenny said quietly. "And he's not as poor as you think. He owns a plantation in Mississippi as big as this ranch."

Hannah's perfectly composed expression changed to avid interest. "Why isn't he there?"

"He likes it here. Out West, I mean."

Hannah smiled. "I'll bet he does."

"Don't even think it," Jenny warned. "He is my employee. That's all."

"Of course it is," Hannah said with mock sympathy. "That's why you're blushing so becomingly and treating his child like your own."

Jenny was blushing because she got flushed whenever Milt was around, but she could hardly tell her friend that. She felt so safe around Milt, so peaceful and secure, whereas Thorne made her feel jittery and unsettled.

"Hannah," she said seriously, "what is the school board's agenda?"

Hannah's expression grew offended. "I'm not certain and I don't like it. Has anyone been out here to speak to you?"

Jenny shook her head.

"They have no right calling a meeting that surely concerns you without talking to you first." She took Jenny's hand and squeezed. "Milton tried to find out more, but the president, Mr. Haynes, only said it was time to meet."

"Without me," Jenny said.

"They knew it would get back to you," Hannah said, "but that is beside the point. It is unethical of them not to consult you first. Come reelection time, I'll let every voter know it."

Not that it would do Jenny any good now.

She shut her eyes. Panic reared again, licking rawly at her nerves. "What if they're going to fire me?" she whispered.

"Just let them try," Hannah challenged. "Jennifer Delaney, you know my father will not put up with such, and neither will Milton."

As much as Jenny wanted to believe Hannah's faith in the men she loved, she knew her friend was speaking from the heart. "They are not on the school board, Hannah."

"Nonetheless, you will not convince me otherwise, Jennifer. My Milton will come through and so will Papa."

It's going to be a lynching.

The sheriff's words echoed in Thorne's mind as he flicked the reins to get the horses moving. He was fairly certain Milton had been right two days ago when he and Hannah had ridden out to El Dorado to warn Jenny about the meeting. In the ensuing time, Thorne had done what he could to even the odds in Jenny's favor, but he had no idea if his plan would work.

Jenny's palms were sweating beneath her gloves. They were white lace, her Sunday best, as was her bonnet. A cloud of choking dust billowed out behind the wagon, but the way ahead was clear, the weather good. She folded her hands together, lacing her fingers tightly in her lap.

"If we hit a rut, you're going to go sailing out," Thorne warned.

She unclenched her hands and held on to the wagon. Her mouth was dry, her heartbeat suspended. All morning her system had been in a frenzy. Her heart had either raced away in her chest or seemed to stop completely, and her mind kept spinning over possible conversations that might take place. Her chest was tight, constricted; it felt as if she couldn't draw a decent breath if her life depended on it.

She looked straight ahead and was silent for a while before asking in an unsteady whisper, "What if they fire me?"

"They won't," he said, but they both knew there was no way to predict what the school board would decide.

"But what—" She put her face in her hands. "I've never been so scared. Not even when I got the letter about Papa and Sam. Papa had been downhearted since Mama died, and I knew he and Sam had fought for something they believed in. I knew they wouldn't want to return to nothing. And I knew they were in Heaven; that's how I got through it."

She took a deep breath, her eyes stark and unblinking as the courthouse came into view. "But this. I won't know how to get through this."

"Yes, you will, Jenny. If it comes down to the worst, you know how to survive."

"But I don't want to just survive!" She wasn't convinced she would want to do anything if she didn't have the school year to look forward to. She enjoyed her summers and holidays, but always there was the greater excitement of being with the children again, of watching their minds grow and expand, flourish in knowledge.

"Why'd you let Jeremiah come?" she asked. "If it goes badly, I don't want him to hear anything."

Thorne had sent him on ahead with Mercedes for very good reason. "He'll be fine."

Thorne's quiet confidence gave her courage. She drew a deep breath as he set the brake, then waited for him to come around to help her down. His hands were strong and welcomed at her waist. She placed her palms on his shoulders and tried to smile.

"Thank you for bringing me. I didn't want to come alone, and I appreciate not having to ask."

"There are any number of people who would have done the same, Jenny," he said as he lowered her, but none would have felt the rush of pleasure he experienced at having his hands at her small waist, at having the scent of her wrap around him like a silk ribbon. She was so close he could see the faint blue veins in her temples, the pale worry that left her cheeks colorless.

It angered him that the self-righteous, moralistic hypocrites could judge her so easily, could worry her so with their threats that her face was ashen. They didn't deserve Jenny for their children, didn't deserve her vigor and enthusiasm and patience. They thought Jenny was unnatural for not wanting to marry the first man to come along, and they couldn't see past their own desires to have her conform to their way of thinking.

His hands lingered at her waist. "Can't have them messing up Jeremiah's education."

Were there others who felt that way? she wondered. No one had come calling to offer support. Even Milt and Hannah had assumed Thorne would bring her.

And so he had.

She placed her hands over his. "Thank you. No matter what happens."

He wanted to pull her to him, to shield her, but he also wanted to do things no self-respecting teacher would allow. He stepped back for her to lead the way inside.

The courtroom was crowded, stifling in the dry summer heat. Every parent who could steal precious time away from work was in attendance. It seemed appropriate to Jenny that the school board had asked to meet here, where they could try and condemn her.

She had dressed in her most severe gown: a dark-blue

serge skirt and a high-necked white blouse. Granny Delaney's cameo was pinned at her throat, a symbol of courage to remind Jenny how brave and sensible and wise her outspoken namesake had been. The demurest edging of lace capped her collar and wrists, as prim as the bonnet she wore.

Her hair, drawn back in a no-nonsense bun, made her eyes appear larger and more innocent than she had intended. In her mirror she looked presentable. To many in the courtroom, she looked young and vulnerable when she entered.

Gathering courage, she surveyed the packed courtroom. Her heart stopped. The children were here. Almost every one of them was lined along the back bench.

Lord, she didn't want them to hear the adults castigate her, didn't want them thinking the worst about her or being forced to side against her. Taking a deep breath, she moved forward, determined to get this over with. The murmurs quieted when she walked to the front and faced the six school board members. Breaths were held; feet stopped shuffling. No one wanted to miss a word.

"Mr. Haynes, members of the school board," she began in a soft, uncertain voice. She cleared her throat and proceeded more bravely. "You have gathered today to discuss me and the future of Little Town's children. Am I to conclude by your choice of venue that I am to be put on trial?"

Thomas Haynes, president of the school board, smiled in a patronizing way. "Now, Miss Jenny, that's not at all the case. We just needed room for all the parents who wanted to have their say."

"Then why not choose the church?" she asked.

"I knew she'd get that smarty mouth going," Elias Waters spouted under his breath. He was eighty if he was a day and nearly blind, but his hearing was keen. He had been the first school board president and held a permanent position, unlike the other members who had to be voted in every two years.

Thomas Haynes had no real excuse for his choice of meeting place. She had hit the nail squarely on the head, even if he hadn't realized his motives when he suggested the courthouse. The school board members were already fairly fixed in their opinions, but an open hearing was the proper thing to do before a final decision was made.

A bit shamefaced, he added honestly, "I assure you, Miss Jenny, if we were not already assembled, I would choose the church. I had no ill intentions in mind at all. I apologize if you thought differently or if it appears that way to others."

He spoke up for all to hear. "This is not a trial but a hearing. We want to give Miss Jenny, the school board, and you parents a chance to speak your minds before we make a final decision. The next term is fast approaching and a decision has to be made."

Davy Manis stood first. Grumpy and ill-natured, he had quit school in fourth grade and still regretted it. "I got me six kids to consider. I'll go first." All heads nodded, even those who knew Davy to be a disagreeable grouch about everything. "I think we need to take a closer look at more than Miss Jenny's morals." More nods followed but no one would meet Jenny's eye. "I git by the schoolhouse at least twice a day. The kids is always outside staring at bugs and looking lazy. Now, I ask you, is that any way to learn them young'uns their reading and writing?"

"I've noticed the same thing," Charity Wilkens piped up in her squeaky voice.

"Lazing around ain't the only thing she's done," Mr. Chancellor added. He had one son in school and another about to be. "I hear tell she lets them kids run wild about every two hours. I know my own boy does; I asked him myself. I recall we didn't get recess but once a day when I was in school. What kind of learning is taking place with them kids out running around all the time?"

A chorus of agreement trickled around the room. It had been a source of whispered contention about town for a while. Riding by the schoolhouse on a nice day, one was as likely to see his child outside as in.

"And what about pictures?" Mr. Perkins asked. "My Jilly brings home more drawings of flowers than she does arithmetic sums."

The murmurs continued, not wholly mean-spirited but decidedly condemning. Jenny felt as if a band were tightening around her throat. The things that made perfect sense to her seemed unorthodox to them. Jilly Perkins was so artistic, it was easier to get through to her if Jenny used art to enhance the girl's other subjects. All her well-laid plans were being shot to the devil, all the teaching devices that had been so highly effective last year had turned into a source of ridicule against her.

Rowdy James stood, hat in hand. "I know it ain't my place, my boys being all grown, but I heard tell Miss Jenny don't even have a hickory stick in that schoolhouse. Now, how can a body keep discipline without a bit of hard persuasion?"

Jenny lunged to her feet, hectic color in her cheeks. "I don't need a stick in my classroom," she burst out. "Children who are well loved and well disciplined at home give me no problem in school."

"What's that supposed to mean?" Rowdy James said, jutting out his chin belligerently.

Thorne strolled forward. He'd had enough of listening to petty ignorance and arguments. He stood off to the side where he could see both the school board and the parents, then raised his hand for silence. The murmurs died away.

The town knew little of the man who went only by the name Thorne. No opinions had been formed, no real assessments made. He didn't drink or carouse, but he didn't attend church regularly either. He was cordial enough when approached, but he wasn't one to share a confidence or offer advice. The women found him handsome and aloof; the men thought of him as a hard worker. No one could say they had gotten to know him as a friend.

Thorne gave everyone time to simmer down, then spoke clearly. "I know that you've made up your minds and I'm not here to change them, but I do have something to say that I think you need to hear." He gave a pointed look at the back of the room where the children were gathered. "Since this concerns the students, I say let them speak."

Murmurs of discord erupted again. This was adult business and adult decisions.

Jenny's face blanched. She didn't want the children feeling responsible no matter what the outcome. She rose to her feet. "Ian, no."

A few in the audience gasped at her use of another name, but most were glued to the unfolding drama.

"Everyone here has a right to know what the children think," he said.

"No." It felt too personal, too frightening to have her students put on the spot. "They're just children."

Thorne gave her an apologetic look. "Yes, but it concerns them directly. If I didn't think it was absolutely necessary, I wouldn't ask them."

"But . . ." she pleaded, then turned to the sheriff. "Tell him, Milt."

Milton sensed Thorne had good motives, Jenny's best interest at heart. "No law against it," he said.

"You scared of what they'll say?" Elias croaked out.

Jenny's shoulders stiffened. She wasn't at all afraid of what the children would say. They had a right to their opinion, but in the long run the adults were not likely to take their opinions into consideration, which would make the children feel responsible.

The air was thick and hot. It had grown so quiet, the parents could hear birds chattering outside. They were torn between anxiety and curiosity.

Thorne didn't wait for agreement and called the first child up. "How about you, Tommy Chancellor?"

The Chancellors stiffened in their seats. Tommy was known as a rascal, always on the edge of trouble. At home it was all they could do to keep him in line.

Tommy walked to the front, looking nervous enough to puke. He sent the crowd a belligerent look. "Miss Jenny tells me I'm not as bad as everyone makes me out to be. She says I'm so smart that my mind just goes real fast." He sent Davy Manis a mean look. "That's why I get to go outside a lot. It's to turn off energy. Miss Jenny says I'll know more than her by tenth grade if she can figure out how to keep me focused in on my schoolwork." His chest was sort of tight and heaving. He looked pleadingly at his parents. "She says I'm just bored with ordinary learning and I'll do fine in university, if she can get me there."

Tommy looked at the school board, his shaky rebellion crumbling. "A bunch of us learn better when we get to go outside and study nature firsthand, instead of keeping our noses stuck in those old books."

Mr. Chancellor looked down, sheepish. His wife wrung her hands in her lap but said nothing. Of course their Tommy was a bright child. Everyone should be able to see that. They were sure their boy had a point about going outside, but they didn't think the rest of the town would agree.

Thorne nodded approval, then pointed at one of the older girls. "Aimee Learner."

The Learners' pride oozed across the room. Aimee had never given them a lick of trouble, and, unlike many parents, they expected only good things from their darling's mouth.

Aimee walked gracefully to the front, her back straight, her chin level, as she'd been brought up. Her face took on a perfect, pained expression. "I am not saying that Miss Jenny isn't a fine teacher," she began demurely. "However, she declares that my intellectual worth is just as important as physical beauty, and my mind is being wasted on frivolity." She gave her parents a wounded look, designed to draw sympathy. "She is very strict on me in my studies, even though I do not plan to go on to higher education. She says that I must realize that an intelligent homemaker is a greater credit to her husband and community than an empty-headed one." Aimee gave a despairing sigh. "I found her words to be unnecessarily cruel. I do my work. She needn't force me to accept her opinions."

Thorne had heard enough from the pampered Miss Learner. His gaze left her and her offended parents and zeroed in on the Evanses. They were good people but struggling to scratch out a meager living. This was one child he would not call forth without permission. Mr. Evans half rose to his feet, paused, then nodded slightly and sat back down to look at his lap.

"Clark Evans," Thorne called.

Clark strolled to the front, ready for his turn. His family had had a rough go of it since moving to Little Town, but Miss Jenny had made the tough days bearable. He faced the town proudly in a suit of clothes half a size too large. "I want to be a doctor." He turned and faced each school board member, then the crowd at large. "Miss Jenny says she has never met a young man more suited to the profession of comforting and healing.

She even borrowed Doc Brown's college texts in order to prepare me for future studies."

No one could quite meet Clark's eyes. Everyone knew there would be no money for college.

Pushing back an angry blush, Clark charged on. "She says I'll be ready for university long before she will be ready to lose me as a student. Right now my family is awaiting word from the governor and others of influence to see if financial help or scholarships will be available for me in the next year. Miss Jenny did that. She wrote to them all."

His son's pride lifted Marshal Evans's head. He rose to his feet. "If Clark don't make it to college, it won't be Miss Jenny's fault." He nodded in gratitude to Miss Jenny, then to James Fitzwilson, the banker, who had already been out to see him at the teacher's request.

Thorne looked around the room. The air was still but no longer filled with expectancy. The men in their heavy black coats were beginning to fidget in the heat, and the women were beginning to feel that perhaps they'd been hasty in siding with the school board. There had been nothing truly blasphemous in the children's words so far, nothing a parent would hate hearing in front of the town. But now he looked over at the Mastersons, concern in his eyes.

"Go ahead," William Masterson said defensively. "Can't be nothing said that we don't already know about our boy. Call him up."

"Billy Masterson?" Thorne asked respectfully.

Billy rose slowly to his feet and shuffled to the front. He looked painfully shy in front of the entire town. He took a deep breath and shoved both hands into his pockets. "Most people say I'm slow," he began. "I am." He looked over at his teacher and smiled. "But Miss Jenny says it this way. She says it just takes me longer to complete my work because I'm so careful. She says I'm a deep thinker who ponders every angle of every problem before finding a solution." He grinned at his pa. "That's me, Pa, a great ponderer."

William Masterson nodded gently at his son.

Billy's brows drew together. "Miss Jenny says that quick decisions and reactions are not my way. I suspect she's right, 'cause I sure do take my time."

Muffled giggles filled the room.

"She says I could be a botanist one day as I love to study living things, maybe even an animal doctor. I seem to do better with animals than people, that's for sure." He looked pleadingly out at the crowd. "I make my grades fair, but Miss Jenny helps me extra so I can keep up with the class, so they won't tease me. But she'd help anyone extra, even the fast ones. I don't know what I'll do if somebody else comes to teach."

Lillian Masterson had tears in her eyes. She brought her kerchief to her mouth, then reached over and slapped at her husband with it. "A botanist," she repeated. "All those bugs and things he likes to collect. No wonder."

Tight-lipped, William Masterson said nothing. Everyone knew his boy was good with animals, but the teacher made Billy sound like a boy with a brain instead of a lumbering fool. He'd never even heard his boy string more than two sentences together at one time, and here Billy had said a whole lot of important things. William could hardly wrap his mind around it with his heart choking up his throat so.

Thorne nodded appreciation at Billy, then looked at the Perkinses. Both eagerness and concern lay in their gazes. Like so many others in the room they had more than one child in school, twice the chance for embarrassment.

"Jilly and Amanda Perkins?" he began. "You two want to come up together or separately?"

The girls walked to the front, Jilly to chastise Miss Jenny, Amanda to commend her.

Mrs. Perkins had a pinched look about her mouth when her daughters were done. Everyone knew Jilly was the beautiful one, Amanda the smart one. The way the girls talked, the teacher had blurred lines a bit, confusing her. Her darling Jilly sounded petulant, while Amanda seemed quite in command of herself. Mr. Perkins simply looked blank.

"Paul Anderson," Thorne started, then stopped. "Never mind. I forgot he isn't here anymore to speak out on Miss Jenny's behalf."

"Mr. Anderson can't be here either," Elias Waters said grumpily.

"What's your opinion, Miss Jenny?" someone shouted from the back.

"Yeah," another toned in. "Let's hear what the teacher has to say about that no-good boy."

"What will that accomplish?" Thorne asked. Though he'd set this fireball rolling, he hoped it wouldn't gain too much momentum. Paul was a touchy subject, but he thought it needed to be addressed. "You have anything to say, Miss Jenny?"

Jenny thought of Paul, all the wasted time. "I failed him," she said quietly.

Thorne gave her a steady look. "I hear he came to school so bruised up, he could hardly walk. I also heard you tried talking to his father about it and the sheriff, even the circuit judge."

Jenny nodded, but she didn't see the point in this. Mr. Anderson was dead and Paul was on the run.

"How," Thorne said evenly, "can you possibly think you failed him?"

Jenny opened her mouth but found nothing to say. Any child lost, no matter what the reason, was a failure in her eyes. She clenched her teeth in despair. Now Paul rode with an outlaw gang, fulfilling all of their opinions of him. She had failed him by not figuring out how to help him.

Thorne looked at the youngest children standing uncertainly in the back. His son was there, sitting on the lap of one of the older girls. "Does anyone else want to talk on Miss Jenny's behalf?"

Half a dozen arms shot up, just as if the children were in the classroom. Thorne hid a smile. "How about you all come up together?"

The six youngest held hands and marched toward the front like they faced a firing squad. Their eyes were huge in their young faces, but their chins were set.

One by one they spoke with simple, endearing child logic. *I love Miss Jenny . . . She don't ever whup us . . .*

She's pretty . . . She's nice . . . We learn everything good, nothing bad.

As soon as Thorne commended their courage, they dashed for their seats, leaving Jeremiah to stand alone.

Small and uncertain, he looked at his father. "What do you want me to say, Pa?"

Thorne felt the same sort of worried pride that the other parents had been feeling. Without a rehearsed speech, his son might say anything. "Just say what you feel, Jeremiah."

His brow knit in concentration, Jeremiah thought long and hard over just the right words. He finally smiled and nodded. "Miss Jenny is the best teacher I ever had. I wish she was my ma."

Thorne choked back a startled laugh along with the rest of the town and gave his son an affectionate nod. "Thank you, Jeremiah. Anyone else?"

When no one else volunteered, the adult voices in the room began to escalate. Everyone seemed to think something should be done, but no one knew what. Thorne picked up the judge's gavel and rapped it on the table.

As soon as the murmurs quieted, he spoke. "What happens to the future of our children will be decided today. Jennifer Delaney is a fine teacher. Her behavior, no matter what some of you think about her unusual methods, is above reproach."

"Well, now. That there's a matter of opinion," Walt Henry piped up just to hear himself speak.

The sheriff glared at his deputy. "Do you want to keep your job?" he asked quietly.

Walt Henry threw his hand protectively over his badge and slid back into his seat.

Thorne looked over at Jimmy Henderson. "Did you lose your job at the bank, Mr. Henderson, because you sneaked a kiss with Miss Jenny behind the schoolhouse?"

Red to the roots of his thinning blond hair, Jimmy stammered, "N-no, sir. I did not."

"Then why should Miss Jenny?"

" 'Cause she broke the rules," Elias piped in. "Jimmy didn't break no rules."

Thorne's brows rose. "That right?"

Elias nodded importantly. "That's right."

"The bank doesn't have a code of conduct for its employees to follow?"

Bank president Fitzwilson rose to his feet. He was a tall man, thin and distinguished-looking. His well-modulated voice carried the ring of authority. "Of course the bank has a code of conduct."

Thorne leveled him with a look. "Does it apply to Jimmy Henderson?"

"It does, sir. But the bank does not feel that Mr. Henderson's actions, though reprehensible to some, did anything that would jeopardize the welfare of our customers."

"But Jenny's actions did."

"That is not for the bank to judge but for the school board to decide."

Thorne directed his gaze back to Elias, the most cantankerous board member. He would not name names unless it became absolutely necessary, but he could make things highly uncomfortable for several pompous fools sitting in judgment. "Tell me, Elias, how does Jenny's behavior compare with that of the men in this town, *in this very room*, who visit Lucy's?"

Offended gasps filled the air. The men were stricken to nervous silence in their seats; their wives were busy trying to cover their youngsters' ears while deciding if they would even admit to knowing that Lucy's brothel existed.

Milton bit back a smile but felt forced to speak. "Now, Mr. Thorne, that might be a bit out of line with the ladies and children present."

Hannah, his demure and perfectly composed bride-to-be, stood up at his side. "No, Milton. I want to know."

Milton watched in shock as Hannah turned, bold as you please, to the rest of the gathering.

"No one wants to admit that Lucy's house of ill repute exists in Little Town, but it does," she said, "and it is being funded by some of you men here."

Hannah's mother was fanning her face as if she would swoon. Her father looked like he had swallowed a sour pickle. "Sit down, Hannah," he commanded.

Her chin, which she knew looked quite lovely in profile, rose a notch. "I will not, Father." She took a deep breath and embarked upon a crusade. "Jennifer is the best teacher this town has ever seen. If she is to be dismissed for her behavior, then I want to know who else will be dismissed for theirs." She smiled warmly at Jenny, then sat back down.

Jenny was hard put not to smile back. If the situation

were not already so volatile she would have been cheering Hannah on.

Stanley Goody stood. He considered himself a fair-minded man, if a bit of a fun-loving scoundrel. "Mr. Thorne, has anyone here ever heard Miss Jenny say a single bad thing to any child in her class?"

Thorne waited long enough to make certain every soul had time to comment. When nothing more was forthcoming, he spoke up. "The only thing I've ever heard Miss Jenny say is that she is responsible. For every failure on the part of any student, Miss Jenny blames herself for not doing her job well enough."

"Well, then," Stanley said slyly, "wouldn't that be reason enough to replace her?" He looked sternly at the crowd. "If she knows she's got faults, maybe we need to find someone more confident of her abilities."

An outcry arose from the gathering. Voices swelled to be heard over each other as the shouts started.

"Ain't a soul here without faults!" someone cried.

"Anyone who says they're perfect is lying."

"Don't need no pompous, stiff-necked stranger in here to teach our young'uns!"

Stanley Goody smiled self-righteously, winked at Thorne, and sat down.

Jenny watched the same people who had been criticizing her moments ago rise to their feet to defend her. Stunned and moved, she looked at each parent, then their children, quietly nodding her gratitude. She had studied theories on behavior in order to better understand her students, but the fact remained that she would never fully understand human nature.

Only With You

The head of the school board took the gavel and rapped it once, twice, then finally shouted to be heard above the din.

"What's it to be then?" one of the parents yelled out.

"I say keep her," another chimed in.

"I don't want my boy stuck inside all day where he can't learn bugs," another defended.

Red-faced, Mr. Haynes rapped the gavel again and stood, then cleared his throat. "Listen to yourselves," he said. "You were condemning her a moment ago and now you are defending her."

"Yeah," Mr. Chancellor said. "We didn't understand before. "This is a mighty good example of a teacher knowing more than the parents."

Haynes ran his finger along the inside of his collar, as if it were choking him. "We still have not resolved the moral issue."

"Oh, yes, we have," Hannah said loudly. "If you're going to fire Jenny, then you had better fire Jimmy Henderson and shut down Lucy's."

The rest of the women rose in a chorus of agreement.

Haynes knew when to retreat. He waited for the woman to sit back down, then cleared his throat. "There is one small problem," he said gravely.

At the pained look on Haynes's face, the courtroom went still as glass.

"We don't see no problem," Stanley Goody said.

Haynes swallowed, looking cornered. "I, um, heard so much outcry from the lot of you that I took the liberty of inviting a Miss Theodora Walker from New

York here for an interview. She arrives in two weeks on the train into Santa Fe."

The color left Jenny's face. A gasping silence hit the room, as if everyone took a breath but forgot to let it out. The terrible quiet beat against her ears. Dazed, people looked about, uncertain what to do, of the exact significance behind Haynes's words.

"It's just an interview," Haynes said weakly. "Miss Walker comes highly recommended, a prized graduate of Mrs. Emerson's School for Proper Young Ladies. She has a teaching certificate—"

Jenny couldn't hear any more. Blinded by a sudden rush of tears and an inescapable knowledge, she rose and fled the courtroom.

Chapter 12

THORNE CAUGHT UP WITH HER HALFWAY DOWN Main Street. She fought like a wildcat when his arms went around her waist, but he knew she wasn't fighting against him. He held on despite her angry twisting and turning, despite the threats and recriminations hurled his way.

"Let me go!" she cried, then resorted to trying to kick him.

He swept her up against him and held tight to protect himself, then began a march back toward the wagon. At the livery he had a wide-eyed boy saddle a horse for him. The courthouse was still in chaos when he lifted Jenny onto the saddle and mounted behind her. Pinning her between his arms, he took up the reins and headed for the solace of the mountains. She fought him for the first half mile, an angry, betrayed young woman with nowhere to vent her ire, then suddenly she turned halfway around in the saddle and pressed fiercely into his chest. Without a word, she clung while tears spilled down the cheeks buried against him.

His arms tightened around her, comforting rather than restraining, and he stroked her back and shoulders, while they galloped through a forgotten stretch of desolate land toward the green foothills.

Her cheek bumped against his chest; her tears soaked his vest. Her hands, fisted in his shirt at his sides, were holding on, holding him, as if he were the lifeline to a world spinning out of control. He felt the quickening of his own outrage. She didn't deserve this, not Jenny. The flash fire of anger that consumed him began to settle into a slow burn that demanded revenge.

He wanted to bash Haynes for his stupid, untimely interference, for being so certain the town would turn against one of its own, for proceeding without consideration for two young women whose livelihoods depended on only one teaching position.

Miss Theodora Walker was not coming to Little Town for an interview. Young women did not travel halfway across the country to a desolate frontier, braving outlaw and Indian attack, without firm assurance of placement. He knew it and, worse, Jenny knew it.

He felt her shudder finally and knew the worst of her crying was over for now. Her feelings were another matter. It would be some time before she could separate Haynes's thoughtless act with her own self-worth. Thorne was fairly certain that the town was in an uproar this very moment and ready to string Haynes from the nearest tree, but the fact still remained that another young woman was on her way to Little Town to teach school.

Even if the town chose to rally behind Jenny, what would they do with Miss Theodora Walker?

Jenny stirred from Thorne's chest, then turned back in the saddle. Facing forward, she leaned against him like a limp rag doll, as if she didn't have the strength to hold herself upright. He rested his chin on the crown of her head and let the clean scent of her wash through him. The gesture was blameless enough, but he was fully aware that she was not family, nor was it their friendship that accelerated the rate of his pulse or heated his blood.

Lust had become constant. For over a month, he had accepted the nagging irritation that ebbed and swelled like the tide, depending on his proximity to her. Today was different, worse. He wanted more than the physical communion of two eager bodies. He wanted to give her comfort and solace, to offer a union of souls that would stand stronger than the desolation of facing the turmoil alone. His chest constricted. To see Jenny in tears—strong, resourceful Jenny—made him crazed. He wanted to smash Haynes to a pulp, but his compassion for Jenny overrode everything else at this moment but comforting her.

He ran his thumb across her troubled brow, longing to do more, knowing he must not. His hunger had a different taste and feel, a wholly different heat. It carried with it a responsibility he was unwilling to accept at this point. The hunger of lust he understood. It was inherent, natural. It gave no quarter but required no permanence.

This feeling was different, stronger. It could lead to disappointment and disillusionment. It lured, then trapped, changing to indifference and cool politeness that made the longest-married couple seem like complete strangers to each other. He refused to examine it further, as if by leaving the emotion nameless, it became stillborn.

Jenny wiped the wetness from her cheek with the back of her sleeve. "I'm sorry," she whispered. "I've made a fool of myself."

"No. Hush."

"Where are we going?"

"There." He pointed to nowhere, a place distant and obscure among the mountain peaks, where she could gather her thoughts and composure and regain some of her spunk.

"They didn't—" Her voice broke. She cleared her throat and continued more forcefully. "They did not invite that other woman out merely for an interview."

"No."

Her heart shuddered all over again, as if the words coming from Thorne held more irreversible truth.

"Oh." She began crying again, soundless tears more wrenching than her sobs because they brought no ease. They didn't exercise or cleanse or comfort. They merely reflected the devastation within her.

"Damn them," Thorne whispered against her hair.

"Don't," she said. "Don't say you're sorry or that it will be all right or that this will work itself out."

He cupped her chin in his palm and tilted her head

back and up to face him. She had the most beautiful skin, lush and flawless and so fair he could see the faint blue veins beneath her closed eyelids. Skin with the freshness of a child's but a woman's beauty.

"It will work out. You have to believe that."

"How can I?" Her voice quavered, then went hard. "I thought the South would win the war. I thought my mother would get well and my father and brother would return home. I thought Uncle Nat would live forever. I thought one day I would marry—" She cut the words off and, with the act, whatever last hope she'd held for Milt. She glared at Thorne, her expression bitter. "I'm done with believing the best. How can you even presume to tell me this will be all right?"

He hurt for her, an actual physical pain constricting his chest. He shied from it in blunt, dramatic fashion, pulling back physically as well as emotionally. His hand slid from her chin and went back to managing the reins. Such intensity was reserved for Jeremiah. Only Jeremiah. Thorne didn't have the ability or inclination to invest so much emotional energy in another person. Yet his hand itched to return to her, to stroke her translucent skin until his hands knew every inch, memorized each texture, savored every softness. He gripped the reins tighter. She didn't need his coddling; she needed his strength.

"Well, it has to be all right, doesn't it?"

The inflection was cruel. Jenny stiffened in the saddle. "Thank you so much for your overwhelming compassion."

"You don't want my compassion, Jenny. You want easy answers, but I don't have any."

"I do not! That's not fair."

Of course it wasn't, but it got her fired up into fighting back. "Nothing is fair. Life isn't fair. Haven't you learned that yet?"

"No!" she cried. "And I'll keep not learning it until it turns out right!" Having just decried her own words, she slumped back again in tired confusion. "You were baiting me."

"Not intentionally." He wanted to rail at her for such misplaced optimism when only seconds before he had been trying to inspire it. He wanted her spunky and fighting, but mostly he just wanted to hold her and make the world behave for once.

"Jenny," he began, but there was nothing else he could say, so he maintained a steady gallop away from the people who so thoughtlessly had hurt her.

The warmth and fragrance of her skin drifted around him. The wind snatched bits of her hair free and flung it across his nose and mouth. A hint of floral-scented soap bathed every stray wisp. She fit into the cradle of his body as if formed for that purpose, her movements even with the rhythm of the horse's gait.

He wondered how she would fit beneath him.

Heat kindled through him. His left arm went across her middle, and he shifted her deeper into the juncture of his thighs, deeper into him. Finally, unavoidably, he didn't try to ignore the sexual cognition growing between them. It would be hypocritical to deny its existence, so he studied it, tried to dissect it as one would a problem that needed solving.

It could create gross complications or, at the very least, some highly uncomfortable nights. He could handle his unsatisfied body, but he found that his spirit also hungered for the intimacy of a woman, *this* woman. He longed for it with the same intensity that he resented it. He didn't want to need a woman. He had Jeremiah for love and companionship and affection. His more basic urges could be satisfied with a quick trip to Lucy's.

So, why hadn't he gone there?

And why was it Jenny's face he saw beckoning to him in the hot night dreams that plagued his sleep? Why was it Jenny's body he imagined, naked and golden in the glow of candlelight, damp from the passion of their lovemaking?

Though the dreams had come more frequently since moving to El Dorado, he'd had them his entire adult life.

But he would not mistake lust for the love she craved, and he knew well how difficult the two were to distinguish when the body was starved for fulfillment.

Jenny sat up straighter in the saddle.

"The terrain up ahead is uneven," Thorne said by way of excuse, and pulled her tighter against him.

Holding her felt right, as comfortable as breathing, but with a sharp expectancy that was growing stronger, biting into his resolve. His forearm rested across her lower abdomen. It would be so easy to slide his hand up her midsection to touch more of her, to fill himself with her goodness. To take both of them beyond an erratic, unstable world. But the escape would be all too temporary. He settled for shifting his arm to her waist.

Her breasts rested just above his sleeve, their full undersides brushing him with every shift in the horse's stride. Her scent was like rain, cleansing and refreshing and bringing new life to his senses amid centuries of dust and legend.

Did he go blithely this way with Jenny? Unaware of the pitfalls of abetting the attraction between them? A rush of heavy desire hit him each time she adjusted her torso or shifted her backside. He knew he should put a stop to it, but her warmth against him was like a beacon calling him home. What harm in a little flirtation, a little temptation?

He realized quickly that the harm lay in the agony of physical incompletion. He was forced to endure in silence the torture he had helped create. With no recourse from his own folly, he pushed the gelding to move faster.

The land rose. Gravity pushed Jenny deeper into the cradle of his lap. Her spine curved along his chest and belly, soft and pliant against his work-toughened torso. Her fragrant hair fell in soft wisps around her face, adding a dainty softness to her features. The tiny pulse at the base of her throat had slowed, and her lashes lay still on her pale cheeks.

Jenny must have slept. When she opened her eyes the sun was low, bathing the canyon in burning splendor. Ocher walls rose on every side, hemming her in, but she could hear rushing water in the distance and knew the passage of rock must give way somewhere ahead. She sat up slowly and pushed her hair out of her face.

"Where are we?"

Thorne reined the stallion in and slid from his back, then reached up and caught her at the waist. "Redrock Canyon."

Jenny planted her hands on his shoulders and dismounted. Her hair tumbled around her face, falling nearly to her waist. Disoriented, she looked around. "What happened to my pins and my bonnet?"

"You didn't have a bonnet. Your hairpins are scattered from here back to town."

She remembered that she had lost the bonnet fleeing the courtroom. Her bottom lip trembled and she bit down hard to still it. Such a silly thing to get upset over, a useless waste of energy. But it felt so huge right now, so dire. She felt tears gathering again and pressed them back. Pulling her hair over one shoulder, she began to braid it into some semblance of order, as if she could right the world by tidying herself.

The whinny of a horse echoed on the wind, and the gelding answered with a neigh and a toss of his head.

Jenny looked around at the vaguely familiar landmarks. "How long have we been riding?" Her voice sounded flat, dispirited and tired, even to her own ears. But she didn't care anymore.

"About an hour."

Startled, she turned toward him. "How could I have slept so long?"

"Trauma, exhaustion?"

She knew the reason didn't matter. His dugout lay

just beyond the next climb, which meant they were another thirty minutes' ride from home. "Jeremiah will be expecting us."

"Mercedes is watching him. I'm not worried about Jeremiah. I'm worried about you."

She shook her head. "I'll be fine, Ian." But her tone was washed out and hollow, less than convincing. "Why did you bring me here?"

"Come this way. I'll show you." He began walking the horse up the steep bank. Jenny followed. When they reached the top, the land flattened out into a wide mesa. "Come around to the back."

Jenny followed, a bit baffled by Thorne's behavior. Her emotions seemed to have dulled with time and sleep. Her earlier shock and panic had settled like a sickness in her stomach. She felt drained, empty of everything but lassitude. They passed the dugout where he had been living only weeks before and the shed where he had stabled her horse that night during the storm.

They reached the other side of a large rock formation and Jenny's breath caught. The mountain fell away gradually. Below lay a sloping meadow with a wide mountain stream. The land was green, rich with vegetation. Perhaps two dozen horses grazed in the glow of a setting sun.

"Whose are they?"

"Mine," he answered. "As is all this land. Jeremiah and I have been living in the dugout to keep expenses down until the land is fully paid for. It will take another year."

"Oh," she said in wonder. The land was glorious, so

lush and verdant, and the horses were of fine, healthy stock.

"Marry me, Jenny."

She gave him a tired look.

"I'm serious."

She spun to face him, shock flooding her features. "You're not."

He hadn't been until the ride up when she fell asleep in his arms, until it made perfect sense for both of them. The hour of sexual aggravation hadn't hindered the decision either, but it had not been made on that unreliable influence alone.

"If you marry me, you won't need the teaching job. My land borders your own. The entire stretch we traveled the night you got hurt is mine."

Her heart pounded, sweeping away the sluggishness of her mind. Though much of the land was comprised of cliffs and canyon passes, the valley stretched for miles and miles. An unbroken connection to El Dorado would be a great advantage to any landholder.

"But I want my teaching job."

"Then keep it."

"I may not have that choice and we both know it." She flung her arms up in aggravation. "Why are you asking me now? Why today?" Her tone was wounded, her eyes angry. He knew she didn't have the resources to fight the all-too-logical suggestion. Her strength was gone, her emotional barriers annihilated. "Is it pity? Don't you dare pity me, Ian Thorne! Don't you dare!"

He grabbed her shoulders, tempted to shake her. "It's

not pity, Jenny. It's mercenary, remember? I want your land and your horses."

Scornfully, she shook off his hands. "You have incomparable land and ten percent of my stock later. You don't need me or my ranch."

He took her shoulders again, in a grip that she couldn't shrug away, and went in for the kill. "Then do it for Jeremiah. He needs a mother, and he loves you, Jenny. More than he ever would have the woman who birthed him."

"Oh." She lost her breath completely. "How . . . how can you fight so dirty? That's not fair, Ian. How can you bring Jeremiah into this?"

His hands slid up and he cupped her face. Though his touch was gentle, it was also uncompromising. "I don't intend to fight fair, Jenny."

"But why—"

His head lowered. She watched, mesmerized, as his gray-green eyes drew closer. It took her another shocked moment to realize he was going to kiss her. Her hands flew to his chest. "Ian, no—"

The words were cut off, smothered by his lips, stripped from her by the hot possession of his mouth. His hand slid around to her nape and held her still as his lips moved over hers with fierce gentleness. "I want you, Jenny," he whispered against her mouth. "More than I've wanted anyone in a long time. This is the right thing to do, for all of us."

She had never imagined such a kiss. Never. Her fantasy dreams about Milt had been sweet, endearing declarations of love and tenderness. Her experiment with

Jimmy had been mildly disgusting. The kiss she and Thorne had already shared had been a mixture of heat and violence.

This kiss was like nothing she had dreamed or anticipated. It was hot and demanding, yet as gentle as a child's wish. It consumed her mind, turning her thoughts to mush, invading her body like heady wine. Sublimely sweet yet agonizingly provocative, the possession of his mouth swept her up in heat and desire. His lips were hard yet soft, weather-roughened and tender. The combination of textures was so stirring her knees went weak and she sagged against him, into him, the power of his body her only support.

Oh, Thorne was good at this, better than she ever would have imagined a man could be. He was skilled and aggressive, taking more than she was willing to give back, yet she had no will to stop him.

Her hands flattened on his chest but they didn't push him away. Instead they held him as tightly as he held her, her fingers digging into the fabric of his vest, her body longing to get as close to him as two people could be. He made a sound against her lips, a feral growl deep in his throat that found an echo in the forbidden recesses of her body.

She answered with a whimper, a hungry, mindless demand for him to stop the assault on her senses. Her lips trembled, unyielding, yet she couldn't seem to rally the willpower to withdraw. His body was warm and strong where it aligned with hers, his mouth heavy and possessive, making her feel both smothered and cherished. Her fingers splayed across the soft leather of his vest, then gripped hard, holding on for sanity. It was a grave mistake.

He groaned again, a desperate purring sound that ignited a sensuality in her that she hadn't known existed, that she hadn't even known she possessed. She jerked in shock at the molten heat inside her. This could only be passion, and it seemed to mirror his own. Her limbs grew heavy, her breath rapid and shallow. A languorous warmth filled her, immersed her frayed nerves in an exquisite, wild craving for his touch, his kisses.

His hands moved over her, pulling, shifting, shaping her into a closeness unhindered by their clothes. Lord help her, she liked it. Liked the sound of his raw desire, the realization that he felt it with her.

No dreams could compare with the reality of Thorne's possession. Nothing in her imagination had been this strong or stirring. She touched Thorne.

Her hands slid up his chest, exalting over the faint definition of muscle beneath his shirt, her fingers absorbing the thunder of his heartbeat. She might pay later with guilt and embarrassment, but for now she reveled in the feel of a man's arms around her, the heat of his closeness, the uncanny combination of comfort and yearning running the length of her body.

Her fingers rose higher, over the hard muscle and bone to the hot skin of his neck, then higher to the dark, golden-tipped curls at his nape. She wound her fingers through his hair and clung tight, leaving herself vulnerable to the full weight of his tall body. His hands found her waist and he took the shape of her like a blind man, his palms slowly gliding over her hips, then back up to her rib cage. They were hungry hands, ravenous as his mouth, but unbelievably controlled and exacting in their purpose. He knew what he wanted, while she felt lost in a maelstrom of need. She rose on tiptoe, nearer, deeper into his passion.

A low groan struggled in his throat, triumph and caution combined. His fingers dug into her lower back and he pulled her tighter than two people could be, then tighter still until she could feel the rampant desire of his body as he moved against her, sought to make them impossibly closer still. But it was not enough, this meshing of leather and cotton, the empty grind of his body against hers in a mocking imitation of what he wanted. Nothing so simple could assuage the hungry fire through Thorne's bloodstream.

He broke contact with a quick jerk, but just barely, the heat of his gruff breathing whispering over her damp, swollen lips. "Marry me, Jenny."

"No," she returned, then began kissing him back, fiercely, hungrily, moving her mouth as he had and pressing back up against him until his arms tightened around her so firmly it was almost painful.

"Jenny, don't," he warned, but she only took advantage of his open lips and kissed him hard. She wanted this escape, being with him, inside him. The only reality was this need. She moved against him, brushing places better left unbrushed, provocative in her innocence. Thorne's will was slipping with alarming speed. Her teeth scraped his bottom lip. The rough, unlearned gesture sent a sharp intake of air into his lungs. Feelings as elemental as fire and rain burgeoned within her. The beat of her own pulse pounded in her ears, her heart, matching the rapid cadence of his.

"Jenny," he warned again, but he was gone, defeated by the heat and innocence of her. He swept the hollows of her mouth with his tongue and felt the moist breath of her gasp, then the acceptance of this new and daring change.

She mirrored his actions as if it were a challenge, and they began a mating dance, an assault on the senses that burned hot enough to meld them, hotter than was prudent.

Too quickly they were moving past the safer elements of flirtation and discovery to the untutored halls of dark passion. His hand slid up her waist, a warning, a chance for her to understand. His thumbs brushed the underside of her breasts. She made a confused sound but didn't pull way, trusting him too much. His guilt was nothing compared to the desire searing him, and his hand slid higher, aching, covering her fully. She went still for a heartbeat, awash in indecision. His hand stirred over her, shocking and intentional. *Now, Jenny. Stop it now.* She was lush warmth in his hands, perfect, so damned perfect.

But she didn't flinch or move away. Instead, her response grew more torrid, her kiss more aggressive. Thorne knew where it would lead. He had no defenses against her honest response, no virtue to end what she would not. In another few moments, he would have her on the ground, her skirts flung over her waist, his body plunging into hers without regard for later. He gripped her upper arms and pushed back, brutally breaking contact.

Her eyes were dewy, her lips swollen and stung with color. It took every ounce of strength within him to keep her at arm's length. "Marry me," he demanded.

"No," she whispered. Her world began to refocus. Thorne's face was hard, his eyes burning. She expected to feel ashamed or uneasy, but she didn't feel any of those things. She felt breathless and hungry and denied something vital. "I want to do that again."

He gave her an unsteady laugh. "So do I. No."

"Why?"

"It's too dangerous." His words puzzled her. He caught the perplexed narrowing of her eyes and proceeded before she could. "Trust me, Jenny, it is entirely too dangerous."

"Why?"

"Because . . ." He slid his hands up her midriff until her breast filled his palm. Her breath caught sharply and her cheeks flooded with color, but she didn't shy away. "See?"

She didn't see anything, except that she wanted him. Badly. Though a part of her knew it was outrageous, it didn't outweigh the other part of her that wanted something else, something more. "But—"

"Jenny!" He caught her chin and tilted her face up. His voice was low, savage. "We are out in the middle of nowhere. No one will come along to rescue you when things get too hot, go too far."

Her eyes flashed. "I don't need rescuing, Ian."

The hell she didn't! He spun her around before he

lost all good sense and held her against him, her back to his chest, his hands safely on her waist. "Do you think it's all just kisses, maybe a few forbidden touches? There's a lot more that can happen, Jenny."

For the first time in too long, she felt alive, lightning-struck and charged, and she wanted more of this energy, more of him. Show me what can happen, her body cried, but her heart knew that wasn't right. His hands shackled her, his fingers strong and firm so she couldn't turn back. She wished he would embrace her again, hold her, kiss her.

"What can happen?" she whispered.

"I think you know."

"Not if we don't let it."

He gave a cynical laugh. "I'm sure not the one who'll stop it."

Even now he felt the urge to run his hands over her, to strip her bare and feast upon the sight of her, to finish what he had unwittingly started in the rawest way. Nothing would stop him from completing the seduction if it went much farther. He didn't have the control if she didn't have the will. Later, when she realized the ultimate destination of their folly, he would be too far gone. A sudden change of heart on her part would mean nothing at that point.

"Marry me."

She tried to turn around but he held her steady. "No. You don't love me."

He ground his teeth in frustration. "I'll love you so good, you won't be able to walk for a week."

She tilted her head back to look at him, confusion in

her expression, then his meaning dawned on her and she jerked her face away. "Real love," she snapped.

He rested his forehead against her hair. "It would be as real as you could stand."

Shivers ran up and down her spine. "You know what I mean."

"Real love is for poets and idealists," he said. Though his tone was not unkind, it was frank. "This is as real as it gets."

She wouldn't believe him. Love had to be real, lasting. She'd built her lonely future on that fact and she wouldn't accept less. Saddened, she shook her head. "I don't believe you."

"It doesn't change the truth."

She jerked from his hold and spun to face him. "What about Jeremiah? Isn't that real?"

"That's parent and child. It's different."

His arms went back around her. He wasn't even certain why. Perhaps he wanted to ease the hurtful truth. Perhaps he just wanted.

The heat of him caressed her, and Jenny's body felt anxious, full of unfinished business. Unconsciously she moved closer. "Ian—"

He stilled her motion with the grip of his fingers on her hips. "Look how much land is here, Jenny. It takes more than an hour to ride it on horseback."

She dipped beneath his hands suddenly and strolled away, her cheeks flushed with agitation. "I don't want to talk about land. I want to talk about you and your foolish assumptions."

"You don't understand," he warned.

She'd seen him with Jeremiah. If any man knew real love, it was Thorne. She searched the strained look on his face, daunted by the fact that he really believed what he was saying. Suddenly she had to make him see he was wrong. It seemed vitally important. She went back to him, into his embrace. "Then tell me. Make me understand."

He took her forcefully by the shoulders. "We have to talk about land or I'll ravish you."

She laughed then, pure unaffected laughter that only stretched Thorne's control to breaking. Because he wouldn't allow her to move, she dropped her head back and looked up at him, the light of mischief and rebellion in her eyes.

"I might like being ravished," she said, "and to hell with the school board and Miss Theodora Walker." She flung her arms around his neck. "Kiss me again, Ian." Her eyes were overbright, demanding. "Kiss me like you mean it."

He pried her arms from around his neck and held them at her sides. "I'm not going to be your misguided attempt at revenge, Jenny."

"But you kissed me first!"

"An error in judgment," he said.

Her face blanched suddenly. "Marvelous! One moment you're asking me to marry you, for completely mercenary reasons, and the next moment you're kissing me as an error in judgment!"

She fought his hold, her voice hoarse, her eyes deeply wounded. "I don't know which is worse, Ian, your greed or your indifference." She jerked free, spun on her heel, and stormed away from him, distraught, exhausted by the turmoil of the past hour, day, and weeks. "At least greed has passion and purpose!" she flung over her shoulder. "If I'm going to be condemned for doing something wrong, I wish, at the very least, that I had done it!"

She had no idea how tempting such words were to a man who was already burning from her touch. "Agree to marry me," he shouted at her, "and I'll kiss you as much as you want."

She stopped dead still, then turned back. "I'm in love with someone else."

His eyes went cold. "Milton Hardaway."

Shock flooded her features. "We're friends."

One didn't look at a mere friend with the hidden emotion Jenny did, the hero worship and suppressed longing. He pushed the thought aside. "No one else knows," he said. "I'm not asking for your love, Jenny, just your commitment."

Hurt, she turned away so he wouldn't see her ridiculous tears and began to march back toward the horse. "You could have at least pretended, Ian. Would it have been so difficult to pretend that you loved me, that you wanted me for just me?"

He flinched. "I do want you, Jenny, never doubt that. But, no, I can't pretend the way you mean." He followed after her. "Is that what you want? Pretty, meaningless lies?"

She looked back at him, her eyes icy and empty. "Yes."

She accepted the fact that she would never have Milt.

Meaningless lies, a fantasy, is exactly what she wanted. She wanted to hear the words, to pretend they were real so as to salvage the lonely future that would forever be devoid of them.

She mounted Thorne's horse in one fluid motion, tempted to leave him behind, but she waited, too chilled inside to care anymore. When he settled himself behind her, she leaned back into his chest.

"Jenny," he warned.

"You won't do anything," she dared. "You're all bluster and intimidation, but no action. You don't scare me anymore, Ian."

"You wiggle your bottom up against me one more time and I'm going to scare the drawers off you."

She tilted her head back, challenge a scornful light in her eyes. "I'm not wearing drawers."

His hand shot down and grabbed her skirt, then hiked it above her knees. Her squeal of protest went ignored as his hand slid over the side of her leg up to her thigh.

"Ian, stop—"

He found the delicate batiste of her unmentionables and grabbed a fistful as his mouth settled against her ear. "Don't ever underestimate me, Jenny," he whispered. "Ever."

She shivered at the dire warning in his tone. She wouldn't.

Chapter 13

Granny Delaney had a few choice words to say on the issues of men and husbands, but she lacked any great opinion on unmarried men in particular. Jenny thumbed through the journal, looking for passages that might shed a bit of light on her situation, but Granny had been married to Colin Patrick Delaney by age fifteen, so little time had been spent in idle flirtation or the exploration of it.

Jenny tucked the journal beneath her pillow and sighed. She hated Ian Thorne. She might love his son as fiercely as a natural mother would, and her traitorous body might ache in secret places every time Thorne got near, but that didn't change her feelings. She hated Ian Thorne with a passion.

Passion . . .

It was an odd word, a strange sentiment. She felt

passionate about many things: her work, her students, the ranch. But she'd never felt passion for a man, not even Milt. Her love for him was soft and sweet and endearing. The way love was supposed to feel. It seemed awkward and unlovely to attach such fierce, consuming emotions as passion to a person who was not family. And it felt dangerous to now associate those feelings with Thorne.

Yet most of their life an intensity, a passion, had marked their time together. The bright swift days of their childhood had been infused with the passion of youth. Running barefoot over the crisp spring grass to the bank of the river, they had laughed and teased with a vigor unfound in Jenny's adulthood. The fleeting seasons of childhood were indelibly imprinted upon her memory. Even now she could smell the rich delta soil, the gray strings of Spanish moss hung from fragrant cedar trees.

Hot sweet summers, cool burnt umber autumns, the mercurial moodiness of spring. When Thorne had been taken by the Comanche, a piece of Jenny's childhood had been stolen, snatched away like a treasure. She had never fully recovered the joy of those early years.

Memories assailed her, coming like bright, sharp prisms of glass to strike at her heart. She could not hate Thorne. Not the boy who had romped and played in the extraordinary, enchanted days of her youth. She longed for those lost years, when the world was innocent and so ripe with possibilities. The yearning only added fuel to her present discontent.

A loud rap came at the patio door. Heat wound

down her body. She flipped onto her stomach and buried her face in the pillow to muffle a moan. Her brain might want to hate the man Ian Thorne had become, but her body didn't know that.

The tap came again, louder and more demanding. She pulled the pillow over her head to drown out the sound. Go away, she cried silently. She wouldn't respond, wouldn't acknowledge him at all. There was nothing he had to say that couldn't wait until a decent hour and the settling down of the discord in her body.

"Jenny, open this damn door!"

She jerked up in bed. "Don't you dare curse at me, Ian Thorne!"

"We've got trouble! Open the door!"

She noted the tone in his voice and flew from the bed. Heedless of her dishabille, she flung the door open and found Cortez, who'd been on watch, seated on a horse, a lantern in his hand. Barkley was shrugging up suspenders as he ran, boots in one hand, holster in the other. The dogs were barking like crazed creatures in the distance.

A knot of fear tightened in Jenny's stomach. "What's happened?"

Thorne moved past her and began unlatching the shutters from the wall. "Lock all the windows and doors. I'm fairly sure it's the Comancheros we ran across. I suspect they've come back for revenge."

"Jeremiah—"

"He's with Mercedes, so is Aunt Tildy. Go! Lock the whole house."

Jenny flew through every room, locking all the

shutters, while Thorne gathered and checked the firearms. There hadn't been any type of raid in years, and she struggled to remember everything Uncle Nat had taught her.

After securing the last barrier, she caught up with Thorne near the patio doors. "How many are there?" she asked.

"Cortez counted six, maybe seven." Thorne shouldered a rifle and a strap of additional ammunition, then opened the door.

"Where are you going?"

"I've got to get out to the horses."

Jenny tried to swallow the dry fear in her throat. "But—" She knew there was little choice. Without the horses, the men wouldn't have jobs. Without jobs, they wouldn't eat. They had been hired for just such work, but they were outnumbered at least two to one and Jenny felt as if she were sending them to their doom. "Ian, wait, I'll come with you."

He paused only a heartbeat, then turned to her, his eyes fierce and direct. "Stay here and take care of Jeremiah," he commanded quietly. "If they get past us, you'll need to defend the household."

"Luis is here."

Though he knew Jenny to be a woman of strength and backbone, she looked young and defenseless in the pristine nightgown, her hair hanging down her back, bare feet peeking beneath the dainty ruffled hem. He read fear in her eyes but no panic.

"My entire life is inside these walls," he said gruffly.

"If they get past us, I need you here to protect Jeremiah . . . to raise him."

Everything in Jenny shuddered at the thought that there could even be such a remote possibility. "Don't let them get past you," she said quietly.

He looked at her a moment, then turned on his heel and left.

Jenny paced from window to window, the rifle at her shoulder, ready. She was capable of hitting anything at which she aimed within a reasonable distance, but she prayed it wouldn't come to that. If the Comancheros got that close to the ranch house, it meant the worst had happened to Thorne and the others.

"Do you see anything?" she called out to Mercedes.

"No, señorita."

"Luis?"

"No, nothing here," he returned.

"Aunt Tildy?"

Matilda Darineau peered out into the darkness with the steady concentration of a sharpshooter. "No Yankees this way."

Mercedes and Luis were positioned at the top legs of the U-shaped house, with Jenny and Aunt Tildy in the base, facing opposite directions. Jenny glanced down beside her. "Jeremiah?" she called quietly.

"No, Miss Jenny," he answered. He pulled a fistful of her nightgown to his face and stuck his thumb in his mouth. "When's Pa coming back?"

"Soon," she said, praying she was right.

• • •

The wait was endless. Time crept insidiously slowly in the darkness, every sound and snap a hundred attacking outlaws. Sporadic shots and the ever-constant barking of the dogs were heard from time to time, but the men didn't return. Rolled up in a blanket, Jeremiah eventually fell asleep beside Jenny on the floor, the tail of her cotton nightrail still clutched in his fist.

Toward dawn Mercedes made the rounds with fresh, strong coffee. "It will be over by dawn," she said. "The evil men won't stay past the light where they'll be exposed."

"I hope you're right," Jenny said. She cradled the warm mug in her hands and breathed in the steamy aroma. Her mind was sluggish, her eyes gritty, but she wouldn't be able to sleep even if all were safe. She sipped the coffee and watched the first fingers of daylight creep over the land. On a peaceful morning the spears of golden pink and lavender would have been beautiful, but now the light was merely vital. She wanted to hurry it along, to will the day into full being.

Her neck and shoulders ached from staying in a fixed position. She tugged her gown from Jeremiah's fist so as not to awaken him and stretched out the kinks in her tired body. The dogs had quieted, and Jenny didn't know if that meant good or bad, but she understood clearly that she couldn't stay on her feet much longer.

Shadows began to emerge out of the incandescent colors of dawn. Jenny shifted the rifle to her shoulder and took aim. The silhouettes changed, took form and substance as men on horseback, indistinguishable as friend or foe. Mercedes ran for her post.

"Luis!" Jenny called.

"*Sí*, I see them."

"Aunt Tildy?"

"Got 'em in my sights," she whispered as she moved beside Jenny.

"Can anyone tell who it is?"

No one could.

Jenny focused on the lead rider. She would pick him off first and leave it to Luis and Mercedes to get the others when they scattered. There were three, galloping fast toward the house. One carried something bulky across the front of his saddle. Within seconds, Jenny recognized Thorne, then the other two.

"Jeremiah, it's your pa."

He stirred in his pallet but didn't fully wake up. Jenny lowered the rifle and hurried to unlatch the shutters, then opened the patio door. Mercedes and Luis met her there.

Thorne dismounted and dragged the bundle from his horse, heaving it over his shoulder. Jenny stepped back, her heart in her throat. "Who is it?"

He pushed past her and headed for the kitchen table.

Jenny's heart began to pound out a sickening foreboding. She searched the other men's bleak faces quickly but Cortez and Barkley were uninjured. She looked back at Thorne. "Who?"

Thorne dumped the body on the table. The young, pale face of a boy rolled limply to the side. "Paul Anderson."

Her heart stopped for a small second. "Oh, no," she whimpered. She rushed forward and pulled the poncho over the boy's head. Beard stubble littered his chin. His hair hung in dirty blond strings that covered his ashen face. His lips held a bluish tinge but his chest rose and fell weakly beneath a blood-soaked shirt. It was Paul, all right, but not the student Jenny remembered.

"Get me a pan of water," she called to Mercedes, "and some soap and rags." She peeled back his filthy shirt to find a bullet hole in his bloody chest. She looked over at Thorne. "Do we have time to fetch the doc?"

His face was cold, his voice remote. "He just tried to make off with your Thoroughbreds, Jenny. They'll hang him as a horse thief."

Her eyes flared briefly in panic, then seemed to level calmly on the three men before her. "I think he was trying to warn us," she said carefully. "In fact, I'm sure of it."

Thorne gave her an incredulous look and his voice held a chilling finality. "No, he wasn't."

She shook her head to deny it but couldn't voice the words with any confidence. "He's just a boy. Help me."

Thorne handed his firearm over to Cortez. They had killed one outlaw and injured several others, who were now on the run. He didn't know when they would be back. "You and Barkley keep watch, just in case." He went to the table and looked down at Paul Anderson. There was so little chance the boy would make it that he hated to drag the inevitable out, but he saw that Jenny needed to do everything possible for the boy.

He ripped Paul's shirt down the middle and pulled it from his shoulders. Turning the limp body over, he found the bullet had exited out the back. If it hadn't hit his heart or lungs, the boy might survive, but he'd already lost a great deal of blood. "If infection doesn't set in he might live, but I doubt it." He glanced at Jenny. "I hope you don't end up regretting this."

Jenny cleaned the wound and bandaged it, then sat to wait. Waiting took most of the morning, but she was not idle. She bathed the boy's feverish brow and checked the bandages regularly, then read to him from the books he had liked most as a student, the ones he had never learned to read well himself.

Failure sat heavily on Jenny's shoulders, brought home more keenly by the fact that Paul Anderson faced a dead-end road if he survived. A poor student and resentful young man, Paul had never been able to break past the barriers he had erected to protect himself. His abusive home life had been beyond repair, and Jenny had not been able to help him see that he had a future.

She was not naive enough to believe that he had one now, that he would change his ways just because he might be given a second chance. But she tried to be hopeful.

Life was so short. However ill-fated the hand dealt, it needed to be played to the fullest. She laid her head back against the chair, so weary of fighting her own struggles. Her future was horribly uncertain now, her options few, but she would not give up the dreams and plans that had sustained her thus far.

She thought of Jimmy Henderson, that meaningless mistake, and wondered if any good could possibly come out of it. She knew why she'd been so foolish. Uncle Nat's death had left her floundering. She saw Milt and

Hannah day after day, knowing their future happiness lay just around the corner, while her own seemed to be slipping away faster than she could stop it. She needed desperately to find a way to correct what had gone awry in her life, find the path back to her own worthwhile destiny.

Mercedes spelled her from time to time, but Jenny couldn't allow Tildy anywhere near Paul Anderson. Her aunt fully believed they had captured a Yankee; she wanted to torture him for information.

By midafternoon Paul began to come around. Jenny fetched a glass of water and helped him drink, then sat down beside the bed. In her most effective teacher's voice, she asked, "How could you dare raid my ranch?"

He stared back at her, his eyes feverish and hate-filled. "Why didn't you let me die?"

"I might yet," she said, "but I want answers first."

"I ain't got any answers, Teach. You know that better than anyone."

Jenny's heart squeezed painfully.

His eyes flared suddenly, then seemed to retreat behind a vacuous shield of indifference. "I killed Pa," he said. "Never doubt that, Teach, or the fact that I would kill you too to save myself."

She wrung water from a cloth and placed it back on his forehead. "You're in no condition to harm me."

In a flash, he reached over and grabbed her wrist in a hard vise. "No?" he rasped. His fingers tightened cruelly. "I could snap you like a twig."

She gave him a bland look, though her wrist was

throbbing. "You and what army?" she asked. "You're so weak now, you can hardly stay conscious."

His eyes teared up, and Jenny wanted to weep herself for this lost boy and his wasted life. "Go to hell, Teach."

"I'll not tolerate such language in my house, Paul." She didn't allow one ounce of her own pain to show on her face. She would have bruises tomorrow, but that was nothing compared to the inner hurt she felt for this boy. "The sheriff knows you didn't deliberately kill your father. That's why he didn't send a posse out after you."

The boy slung her hand aside and laughed bitterly. "He'll send one as soon as you tell him I'm here."

"I haven't decided what I'm going to do yet."

His eyes flared with a pitiful spark of hope, then dimmed. "Never figured you for a liar, Teach."

She shrugged. "And I never figured you for a fool, Paul."

She knew he was tired, sick to death of life and running. It was etched all over his face, but she also knew he was scared of the grave. It was the only leverage she had to convince him to get better. The essence of him seemed to be fading out in waves of gray, and she didn't know how to keep him fighting. "You have to get better, Paul."

Thorne stood outside the doorway, listening to the exchange. He didn't trust Paul Anderson as far as he could toss him, but he knew the boy was too injured at this point to do much harm. Jenny was up to her old tricks again, trying to help angry young men who didn't want help. This boy wasn't a displaced orphan she found in the cold but an outlaw to the core. His worthless pa had made him that way, and Thorne suspected it was too late for Jenny to reconstruct the boy with kindness and expect it to transform him to any degree of humanity that would stick.

He tucked his hand inside Jeremiah's, then rapped lightly on the door frame. Jenny looked up. Her eyes were tired, her face wan. "I'll sit with him awhile," Thorne said. "Why don't you and Jeremiah go get some sleep."

"But it's daytime!" Jeremiah made a commendable effort to wail out his disagreement but his voice was fuzzy, his eyelids were so heavy he could barely keep his eyes open. "C'mon, Miss Jenny."

She nodded and rose, grateful for the reprieve. "Don't let Aunt Tildy near him," she warned, then glanced back at Paul. "She's not fond of Yankees."

"I ain't no damn Yankee," he said.

"Try and tell that to Aunt Tildy," she returned.

Thorne cocked one eyebrow at the young outlaw. "I don't think Tildy will cause him too much grief. I won't let her anywhere near, unless he refuses to answer my questions."

Paul Anderson stared up at the tall, imposing man. He was in no shape to flee, much less from a person twice his size, but belligerence had been bred into him from the cradle. "I ain't answering nothing."

After opening her arms for Jeremiah, Jenny scooped him up when he stumbled forward. His head immediately went to rest on her shoulder. "I'll only be an hour or so, Ian. Don't torture him until I get back."

"I'll try not to," he commented.

"Promise me."

He wanted to ease the strain on Jenny's face but he wouldn't lie to her. "Can't do that, Miss Jenny."

She stamped her foot, tired to the bone and frustrated by every awful thing going on in her life. "Then I'll stay right here."

"Go," he said gently. "You're dead on your feet." He watched her hesitate, then turn, his son's small head bobbing on her slender shoulder as she made her way down the hall. Jeremiah looked so natural there it twisted his gut. The innate goodness in her was more than his mind could take in. What would happen to his son when they left the ranch to make another life? What would happen to Jenny? He pushed the thought aside to get down to the business at hand. He waited until Jenny disappeared around the corridor, then turned and smiled at Paul Anderson. "We're going to have us a little talk, outlaw."

Moonlight lit the fountain. The water splashed and sparkled like liquid diamonds in the black night. The tangy scent of Thorne's tobacco was the only hint of his presence.

"You move like a cat," Jenny said, then watched as he emerged from the shadows to sit beside her. "Will the other outlaws come back?"

"Not tonight," he said. "We nicked four of them, nothing but a scratch on two, but two others were wounded pretty badly. They'll bury their dead, then rest and regroup before coming at us again."

Jenny put her face in her hands. "What a mess." She had rested long enough to be physically restored, but the emotional toll of the past few days was wearing on her. "Are there more of them?"

"No, just the seven that attacked last night. From what I can gather from the Anderson boy, they have more foolishness than brains and are fairly disorganized." He took a drag on the cigarette and watched smoke curl slowly into the night sky. "We sure don't need for them to join up with someone smarter, though."

"Is that likely?"

"It's hard to tell. They'll be licking their wounds for a week or so, but I wouldn't count out the possibility in the future."

Jenny sighed and stirred the fountain. The stones still held some of the day's heat but the fresh water was chilly. "Do you think Paul is reformable?"

"Why?"

She shrugged, knowing Thorne wouldn't like the idea. "I just wondered, if I put him to work—hard, honest work with a decent wage—if he would prove trustworthy or if he would betray me."

"I don't think you can take that chance, Jenny."

"I don't want to fail him twice," she whispered.

"Jenny," he warned.

"No, listen. No one knows he rides with that gang. If he were to go to work here, prove himself, the town would eventually forgive and forget."

"They'll try him for his father's murder."

"They can't prove anything. Besides, I know he didn't do it."

Thorne threw up his hands in disgust. "Even the boy doesn't claim that. How can you know?"

"I just do." She shook her heard, grieved. "You didn't know him like I did, Ian. You didn't see him day after day, struggling to be a proper student on little food or sleep, wearing threadbare clothes that were either too large or too small, always bruised from his father's fist."

"I saw him plenty," Thorne said. "I saw him steal anything he could get his hands on when he thought no one was looking. That was the problem, Jenny. Everyone felt so sorry for him that they pretended they didn't see. They kept looking the other way until he got bigger and tougher, old enough to know better."

"Then they turned on him," she accused.

"No, they just quit making excuses for him."

"I don't see it that way," she said.

He knew she didn't. That's why he wanted her for Jeremiah's mother. It had become so clear to him over the past few days. She would raise his son right, defend him to the death, and love him without reserve. Conventional good sense didn't have a chance when Jenny did things from the heart. Although wisdom was essential in raising children, Thorne would take her generous heart any day as the perfect complement.

And the fact that as his wife she would share his bed made the idea just that much easier. Now, if he could only convince her that a union between them would benefit them both. He knew his offer had been abrupt, not the sort of thing a passionate woman like Jenny would take to heart. Perhaps if he courted her like the suitor she deserved, pressed the physical advantage that lay sleeping within her, he could get her to see things his way. She didn't love him, but she desired him.

Moonlight wound like silver streamers through the wisps of hair around her face. Her long braid hung down her back, tied at the end with a girlish pink ribbon. Thorne picked up the heavy rope of her hair and pulled the ribbon free. The braid fell apart in his hands, a silky cascade of fragrance.

Jenny immediately pulled back. "What are you doing?"

"Playing with your hair," he admitted. He pulled it back into his hands, ran his fingers through the long tresses. "You have the most beautiful hair."

Jenny's heart leapt strangely. "Have you lost your mind, Ian?"

"Thorne," he whispered, bringing her hair to his face. He inhaled her scent, allowed the deep auburn mass to spill through his fingers. "Let me brush it for you."

"No." She snatched her hair back, discombobulated. "What's gotten into you?"

He took her chin, tipped her face up. "You."

"Oh, no—" she began before his mouth descended on hers.

The kiss was short, sweet, horribly unfulfilling.

"Ian—"

"I know," he said gently. "You're in love with Milton."

Milt was a foolish, impossible dream and one that had never seemed so far away as now, when all her senses were taken up with this one man and the seduction of his soft words, the tenderness of his kiss.

Thorne laid his hand on her chest, just above her left

breast. "Does your heart beat like this when Milton kisses you?"

Her heart was running away with her. "He doesn't kiss me."

His hand slid lower. "But if he did, would you feel like this? So flushed and unsteady and wanting?"

With a will of its own, her body lost composure and leaned into him. "Ian, don't." She moaned.

His lips whispered over hers, "Don't what, Jenny? Don't make you feel this way?"

Hot. She was so hot inside he must feel it through her clothing. "Don't do this," she begged. She took his wrist, tugged on his arm, then almost cried out when his fingers curled in, touching her intimately.

His hand slid away. "All right, I won't," he said, "if you'll let me brush your hair."

He was making her insane. "Fine, brush my hair," she said, breathless and aching.

He left her for less than a minute as he retrieved a hairbrush from the dresser in her room. She was still in the same, semisuspended position when he returned. He sat beside her, then turned her slightly and began to stroke her hair in long, idle sweeps.

The attention felt heavenly. That something so simple could bring such exquisite relaxation was amazing to Jenny. "Will you do this every night?" she whispered.

"Only if you marry me."

"Darn."

"I know a lot of other things that feel even better," he said.

The dark teasing in his voice beckoned her, an odd

reaction in the deepest parts of her body. "Ian," she returned, her voice sounding tortured. "I need you. The ranch needs you. Don't make me fire you."

He brought the brush down slowly through her long hair. "Do what you have to, Jenny, but do it quickly. I've already warned you I won't fight fair."

"But I can't afford to lose you."

He laid the brush on the rim of the fountain, then began kneading her neck and shoulders. His fingers were strong and deft, and the stiff tension in her body began to melt away at his touch.

"Why are you being so stubborn?" he asked. "Do you think a knight in shining armor will come along and sweep you off your feet?"

"Maybe," she said defensively. Out West where it was miles between ranches and days between towns, a woman was fortunate just to find a mate she liked. Being choosy was for city girls with greater prospects.

His hand drifted around her rib cage and gathered her intimately against him. "How do you know we're not in love?" he asked against her ear.

"We're *in heat*," she argued, squirming to get loose before she melted into a boneless puddle at his feet. She turned suddenly and took his hands, holding them tightly. "And it's indecent," she added, distressed. "It makes me feel wanton and guilty."

"You didn't feel that way the other day."

She looked down. "I've had time to compose myself."

He threw up his arms in surrender. "Fine. Hands off, for now."

She searched his face for hidden emotion. "Don't you want the same thing?" she asked. "Don't you want to find someone you're truly in love with, someone who moves you, who makes each day worthwhile?"

He crossed his feet at the ankles and leaned against the rim of the fountain. "I don't believe that exists, Jenny. Or at least it doesn't last."

She felt a deep sadness inside her. He had spoken with such cold finality. "It does exist," she said. "It has to."

He laughed sharply. "For poets and fools, maybe, and sentimentalists who don't know the difference."

His tone made her ire rise, and she hit home with the one thing he couldn't deny. "What about Jeremiah? Isn't that love?"

He looked at her, his eyes as fathomless as the darkness. "I've already told you. What I feel for Jeremiah is the only real love. And it's more than mere words or collections of rhyme. The love of a child has complexity, depth, and dimension. It can't be described or contained by something so simple as words."

"But you can't feel that way for a woman," she accused sarcastically. "That's ridiculous."

"It's not possible," he agreed with pure conviction. "I've already tried it."

Frustrated, Jenny turned to face him. "You're talking about Jeremiah's mother."

"Yes."

"Did you love her at one time?"

"Yes. Very much, or so I thought, but it didn't last, Jenny."

His words hurt her. What had this woman done to him, this woman he had loved so much that the absence of it soured him on the emotion? "What about your parents? Don't you remember—"

"They were so civil to each other. Going through the polite motions of a married couple. After my mother's fifth miscarriage, they never shared a bed again."

Shocked, Jenny's chin dropped. "How do you know that?"

"Servants talk, little boys listen."

"But—"

"Marry me, Jenny." He reached over and threaded his fingers through the hair at her temples. His thumbs stroked her cheeks. "Marry me and be Jeremiah's mother. Don't fill your mind with the rest."

She was tired, so frightened of the future. Milt would be Hannah's husband forever in only a few weeks. There was no reason beyond the obvious not to marry Thorne, but even worse than that, she knew she couldn't bear to lose Jeremiah. Stubbornly she refused to acknowledge the odd stirrings in her heart whenever Thorne kissed her, the clamorous way her body reacted when he touched her. Even more confusing, the serenity and contentment when she heard his voice, when he spoke to her as a friend, an equal.

"A marriage of convenience?" she asked.

He took a deep breath. "No. Not the way you mean."

She didn't like the idea of the marriage being so

"convenient" for him while lacking what she wanted most in marriage. "What if I won't agree to anything else?"

"If that's the way it has to be." He shrugged. "I can manage it for a time."

She looked away, embarrassed. "How long a time?"

"Until you're ready."

How would she know that? She couldn't actually see herself approaching Thorne to inform him that she wanted to follow through with the lurid thoughts that entered her head often. "What if I never am?"

He gave a visible shrug that meant nothing and everything. "You want children, don't you?"

She looked up, hope in her eyes. "I . . . yes."

His fingers followed the silky curls over her shoulder and down her arm. "There's only one way to accomplish that, Jenny."

She felt as if her insides were melting. "All right, I'll marry you for Jeremiah and the sake of the ranch."

His hand slid over hers, lacing their fingers. "And for future children."

She gazed off into the distance, into a future that stretched as far as the vast, desolate land surrounding them. There lay destruction and hope, hope as big as the mountains.

Her chest felt tight, every cell in her body alive. "Later. Maybe."

He leaned in until his lips brushed hers, the merest breath, the most tempting promise. "Sooner than later."

"I don't—"

His lips brushed hers again, absorbing the words,

carrying them away to her cheek, then down the side of her neck. His fingers flexed on hers, tightening until it was almost painful. Suddenly he released her and backed away with a strained laugh.

"I have a feeling that this is going to prove to be a most *in*convenient marriage."

Chapter 14

Everyone had gathered in town for a social event, but instead of the normal exchange of pleasantries, the men were mingling with Lucy's painted women, while Hannah laughed flirtatiously with every man who passed by. It was a ghastly performance of unfaithfulness and perversion. Wives stood off to the side, quilting and baking and gossiping, seemingly unaware of their husbands' infidelity, while the men boldly caressed the misguided women.

The dream made no sense whatsoever, but it was vivid and hurtful to the girl who watched from the lantern-lit edges of a wooden platform. The girl was Jenny but a younger version, more insecure. She awaited her turn patiently, her chance to be spun like a ballerina across the sawdust-covered dance floor by a dashing gentleman.

The turn never came. Time and again she was passed over, even when she found the courage to smile and wave, even when she called out Milt's name, then Thorne's, in the hopes that one of them would notice her solitude and ask for a place on her card. But the card, an overlarge scroll that dangled from her wrist by a ribbon, remained empty for all the town to see.

Hannah smiled and everyone turned. She danced first with Milt, then Thorne, then Jimmy, her face ethereal in the golden glow. Amid whimsical laughter, she spun across the floor, every turn revealing the face of a different partner vying for her attention. Then Lucy strolled by with a string of her ladies, their clothing and makeup so garish it seemed that every spark of light was captured on their faces. She glared at Jenny, gloating, as if she knew the secrets to claiming manhood and would not share them with a shy girl.

The school board and members of the town council stood off to the side, unconcerned by what was transpiring before their eyes. They nodded cordially at Hannah and Lucy, but their eyes held only censure for Jennifer Delaney, the spinster who couldn't lure a man.

Jenny moved closer to the throng and tried to talk to her friends, to join in the dance, but the men ignored her, almost trampling her in their indifference. She called to them again but they only smiled, a mocking smile without warmth or sincerity. Then Paul Anderson appeared in a blood-soaked shirt, a cruel twist to his lips, and dragged her onto the dance floor.

The town turned away.

"Wait," she called. "Wait! I am engaged to be married."

They all laughed and kept their backs turned.

"Ian, tell them," she called. "Tell them we are engaged!"

Jenny awoke suddenly. Sweat drenched the bed sheets that tangled around her legs like a trap. She kicked free and sat up, pushing her damp hair out of her eyes. The music still played in her mind, a haunting refrain that seemed to echo her discontent.

She was exhausted, irritated, and confused. Why should she care if Thorne and Milt danced with Hannah or Lucy's girls while she withered and faded into the background? She crawled from the bed and splashed her face with cold water, trying to shrug off the fogginess in her brain and the lingering loneliness in her heart.

It was just a dream. She was not that pitiable girl standing alone in a room full of people, unnoticed and unloved. She had friends and family members who were as devoted to her as she was to them. She'd had two offers of marriage. Though neither one had been overly serious or based on undying affection, she could still claim two.

She sat back on the side of her bed and dropped her chin in her hands. Paul Anderson, lying between life and death in her guest room, had quit school and joined up with a Comanchero gang that had tried to steal her horses. The school board was bringing in a new teacher.

Thorne had kissed her and asked her to marry him, yet Milt—the man she loved—didn't know she was alive.

She could hardly believe the bizarre turn her life had taken. Her senseless dreams were nothing compared to the confusion of her real life.

Dressing with care, she donned a brown skirt, white blouse, and leather vest. A well-worn Stetson covered her hair and would keep the sun out of her face on her trip to town. She needed to talk to Milt, to find out what Paul Anderson's chances were if he went to trial for murder. And she had to do it in a way that would not arouse suspicion.

Mercedes met her at the breakfast table with a disapproving glare. "After the night we have had, señorita, you are thinking of going off to town alone?" She looked up when Thorne entered the kitchen and met him with the same uncompromising stare. "Tell her, Señor Thorne. Tell her she must not do it."

"Must not do what?" he asked.

Jenny looked up and their eyes met. Something passed between them, awareness or challenge, something that had not been there before last night. She curled her fingers in to keep from pressing them to her lips, shying from the memory of his words and touch. Disconcerted, she looked away.

"Tell Mercedes," Jenny said, "that I will be fine. That the bad men have run off to lick their wounds and they certainly have not gone in the direction of town."

Thorne looked at both women in turn, then shook his head and sat down at the table. There was a faint blush on Jenny's cheeks, an odd reserve. "Why do you need to go to town?"

"To inform Milt about the outlaws."

"Ah, Milt." A little of stab of jealousy hit him, completely uncalled for but there nonetheless. It made him irritable. "You can inform him of our . . . other news as well."

Jenny's head jerked up. "Me?"

He gave her a cool look. "Who better?"

Who better indeed? She closed her eyes briefly to block out his stare. She felt guilty and oddly unsteady. Things were moving too fast but she didn't know how to stop them, or even if she should.

Mercedes set down a fresh cup of coffee with a grumble. "Tell her not to go, Señor Thorne. It is too dangerous."

Thorne touched Jenny's hand, forced her to look at him. "Is it too dangerous, Jenny?"

She shook her head silently, adamantly.

He rose from the table, as cold and forbidding a man as she had ever seen. His coffee sat untouched. "I have work to do."

Jeremiah skidded into the kitchen, still in his nightclothes. He scrambled up into Jenny's lap. "Let me go with you, please."

Jenny took his face in her hands and gave him a big kiss on the nose. "How do you know where I'm going?"

"I heard you say town. Let me go."

She glanced at Thorne, then away. "Not today. But I'll bring you back a candy stick. All right?"

"I won't be in the way," he pleaded.

Her heart melted. "I know you won't, honey, but I have business to tend to and you would get bored and restless and very tired."

"But, please—"

"Jeremiah, enough!" Thorne's sharp voice surprised them all.

Jeremiah's bottom lip trembled. Jenny hugged him tighter and sent Thorne a hurt look. His eyes were cold, remote, his body tense. She wondered if it was merely the obvious trauma of the past night or if it was her. Did he discover after a night of rest that their decision to marry had been made in haste and out of exhaustion? Worse, did he regret it?

She could read nothing in his eyes but a strange hardness. Her spine stiffened and her heart closed off in self-protection.

Aunt Tildy rushed into the kitchen, looking frazzled. Her nightcap was askew and there were dark circles under her eyes. "Do you know that Yankee is still alive?"

Jenny tore her gaze from Thorne's. "He's not a Yankee," she said tiredly. "He's an outlaw." She winced at her own words, then smiled softly. "Aunt Tildy, I would never let a Yankee within a hundred yards of you."

"Then who is that boy lying shot in the guest bedroom?"

Mercedes brought Tildy a cup of coffee. "Tell her, señora. Tell the señorita she should not ride into town with outlaws about."

Jenny groaned and put Jeremiah in his own chair, then turned to her aunt. She didn't need this after the night she'd had. "Do you remember Paul Anderson? He was one of my students."

"Not the son of that no-good drunkard by the same name!" Tildy said, aghast. "Trash, nothing but trash."

"The very same."

"Oh, my. We don't serve his kind in the house, dear. Your mother will have a fit when she hears of it."

Jenny suppressed a groan. Her nerves were fraying, and she didn't know how much longer she could hold her patience together. "Think of him as a guest, Aunt Tildy, a lost soul in need of missionary kindness. He was my student. I can't just abandon him." She rose from the table and straightened her aunt's nightcap. "At this point he's not dangerous because he's wounded. I don't know what he'll do when he's well. You should probably stay away from him."

Matilda Darineau got that faraway look in her eyes, the belle of the ball, the gracious Southern lady. "But we've a duty," she argued. "A Delaney does not ignore guests."

Jenny closed her eyes briefly. "Just promise me you'll be careful."

Tildy rose with a purpose and piled a plate high with eggs, bacon, and biscuits. "I think I'll go see if I can get him to eat."

Jenny hesitated, then decided it wouldn't hurt to have her aunt mother Paul a bit. *Watch her,* she mouthed to Mercedes, then added aloud, "I'll be back before noon."

Mercedes shook her head. She sent Thorne one last reproving look for not interfering, then wiped her hands on her apron and picked up Jeremiah. "Come with me, *niño*, where you will be safe. Everyone else in this family *es muy loco*."

Jenny had not been back to town since the school board hearing. The ride out would have been more pleasant if the past night had not taken its toll and her mission had not been so distressing. She returned Deputy Sheriff Walt Henry's overzealous wave from the rocking chair in front of the general store and marched straight to the sheriff's office. Milt was poring through a stack of newly arrived wanted posters. Jenny's heart squeezed a little as she studied him in silence for a few seconds before making her presence known.

He was a handsome man, and a good one. Hannah could do worse. Her friend had devoted years to the task of becoming a proficient wife and mother. Hannah was perfect for Milt and would make him a good helpmate. Even knowing this Jenny couldn't stop the envy from constricting her chest. She had loved Milt so long, she didn't know how to stop, even when she knew Hannah was the better choice.

She cleared her throat. "Good morning, Sheriff."

Milt looked up and smiled, rising instantly to his feet. "Mornin', Miss Jenny. What can I do for you?"

"Sit," she said, waving him back down. "I need to ask a question in confidence and I need your word that this conversation won't go any farther."

His expression darkened. "You in some kind of bind, Jenny? You know I'll do whatever—"

"No," she interrupted. "It's not me. I need some advice about the law."

Milt laughed lightly. "Best take your questions to Harley Cranberry over at the law office."

Jenny shook her head. "He'll charge too much for his time. Besides, this is a question for the law, not lawyers."

Milt propped one hip on the side of his desk. "Shoot," he said.

"If Paul Anderson were to show up in Little Town, would he be arrested for the murder of his pa?"

Milt rose at once and approached her. "Do you know the whereabouts of that boy?"

Jenny smiled, guileless and beguiling. "It's just a question, Milt. I got to thinking about it after the school board hearing. What would the law do if Paul showed back up here?"

"Bring him in for questioning, that's a given. As far as the other goes—" He shrugged, then walked over to a cabinet. After pulling out the written report on Paul senior's death, he scanned the page quickly. "That would be up to the sensibilities of the town, I imagine. I don't have enough evidence for a judge to convict him right off, but public outcry might demand a trial."

Jenny nodded. "Thanks, Milt. Give my love to Hannah."

"Hey, wait." He came around the desk and looked down at Jenny in a manner so tender it made her heart hurt. "How are you? We haven't seen you since the school board fiasco. The town's in a snit. They're ready to string Haynes up by his ears and his cronies with him."

"Good," she said, then felt a bit guilty for having the sentiment. "When does Miss Walker arrive?"

"Another week or so. Travel is unpredictable."

Jenny nodded, resigned. In another week a teacher would be here to take her job; in another month her best friend would marry the man she loved. Her ranch had just been attacked by outlaws and her best horse stolen. She looked up and smiled wryly. "You know, Milt, I'm really not having a very good summer."

Milt nodded in concern. "Don't worry about Miss Walker, not yet."

"Actually, I'm not," Jenny admitted. "I've got too much else to worry about right now." She pulled a sheet of paper from her reticule and placed it on his desk. "I almost forgot this. Here's a list of names and descriptions. We were hit by Comancheros last night." She lifted her hand when Milt lunged for his gun belt and hat. "No one was hurt at my place, and I don't think they made off with much." She smiled sadly. "But they did get Bulle and she's due to foal anytime."

"Foal? But it's not—"

"It's possible," she ground out.

"I'm sorry, Jenny. As soon as Walt Henry gets back from the general store, I'll follow you to the ranch and look things over."

Jenny shook her head. "No need. Barkley and the

others got a few good shots off, so you might have the doc be on the alert for late-night visits from strangers, even though I don't think they would dare come near town." She pulled her riding gloves back on. "Give my love to Hannah."

"You've got that boy at the ranch."

Jenny's face paled. "I don't know what you're talking about."

Milt shook his head. "You're like an open book, Jenny. Your face mirrors every emotion. I knew something was up the moment you walked in. My guess is he got himself injured and you haven't decided what to do about him."

Jenny blew out the breath she was holding. "He's just a boy, Milt."

"Yeah, one that tried to make off with your stock."

"I'd never testify to that," she warned.

Milt sighed in vexation. "I'll come out, get some information from him, then see if I can track down the others."

"I won't let you hang him, Milt."

He smiled sadly. "I hope you won't regret it, Jenny."

She looked away. He had that tender, concerned look in his eyes that always turned her insides to mush. "I won't, Milt."

"Hannah and I are having lunch over at the café in about an hour. Why don't you join us?"

She dared to look back up, to absorb every feature of a face that would never belong to her. "I have to get back to the ranch, but thanks anyway."

"How bad is he hurt?"

"Bad," she whispered, "real bad."

Jenny was well aware that she had only until Sunday to figure something out. By the time the church service started, everyone in town would know from Aunt Tildy that Paul had been her "guest" for the week, and they would demand some type of action on the sheriff's part.

"I'll see you later," she said.

"I'll try to get by this afternoon to question him."

"If he's up to it."

Jenny stopped in at the general store to pick up a few supplies and Jeremiah's candy. Wolf was rolling a huge pickle barrel down the aisle.

"Good morning, Wolf."

He looked up with a start, then smiled. "If you had been an Apache, Miss Jenny, I would be scalped just now."

"I didn't mean to startle you," she apologized.

He shook his head. "I just had my mind on other things. Come sit, I have fresh coffee."

"No, I mustn't tarry. I just wanted to stop by and say hello."

" 'Hello' you can say in a wave from the street." His gaze was warm but knowing. "So, Miss Jenny. What is the news this day?"

She plopped down on an overturned wash tub and sighed. "Bad news," she said.

She was just about to regale Wolf with the story about the Comancheros when Walt Henry came through the door. "Hey, Wolf, is Miss Jenny still—" He stopped and grinned, almost tripping over her. "I guess you are." He stuck out an envelope. "This just came by mail. I told Clarence I thought you was still in town."

Jenny took the letter. "Thanks, Walt Henry." She opened it to find another request from the army for thirty more saddle-broke horses. Her uncle had negotiated yearly with the army, and the added contract was a relief. She slipped the letter into her purse. "Good day, gentlemen."

Walt Henry's jaw dropped. "But it looks so official. Ain't you gonna tell us what's in it?"

Wolf slapped at Walt Henry with the tail of his apron. "None of your business. You are as nosy as a spinster in a—" He flushed dull red. "Sorry, Miss Jenny."

"No offense taken," she lied, then marched out.

Pique put a nasty taste in her mouth. Spinster, indeed! She pursed her lips, but instead of heading for her horse, she headed straight for the café where she found Hannah sipping tea.

"Jennifer!" Hannah stood, embracing her friend in a fierce hug. The faintest hint of rosewater filled the air like a refreshing breeze. Hannah's gown was starched white cotton with delicate embroidery around the hem and sash. As usual, she looked fresh as springtime.

Jenny glanced down at her own dull, travel-dusty attire and refused to wonder for the hundredth time how her friend managed to stay so spotless. Her own boring garments were serviceable but fashionless.

"Hello, Hannah," she said warmly. "I've missed you."

She meant every word. The two met for tea every

afternoon after school let out to catch up on the day's happenings, but the ritual stopped when the term was over. Jenny's stomach made a strange drop as she took her friend's hands in her own.

"I have news, Hannah, and I wanted you to be the first to know."

Wide-eyed, Hannah leaned in. "What is it, Jennifer?"

Jenny took a deep, fortifying breath. "I'm going to be married."

It took Hannah a moment to formulate the words, then her face lit up. "Oh, Jennifer," she breathed, "is it that handsome Mr. Thorne? Tell me it is."

Jenny smiled, ridiculously relieved and gratified by Hannah's reaction. "Yes. I've agreed to marry Ian Thorne."

"Oh, Jennifer!" With genuine glee, Hannah flew around the table and wrapped her friend up in a joyful hug. "I'm so happy for you! When? Have you set a date?"

The tears in Jenny's eyes had nothing to do with happiness but Hannah wouldn't know that. She nodded, her mind racing at her friend's eagerness and joy. "We've decided on . . . next week."

Hannah reared back. "Next week!" she cried bluntly. "Have you lost your mind, Jennifer? We can't plan a wedding in a week!"

Jenny's face paled. "I . . . we aren't going to plan anything elaborate. Just a small ceremony."

Hannah dropped her face into her hands. "Forgive me, Jennifer, I forgot that you are still in mourning for your uncle." She looked up. "What a thoughtless nincompoop I am. Say you forgive me."

"Of course," Jenny responded, relieved she hadn't had to come up with a plausible excuse for having such a quick, simple wedding. "Do you think the town will understand?"

Hannah patted her hand. "Of course," she said sincerely, then charged straight ahead without warning. "Now, let's put our heads together. A simple wedding on short notice is a wedding nonetheless and no excuse for shortchanging the most important day of your life."

For the next hour Jenny's mind reeled in terror as Hannah planned out every detail of a hasty marriage with the most exquisite proficiency Jenny had ever witnessed. If she had been uncertain about her commitment or Thorne's when she walked into the café, she was convinced when she walked out. There was going to be a wedding in a week, and, with Hannah Thompson in charge, there was no turning back for either of them. By the end of the hour Jenny understood that all she and Thorne had to do was show up in appropriate attire with a license.

Still dizzy from the impact, she left before Milt showed up for lunch. She couldn't bear sitting across from him and having to listen to his congratulations and well-wishes for her future. There was a sinking hole in her chest where her heart should have been, and it felt unbearably hollow and achy.

• • •

The clouds were lowering when she reached the ranch. They had been swelling all day and the sky didn't bode well for the evening ahead. Jenny bypassed the house and rode straight for the pasture. She would need to help Thorne get the horses in before the storm hit, or they'd risk losing too many if lightning panicked them.

The wind tore at her hat and sent it sailing across the pasture. She leaned into the bluster and forged ahead. Lightning had begun in the distance, a stunning display of nature's brilliance, if all one needed to do was watch from the safety of a cozy fire. Jenny didn't have that luxury, however. If the horses spooked, they could stampede, carrying the herd away from safety in a death frenzy. It could take days to round up the strays.

With the added army contract, she couldn't afford to lose a single horse. Using the dogs, Barkley worked to close into the corral the semitame mustangs they had already gathered for the original contract. Cortez was rounding up Thoroughbreds, while Thorne had ridden farther afield to steer the grazing quarter horses toward a walled-off canyon where they would be hemmed in and protected from the worst of the storm.

Jenny rode out to help him. He was working without the advantage of gate or fence, and the spooked horses were fractious and uncooperative. She signaled Thorne, then circled out, and they began to work the horses toward a canyon pass, moving them in an ever-tightening group to the opening. When the lead horses began to enter, the others followed more peaceably.

Rain had begun to fall, a moderate downpour less threatening than the bold streaks of lightning followed by deafening thunder. Thorne rode up and leaned into Jenny to be heard over the roar. "I've got to go see to my own horses," he yelled. "Get back to the ranch before the rain begins in earnest."

"No!" she called back. "You can't do it by yourself! I'll help."

He grabbed the reins of her horse to keep her from riding off. The wind tore at them both, snatching their words into oblivion. "The valley is safe enough," he called, "I just need to check for strays."

She knew it would be twice as hard if he tried to manage it on his own. The rain was coming in from the east so they still had a little time to attempt to get over to his valley before the worst of it overtook them—if they didn't sit around arguing. She pulled on the reins, then turned her horse sharply west. "Giddy-up," she called.

Thorne followed, both angry at Jenny's stubbornness and grateful for the help. It was unlikely they could reach the valley in time to do much good, but he had to try to get the horses to higher ground in case a gully-washer swept down from the higher reaches.

They made decent time with the wind at their backs, but the downpour had begun to overtake them by the time the horses came into view. Most had moved to higher ground but a few stragglers had become confused by the lightning repeatedly illuminating the sky. Thorne rode toward the skittish horses, while Jenny tried to decide which paths would be the most dangerous should they bolt. She rode near the most obvious in an attempt to steer any stragglers away.

The rain thickened, coming down in stinging sheets,

blinding in its intensity and chilling to the bone. Her clothing was drenched through and a sense of foreboding began to creep in with the frigid chill. A murky darkness rode in with the downpour and covered the land in dangerous, depthless shadows that would make riding safely impossible. When she could no longer see Thorne clearly or even make sense of her surroundings, Jenny slid to the ground and began to lead her horse toward a rock overhang that she hoped would offer better protection.

Beyond the storm it might have been daylight, but here darkness had fallen with a vengeance in colorless tones of black and gray. Shadows lengthened and merged to reveal a gaping hole in the canyon wall, a cave with an opening large enough to lead the horse into. Jenny ran her hand along the rock wall, feeling her way with hands and feet to determine the solidity of her surroundings. There was nothing but darkness and a deeper absence of color that warned of plunging depths in the land.

She tethered the horse by looping the reins over a large rock and crept back to the opening, then crouched under the overhang and waited for lightning to strike and reveal her situation. With the first illumination, she saw Thorne struggling against the wind in the descending gloom. He seemed to have done all he could for the horses and was searching out a shelter.

Calling out would be useless. The wind tore at her, stealing breath and words before they were even formed. The hat protecting her face was gone, lost somewhere on the ride out. Her hair hung in a sodden braid down her back, while loose tendrils clung to her lips and cheeks. Her teeth were chattering violently against the cold.

Another flash of lightning exposed Thorne headed straight for her. She scrambled to her feet and called to him, hoping the wind would not confuse the sound. There was little chance that he could hear her but she screamed anyway, as if the intent alone could propel him forward.

He made steady progress, each lightning bolt bringing him eerily closer, though not in any manner familiar to Jenny. Blocks of space at a time, he appeared, like some nightmarish phantom who floated in nearing snatches of light and night. Suddenly he was upon her, climbing up onto the ledge, dragging his horse with him.

Jenny grabbed his shoulder to make her presence known and he jerked suddenly, then shouted something lost on the wind and pulled her under his arm, as if relieved to find her safe. He led his horse over to shelter next to Jenny's, then drew her deeper beneath the overhang and into the darkness. Black and a chilling cold surrounded her, but the force of the wind faded and the roar of thunder gave way to a distant echo, then finally to silence.

Jenny clung to Thorne. She had no idea where she was or what lay ahead. He moved with cautious confidence, a man familiar with his environment but uncertain in the sunless storm. He had obviously been to the cave before, but still he had to move in slow, careful inches. They finally moved deep enough in that Jenny could no longer feel the buffeting wind or drenching rain.

Shivering, she stopped and breathed a sigh of relief.

She hadn't realized just how tired and scared she was until that moment. But relief became the new enemy, replacing the driving force of fear. Once safe, she began to feel the cold in earnest and the grueling exhaustion that stripped the strength from her bones.

"Ian?" she called.

"Here," he returned. He fumbled with a match, swearing when it flickered, then died. He knelt down and swept the floor for dry litter, finding straw and old bedding in a crevice. Striking another match, he touched it to the moldy hay and made a small torch to illuminate the dwelling long enough to locate his supplies.

On a ledge three feet away, he took down a lantern and lit it, then pulled down a large, bulky pack. Inside were several cans of beans, hardtack, beef jerky, and a tin of biscuits. He took down a bedroll and spread it out for Jenny.

She was still standing in the same frozen position, shivering from head to toe. "Here." He moved toward her, casting light in wavering shadows along the walls. He took her arm, then led her over to the blankets. She moved like a wooden doll, all stiff limbs and jerky movements. He put the lantern on a ledge, then set about rubbing her arms with brisk motions.

"You have to get out of these wet clothes, Jenny," he warned, then prepared himself for a battle she would lose.

Instead, she shocked him by nodding. "You too."

He smiled, a decidedly wolfish twist to his lips. "Ah,

you planned this and I didn't even know I was being lured."

Her body quaking, she nodded. "Yes, I command storms to my advantage." Her smile weakened, then changed suddenly to a fixed expression of fear. She grabbed onto his arms when a roar sounded outside. Water suddenly gushed down the rock canyon past the outside of the cave. Illuminated by the lightning, the mud slide was a violent display of elemental fury that would have killed Thorne and his horse had he not made it inside only moments before. Jenny gripped him tighter. Her teeth were chattering uncontrollably and she felt as if she would be ill. "Did . . . you know?"

He nodded, his features hollowed and sharpened in the flickering light of the torch. "I knew the possibility was there. I've been in this canyon before during a gullywasher. I lost half a dozen horses last spring."

She shivered again, a combination of fear and cold and regret. "You could have died."

He began to unfasten the buttons on her vest. "You need to get dry, Jenny." He slid the vest from her shoulders, then pulled her hair to the side and wrung the water from her braid. Reaching beside her, he picked up a blanket. When she went to grab for it, he jerked it back out of reach. "It needs to stay dry," he explained. "Get out of everything wet, even your undergarments if they are soaked, then I'll give you the blanket."

"Turn around," she said between shivers, but she was already unbuttoning her blouse before he had rotated fully. She peeled off her outer garments but hesitated when she reached her skivvies.

"Everything," he emphasized, as if sensing her dilemma.

She shucked her clothes before embarrassment got the better of her, then reached around him for the blanket.

It took every ounce of control within Thorne not to turn.

Chapter 15

THE LANTERN GAVE OFF HEAT AND LIGHT. JENNY huddled near it, extending her hands to capture every ounce of warmth possible. The blanket was scratchy against her bare skin but it was dry, and that counted more than buckets of pure gold at the moment. Thorne sat beside her, staring fixedly at the leaping lantern flame. He had stripped off his wet clothing as well and had a blanket wrapped around his waist. His upper torso was bare, and Jenny's gaze kept roaming back to the superb width of his shoulders, the trim corded muscles of his belly.

He didn't seem to feel the cold, and any sense of modesty appeared nonexistent. Where Jenny was decidedly uncomfortable with her present state of undress, Thorne seemed perfectly untroubled. As easy as you please, he had begun to strip off his wet garments without warning, forcing Jenny to turn away hastily lest she see more than was proper or necessary. The intimacy of it had nearly driven her into a fit of apoplexy. He had laughed when she mentioned it, so unconcerned in fact that he had made her feel foolish.

The glow from the lantern made dancing patterns on the cave wall. Jenny turned toward Thorne and watched the play of light and shadow on his face. Such a handsome face, rugged yet noble. It suited the varied and complex existence he had led. Plantation gentleman, Comanche brave, rancher. Each had left its mark. "How long will we be here?" she asked.

"I won't know until daylight."

His voice was cold, a bit remote. She wished he would move closer to her and help ward off the prevailing chill in the cave. She went back to studying the flame and casting sideways glances at his musculature. His shoulders were broad, his body lean. There was no excess, yet he was strong and finely built. So appealing, it was hard to tear her gaze away.

She pulled her blanket more firmly around her. Exhaustion had begun to creep in, and she was feeling touchy and out of sorts. "We're getting married next week."

His gaze cut sharply to her. "Oh?"

"I told Hannah when I rode into town. The whole universe will know by tomorrow."

Heat slid over Thorne, making the darkened cavern seem too warm, too confining. He was trying to maintain his distance but it was all he could do not to reach for her. He had found himself covertly watching her, savoring the rain-dampened mass of her hair, the way her profile glowed in the meager light, the graceful curve of her neck and the unconscious seduction of her soft lips. Just as the storm raged without, he could feel the violence within, sensations and needs that pushed against his control.

They were an engaged couple alone in the dark with only a blanket to cover their nakedness. He couldn't have planned a better seduction, except for one small complication. The bride-to-be was not enamored of the groom and already skittish of any advance.

"Want to play Adam and Eve?" he asked.

It took Jenny a moment for the insinuation to seep in past her tired mind. Shocked, she laughed, dropping her forehead to her knees. "The Garden of Eden was never this cold or dark."

"I can warm up paradise."

She shook her head. "You're an evil man, Ian Thorne."

Aye, and a horny one, but he didn't think she'd take kindly to that announcement. "Not too evil," he said. "A bit . . . hungry, perhaps."

Hungry. Was that the appropriate term for what she was feeling as well? The intimate quiet, the muted candlelight, the feel of dry wool against her sensitive flesh. Thorne. All elements seemed combined to establish a restlessness inside her, a deep energy and dissatisfaction in juxtaposition with her tired body.

She peeked at him beneath half-lowered lashes. "There's food in the pack."

He gave a wry smile. "Food won't do it."

She almost asked what would but didn't dare. She felt edgy and too vulnerable. Jenny was glad Thorne was with her here in this dark, dank place. He made her feel safe and protected on one level but wholly threatened on another. She knew better than to allow the teasing to go too far. She sensed he was holding back some part of himself with iron restraint. She lost herself again in the swaying dance of the lantern flame.

"It's so cold."

That was all it took. He scooted over until his shoulder bumped hers. "We're both naked beneath these blankets, Jenny. Doesn't that make you just a little curious?"

"About what?" she returned without thought, then blushed. "I mean no."

"About what's beneath. About our differences."

"No!" The word was adamant, as it should be, but her heartbeat had picked up a funny rhythm.

He nudged her. "Not even a little curious?"

It made her a lot curious. She pressed her face into her knees and let the warmth of her own breath keep the chill at bay on her cold cheeks. "Not even a little," she lied.

"Do you remember when I was ten?" Thorne continued. "You would have been . . ."

"Five. And, no, I don't remember the incident you're going to bring up and embarrass me beyond redemption."

His laugh was quiet, a deep rumble in his chest that sent fresh chills along her arms. "Show me your John Thomas and—"

"Hush, Ian."

"I'll show you my . . . what were you going to show me that day?"

Her face was burning. "I wasn't talking about *that*. I have a birthmark—"

He leaned in close and whispered, "Yes, I've seen it. It's a stunning birthmark, shaped like a butterfly."

"You took my words the wrong way."

"I've always wanted to touch it."

She jerked involuntarily, then hugged her knees more tightly to her chest. "*You* got embarrassed and wouldn't show me anyway."

"I'm not embarrassed now."

Jenny's breath stilled in her chest. "I don't think we should talk about this."

"Why?"

The word was a mere murmur along the shell of her ear. It sent heat spiraling down her spine and made her toes curl. Though the approach was subtle, seduction cloaked in friendship and humor, Jenny recognized it nonetheless. Her body was attuned to him, to the nuances of his deep voice, to the warmth radiating from his bare skin. She felt the impact of it in every cell of her being. It would be so easy, too easy, to lose herself in the heat and strength of his arms. She looked at him, frank and without reserve.

"Do you love me, Ian?"

She couldn't see him clearly in the darkness and he didn't pull away physically, but she sensed his immediate withdrawal. Her heart contracted with a twinge of pain.

"I could love you until dawn," he replied with a touch of sensuous evasion.

"But will you love me after?"

"Jenny."

Her heart chilled. She rested her cheek on her knees and looked at him. "Will you ever love me?" she whispered.

Her sad words made him restless and irritated. He lunged to his feet, gathering his blanket tightly around his waist. "I need to check the horses."

Lantern light played over his face, enhancing the dark shadow of his jaw. He was handsome enough to steal her breath, but the measure of a man was not taken in bone structure and flesh. Her words came out brave but a hint of sorrow lingered in her eyes.

"How can we bear to spend the rest of our lives together without love?"

"The love you're talking about doesn't last," he said bluntly. Though his tone was not unkind, it was firm. "We have friendship and respect and mutual goals. We don't need to concentrate on the farce of physical attraction that people mistake for love."

His words wounded her to the core. "Mistake? You call love a mistake?"

"I call it lust. It exists, it's real, and it's highly necessary for attraction and procreation. But it's not love and it doesn't last. If you know that ahead of time, you won't be disappointed later."

Her anger rose at his superior tone. "You're wrong, Ian. Love is real. It exists. We choose to expand or retract it, to nurture or destroy it. And it can last."

"Prove it, Jenny," he said quietly.

Her words faltered. She couldn't prove it, not

exactly. She couldn't think of one couple for whom love had remained the driving force in their lives. Though her mother and father had been civil until death, theirs was a marriage arranged by their families, built and maintained on duty and commitment. It had been a good marriage, strong in things that counted, but never had she seen the tenderness and adoration that she imagined lovers would exude.

Granny Delaney's marriage had been much the same, as were most of the marriages with which Jenny was familiar. She was certain Hannah and Milt loved each other, but their years to affirm it were ahead of them.

"I don't need to prove it," she said in defense, but there was a terrible, empty place expanding inside her that needed to be filled with the truth of her convictions. She had built her future on the idea that she would one day love and be loved, romantically, an everlasting commitment. Against social censure, she had remained unmarried for that very reason.

She huddled down tighter in her blanket and stared at the lantern, its mesmerizing warmth. His words chilled her to the bone, and she couldn't shake the frightening realization that she was going to be stuck in a loveless arrangement the rest of her life.

He took the lantern with him to check the horses. Ensconced in the darkness, every sound was magnified a thousand times, every rustle a snake or scorpion. The small cavern seemed bereft without him. She felt lonely with him gone, deprived of the simplest, elemental necessities.

Thorne was wrong. He had to be. If he loved Jeremiah

with an undying, unconditional acceptance, he could one day love her the same way.

Her eyes widened in shock. She had agreed to marry him only because her future was at stake and the man she loved was marrying another. Why, then, was she so determined that Thorne should fall in love with her? The thought had come from nowhere, but once formed it would not abate.

He returned and placed the lantern on a low ledge of rock, close enough to shed light and some warmth but not near enough to knock over during the night. Jenny stared at him as if he'd sprouted horns.

"What?" he asked. His eyes narrowed on her odd expression. "What's churning through your mind, Jenny? You look like you've seen a ghost."

She shook her head, at a loss for words. Fear clogged her throat. By marrying Thorne, she was setting herself up for lifelong failure. She could feel the desolation, the reprehensible longing that had marked most of her adulthood. What if he could never love her?

Her hands fisted in the blanket. She wasn't wrong. Love did exist. Life held no meaning without it. She knew this as sincerely as she knew the order of nature. The sun would come up in the morning, the moon would rise at night, the seasons would change. For all of nature's arbitrary ways—flash flood, drought, pestilence—the elemental laws remained constant. But what if Thorne did love one day, discovered too late that Jenny had been right? What if he loved another and found himself trapped in marriage with her?

Her head spun with questions that had no answers,

yet something inside her intrinsically changed, as if for the smallest moment she had seen a burst of light. But the illumination was too quick to catch and understand. All she could think of was the lonely years ahead, of Thorne not loving her, not loving anyone but his son.

She could not, would not, chance becoming that woman—lonely, pitiable, and unfulfilled. The true spinster.

Unless . . .

"Ian," she whispered, "do you believe a man can change?"

"Anything is possible," he answered without much conviction.

A spark of renewed hope lit inside Jenny. "Ian Blackwell Thorne," she repeated, rolling out the words with a hint of impish flirtation.

Her new tone caressed his raw nerves and very masculine impulses. She made the syllables sound as if she were running her tongue over them. "Jennifer Delaney," he said, wary but intrigued.

"Exactly what does it take to change a man's mind about matters of the heart?"

Her words were challenging, seductive. His body drew tight as a stretched bowstring. "A miracle."

She smiled like a sweet, satisfied kitten. "I believe in miracles."

With only the dark and cold for comfort, the heat emanated from her, drawing him in. Her face was pale in the lantern light, hair falling around sleek bare shoulders like a cloak of dark fire. She had lost her family, her job, and was about to lose her ranch. Yet she believed in miracles. For one savory, fleeting moment, while studying her face by the light of a lone flame, so did he.

He moved back beside her, at a loss to understand what was going on inside her mind. Their shoulders touched but he wanted more, wanted her. Yet he wouldn't spout false platitudes in order to have her. If she came to him it would be of her own free will, her eyes open and aware. "Are you still cold?"

"Yes."

"Here, lie down." He helped her get comfortable, then lay beside her, his front fitting along the length of her side.

She lay on her back, the warmth of his larger body helping to shield her from the worst of the cold. She turned her face toward him. "This will definitely ruin my reputation for good," she said.

"You are decidedly compromised," he agreed. "Want to make it official?"

The idea was tempting, but she only smiled at him.

His lips dropped to her forehead; he couldn't seem to help the impulse. "You have a fragrance . . . I can't describe it."

"Wet hair and horse."

He laughed lightly and ran his lips down her cold cheek to the tender spot beneath her ear. "I don't like this idea of a convenient marriage."

"Are you backing out?"

His lips slid over her neck, raising goose flesh. "No, just reassessing. By convenience, do you mean no conjugal visits?"

Her cheeks heated up but she played her trump boldly. "No conjugal visits." She turned to him, her chest fitting so perfectly against his. "I can't commit my body and not my heart."

"Hogwash," he returned. His hand trailed over her shoulder and down her arm to the narrow indention at her waist. His thumb made lazy circles there, but she felt the effects all over. "Let me show you just how easy it is."

She closed her eyes briefly. His touch was delicious and she wanted to partake of all he was offering, but she knew it would be a wasted feast. Like a meal of candy, it would be sweet for a time but would never provide what she really needed to survive.

She pulled his hand from her waist and brought it to her lips. "We were friends once, then enemies. I don't know what we are now."

"You'll be my wife, Jeremiah's mother."

"Fine," she said.

"The mother of my future children."

The thought made her heart quiver. "Not without love."

His expression changed to cold calculation. "Do you love me, Jenny? Can you honestly say you've forgotten Milton in all this?"

"I . . ." Her heart sank. Was she demanding the very thing from him she couldn't give herself? She hadn't forgotten Milt, she had given up on him. He had no place in her future. The knowledge was a sweet sorrow that, oddly, held little impact on her senses.

"Don't," he said, and put a finger to her lips. "Either

way you answer, you lose. If you still love Milton, then there's no room in your heart for me. If you don't, if you've so easily set your affection for him aside, it only proves what I've been saying all along. Love doesn't last."

She turned her cheek to the hard pallet beneath her. "You're right, Ian. Either way I lose. But so do you."

Jenny was wrong. He was getting exactly what he wanted, except for the use of her body. He reached out and touched her bare collarbone with a callused finger. Her skin was chilled and soft. He curled his hand over the hill of her upper arm, running his thumb along the fine bones of her shoulder.

"I know you want more children."

Desperately. She wanted them desperately, but she wanted so much more. "I want everything," she said without regard for how foolish she might sound. "A knight on a white horse who will sweep me away and love me forever."

"Fairy tales. Fantasy."

"Yes," she whispered. "I'm so cold, Ian."

He pulled her closer, their blankets feeble barriers. He could feel every outline and inch of her curvature, every hollow and rise. He wanted to be with her, inside her, to merge their beings until their heartbeats were one, their breaths purled out in unison.

"I'm no knight, Jenny, just a man."

She felt his hand at the small of her back, pulling her closer, deeper into him. However improper, she wanted to be there, safe and protected by him, stirred by the masculine virility of his body in such a compromising situation. But as badly as she wanted everything he offered, she placed a hand to his chest.

Jenny Delaney might be wanton and foolish and full of dreams, but she was not stupid. She would have a wedding ring on her finger before she even considered casting her morals to the wind.

"Kiss me, Ian," she said softly. "Kiss me like you love me, then I'll go to sleep."

He didn't want sleep, he wanted her, but he would never take advantage of her vulnerability. "You have no idea how dangerous that would be right now."

"I don't care," she said. "You're a strong man, Ian. I'm certain you can control yourself enough to grant me that one wish without me having to suffer the consequences."

His grin was pained. "You have entirely too much trust."

She gazed into his eyes. "Only with you. I trust only you."

His smile faded. "Don't, Jenny. You'll only end up feeling betrayed."

She felt betrayed now. By her body, her mind. By the fact that love seemed forever out of her grasp. She had never felt this way about Milt, had never wanted him as badly as she wanted Thorne. The prospect was frightening. Although she had adored Milt from afar, she had never staked her future happiness on him.

"Kiss me anyway. Pretend."

A muscle moved in his cheek. "Is that what you were doing with Jimmy Henderson? Pretending?"

She had never felt this for Jimmy. "Jealous?"

Was he? Thorne didn't see Jimmy Henderson as a threat to his masculinity or Jenny's affection, yet the thought of that man getting anywhere near her lips sent an irresponsible streak of rage through him. "Maybe just a touch."

"Ah." Satisfaction purred in her throat. "I like that." She reached up and traced his jaw, entranced with the dark stubble of beard along his strong chin.

He pulled his head back and grabbed her hand. "I'm warning you, Jenny, I'm too close to the edge."

His hold was painful, his eyes intense. A trickle of fear moved through her. "The edge?"

"The very edge. If I kiss you and touch you, take *you* there, there might be a problem."

She swallowed. "What problem?"

"Control."

She was deeply embarrassed to find that she liked the thought of Thorne losing control. Strong, pragmatic Thorne, who thought he knew all the answers. "I don't think you would . . . forget yourself."

"But what if I can't control *you*?"

She buried her laughter in his chest. "Not a concern. Just the thought terrifies me." She lifted her face to him. "Kiss me, Ian. Pretend for me."

He didn't have to pretend to want her. Need was in every touch, every breath he took. His lips were tender as they met hers, his hold secure, but he didn't dare touch her in any other way. If she couldn't have his love, she at least deserved his honor.

"What are you terrified of?" he said against her lips.

Jenny reveled in the taste of him, the warmth of their

bodies closely fitted. "Everything," she murmured, but as the pressure of his mouth increased, as his tongue boldly swept her lips, she rapidly lost all maidenly concerns. There was no town, no school board, nothing. There was only Thorne and this burning need inside her.

She made a sound, a deep craving, and his mouth moved overs hers, hot and aggressive, almost ruthless in its purpose. She found herself taking and taking, then answering his savagery in kind. He was right about the edge. The closer she got, the more she wanted to go there. She was losing herself to the wonder of his mouth, the gruff sounds coming from his throat. She had never felt so desired and desirable. Her hands gripped his shoulders but she wanted to run them over his chest and belly, to touch his thighs.

The thought shocked her. She'd never touched a man's thighs in her life, had never even thought about it. She didn't know if such behavior was allowed. She shivered, then followed his lead, running her hands down his arms, but too soon she wanted more. She dared to go further and slid her palms over his exposed sides.

She felt him quiver, felt the muscles of his belly contract. His skin was hot and firm beneath her fingers. He made a harsh sound, began to touch her in return, and she reveled in the power of it, the overwhelming sense of right. His kiss grew rougher, more demanding, and his hands began to search the smooth skin along her shoulder. She kissed him back with the same intensity, the same want, daring to run her hands up his chest, to fill her palms with the strength of him.

His left hand spearing through her hair, he held her

close for the tender aggression of his mouth, while his right hand explored every inch of available flesh. His touch was gentle, persistent, demanding. He couldn't get enough of her soft skin, her slender curves. He wanted, needed, more and pushed her blanket down until it bunched at her waist, baring her midriff. She recoiled instinctively, whether from the cold or exposure he wasn't sure and at this point didn't care. He pushed her hands aside and touched her intimately.

Jenny gasped aloud as his hand covered her, took the weight of her naked breast in his palm. "Ian, no . . ." Her mind rebelled at the liberty but her body arched into him, abetting him. She knew this was going too far but she seemed helpless to stop it when she wanted him so badly, wanted him to continue.

"Yes, Jenny," he said, his voice rough and tinged with urgency. "See how good it is."

His hand cradled her, shaping, then brushed her in warm circles until she thought she would cry out with the exquisite agony of it.

Achy and alive she pressed into him, needing more, needing him. His teeth scraped her jaw as his mouth left hers and he began a devouring trail down her throat, slowly, consuming every inch as if starved. He made her feel cherished as his mouth continued over her shoulders, his teeth nipping the tender flesh almost to the point of pain, his tongue making moist forays along her collarbone to soothe the small hurt. Then his mouth drifted lower, to the round curve of her breast. *Ah, no, he wouldn't.*

But he did.

His mouth touched her breast, light as a whisper, and he watched her face, her struggle to reject or accept the intimacy.

"Ian!" She gasped. "What . . ." Then he took her into his mouth, like a baby would, kissing and suckling until she was mindless, her body burning and twisting against him.

She could feel him through the bunched woolen blankets, could feel his hard body pressed along her belly, hips, and thighs, but it wasn't enough. She couldn't seem to get close enough and kicked at her blanket, wanting her skin next to his, wanting his heat and intensity. Yearning and yearning—

"Jenny, no!" The command was abrupt and severe. Thorne grabbed her blanket and jerked it back over her body.

She blinked, tried to recall herself, then flushed at her wanton behavior. She was naked as a newborn, her flesh against his, shielded from sight by the blanket he had hastily grabbed but not shielded from touch.

His body was hot, powerful, tense. She whispered against his lips, "I guess we're too close to the edge?"

He was there, past, falling into a place of no return. He knew with a little coaxing he would have her there as well, but it wouldn't be fair, wouldn't be right to take her the first time in a cold cave on a bed of dirt and stone. His breathing ragged and uneven, he gripped her hard, pressing her cheek to his chest, and held on for dear life. "Sleep. Please."

Jenny sensed his struggle. It mirrored the sensual upheaval in her own body. "What did I do wrong?"

"Nothing. You did everything right."

"Then why?"

He wasn't strong enough for this. His desire had turned savage and all-consuming. In another second her wants wouldn't matter. Neither would her inhibitions or protests. Or her dreams. They would mean nothing. He couldn't give her the love she sought but he could give her this, his restraint, his respect until their wedding night.

He pushed her blanket between them, needing the barrier. "I'll ravage you, Jenny, I swear. I won't stop. Please go to sleep."

Her body felt ravaged already, hurting, wanting more. He sounded fierce, tortured. But his concern was for her. It meant something. Something important. Maybe he didn't love her, but he cared for her. If not, he would have taken her without regard for her feelings. Everything he had done for her lately showed a deep caring.

Oh, Ian. I think I'm falling for you, and it scares me. What if he was right? She had certainly lost sight of her affections for Milt in all this. What if love was a farce and lust the only reality, one that would, indeed, fade with time. Was Thorne right? Did love not last?

Or had she just not recognized it until now? Uncertain of everything but the fact that her body felt as desolate as her heart, she closed her eyes and listened to his racing heartbeat thrum against her ear. But the tension did not abate.

"Why did you stop?" she asked.

"It wouldn't be right," he said harshly.

"If you don't love me, then why does it matter to you what's right?"

She was going to drive him insane. "It matters."

"Why?"

Because she was good and honest, giving and sincere. He wanted more from her than he was willing to give in return, and it wouldn't be fair. Once they were married and she had his name and protection, she would feel better about a physical union. If he had her now, in the dark and cold, she might feel cheated in the morning. He didn't want to hurt her, and he was greedy as well. He didn't want her bringing regrets to the marriage bed.

He stroked her hair, willing his body to calm. "I don't want a marriage of convenience, Jenny."

She smiled secretly. "Are you backing out?"

"No. I want to renegotiate the rules."

"I can't do that, Ian." Ridiculous man. He had her now, if he just knew it. But if she had realized that he cared for her more than he wanted to admit, she thought it much more important that he realize it. And she knew, as badly as she yearned now, in the blinding light of day she would regret settling for less than a full commitment from him. She snuggled her face into his chest and pretended to drift off to sleep.

Thorne roused before dawn. Jenny murmured her discontent, then curled back in to the warmth of his chest. "Jenny," he said again, shaking her.

"Ummm."

"The storm has been over for hours. If you want to avoid talk, we need to sneak back before daylight."

No one at the ranch would divulge her personal business to the outside world, except . . . "Aunt Tildy!" She bolted straight up. Her blanket fell in a heap around her waist and she scrambled to pull it back up. It was still dark, the lantern light murky and unrevealing, but her cheeks flamed when she caught Thorne's appreciative stare.

"Very nice," he said, which made her blush all the more.

She climbed to her feet but dread stopped her in her tracks. "I don't want to put those wet clothes back on."

The vision of her riding naked through the canyon made him dangerous. "They're a little drier," he said with a hint of irritation. He had already struggled into his damp trousers and shirt and was perfectly miserable. "Leave off the undergarments."

Jenny agreed, but by the time she had her blouse fastened, she wished she hadn't. The fabric was thin, especially when damp, and needed her unmentionables for modesty. Without a layer of petticoats, her skirt clung to her legs like a second skin.

Thorne's perusal was blatant and appreciative. He lifted the lantern higher to cast a broader light and made no effort at all to hide his interest.

"Stop it," Jenny demanded, and would have stomped her foot except for the added view it would have afforded him.

Thorne answered by pulling her into his arms. "One week. Then I get to look all I want."

She shook her head, modest and delighted. "Not unless—"

He stopped her words with his lips. "We're changing the agreement."

"No, we're not, Ian—"

He stopped her again with a brief, perfunctory kiss. "Yes, we are." His words were cold, firm and final. He stepped back and finished rolling the rest of their belongings into the blankets.

She watched him with an astonishing sort of excitement building inside her. Fear, challenge, and a strange feminine satisfaction infused her with determination. "Nothing has changed."

The hell it hadn't. He had spent a painful, restless night lying next to her. He wouldn't spend another. She wanted him as much as he did her, and he planned to take full advantage of it. "Everything has changed."

She did stomp her foot at his superior tone. She couldn't help it. "What?"

"You want me as badly as I want you. And I mean to have you. It's as simple as that."

The gall of the man. "Do you love me, Ian?"

His head whipped around and he speared her with a hard look. "No."

Ice splintered through her, so painful she thought she would cry out, but she held on to her composure with hard-won dignity. "Then nothing has changed."

As soon as the word left his mouth, Thorne regretted it. He didn't want to hurt her, ever. He was tired, aroused, chafed raw by his damp clothes. He wanted to be what she needed, what she deserved, but he couldn't lie to her. They could have a stronger marriage than the one he'd had with Allissa, could build a better future, if Jenny knew beforehand the reality and nature of affection. Respect and mutual goals would carry them through the years. Lust would dwindle with proximity and age. He didn't want her disappointed, her dreams shattered, as Allissa's had been. As his had been.

"I do care for you," he admitted.

But she had moved out of reach, braced and untouchable. "It's not enough," she said coldly.

The path was slippery and deceiving in the pearlescent dawn. The sky was awakening in the distance but below shadows covered the land and made the footing unpredictable. Staying flat against the canyon wall, they led the horses down the narrow stretches and winding paths until they reached flatter ground.

They would never make it back to the ranch before dawn, but they might arrive before anyone began to stir and realized they hadn't come in the night before. Growing chilled in her damp clothing, Jenny mounted her horse and wished she still had Thorne's warmth to cling to.

The ride back was miserable. The air was cold and infiltrated her body to the bone. Midafternoon would be scorching, but at this moment Jenny was convinced she would never be warm again. She clenched her teeth against their infernal chattering and rode as fast as she dared in the unstable light.

Once they reached the ranch, Thorne had Jenny dismount near the house, then he took both horses on to the barn. She hurried across the patio and slipped into her room. The house was silent and warm, the layers of blankets on her bed calling to her. She stripped her damp clothes off, shrugged into a long cotton nightgown, then slipped between the sheets. She'd made it home before the house awoke, but there would be some explaining to do come daylight.

"We were so worried, señorita!" Mercedes had kept up a steady stream of chatter since realizing Jenny had made it home safely. She bustled around the kitchen, refilling Jenny's plate and coffee cup with nervous relief. "Luis went looking but he could not find you anywhere. Cortez and Barkley did the same."

"I'm sorry," Jenny said, averting her eyes. "We were trapped in the canyon. We had to wait out the flash flood before we could ride back."

"Oh, such a dangerous thing. Luis lost a brother, you know, many years ago in just such an accident. Why did you take such a risk?"

"The horses," she said.

"But that is man's work, not yours."

Jenny shook her head. "It's everyone's work if we want to survive." She lifted a hand. "Mercedes, sit down. I need to talk to you."

Mercedes stilled her anxious puttering and slid into the chair beside Jenny, her fingers clenched around her coffee cup.

Jenny reached over and laid her hand over her housekeeper's. "I'm so sorry you worried." Mercedes' eyes filled with tears and Jenny squeezed her hand. "I have good news. News I think you'll like. Ian and I are going to be married."

In the span of a few seconds, Mercedes' expression went from interest to confusion to shock. "Luis will have Señor Thorne horsewhipped for what he has done!"

"What are you talking about?"

Mercedes burst into tears.

Stunned, Jenny sat back, at a loss for words. Luis walked in at that moment and she hurried him over. "I don't know what's wrong."

Luis went instantly to his wife and wrapped her in his arms. "*Mi espousa*, what is this?"

Mercedes looked up, tears streaming down her face. "Our Jenny is gone all night, then comes back saying she is getting married. I think that Señor Thorne has taken advantage of her."

Luis leapt up, outraged.

"No!" Jenny burst out. "He did nothing."

Mercedes shook a finger at her. "I was not born tomorrow, señorita."

"Yesterday," Jenny corrected softly. "The plans were already made, even before the flash flood. I told Hannah yesterday in town. We planned the whole wedding."

Mercedes cried harder. "You tell the town before you tell your own family!"

Bemused, Jenny turned to Luis for understanding.

He shook his head. "She is upset because she thought we lost you last night. We heard the rumbling in the hills and knew what was happening. It is only the relief and shock she is feeling now." He wrapped his wife up tighter and whispered soothing words in Spanish until she quieted.

Jenny watched in silence, feeling intrusive, but she couldn't tear herself away. Watching these two share confidences and concerns, these two who had been married since they were teenagers, she realized one very important thing. Love could last. Through good times and bad, through trauma and joy. If love existed, it could last.

But how did one create love where it did not exist?

Chapter 16

Paul Anderson was weakening. Jenny pulled out Granny's journal, found her "receipt for the sickly," and followed it to the letter. She took the required pound of beef, skimmed the fat, and cut it into small pieces. After placing that into two quarts of water, she set it on the stove to boil.

"Whatcha doing, Miss Jenny?"

She turned, brightening at the sound of Jeremiah's voice. "Making a broth. Want to help?"

He nodded and lifted his arms to be picked up.

She lifted him up and showed him the beef bits in the pot. "We have to let it boil down to about a quarter of a pint."

He nodded sagely but quickly lost interest when the water just sat there with pieces of meat floating around. She took sympathy on him and sat him at the table.

"Why don't you wash your hands and roll out some dough for biscuits?"

He nodded vigorously and scrambled over to the washtub. Within minutes, he was up to his elbows in flour and Jenny's pot was boiling. The aroma of beef broth filled the warm kitchen, bringing a contentment despite the troubled situation. But Jenny basked in the small respite, allowing the comfort it brought as a buffer for what lay ahead.

As soon as the water boiled down, she added a tiny bit of salt, then let it cool. After skimming off the remaining fat, she reheated the broth to an edible temperature.

But no matter how much strengthening beef broth they spooned down Paul's throat, no matter how often they cooled his feverish brow, he was growing weaker by the hour. Infection had set in. Fiery red streaks ran out from the center, and putrid fluid oozed from his flesh. They cleaned the area, searched for bullet fragments, even washed it with whiskey to disinfect it, but nothing worked.

Other than an occasional twinge of pain or swear word, Paul was no help. He seemed content to die. No matter how Jenny coaxed or argued or pleaded, he made no effort to rouse and fight the sickness consuming his body. Without a will to live, he stood little chance of surviving.

Once he was asleep, Jenny sat in the chair beside his bed and opened Granny's journal, scanning to the place she had left off. Granny claimed that a woman's day was one part work and three parts worry. While men exhausted muscle and mind with their daily activity, it had fallen to the women to exhaust the soul.

Staring at Paul's wasting form, Jenny recognized the validity of Granny's statement. Truly, her soul was exhausted, and worry was an ever-constant enemy that also sapped her strength. She didn't know what to do, how to convince her former student that he must fight back.

She closed the journal softly, then rose and carried out a pan of water and soiled towels. Granny claimed that a woman should partake of her own destiny, but it was hard to be brave and untroubled when her job had been taken from her, the student she had already failed once lay dying in her house, and the man she was to marry would never love her.

I'm changing the agreement.

Thorne's words echoed, strumming some sensual cord inside her she hadn't even known existed. "Granny," she whispered. "How am I going to muddle through this?" Resolute, she set her chin. She might not be able to help Paul Anderson, but she would not give up on Ian Thorne or her dreams. Not only would she partake of her own destiny, but she would take charge of it.

With equal parts nostalgia and nerves, Jenny pulled her mother's wedding gown from a trunk. It was one of the few things the Yankees had allowed her to take from River Run before burning the plantation to the ground. She had been allowed a few portraits also but not the gilded frames that had graced them. Nor had she been allowed her mother's and grandmother's jewelry that was to be her legacy. Those items would fetch too fair a price to pay any mind to their sentimental value.

She pulled out the hopelessly wrinkled dress and shook it, then crushed it to her. It would be beautiful once laundered, but for the second time it would adorn the body of a woman doing her duty in marriage, rather than one following her heart.

"Señorita," Mercedes called. She poked her head in, then gasped. "Oh, your mama's beautiful marriage dress, *sí*?"

Jenny smiled. *"Sí."*

Mercedes reached for the gown. "I will launder it for you. It will look as new as the day your sweet mama wore it."

Jenny handed it over, grateful for the help. "Did you need me?"

"Oh, *sí*. The sheriff is here. I didn't know what to tell him about the outlaw boy."

"No need to tell him anything," Jenny said. "He knows about Paul Anderson." She searched out the wedding veil from her trunk, then added it to the gown in Mercedes' arms. "I'll go talk to him. Have Luis find Ian. Milt may want to speak to him too."

The sheriff was sipping coffee at the kitchen table when Jenny walked in. "Please, don't get up," she said as he rose to greet her.

He stood anyway, manners inbred from his mama's knee. "I hear congratulations are in order."

Jenny forced a smile. "Thank you, but they can wait. I know you are here to talk about Paul."

"Unfortunately, it's worse than that." Milt sat back down. "Doc was taken last night, Jenny, right from his bed."

"No." Jenny's hand went to her mouth. Doc Brown was a hearty man but not a young one. "You think it's the Comancheros?"

"I'm fairly positive. I need to talk to that boy, Jenny, and see if he'll tell me where their hideout is."

Thorne stomped sand from his boots outside the kitchen door.

Jenny turned at the noise. "They got Doc Brown."

"So I heard." He entered, addressing the sheriff. "The boy's in bad shape for questioning. I don't think he'll make it through the morning."

Jenny's eyes welled up. "Don't say that."

Thorne gave the sheriff a pointed look. "Unless he's a good liar, I got the general area of their hideout from him two nights ago."

Milt rose and grabbed his hat. "How many?"

"There can't be more than three left who are healthy, maybe only two. The fewer men you send up, the better chance of getting in."

Milton understood where Thorne was leading. "You ready to ride?"

Thorne grabbed his gun belt from the coat rack. "Yep."

Jenny looked at both men, panic beating with her pulse. For different but valid reasons, she loved both men and respected them with a fierce protectiveness that rose up at the thought of the danger they would be riding into. She wanted to shout at them not to go, not to endanger themselves, but it was Milt's duty to the citizens of Little Town and Thorne's to the ranch that drove them. The two things that Jenny loved most about them would put them in imminent danger.

She clamped her mouth shut and set about fixing them as much food as they could comfortably carry. It took less than a half hour for them to ready the horses for an indefinite amount of time.

She stuffed provisions into Thorne's saddlebag, then handed it to him. He took her hand, stared intently down at her face, then pressed a hard kiss on her knuckles. She made an unconscious move to touch him, to say something, but he was gone.

As soon as the men had ridden out of sight, Jenny picked up Jeremiah and held him so tightly he squirmed.

"Miss Jenny, you're squishing me!"

"Sorry," she whispered, and closed her eyes against the rising sting behind her eyelids. She put him back down at the table with a ring to cut biscuits, then went to see what she could do for Paul. She had to stay busy, to keep her mind and heart from dwelling on Ian and Milt, but it was nigh impossible.

Aunt Tildy was wringing out a cloth when Jenny walked in. "He's not responding well," she said with unusual clarity. "He won't fight."

"I know." Jenny walked over and put a hand to his hot brow. "Paul," she said, "you need to listen to me." She leaned in close. "I talked to the sheriff. You will not be charged with your father's murder. They don't have any proof to convict you."

He seemed to stir but did not awaken. His brow was

dry and burning; his cheeks bore the incongruence of being both flushed and wan, the look of the severely ill. Jenny remembered Uncle Nat looking much the same way before he finally fell into the final, laudanum-induced sleep from which he never awoke.

She grabbed Paul's hand and squeezed. "Please," she begged, "you're so young. You have so much life ahead of you." She didn't know how to convince him, how to get through to him. She wondered if it were too late to try.

"Señorita?"

Jenny turned at Mercedes' whisper. "Yes?"

"I know a place, a small church, empty now. It is said that the Virgin Mother visits there to heal the sick."

Jenny was willing to try anything. "Is it within riding distance?"

"*Sí*, a half day, but I don't know if Señor Paul will make it even that long." Her brow creased with concern. "If he lasts the night, we will have Luis take us in the wagon tomorrow."

Jenny felt a terrible urgency to leave now but knew the idea was foolish. If there were miracles for Paul, they could just as easily be performed at El Dorado ranch than at some forgotten shrine.

By midafternoon her worst fears were confirmed. There were no miracles for Paul, or even any added time. With a peacefulness that had never marked his short turbulent life, Paul Anderson slipped quietly into the next.

Jenny had no tears. Her eyes were dry and hard, her soul callused. She shut herself off from the grief and failure. She wanted to cry, to scream, to rail her frustration at God, but another part of her took over, a person removed and untouched from the helplessness and tragedy that had befallen Paul. She reined in her emotions, but it was a fragile control.

With efficiency, she helped Mercedes prepare the body for burial, while Cortez and Luis dug a grave, and Barkley made a coffin of fragrant pine. She would not use the undertaker in town or even ask for the services of the reverend. She wanted no one who would judge in death what Paul had been—or failed to be—in life.

She tried to explain to Jeremiah what was happening, but he was young, and she didn't know where his beliefs lay. What had Thorne taught him about life and death and spiritual matters? She didn't even know how much of her ill-constructed conversation he absorbed until they stood outside at twilight laying the last of summer's wildflowers on the mound of earth.

They bowed their heads for a final prayer, then Jeremiah slipped his small hand in Jenny's and looked up. "It's all right, Miss Jenny. He's with Jesus now. Nothing is ever gonna hurt him again."

Jenny burst into tears.

Hannah rode in at dusk, her eyes red-rimmed from crying. She marched right into the kitchen and plopped down at the table.

"I couldn't stay away," she said. "I'm so worried about Milton, I can't eat or rest. All I can do is weep. I told Mama I'm going to wait right here until Milton comes back." She took her first good look at Jenny. "What's wrong?"

"We just buried Paul Anderson."

"Paul Ander—? The boy from school? The one who—"

"He didn't kill his father!" Jenny said viciously.

"I know." Hannah reached for Jenny's hands. Taking them in her own, she said softly, "Milton told me he thinks the old man shot himself in a drunken mishap. Paul found him a few hours later, but instead of getting help, he left his father to die."

Jenny pursed her lips. "Some would call that murder."

"Some might," Hannah agreed, "but some think the boy was justified in his actions."

Of every awful thing that had happened over the past few days, it was those few words of acceptance that were almost Jenny's undoing. Folding forward onto the table, she buried her face in her arms. "He was so young, Hannah."

Hannah rushed over and clutched her friend's shoulders.

"It's just not fair," Jenny continued. "He was only sixteen, he had an entire life ahead of him." She reared back, her eyes vehement. "I will never let that happen to another child. Never!" She pushed back from the table and stood, eyes dry and earnest. "I don't care what I have to do, what laws have to be changed, but I'll never let that happen to another one of my students."

Hannah was intimidated by the light of insurgence in Jenny's eyes, but she admired the determination. "Never again," she echoed meekly. "I'll help you, Jennifer. Father knows more politicans than the president."

Jenny's lips trembled but her jaw was set. "I mean it, Hannah. This won't be a Sunday social."

Hannah drew herself up primly. "I know, Jennifer. Contrary to popular opinion, I do have a brain behind this pretty face. And I do choose worthy causes from time to time on which to expend Papa's money and influence."

Her heart contracting, Jenny smiled sadly. "I know you do, Hannah, and you are also the very best friend anyone could have."

"Exactly, Jennifer," Hannah said. "I agree completely. Now, sit down so we can plan how to go about it."

They sat but their planning was halfhearted as they waited out the long vigil. Rationally, Jenny knew Milt and Thorne could not possibly be back for days, but she and Hannah counted each hour as if it were the very one in which the men would return safe.

Midnight came and went, a mere tick of the clock for the two who were still wide awake. The rest of the household had long since retired, but Hannah and Jenny sat outside at the fountain, wrapped in blankets against the chill. Both were impossibly tired but neither could sleep, and neither wanted to be alone with her fears. The day had taken an enormous toll on Jenny's emotions, and she had never been so grateful for Hannah's friendship.

"They will come back," Hannah said with quiet fortitude, and Jenny realized that her friend's strength was being upheld by bravado.

"Yes, they will, Hannah. You must believe that."

"I do," she whispered, but her voice cracked and she refused to say another word for fear of disgracing herself and not upholding her end of their unspoken support.

Neither wanted to indulge in a fit of tears and fears, so they spoke of important things, such as women's suffrage and the mistreatment of children, and simple things, such as ingredients for face cream. But they avoided speaking of the two men riding through the night after murderous outlaws until the strain was too much.

"I can't bear it," Hannah whispered. "I love Milton so much, I just can't bear this!"

"He'll keep safe," Jenny said, but her own fears for Thorne were threatening to surface.

Hannah looked at Jenny askance, frank and unashamed. "He kissed me before he left, but all I could think of was that I wanted more, that if anything happened to him, I would never know what it was like to . . . love him." She looked away. "To love him as a man, a husband."

Jenny nodded, the same realization seeping into her own thoughts. She'd had her chance with Thorne in the cave. What if that was the only chance she'd ever get?

Hannah stood, too restless to remain idle. "Have I shocked you?"

"No." Jenny shook her head. "That's the way it's supposed to be."

"I miss him so much," Hannah said wistfully. "Even when he's only at work, I can't wait to see him. I think about him all the time. I daydream about how it will be for us. I think about what our children will look like, if they'll be boys or girls or both. I try to imagine what kind of father he'll be, and I see our grandchildren one day, sharing the holidays."

A terrible, wonderful suspicion was growing inside Jenny. She'd never felt any of those things for Milt. She harbored affection and friendship, she had even imagined him taking her hand and making sweet declarations of love. But she'd never considered the marriage act or begetting children with him or growing old together.

A gasp rose in her throat, and she quickly covered it with a cough. She didn't love Milt. She had never loved Milt. He was a friend, a confidant, a man to be admired. But he was not the man she wanted to marry.

For four days Hannah stayed with Jenny, helping with chores, planning her friend's wedding, and keeping watch on the horizon for riders. Being opposites in many ways, they found they worked well together, complementing each other's strengths rather than compounding their weaknesses.

"I think you should consider a wedding at the church for those like Mr. Elias who can't travel far from home but a grand reception here to mark the momentous occasion for those of us who can."

"All right," Jenny agreed halfheartedly. "But nothing too elaborate. I don't have the provisions for it or the time." She was worried about the men. The wedding plans helped take her mind off their safety, but it also kept reminding her that she would soon be married to a man who didn't love her. She didn't think Thorne would want anything extra done for their "convenient" wedding.

"Everyone will bring something to share," Hannah said, "and I'll help with the rest." Paper and pen in hand, Hannah stopped and eyed her friend with a straightforward frankness that made Jenny want to duck. "Are you in love with Mr. Thorne, Jennifer?"

"Whyever would you ask such a thing?" Jenny returned.

"I thought not." Hannah *tsk*ed gently. "Are you certain you want to go through with this?"

"Yes!" At least Jenny could answer that honestly.

"For the rest of your life?"

She paled. "No." She closed her eyes briefly. "I don't know, Hannah." She lunged from the sofa and paced the sitting room, agitation in each stride. "Everything about this arrangement is perfect."

"Except for the part in the ceremony when you vow to love and obey until death do you part?"

Jenny winced. "I do love Ian in my own way. I've known him forever. As children we were friends. I admit that I don't know the man he has become, at least not well, but that man has my respect." She looked up, fear and confusion in her eyes. "And I love Jeremiah without question, and he so needs a mother, Hannah. This is the right thing to do."

"For whom?"

"For all three of us," she answered with conviction, and for the first time she began to believe it. Her heart shivered, then lightened with a fledgling ray of hope. "For all of us."

Hannah pressed her hands together. "I pray you are right, Jennifer. How does Mr. Thorne feel?"

Jenny smiled. "He wants me for my horses."

Hannah's eyes widened in horror. "Jennifer—"

"Actually, he wants to combine my resources with his. Putting our land and horses together will be wise for both of us financially. And he wants a mother for Jeremiah." Jenny smiled softly, keeping her pain back. "He's never been anything but honest with me, Hannah, another thing in his favor."

The consummate friend, Hannah nodded and gave up. "Love, even that of friendship, respect, and honesty. There are worse things upon which to build a marriage, Jennifer."

"I know," Jenny agreed.

"Pa!" Jeremiah came tearing through the sitting room headed for the kitchen.

Jenny caught him up in one arm before he could race through the door. "Wait," she pleaded against his squirming. She ran to the window. She could see the riders in the distance, but they were too far away to identify. "Not yet, honey. We don't know who it is."

For good or evil, there were three of them, but only two were riding upright. One was slumped over his horse like a rag doll. Jenny's heart rose to her throat when Hannah stepped up beside her and slid an arm around her waist.

"Who is?" Hannah asked calmly, too calmly for the grip she had on the waistband of Jenny's apron. "Who is it?"

Jenny noted the shrill tension underlying the words.

"I don't know yet," she answered, her own words strained. "I can't tell—" Barkley and Cortez seemed to burst from nowhere and run toward the riders. Jenny scooped Jeremiah up onto her hip and headed for the door. "Mercedes," she called as she ran. "Mercedes!"

"*Sí?*" The housekeeper hurried from the kitchen, wringing her hands in her apron. "Is it Señor Thorne and the sheriff?"

"Yes, and someone is hurt." But she didn't know who.

"Holy Mary," Mercedes prayed, "not someone else."

"Get the bandages and heat some water." There was a terror in Jenny's soul unlike any she had ever experienced. She felt alternately hot and cold, shaky and transfixed. She did the right things as she tore strips of sheets for bandaging, made the right movements as she gathered ointments and salves. But less than a week ago they had brought Paul Anderson to the house in much the same way, and she didn't think she could hold up under another funeral, not if it were Thorne or Milt. Her stomach clenched with fear, and only the necessity of motion kept her going.

She spun toward the door at Hannah's wail and knew instantly that the man slumped over the horse was Milt.

Tears flooded her eyes. Tears of pain, of relief.

Chapter 17

Thorne had Milt's shoulders, bearing the brunt of his weight, while Cortez helped carry his feet. Doc Brown followed behind, thin and shaken from his ordeal, but his eyes were alert, his hands ready for whatever must be done. Jenny swung the door wide and, for the second time in a week, made a place on her kitchen table for a wounded man.

Doc Brown nodded as he approached. "Miss Jenny."

She stared at Milt's unconscious body. "How is he?" Her voice came out reedy and thin.

"Lucky to be alive." Doc limped past her with a scarred medical bag in his grip.

He was a cagey old man with a penchant for sarsaparilla tea and one shot of whiskey at the end of a long day. Watching him shuffle arthriticlike into the room, Jenny suspected he hadn't had either since being kidnapped.

She pulled Mercedes over and asked her to ready a few cups of tea, then returned to the table.

Hannah was already tearing more sheets into strips for bandaging.

"What can I do, Doc?" Jenny asked.

Tired and surly, he looked up. "Pray. He's gut-shot. No chance without a miracle, Jenny girl, so git to prayin'. And get me some gol-dern whiskey."

Jenny blanched and turned away. She didn't have any whiskey in the house, and she knew there was a bad shortage of miracles at El Dorado these days. Hannah was sobbing quietly in the background. They both knew what gut-shot meant, how hopeless the words. She needed to go to Hannah, but her own heart was caving in and she didn't know how she was going to get through the next few hours.

She spun toward Cortez. "Has Barkley got any whiskey?"

"I do."

Jenny's attention jerked to Thorne. She was so grateful he had walked in under his own power, she had dismissed him and turned immediately to the injured man. But the sight of him now, dusty and travel weary, with deep grooves cutting into the corners of his mouth shouted loudly that he was in pain too. She scanned him quickly from head to toe but found nothing obvious. "Are you hurt, Ian?" *God, please don't let him be hurt too.*

"I'll be fine. The whiskey's in the trunk at the foot of my bed."

"I'll get it," Hannah said, then ran from the room.

"But you don't know where—" Jenny's words met the trailing sash of Hannah's apron strings.

"She'll find it," Thorne said. He held his side tightly and limped away from the table where he had laid Milton.

Jenny went to him. "Where are you hurt?"

He shook his head. "It was a sucker punch. The guy blindsided me with a branch. I'll be fine."

Jenny pulled out a chair for him. "Sit down, please." He did as she bade, his lips white-tinged at the edges. "Are your ribs broken?"

He eased down into the chair and let his breath out slowly. "Milton's bad." His green eyes stayed intently on her face, as if searching for something. His shoulders heaved in a weary sigh. "I'm sorry, Jenny."

Jenny's voice quivered over the tears in her throat. "I know. Doc says we need a miracle." She let out a ragged gasp of breath. "But I just don't think there are any."

Thorne clasped her hand. "Sure there are, Jenny." His eyes were glassy with pain but they never wavered from her. "You're a miracle."

She shook her head, then pressed his hand to her lips. "Paul died."

Shock rocked through him. His face creased in regret for Jenny and a young life wasted. "I'm sorry."

Tears clogging her throat, she glanced over at the table, then away. "I can't do this again, Ian."

There was nothing he could say, no words of comfort that wouldn't be a lie. "Don't give up on him yet."

Grim-lipped, Hannah walked back into the kitchen with a bottle of whiskey. She refused to look at Milton or ask a single question. Instead, she fetched several glasses and poured. She took the first to Doc Brown, the second to Thorne, then poured a third for herself. She downed it in one gulp, quivered all over, then turned and walked from the room.

Jenny started to go after her but was afraid the doc would need something, and she wanted to stay close in case Thorne did as well. Hannah was sorting through things her own way, with efficiency, organization, and action. She wouldn't fall apart until later, when no one needed her, when no one was looking.

Doc Brown worked on Milton for over an hour. He had his medical bag and surgical instruments, and he had faith. But there was little else going for the sheriff at that moment. The bullet had ripped through his insides, but the major organs were intact. Doc did what he could, which was considerable, but Milton had lost an inordinate amount of blood. The fact that Doc had poked and pulled and stitched for an hour without Milton needing a drop of chloroform was not a good sign.

Once done, Doc washed his hands, then shuffled outside to breathe the clean, bloodless air of evening.

"Doc?"

"I'll take that tea now, Jenny."

Something in his tone warned her not to ask what Milt's chances were. She stood in the last vestiges of twilight, breathing the cooler air and wishing that she could fix everything, that she could turn back the clock and change time. Suddenly the fact that Miss Theodora Walker was arriving any day now to take her teaching job seemed a piddling thing. She had a ranch with potential, an honest man to marry who could work it, and a ready-made son whom she loved. Everything except the man on her kitchen table seemed trivial now.

"I'll get your tea, Doc," she said softly to his bent shoulders. "Are you all right?"

"Just tired, Jenny girl. Hell of a day."

She put a hand on his thin shoulder. "Mercedes made up a room for you. Would you like your tea there?"

"More than a wagonload of gold." He laid his hand upon hers. "Care if a crotchety old man takes a bit of strength from a pretty young girl?"

She smiled. "If I see a pretty young girl, I'll get her for you. Until then, you'll have to make do with me."

He chuckled and placed his arm on hers for support. "It's time Little Town got one of them fancy city doctors with all the newest ways."

"Ha," Jenny scoffed. "What would a city doctor have over you?"

"Youth," he grumbled emphatically. "I'm too old for this, Jenny girl. In my heyday, I'd have whipped those no-accounts, got myself loose, *and* sewed up the injured. Sure wouldn't have needed no sheriff comin' along to git himself shot."

Her heart trembled at his failing voice and the terrible regret there. "Let's get you inside. I'll have Mercedes bring in a supper tray with your tea, and you just ask for anything else you need."

They crossed the patio at a slow but steady pace, the fate of the man inside wearing heavy upon them both. "Miss Hannah's gonna be in a bad way if Milton doesn't pull through," Doc said quietly.

"She'll be a rock," Jenny said. It was the one thing a person could count upon most with Hannah. Struggling over her own fears, Jenny whispered, "Can he pull through, Doc?"

He paused at the bedroom door and glanced up at the stars. "In seventy some-odd years, I've seen everything," he answered. "Some of it good, some of it bad, and some of it unexplainable." Trembling with fatigue, his arm swept out in a wide arc, encompassing the land. "It only takes a miracle, Jenny. Not such a momentous thing to the Almighty who created all this."

Jenny's heart constricted. Both hope and despair warred for dominance within her spirit. She opened the door and urged Doc inside, then turned down his bedding and checked the washstand for fresh water.

He made his way over to the nearest chair and sighed as he dropped down into it. "He's lost a lot of blood, but that wound wasn't near as bad as I first thought. That's something, and Milton is strong."

Jenny forced a determined smile and nodded. "Better suited for catching that miracle when it comes by."

She returned to the kitchen to find it empty, save for Mercedes, who was preparing supper.

"Where is everyone?" she asked in a shaky voice.

"They have moved the sheriff to a bedroom. Miss Hannah is sitting with him now." She looked up from the pot of chili she was stirring. "Señor Thorne is with Jeremiah, Barkley and Cortez are putting the horses up for the night, and I have sent Luis to the doctor's room with tea and food. And you, señorita, are about to sit right here and have something to eat."

Jenny looked at the table where Milton had been lying in his own blood only minutes before. She shuddered slightly. "I can't—"

"You can and you must," Mercedes said sternly, then broke into pleading. "*Por favor*, señorita, you must keep your strength up."

Jenny knew it was true, but she could not force even a morsel in the kitchen. "Fix several plates and I'll take them around to everyone," she said. "Then I'll eat as well."

Mercedes loaded up several platters with cheese, fruit, and bread, then ladled out steaming bowls of chili. The aromas wafted up and blended to bring a false normalcy back to a kitchen that had been filled too often lately with the odors of a field hospital.

"Here," she said, handing over the largest tray. "Take this one to Señor Thorne and Jeremiah. I'll take Miss Hannah's and sit with her for a while."

Jenny accepted the tray, then paused. "We need to make more of that restorative beef broth," she said with a confidence that belied the anxiety in her heart. "Milt will need it tomorrow."

Mercedes opened her mouth, then closed it and nodded briskly. "*Sí*, we will do that."

Taking a deep breath, Jenny marched from the kitchen. She carried the tray to Thorne's room and paused outside his door. She could hear plaintive concern in Jeremiah's voice, followed by Thorne's attempt to soothe him. She rapped lightly to make her presence known, then pushed the door open with her foot.

Thorne rose at once, wincing at the jolt to his ribs,

but Jenny waved him back and carried the tray over to the table.

"Miss Jenny," Jeremiah said with concern, "the sheriff got shot."

She knelt down for eye level with him. "I know. Doc Brown says we need to pray hard for a miracle."

Jeremiah nodded. "Me and Pa already did." He glanced up at the table, trying to mind his manners, but the growl in his stomach got the better of him. "Something smells good," he said hopefully. "Something smells like my supper."

Jenny smiled and opened her arms for him. He ran up and she lifted him into a chair. "It is your supper." She glanced up at Thorne. "And yours. How are your ribs?"

He shrugged, then wished he hadn't. "They've been better." He made his way less enthusiastically to the table and eased down into a chair.

"They need to be wrapped," Jenny said with concern.

"I'll locate Doc after we eat," Thorne agreed.

"I can do it," Jenny offered. "Doc is past tired."

Thorne was beyond tired as well and hurting, but he found he liked Jenny fussing over him. Although pestering at times, a woman's attention also gave a man a feeling of being coddled and cared for, and he needed some coddling just now. The scene at the hideout had been ugly, and it was a wonder any of them had escaped. The Comancheros had not been particularly smart, but they had known enough to move their hideout after Paul was taken. Thorne and Milton had stumbled onto their new place by mistake, which had given the outlaws a momentary advantage.

Roused from their nest like vipers, the Comancheros had struck swiftly and blindly. Once the initial surprise was past, Thorne and the doc had been able to take care of the two remaining outlaws in short order. A third had gotten away, running like a coward from the first shout of alarm, but they couldn't go after him with Milton shot, and they couldn't stay lest the outlaw meet up with companions deeper in the mountains and decide to come back.

Thorne rested his head against the high-backed chair and watched Jenny talk with his son. She had on a butternut skirt and plain shirt. Her auburn hair was pulled back into an untidy braid that swung back and forth with her movements. The curling ends shone glossy as ripe cherries in the lantern light. If all went as planned, he would be married to her within the week.

The thought sent a shiver of heat and uncertainty through him. The heat was easy enough to define, but the uncertainty, especially for a man of his unquestionable calculation, was not as clearly understood. When he had realized how much Jeremiah loved and needed Jenny, he knew he should pursue an alliance. Together they could pool their resources and strengths. It was so logical, he couldn't ignore it.

But Jenny defied logic. She was a strong, courageous woman, and she had dreams: a fairy-tale courtship and marriage, children with a husband she adored. She was destined for disappointment, and he hated that. He wanted her happy, content.

Fatigue and frustration diminished his appetite. He pushed his bowl aside in favor of studying his betrothed.

She was an attractive woman and strong enough to shoulder the burdens of this rough land, but her heart was tender, her soul passionate. He didn't want to be the one who caused her dreams to collapse.

"Are you ready?"

Her soft voice filtered through his exhausted mind. He hadn't realized he'd closed his eyes and dozed until he opened them to find her standing over him with an arm full of bandaging. He sat upright too quickly, then recoiled from the pain.

"Where's Jeremiah?"

"Asleep," she said, and nodded toward the bed. "I gave his room to Doc Brown."

His son lay curled in the middle, swallowed up by a quilt. "How's Milton?"

"Still alive," she said, and they both knew it was the best and only thing to be said for his condition at this point. Her eyes were tired, her brow creased with unspoken fear. He didn't like seeing her so drained and worried. "I'm going to spell Hannah after I finish with your ribs."

Thorne nodded and began unlacing his shirt. It was a soft tan chamois, nice against the skin, but unfortunately it had to be pulled over his head. "Have your way with me, then," he said, "but be gentle."

"I will," she said sincerely.

He grimaced. She hadn't even understood the double entendre. Bracing against the pain, he pulled his shirt off, then draped it over a chair.

Jenny's cheeks heated up at the sight of his naked torso. He was a beautiful man in a rugged way, strong and lean and hard. A thin scar ran down the right side of his chest. Old and well healed, it was obvious someone had taken time to care for the injury. There were other faint nicks and bruises, some old, some new. All a testament to the hard life he had led.

Jenny touched the scar lightly. "What happened?"

He didn't remember exactly which incident had caused that particular scar, but he did know that her touch was warm and compassionate. The urge to lean forward and lay his head on her breast, the need to find some sort of comfort after the harrowing day was almost overwhelming. He placed his hand over hers and dissolved into the gentle, caring touch of a woman. This woman. With the gesture came heat, a slow inappropriate flood of desire that far outdistanced his pain. Her fingers moved down the thin scar, sending another pain to throb with his pulse.

He felt foolish for stumbling onto the outlaws' hideout. His skills as a tracker were well developed and there was no excuse for the sloppy way he and Milt had gone about rescuing the doc. He had been arrogant and overconfident, and he knew better. Stealth and intelligence had been drilled into him as a Comanche son. Life and death hung in the balance for Milton, and part of that was Thorne's fault.

He held Jenny's palm pressed flat to his chest. "Feel that?" he asked.

Her mouth went dry. "Your heartbeat?"

He nodded. "It beats for you, Jenny."

She laughed aloud, which he had intended. He wanted to take the worry from her, if even for a moment.

"Are you a charmer now?"

He made a face. "I'm courting you. You could act impressed."

She sobered. "It takes a lot more than words to impress me, Ian. Going after the men who kidnapped Doc, that impresses me. The way you raise Jeremiah impresses me. The way you stood up to the school board on my behalf impresses me."

"But not my manly heartbeat?"

She could feel the steady thunder of his pulse beneath her palm. There was no hint of softness in his sculpted chest, but his skin was smooth and warm. His shoulders and belly were a combination of work-toughened ridges, tight muscle, and tendon, all fitted together with graceful symmetry.

"I'm impressed," she admitted.

He moved her hand down over him in a caress. "How impressed?"

"Mighty impressed that you can think such immoral thoughts while injured," she said dryly.

He sent her a half smile. "A woman's touch is the only thing that will get me through this."

"A woman?" she scolded. "Any woman?"

"Just you. Trust me when I tell you Mercedes would not have the same effect on me."

She smiled. "Mama said never trust a man who says 'Trust me.'"

He did feel good, all strength and heat. Strong security after a traumatic week. Reaching around him, she began binding his ribs as tightly as possible yet still allowing him to breathe.

He closed his eyes against the shiny elegance of her hair swaying back and forth as she moved, the perfume of her skin in such close proximity, the perfection of her features. Her beauty was rare—clean, classic lines unenhanced by cosmetics and unravaged by the elements of a harsh climate.

When she was done, he tested a deep breath and sighed with relief. "Better," he said. "Thank you."

"I'm sorry it took so long to get to you."

He took her wrist. Her bones were tiny beneath his hold, too delicate for the weight of work and worry she'd had to carry lately. "I'm sorry about Paul."

Her eyes welled up but the emotion was prompted partly by sheer exhaustion. "I just don't know if I can bear another—"

"Milton's got more reason to live," Thorne said, "more reason to fight. And he's got the doc here to help."

She knew his words were meant to comfort her. Whether he believed them or not was irrelevant. At that moment, she appreciated the gesture as it was intended.

"Will you be all right?" she asked.

"Will you stay if I say no?" he asked. There was a hint of roguish levity in his tone.

She knew he was teasing and it helped. "You're an evil man, Ian."

"I won't deny it," he said, then added gently, "Go to Milton."

She nodded, and he felt a spark of jealousy. It was

foolish and oddly insecure of him to ask her to forget that her Prince Charming lay at death's door in another room. Whether she fancied herself in love with Milton or was merely his friend, she needed by her very nature to make certain everyone in her house was receiving the best of care.

"I'll be back to check on you," she said, going toward the door.

"Just send Luis," he requested.

She paused, perplexed. "Why?"

Thorne smiled dryly. "I need help with my . . . boots."

"But I can—"

"And my pants."

"Oh."

The word was a mere breath of sound, the color on her cheeks enchanting. "Yeah, *oh*."

"I . . . if I close my eyes . . ."

"Luis is fine. I can wait."

"If you're sure," she hedged.

He gave her a reflective look. "The first time you take my pants off, Jenny, I want it to mean something."

She opened her mouth to speak, then closed it and fled from the room.

Milt seemed much the same as when she had left him. His face was pale as death, his body just as lifeless. The steady rise and fall of his chest was the only reassurance that he was still with them. Hannah sat by his side in a rocking chair Aunt Tildy had thoughtfully found for her. Her eyes were stark and dry upon the knitting needles clacking in her lap. A flood of soft yellow yarn poured over her knees to the floor.

"How is he?" Jenny asked.

Hannah glanced over at the bed. "Doing as well as can be expected," she said woodenly, then turned back to her knitting. "It will be up to God's mercy to see him through. Doc says if he makes it through the night, there is a good chance he'll live."

Jenny nodded. "Can I get you anything?"

Hannah paused, shuddered, then looked up. Tears filled her eyes and threatened to spill over. "Can you send word to Mama in the morning?"

"Of course." Jenny knelt beside the rocking chair and took the pile of yarn in her hands. "Are you making a . . . shawl or blanket?"

Hannah looked down at the ridiculous trail of yellow and burst into tears. It was less than six inches wide but must have been six feet long. "I've lost my mind, Jennifer."

"No." Jenny took the pile of yarn and rolled it up. "You have more important things to think about."

"But this will all have to come out!" Hannah wailed softly.

"Hannah," Jenny whispered.

She buried her face in the pool of yarn and wept until hoarse. Jenny sat by her side until the worst of it was over, then found Hannah a damp cloth to wash her face.

"Oh, Jennifer," she whispered for the first time. "What will I do without him? How will I go on?"

Every word sent daggers of anguish through Jenny's

heart. She didn't know how to answer her friend's question. How would Hannah go on? Elegant, proficient Hannah who had loved Milt so long and prepared diligently to be his wife. And how could Jenny offer words of comfort when she hurt so badly herself?

Over the course of the last four days, one thing had become startlingly clear and confirmed now. If Milt died, Jenny would not. She would grieve with untold anguish, and she would mourn a life wasted in its prime, but she would not be undone.

She looked at Milt, at his precious face, his dear countenance, and realized she did not love him. She admired him, she cared for him, she cherished him as the dearest friend. But she did not love him as a woman did a man she would marry, a man with whom she would spend her lifetime.

"You mustn't give up hope, Hannah," Jenny said fiercely. "You just mustn't."

Chapter 18

DAYLIGHT BROUGHT WITH IT THE SWELTERING HEAT of Indian summer. Cool fall days were little more than a distant wish as Jenny stirred the fountain with her fingertips.

Milt was still alive. Not only had he survived the night, but he had roused at dawn, delirious and cursing like a drunkard. He had said things Hannah wouldn't repeat, even to her best friend, but the fact that he had come out of his stupor was a most positive change, along with the fact that he was resting peacefully now.

Jenny was not. Her mind was a turmoil of conflicting emotions and a dawning awareness more frightening than anything she had ever faced. She had loved Milt for so long. But romantically he was Hannah's, and that was just the way Jenny wanted it.

When the three had ridden in, she'd rushed to do

what she must for Milt, but it had been Thorne whom she fretted over, Thorne to whom she had wanted to rush and make certain he was all right. Thorne to whom her heart and compassion had been committed.

Ian Blackwell Thorne didn't believe in love, and Jenny was forced to wonder if she did now. How could her affections have been fixed upon one man for so long and now her mind be so preoccupied with another?

The answer came softly and not at all startling. Sometime over the past few months she had fallen, head over heals and irreversibly, in love with Thorne.

The thought made her stomach contract with fear and longing and a desperate sense of neediness. Where there should have been joy, there was turmoil. Happiness was soured with doubt and longing. What she had felt for Milton was a child's form of adoration, hero worship compounded by loneliness. What she felt for Thorne transcended all her known ideas about love and sent her heart plunging down a dark tunnel of the unknown. Her feelings for Thorne challenged every thought she'd ever had about the feelings a woman held for a man. What she felt for Thorne wasn't the sweet adoration she'd harbored for Milt. And it wasn't innocent.

Though not easily defined, it encompassed several shocking elements. It was grasping and self-serving yet demanded charity. It shook the foundation of her life and long-held beliefs; it shattered her emotions. And somewhere beyond the sublime wonder and realization that she had loved him since childhood and the earthy grittiness of adult yearning, she realized that true love was something holy, for her spirit ached with grief.

Thorne didn't believe in love everlasting. How could Jenny, now so hopelessly enamored, bear spending a lifetime with a companionable stranger? How could she, after coming to the end of a long road of searching for him, bear to know that he brought only the most superficial of emotions for her to this marriage of convenience?

The main source of her confusion walked out of his bedroom door. He moved with confidence but care, his stride diminished by the pain in his ribs.

Jenny smiled with sad concern and a terrible ache in her heart. "Can you rest today?"

He shook his head and again watched her with a curiously intense manner. He'd been doing that often since returning to the ranch. Sometimes she thought there was wonder and expectation in his gaze. Yet, if anything, he seemed more aloof.

"I've been gone too many days already," he said.

She rose from the fountain and went to him. "You can't work like this. It will only make things more difficult for everyone if you get worse."

He looked toward the house and the bedroom where Milton lay. "He needs you more than I do."

Despair flooded her. "He has Hannah and Doc. He doesn't need me, but you do." Her eyes pleaded. "It's foolish for you to try to work in your condition. I forbid it."

He gave her a dry look. "Don't pull your teacher's voice on me," he said. "It might work on Jeremiah but it won't work on me."

She lifted her chin haughtily. "I'll have you know that voice has worked on many a grown man in town."

His eyes darkened a trace and his gaze made a quick inspection of her. "It wasn't your voice, Jenny, that made them weak in the knees."

Something hot ran through her at his intimate look. "What do you mean, 'weak'?"

"You'll figure it out," he said, "eventually." He tipped his hat and headed for the corral.

"Weak!" she called after him. "You make it sound like I gave them the influenza!"

His shoulders shook from silent laugher. He was crazy about that woman. Absolutely, head over heels crazy about her. He just couldn't help himself. "Marry me, Jenny," he tossed out in parting.

The words went straight to her heart. She tried to smile but the newness of her love was like a two-sided mirror reflecting both the pain and wonder of her discovery. "As soon as you're better."

He paused in midstride, then looked back over his shoulder. "I can walk down a church aisle and say a few words just fine."

Hope ebbed and flowed. "It's not just a few words, Ian. It's a lifetime commitment."

He stiffened visibly but sent her a cocky grin. "Don't remind me."

His words hurt, though she knew he hadn't intended for them to. Her smile became overbright, adoring. "Are you changing your mind?"

If his ribs didn't hurt so badly, he would have laughed. "Not on your life."

Our life, she thought. For him, marriage was a preferable alternative to his single state. To her, it had become everything. His words challenged and frightened her. He might want the convenience of a helpmate, but she wanted a loving husband in the realest sense of the word.

"Do you love me, Ian?" she shouted.

"From dusk to dawn," he answered without turning back.

Indignation rose within her. Winning Thorne's heart was suddenly the most important thing in her life, and she would have to build some sort of strategy to accomplish it. Feeling both bold and shaky, she took a deep breath. "When?"

He paused again. "When?"

"When do you want to get married?"

He eyed her suspiciously. "I thought you had it all worked out."

"Not the exact date."

He seemed to hesitate. "I suppose you'll want something fancy."

More than anything. Her whole life she'd imagined herself walking down an aisle in a cathedrallike setting wearing a glorious gown and carrying a bouquet of orange blossoms. "I don't guess that's practical."

He hesitated, then sighed. "I don't want you to feel cheated, Jenny."

"It's not the ceremony that makes a marriage, Ian."

He didn't know what had gotten into her, and there was no time this morning to try to figure it out. His ribs were hurting like hell, and bantering nonsense back and forth wasn't helping any. "Make whatever plans you want," he said. "I'm easy to please."

• • •

Never, not in ten thousand years, would Thorne have suspected that his parting words would have such a swift effect. He returned to the ranch at sunset to find the reverend, prayer book in hand, standing beside Jenny, Hannah, Tildy, Mercedes, Luis, and Jeremiah. They were all awaiting him.

"Get changed," Jenny said. "The reverend will marry us this evening."

For the briefest moment, he thought it was a joke, but the reverend's earnest face and Mercedes' quiet, joyful weeping made it all too real.

"It's all this ruckus," Aunt Tildy said in soft apology. "Can't have a big shindig with the sheriff lying at death's door and outlaws still on the run. Likely be Yankees next."

Thorne looked at Jenny. He wanted this, he reminded himself, wanted her. But he hadn't expected everything to happen quite so fast.

"The reverend's only here a few days," she said quietly, uncertain now at the reservation on his face. "It'll be a month before he gets back."

Thorne nodded. "How is Milton?"

She didn't know how to interpret his look and decided not to try. "Improving," she said. "Maybe there are miracles at El Dorado after all."

Thorne looked at each person present, then held out his hand to Jeremiah. "Come with me a moment." He hadn't talked to him, hadn't let his son know what would take place or even considered Jeremiah's opinion.

That Jeremiah loved Jenny had been evident a long time, but Thorne had wanted to be the one to tell him, to gauge his reaction to such a monumental change in their lives.

He took his son to his bedroom and stood him on the high bed. "Do you know why the reverend is here?"

Jeremiah nodded eagerly. "So you and Miss Jenny can get married."

"Do you know what that means?"

"Miss Jenny will be my ma and you will still be my pa and we'll live here forever." He paused, concerned. "Are you mad, Pa?"

He forced a smile. "No, I just want to make certain that you understand what's going on and that you approve."

"I 'prove." Jeremiah nodded readily, then paused. "What's 'prove?"

So sincere and eager to please, so precious. "Do you want me and Miss Jenny to get married?"

Jeremiah beamed. "Yes, sir! I like this house lots better than ours and I like Mercedes' cooking *way* lots better than yours."

If that's all marriage was, they'd have it made. He swung Jeremiah off the bed, smiling ruefully. "Then let's get dressed."

They married at sunset by the fountain. The world was on fire, vivid in every spectrum of color. The mountains rose in the distance, their tops bathed in pink-gold flame, the valley a vastness that spread into the indigo shadows of twilight.

Jenny was stunning in her wedding gown, sending a streak of cowardice through Thorne. He didn't want a sexless, convenient marriage. It had been a mistake to agree to Jenny's terms, thinking she would eventually come around, but it was too late now to back out.

Their vows where exchanged in the clear cool whisper of evening, their voices steady and sure, even if their hearts were not. Mercedes wept softly in the background, while Luis held her hand tightly in his own, both repeating the promises silently in their own hearts.

Jeremiah stood next to Hannah, restless but obliging his father's wishes. He was done standing still and ready to go back to the kitchen where Mercedes had been baking special treats all afternoon. He shifted from one foot to the other, fighting to be as quiet and obedient as the others. "Miss Jenny sure looks pretty," he said in an overloud whisper.

Everyone smiled. Then Thorne was turning to Jenny, admonished by the reverend that he might now kiss the bride. It was short and sweet, a mere meeting of lips to satisfy the ceremony. It would never be enough for Thorne. How long before it wouldn't be enough for Jenny?

They turned as one to smile at their guests and were instantly enfolded in hugs and handshakes and congratulations.

Hannah slipped away as soon as possible to go sit with Milton.

• • •

Thorne and Jenny had drawn the night out as long as possible. Finally it had fallen to the others to take themselves off to bed when they realized the newly married couple seemed to have no intention of doing so. It was awkward and embarrassing, but Jenny figured there were worse things than having the whole house speculate on what she and Thorne would be doing behind closed doors, if they ever got there.

There was no question of her going to her own room. She knew at least a pretense of sharing his bed was expected. But she hadn't reckoned she'd feel so jittery about it.

She turned out the lamp in her room where she had placed Jeremiah, then leaned over and kissed his forehead. He'd fallen asleep hours ago on his father's shoulder, but Thorne had just put him in bed. "Will he wake?" she asked.

"Not likely," Thorne answered. He knew she was self-conscious, maybe a bit worried, dragging out the time until they would have to be alone. "You scared, Jenny?"

She looked up sharply. "No. Should I be?"

He smiled, that lazy half smile that said he knew she was feeling skittish. "No." He pulled the covers up snugly to his son's chin. "Why don't you go on to my room?"

"Yes." She'd get that part out of the way, at least.

She did as he bade, crossing the courtyard in the still night air rather than going through the quiet house. The sky was clear, the stars brilliant overhead. She loved the hush of late night, when the world had put itself to bed and only the night creatures dared intrude on the silence. She stepped inside Thorne's room and approached his bed, then realized she didn't have her nightgown. She turned to find he had followed, candle in hand, its light the only illumination in the dark room.

His expression was solemn, his eyes intense. "What's wrong, Jenny?"

"Nothing. I forgot my nightgown. I'll just go—"

"You won't need it."

Her heart stilled, then began to race. "Ian . . ." Her hand lifted, as if she would say more, then fell to her side. "Our agreement . . ."

He placed the candle on the bedside table, then turned to her. "I don't want any part of it. You don't either, if you're honest with yourself."

She took a deep breath, exhaled slowly. "Do you love me, Ian?"

He thought of a flippant reply but decided against it. "We're married, Jenny. It's enough."

"Not for me," she whispered, aching inside.

"How long, then?" The words were curt, harsh.

She met his gaze with honesty. "I don't know." How long would it take him to feel the way she did?

He closed his eyes briefly. His ribs hurt too badly to argue the point for a day or so, but the healthier parts of him wanted an answer he could live with. "Go get your gown," he said.

He was sitting on the edge of the bed when she returned, his shirt and boots on the floor at his feet. His bandages stood out starkly in the dim light against his bronzed skin, a reminder.

"How are you feeling?" she asked.

"Good enough to make love to you, but too bad to wrestle for it."

Her blush was becoming if unwelcome. Her white cotton nightgown was prim, covering her from head to toe, and prissy with lace at the neck and cuffs. He chuckled ruefully.

"You look ten years old in that getup."

She took exception to his teasing. "This is perfectly proper."

"It is that," he stated. "Just what a man wants on his wedding night. A perfectly proper wife."

Her chin rose a notch. "What is that supposed to mean?"

He shook his head. "Nothing, Jenny. Come to bed."

She took one step forward, then paused. He had risen and was unbuttoning his pants, right there in front of her. "Perhaps I should wait . . . outside."

He looked over to see what had her stammering and found her eyes fixed on his hands. He glanced down and realized the source of her hesitation. He smiled. "No need to get all shy now," he said.

"Aren't you?"

"Nope." He pushed the buttons through, then began to slip the trousers down.

With a squeak, Jenny spun in a half circle, presenting her back.

"We spent an entire night in a cave, naked."

"It was dark."

"What are you afraid to see?" he asked.

"Nothing. Everything. Aren't you even a little embarrassed?"

"Why should I be?"

"I don't know." Truthfully, she didn't. It just seemed that he should be as nervous as she. "We're practically strangers."

"Most newly married couples are."

"I suppose."

"Come here, Jenny." His voice was dark, no longer teasing.

She turned slowly to find him in the bed, holding the covers out for her. His chest and shoulders were bare above the quilt. She didn't know about the rest of him beneath. She told her legs to take that first step forward, but they wouldn't obey. "What have you got on under there?"

"I won't ravish you," he said.

"That's not an answer."

"Come here."

She hurried before her courage failed and crawled beneath the covers. Lying still as a stone, she stared up at the ceiling. "I'll never be able to sleep."

"I know how to help you."

The suggestive timbre of his voice made her laugh. "Are you trying to seduce me, Ian?"

"Are you willing to be seduced?"

"No."

He cursed mildly, sighed, then rolled over, presenting his back. "Good night, Mrs. Thorne."

She lifted the covers gingerly and sneaked a peek at his bare backside.

"Like what you see?"

"Good night, Ian."

Daylight brought an awkwardness that could not be helped. Jenny hated facing the household and their suppositions but knew she couldn't ignore them. She hurried to her own room to dress, then went to the kitchen to help with breakfast.

Mercedes *tsk*ed lightly. "You should not be in here so early on your first morning together."

"Ian's already out with the horses," she said. He'd boldly climbed right from the bed at dawn, not an ounce of shame for his nakedness, and dressed with an economy of movement, if not discretion.

The housekeeper made a grumbled reply about men, then placed platters of eggs and sausages on the sideboard. Biscuits and jam followed. "No proper honeymoon, no special time to get to know each other. It is not right, señora. You should have gone away from here for a day or so, to Santa Fe maybe."

"We couldn't afford the time," Jenny soothed. "One day maybe." One day when they were truly man and wife, when Thorne loved her as she believed she did him. But what if he was right? What if love was so fallible that one could fall out as easily and uncontrollably as one fell in?

Jenny fetched a pitcher of milk and brought it to the table. "Have you always loved Luis?" she asked.

"Of course," Mercedes answered. "What a question to ask someone who has been married as long as we have."

"So there was never a time when you questioned your love, your devotion to one another?"

"Oh." Mercedes nodded wisely. "*Sí*, there have been a thousand times when love was questioned. Marriage does not alleviate problems, sometimes it even compounds them, but the love is what sees you through. Sometimes it is the only thing left after the first fires burn low." She looked at Jenny kindly. "If there is commitment, love will not fail. A man's passion for his wife will dim, and hers for him, but love will rekindle it time and again."

They could hear the men approaching the house and set the conversation aside. But Mercedes' words were not forgotten as Jenny set the table. Perhaps it was wrong to turn Thorne away. Perhaps it was the only way to prove to him that her love would remain constant after the first fires dwindled.

Or perhaps it would have the opposite effect. If she gave herself to him, would he have all he wanted out of marriage and have no reason to seek a deeper understanding and communion?

"Good morning."

Jenny gasped and turned. Milt stood in the doorway, pale but on his feet, smiling.

"Oh, Milt," she said. "Should you be up?"

"He insisted," Hannah scolded, but she was smiling thinly at his accomplishment.

"I'm so hungry I could eat my horse," he said. "Mercedes' cooking brought me running."

Mercedes smiled hugely. "Oh, Señor Sheriff! You go lie back down and I will bring you too much food to eat."

Milton shook his head and hobbled over to the table. "I can't stay in that bed another minute, but I will sit down."

The men were coming through the back door, hanging hats and coats on the rack. They stopped when they saw the sheriff.

"The streets are safe again," Barkley said, and had them all chuckling.

"You sure you should be up?" Thorne asked. His tone was neutral but Jenny detected a forcefulness in his voice.

Milton nodded. "I had to." He was too pale for comfort, and the short walk was beginning to take its toll. "I need you to do me a favor though, before I fall flat on my face." He reached over and took Hannah's hand in his. "I want you to go to town and get the reverend before he leaves. I don't want to wait until next month to get married."

Everyone smiled and began to congratulate them at once. Everyone except Hannah.

"No." It was a mere rasp of breath, yet audible. She rose to her feet and pulled her trembling hand from Milton's. "No," she repeated with stark, icy calm.

Milton gazed at her with hurt. "I'm sorry, Hannah. I thought, I didn't consider . . . a large wedding would be important to you."

She seemed to shake herself free. "We made so many plans, Milton."

"I know. I'm sorry." He looked up at Thorne, ill at ease now and feeling the trying effects of getting up too soon. "Forget it."

Hannah ran from the room. Jenny ran after her.

It is time we women challenge ourselves to become, not the missish mice of indecision and meekness but partakers of our own destinies, makers of the decisions affecting our lives. A woman who worries overmuch is like a sickness invading her own home. She must move forward and overtake the troubles of her day.

I fully expect men will grow accustomed to the improved woman with time.

—Granny Delaney
Granny's Journal
12 May 1780

Chapter 19

A FRIGID RAGE GRIPPED HANNAH. "NOT NEXT MONTH, not ever!" she said.

Jenny shivered at her friend's uncompromising tone. Disbelief lay like a barrier between them. "But why, Hannah? You've waited so long, made so many plans."

Eyes dry and cold, Hannah looked out at the mountains in the distance. "I cannot worry day after day if he will come home to me. I cannot go through this again."

Jenny only stared, at a loss for words. "But you knew this could happen."

"No, I didn't." Hannah began to pace. "Realizing the possibilities and experiencing them firsthand are two entirely different things, Jennifer." She spun around. "I won't do it."

Jenny struggled for air. "You can't do this to Milt, to yourself. You love him!"

"I need order and predictability. No matter how carefully I plan, I will never be able to protect Milton. How long do you think love will last," Hannah fired back, "if I am forced to live in this constant state of worry and anxiety?"

"A lifetime," Jenny cried softly, but knew Hannah had set herself against any such sentiment. She gripped her friend's upper arms, hard. "What if the worst happens, what if you only have him for a week or a month? Wouldn't it better than not having Milt at all?"

Hannah's face crumbled. "I can't, Jennifer. I love him so much but it's just too painful."

Loving was painful and glorious and uncertain. But Jenny also knew her friend would be in no less agony if she left her beloved. "Please, give it time, Hannah. You're exhausted. It has been a trying time for us all but, please, at least promise me you'll give this some thought before you tell him."

Hannah shook her head. "He's on his feet. I'm returning home this morning." She spun away, her shoulders rigid as she marched from the room.

Thorne stood in the doorway, an unwilling audience. Jenny caught sight of him as she brushed away tears. "So," he said, his jaw tight. "Now Milton is free . . . and you are not."

Shock flooded her features. Jenny shook her head, denying him, but her throat was too constricted to speak. The dreams of two of the people she loved most in the world were crumbling to dust.

Thorne grabbed his hat from the rack and slammed it

on his head. "I've got work to do," he said with a hint of disgust.

He stopped short in the doorway. Milton stood there, looking worse than he had when they carried him in. "She has left me," he said. "Hannah has left me." His voice was gravel, his expression stupefied. He held on to the door frame for support, but he was fading fast.

"Oh, Milt." Jenny rushed to him, shoving her shoulder under one arm to keep him on his feet. "Help me," she demanded of Thorne.

Thorne braced Milton upright until they got him seated in a chair. He sent Jenny a cold, removed look, then silently left the house.

Jenny watched him go, knowing what he was thinking, knowing he was wrong. She considered going after him, but what could she say? If she protested that she didn't love Milt, it would only confirm Thorne's belief that love didn't last.

But she had never loved Milt, not as anything more than a friend. How could she explain to Thorne that she had mistaken the emotion? He would only assume that she was mistaking her feelings for him as well.

She knew better. She knew. It was a knowing in her heart, her soul. A feeling as lasting and profound and elementally necessary as the air she breathed. But she had to find a way to convince Thorne.

He didn't come home for supper.

Jenny waited and waited, then gave up when dusk turned to twilight, then full dark. She had tucked

Jeremiah into bed, then changed into her simple, virginal nightgown. There wasn't much about her to entice a man, but she was going to try it anyway. She had something to prove and this was the only way she knew to go about it.

By the light of a lone candle, she brushed her hair out until it crackled, then crawled into Thorne's bed. Her stomach was a mess, but she figured it was that way for most women on their wedding night—their real wedding night. She folded the covers back to her waist and sat propped against the pillows, a silly untried girl with her heart beating hard against her ribs. Within minutes, she climbed from the bed, too restless to sit, growing angry because she was worried now that Thorne had not returned.

The door opened suddenly and she spun around. Thorne stood there, looking tired.

"Where have you been?" she demanded.

His gaze swept her, bold and without emotion. "Where's Milton?"

"Gone home with Doc's help."

"I see. You couldn't make him stay."

Anger reared like lightning. "I didn't try."

His shoulders slumped slightly, barely visible, but Jenny was attuned to every nuance of his expression.

"The marriage hasn't been consummated," he said. "You could have it annulled."

Her anger receded fast to be replaced by fear. "Is that what you want, Ian?"

He raked his fingers through his hair, then let his arms

hang at his sides. "For you, Jenny. If that's what you want, I won't stand in your way."

Tears stung her eyes. She wanted to hit him and hug him, and gather him so close he could not escape. She ground her teeth instead. "Do you love me then, Ian? Do you love me so much that you would step aside for my happiness?"

His hands balled into fists. "You know how I feel, Jenny. Don't try to twist this into something else."

"I thought you wanted me," she whispered.

"I do." More than any woman he had ever wanted in his life.

"But you'll give up the ranch and Jeremiah's future and me, just so I can be happy with another man?"

Like hell he would! "Look—"

"No, you look," she said, advancing until they were nearly chest to chest and she had to tip her head back to rail at him. "I love you, Ian."

He lashed out, mindless and hurting against his will. "Like you loved Milton a week ago?"

"No," she said softly, painfully. "Never like I loved Milt. That was friendship, a girl's infatuation."

"Well, you can have him now."

"I don't want him, Ian. I want you." Her eyes were fierce and glowing. "You do love me, Ian Thorne. Whether you want to admit it or not. Whether you even know it yet or not, you love me just like I love you. I don't want Milt, I want you." She took a deep breath for courage. "I made a mistake misreading my affection for him, but you made a mistake too, thinking love can't last. It can. It will, if we give it a chance."

He hadn't moved, hadn't blinked. She knew he didn't want to hurt her, but she was hurting anyway. What if she was wrong about him, and he felt little more for her than the friendship she had felt for Milt?

She struggled against tears and tried to make her voice confident. "So, what are you going to do about it?"

God, she was beautiful, standing there awash in moonlight, her deep auburn hair all tumbled down to her waist. "You don't know what you're saying, Jenny."

"I know exactly what I'm saying. It's you who are confused."

He took a step toward her, knowing if he took another she would be in his arms and there would be no turning back. "You'd better be sure about this."

"No," she whispered, "*you'd* better be sure. I plan to love you for the next fifty or sixty years on this earth, then for eternity. I think you're the one who'd better be sure, Ian."

He knew he wanted her. Desire was a constant ache twisting his insides. But he also knew he could be happy with her. On this ranch or in some hovel in the desert, he knew that he could be happy if she were by his side. Was this it then? Was it really so simple? What happened when passion had run its course, and old age and companionship were all they had left?

The truth struck, a shattering whisper in his heart that splintered his long-held beliefs. He would still have Jenny. Whether aged and infirm or cantankerous and hardy, as long as Jenny was with him, he would be happy. He would be fulfilled and content and strong enough to endure whatever life threw their way. Without her, he would be nothing but a lonely, wasted old man.

Jenny saw a change in his eyes, a subtle new awareness. Her heart beat faster. "Do you love me, Ian?"

He smiled.

"Will you love me forever?"

"Longer."

Her breath pooled out softly. "Then show me."

In two steps, he swept her up in his arms. His mouth captured hers, sweetly, savagely, a meeting of minds and hearts and souls. There was a completeness to their kiss, an offering and a promise. She lay her hand along his strong jaw and looked into his eyes.

"This won't go away," she said. "You're wrong."

"I hope so." With Jenny, he was willing to risk it.

"I know so." For all her brave words, her heart thudded with a trace of uncertainty. She had to be right. Their future depended on it. But the present was where they would start. She ducked her head into his chest. "I'm nervous," she whispered.

"Not you."

"Yes." She peeked up at him, feeling so right yet so fragile.

"I love it when you blush, Jenny."

She pulled back to look at him. "Guess you'll get plenty of those tonight."

Heat streaked through him, dangerous but delicious. So powerful it shook him. "Don't be afraid."

"Easy for you to say. You know what to expect."

"I know what I want."

She shivered at his tone. "Tell me."

He let her slide down his body, every inch of her setting fire to every inch of him. He took her face in his hands and brought their lips together again. "It's too late for words."

There was fire inside her, burning like nothing she had known before. "Tell me anyway. Tell me what to do to make it right."

"It's already right," he said. Unbelievably right. His hands slid over her, strong and sure, lifting and turning so that she was against his chest, his heartbeat in counterpoint to hers. He lay her on the bed, then backed away and began unbuttoning his shirt.

She watched him, her eyes bright and curious despite the becoming blush on her cheeks. He hesitated at his pants, giving her time to turn away, but her gaze stayed fixed on him, bold as she could make herself in this unknown realm of passion. He sat on the side of the bed to remove his boots and socks, then his pants and undergarments. Still she did not turn away, though her heartbeat had quickened and a dewy uncertainty now lay in her eyes.

She reached over and touched his chest. "You are so handsome."

With a half smile, he placed his hand over hers. "Hardly." His look changed, became hot. "I love it when you touch me, Jenny."

"I wanted to, in the cave . . . more than I did."

He closed his eyes a brief second for composure. "You can, all you want."

"Where?"

"Everywhere."

She wasn't certain where to proceed with such liberty, but she did as she wanted. She traced the musculature of his chest and belly and felt him draw breath. She wondered if he had meant his words. Could she really touch him however and wherever she wanted? She slid her fingers through the hair on his chest, delighting in the feel of rough hair and smooth skin. His expression changed to a combination of pain and pleasure.

He leaned over her, bracing his hands on either side of her hips. His fingers curled into the quilt, gripping for life, while her hands found the shape of his torso. She smelled of flowers, something light and arresting. He inhaled the fragrance deep into his lungs, where his feelings for her were lodged, so new and expanding there didn't seem to be enough room for them. This was Jenny, his Jenny. He realized he'd been too afraid to hope for more, too afraid to open his heart and hand it over to her safekeeping. Too afraid of the power she possessed to destroy him.

Her hand drifted down, tentative over his hip to see what he would do. He exhaled sharply and lowered his mouth to hers, lightly, the merest touch of flesh. He didn't dare touch her elsewhere, and braced himself on his arms and gave her time to explore, to come to know him as he planned to know her. Her fingers discovered the shape and strength of his waist, his hips, the ways they were different.

"I've wanted to do this for so long," she admitted. "Even before the cave."

Her palm skimmed his thigh, bold and uncertain, and

he made a sound of approval in his throat that turned to a deep growl when she brushed his arousal.

"I'm sorry." She jerked her hand back, embarrassed.

He dropped his forehead to hers, smiling. "I'm not, but if you want this to last longer you might want to throw your arms around my neck. Now."

She did as he bade. "Why?"

"Remember the edge? Control?"

Her eyes were luminous. "I want you to lose control, Ian. I want to know that I caused it."

Too fast. Too much to know that she wanted him that way. There were a few things he wanted too. "I'm going to take your nightgown off."

Her breath came fast, anxious. "Will you put out the candle?"

He would do anything for her, but the sight of her was more than he was willing to give up easily. "I want to see you," he whispered. "Don't be shy."

She wanted him too, to feel him against her, to know how they fit. "I can't help it."

He released the tiny buttons at her neck. "Do you remember when we went for a swim? I could see right through your dress. I thought I would go mad with desire." He reached down and lifted the hem of her nightgown, talking steadily to keep her focus off what he was doing. "I had to stay away or embarrass myself."

He tugged the gown over her head. She suppressed the instinct to recoil and gripped his arms to keep from covering herself.

She was glorious in moonlight, her unbound hair the

only color surrounding her pale face, her limbs long and well shaped.

"So beautiful," he said, bringing her gaze to his. He laid his hand over her heartbeat. "And I've wanted to do this for so long." His mouth captured hers in the way his body wanted to, hot and sleek and hungry. His warm palm brushed over her, slowly, so slowly, every inch from her neck to her waist in the most lazy exploration. She felt her shyness recede bit by slow bit into a restless desire that matched the need in him.

"Oh!" She gasped when his mouth drifted down, replacing his hands, tracing blindly everywhere he had already touched. Her throat, the underside of her arm, her breast. Her heart thundered, eager for more, and she realized her imagination had been a poor thing against the reality of loving him. The shadow of his beard scraped her belly and she stiffened as he continued to trail kisses lower.

"Ian," she rasped.

"Don't be shy," he murmured into her flesh.

He forced himself to go gently, careful on this first night, but the vision of what lay ahead for them was as hot as the fire already consuming him. His hands wandered, almost aimlessly, over the lush contours of her shape, the indention at her waist, the gentle slope of her belly, the slender curve of her hip. She startled easily, and he tenderly sought to draw her away from modesty until she was as eager as he, as hungry to experience all that awaited them.

Jenny didn't know whether to worry more about his hands or his mouth. Both seemed to be everywhere, soothing, pleasuring, stirring. Then he touched her low, and she gasped, her entire body flooding with heat and embarrassment and wonder.

"No, don't pull away," he coaxed. "It's just me, Jenny. I want all of you." He stroked her until her breathing grew rapid, until her hands were clutching at him.

"Ian," she pleaded.

He lay alongside her, testing his weight against her slighter frame. She gripped him as a drowning woman would, all arms and legs and desperation.

With hearts and hands and dreams they came together, their bodies perfectly fitted. He moved to enter her with care and a hint of regret for the pain on her face, but she held him, her eyes fixed on his. She would not allow herself to retreat in misgiving when she wanted him so badly.

He lay still, his weight heavy on her and in her, concern in his eyes. "Are you all right?"

She nodded, her throat tight with emotion. She felt full, overwhelmed, and so in love she didn't mind the sharp burning pain nearly as much as the thought of him leaving her.

"It will get better," he promised, and kept perfectly still, allowing her time to adjust. "If it doesn't I'll stop." He kissed her lightly, and she managed a smile.

"If you stop, I'll die," she said.

Passion overcame him; his body screamed for fulfillment. In agony he held back, waited for her discomfort to ease, and touched her in ways to help it along, to take her from the first blunt contact to the searing need for completion. His hand swept her back, down the tight muscles of her buttocks and thighs, urging her gently to relax.

She began to ease, to reach for him, running her fingers through his hair, sculpting his face, touching the lines of strain on his brow.

He turned his face into her hand and kissed her palm, then lowered his head. When his lips touched her breast, she arched on a ragged breath and he took her into his mouth and suckled until she was bowing into him, taking him deeper, completing the joining of their bodies.

Then they were moving together, her cries high and raspy as her body reached for the fever he offered. The world around them subsided into the pinpoint of light that was her face, her love, and he gave everything he was, everything he had thought impossible to feel, up to her safeguarding forever.

The night wind moaned outside, lonely, but the two lying peacefully in each other's arms heard nothing but the echo of their fulfilled heartbeats.

"Come daylight, I have to go into town," Jenny said.

He stopped playing with her hair and rolled to look at her. "Why?"

"To tell Hannah what she's missing."

Thorne chuckled quietly. "You'll scare her proper sensibilities to death."

Jenny buried her face in his chest. "That's why you didn't tell me?"

"No. I didn't tell you because everytime you brought it up I wanted to ravish you."

"I don't think Hannah will want to ravish me. I hope she'll want to ravish Milt."

"It's not the same."

"Not without love," she agreed. "Do you love me, Ian?"

"I love you, Jenny."

She smiled, smug and drowsy and content. "I knew it."